Praise for th............Claudia Carroll

LEABHARLAN..............story ... A very modern
....and ...mour'

Sheila O'Flanagan

'Full of warmth, humour and emotion, this is a wonderfully
written, unconventional love story that charms from the very
first page. I adored it and didn't want it to end. Read it – I
guarantee you'll love it'

Melissa Hill

'It bubbles and sparkles like pink champagne. A hugely enter-
taining read'

Patricia Scanlan

'An emotional roller-coaster ride . . . keeps the reader wondering
until the very end'

Irish Independent

'Claudia Carroll has done it again, with a heroine you just want
fate to smile on'

Heat

Readers adore the novels of Claudia Carroll – here
is a glimpse of just how much!

'I was holding my breath . . . the story really **touched my heart**'

'**Fun, breezy**, and kept me guessing and oohing and aaahhhing
until the end!'

'Truly **captivating**'

'Will lift your **spirits**'

'If you love **page-turning women's fiction with depth** then this
book is for you!'

'I so enjoyed this **unusual story** of friendships and love'

'Very fresh and **brilliantly plotted**'

'A total page-turner with **companionship, fear, laughter,** and a
whole bunch of other emotions that will take you on **a journey
like no other**'

'Officially one of my **favourite books of the year**!'

'Some **sobs**, but lots of **laughter** and **joy**'

All She Ever Wished For

Claudia Carroll is a top-ten bestselling author in the UK and a number one bestselling author in Ireland, selling over 670,000 copies of her paperbacks alone. Three of her novels have been optioned, two for movies and one for a TV series on Fox TV. In 2013, her tenth novel, *Me and You,* was shortlisted for the Bord Gais Popular Choice Irish Book Award. She was born in Dublin where she still lives.

All She Ever Wished For

Claudia Carroll

avon

AVON

A division of HarperCollins*Publishers*
1 London Bridge Street
London
SE1 9GF

www.harpercollins.co.uk

A Paperback Original 2016

A catalogue record for this book is
available from the British Library

ISBN-13: 9780008140724

Set in Minion by Palimpsest Book Production Limited,
Falkirk, Stirlingshire

Printed and bound in Great Britain by Clays Ltd, St Ives plc

MIX
Paper from
responsible sources
FSC™ C007454

*This book is warmly dedicated to a very special lady,
who will be much missed.*

For Eleanor Dryden, with love.

PROLOGUE

Valentine's Day, Dublin
Two years ago

In this day and age, is there anything that says 'I love you' more than a Chubb padlock fastened tight onto a bridge? And like a growing number of landmarks around the world, the Ha'penny Bridge is only coming down in them. You'll often catch couples sneakily fastening locks to the metal grills on either side of the bridge's arch, pledging undying love (weather permitting), then tossing the key down into the River Liffey beneath.

Every red-letter date in the calendar without fail, you can be guaranteed the Ha'penny Bridge will groan under the weight of all these tiny little love locks, with particular spikes around Valentine's Day and New Year. After all, it's a romantic and slightly different way to show your commitment to that someone special, isn't it? Plus it sure as hell beats a bunch of overpriced red roses from Tesco.

But every so often you'll see a forlorn single revisiting a lock, maybe touching it wistfully, then sadly walking away. And you'll find yourself wondering what their story could possibly be.

1

Like tonight, for instance.

A woman was standing tall and proud beside one such lock and from behind you'd think absolutely nothing at all was the matter with her. She had choppy, blonde, bang-on-trend hair and stood ramrod straight with her head held high as she stared out over the Liffey swirling beneath.

It was only when you caught her profile sideways on, you could see how upset she was. This woman looked all out of place here; there was something way too regal and composed about the way she stood all alone on the bridge, while backpackers in puffa jackets and exhausted tourists barged past her on their way to and from the pubs and restaurants of Temple Bar.

No way was a lady this classy and elegant on her way to some booze-up or hen night in Temple Bar, that was for certain. She was older, late thirties at a guess, slim and elegant in red-soled Louboutin high heels and huddling a blonde fur coat around her shoulders, to ward off the icy February rain and chill. Real fur too, you could tell at a glance. She had no umbrella either, but didn't seem to care that she was slowly getting drenched. Instead she just stood right beside the lovelocks, staring out over the river and clinging onto the coat; silent, unchecked tears running down her coldly angular face.

But if this lady thought she was passing by anonymously and completely unnoticed, she was wrong. At that exact moment, a much younger woman taking a short cut across the bridge spotted her, and even though she was running late for a movie screening, suddenly found herself stopping dead in her tracks.

Because she'd recognised the lady standing proudly beside all the lovelocks. As would anyone who'd bothered to look closely enough. This was Kate King, *the* Kate King. There was hardly anyone in the country who wouldn't have known who she was, barring if they'd lived inside a cave for the last fifteen years.

Everyone knows a Glamazon like Kate King; or at least, everyone thinks that they do. She's the type who's forever in the papers flaunting her statement homes – and yes, that's homes plural – or gracing high society dos, or else maybe perched on a TV sofa discussing her 'charity work'. Always glossy and smiley and skinny, with her filthy rich husband never too far from her side. Kate King really was the woman who had it all.

But why the woman who had it all was now crying on a bridge in public in the lashing rain was quite another thing. It was a bit like stumbling across the Queen bawling her eyes out over the Thames; one of those things that you just couldn't imagine happening.

Tess hesitated. She was dead late for the movie now and Bernard would probably be furious with her, but it felt wrong to just walk by when there was someone beside her clearly distressed and needing help. Kate King really did seem to be in a right state; supposing she was on the verge of doing something stupid like throwing herself over the bridge? Then Tess would have to read all about it in the next day's papers, knowing that she might have been able to do something, but instead chose to keep on walking, just so she could be on time for some obscure Mexican art house movie that Bernard insisted on seeing.

'Excuse me,' she said gingerly, approaching the lady. 'I'm so sorry to bother you, but are you OK?'

Kate King turned sharply to look at her and Tess was shocked to see two puffy, red eyes with mascara running

3

all the way down that famously beautiful, sculpted face. You never saw a woman like this looking anything less than flawlessly composed and immaculate in magazines and on the telly. Tess almost wondered if this could possibly be one and the same person.

No response.

'Maybe you'd like me to get you a taxi?' Tess asked her gently. 'You could shelter under my umbrella till we find you one?'

'Please just go away,' came the clipped response.

'But you're getting soaked!'

'I don't care.'

'Oh, well . . . sorry to disturb you,' said Tess, taken aback. 'I only meant to—'

'Look, I'd really like some privacy. Can't you just leave me in peace?'

Her tone was brusque now, dismissive. She meant what she said. So Tess backed off, wondering what the hell could possibly have gone so wrong in Kate King's flawlessly perfect A-list life that someone like her was left all alone and sobbing on the Ha'penny Bridge in the pouring rain. For a split second, she hesitated, overwhelmed with guilt for leaving and walking away. Should she turn back? Maybe try to engage with her a bit more?

'Whoever you are,' Kate King said, sensing Tess wavering right by her shoulder. 'I'm sure you mean well, but I'd really like you to move on.'

So, left with little choice in the matter, Tess did as she was told, shook the excess rain off her umbrella and quietly went on her way.

She could barely concentrate on the movie though. Instead, all she could do was think about Kate King, and wonder.

KATE

The Present

And so it was happening. Now. Today. This morning. There was no getting out of it and certainly no turning back. At that thought alone, she felt another huge, violent stomach retch and this time barely made it as far as the bathroom. Her third time to throw up so far today.

Oh Christ, she thought, slumped against the bathroom floor – for a brief, fleeting moment savouring the cool feel of the marble tiles against her skin – have I really brought all this on myself? Have I really been that stupidly short-sighted? Isn't there any way out of it?

She felt as weak and useless as a butterfly pinned to a card. But like a character in a Greek tragedy, the inevitable was slowly coming to get her and there was absolutely nothing she could do about it.

If it's any small consolation, she thought bitterly while she waited on yet another wave of nausea to pass, you've got absolutely no one to blame but yourself.

TESS

The present

What would Kate Middleton do?

Easy, I thought, fidgeting with the letter that had just arrived and forcing my shaky legs as far as the bedroom window for a few nice, deep, soothing breaths. Kate Middleton would stay serenely calm and at all costs not let a potential disaster like this get to her. She'd call Carole and Pippa who would instantly rush around to her side with wise words of wisdom and support. She'd book herself in for a nice, relaxing blow dry, shoehorn herself into a neat little coat dress from Reiss, then get back out there, arm clamped onto Prince William's with a bright smile plastered across her face.

It's impossible to plan any wedding without a blip and it would seem that this is mine. So now I just have to figure a way out of it, that's all.

'*Oh, I'm a lumberjack, and I'm OKAAAAYYY!*' I hear my dad warbling from out in the back garden, as he waves the hedge trimmer in huge threatening swoops, Darth Vader-style. All to the soundtrack of electronic buzzing that's only marginally more deafening than that instrumental bit in

Fatboy Slim's 'Praise You', and Christ alone knows that's bad enough.

'Jacko? You'll do yourself an injury!' Mum yells from the kitchen window. 'If you lose a limb cutting back those bushes, you needn't come crying to me, you roaring eejit.'

'*I cut down treeeees, I wear high heels, suspenders and a braaaaaa! I wish I'd been a girlie, just like my dear Papa!*' Dad keeps on screeching in a surprisingly passable baritone, considering that Mum never tires of reminding him how useless he is in all other walks of life.

'And where's Tess gone? I thought she was out there helping you?'

'She was meant to be, but she vanished the minute the post came,' Dad shrugs. 'More wedding shite, I suppose.'

I can hear the conversation as loud and clear as that. The only problem is that as I'm listening, the four walls of my bedroom tilt a bit and I suddenly have to focus very hard on breathing.

In for two, out for four, in for two and out for four . . .

'Tess, are you in the loo?' Mum yells up the stairs. 'You've been up there for ages. Are you a bit constipated, do you think?'

'No, Mum,' I somehow manage to squawk back down at her, in a voice I barely even recognise as my own.

Stay by the window and keep breathing, just keep breathing.

'Well I think the base of the wedding cake is nearly done, are you coming down to do a Mary Berry on it?'

'Did I hear you say wedding cake?' Dad butts in from the garden, switching off the hedge trimmers. 'Ahh lovely, you can cut me a nice, juicy, big slice while you're at it. I'm starving.'

'It's not for you, it's for the guests; I wouldn't waste it

on you. Now you just pick up those branches and stop annoying me,' is Mum's comeback, as she slams the kitchen window firmly shut.

All this is for me, I remind myself, trying my damnedest to blank out the letter that's just arrived; this curt, five-line letter that's just caused my whole world to shift on its axis. Which side is it if you're having a heart attack? I wonder. Left or right? Because right now my breath will only come in short, jagged shards and the tightness around my chest is almost making me want to black out.

Twisting the letter in my hand, I force myself to keep on breathing and look down onto the garden, to the grass, the leaves, to my mother's petunias in full bloom, to the peaceful, lovely sight down below. To absolutely anything that might take my mind off this.

Exactly half an hour ago, I hadn't a care in the world. There I was, out the back helping Dad with the garden, mowing the lawn and picking up dead leaves. Half an hour ago, I was happily bustling in and out of the kitchen checking on the wedding cake base and trying to convince Mum to relax and leave me to it. That I'd take care of everything. That getting married at home needn't be the huge stress-inducing nightmare you'd think. That I could expertly organise my wedding reception in our own back garden and that I could easily manage all the catering myself. That with a bit of imagination, Bernard and I could have a simple, intimate, homely wedding and save ourselves a complete fortune in the process.

No, not now, this cannot be happening now.

I have a marquee arriving in a few weeks' time, for God's sake. I have fifty-five guests and counting descending on us and I still have to do all the marinades before the big

8

day. I have to hire the glasses, cutlery and dinner plates, and that's before I even get started on the flowers. I somehow have to get twinkly lights dangling all over our back garden, so it'll look all magical and elegant when the sun sets. I have all my pals roped in to help me with what little free time they can spare. I have lists and more lists and daily targets that, until a short half an hour ago, I was confidently on top of.

From the minute I convinced Mum, Dad and my sister Gracie that we could have the reception here, I've been at pains to reassure them that a home wedding needn't be a nightmare. That it could all be simple and stress-free and just beautiful.

'We'll put on one helluva show,' I proudly told my family.

'. . . and not disgrace ourselves in front of the Pritchards,' Mum finished the sentence for me, with just a tiny bit more ice in her voice than I'd have liked. 'Because, frankly, I could do without that snobby shower looking down their noses at us any more than they already do.'

'Now Mum, it's not a "who lives in the posher house" competition,' I told her as soothingly as I could. 'I don't want my wedding to be about the haves and the have-nots. It's going to be simple and small and more importantly, cost-effective. Have you even seen what hotels charge for wedding receptions these days? Thirty grand and upwards! And that's before you even buy a bottle of water for your guests. Besides, the Pritchards will be dream wedding guests, wait till you see.'

'Hmm,' Mum sniffed doubtfully. 'Well, if I have to listen to one more patronising remark out of them, I'm warning you, Tess, I won't be held responsible.'

The Pritchards are my future in-laws, you see, and in

sharp contrast to us, they live in an elegant two-storey, over-basement, Victorian redbrick statement home in Donnybrook. They've got about five reception rooms that they hardly ever use, including a drawing room, a conservatory and a sitting room with dusty hardback books piled everywhere which they insist on referring to as 'the library'.

My family, however, have none of the above. And so for one day and one day only, our modest and very ordinary little semi-d in an estate full of houses just like it, is about to be transformed into fairyland; a bit like a low-budget Santa's Grotto on Christmas Eve.

At least, until half an hour ago, that was the plan.

I stick my head closer to the window, savouring the lovely, soothing spring breeze and as the minutes tick by, gradually begin to feel more and more composed. Better. At least now my heart rate seems to be heading back down into double digits. Definitely better.

OK, I try my best to think calmly and rationally, gulping in one last mouthful of fresh air before snapping the bedroom window shut. So according to this letter a major problem has arisen, but I'm going to deal with it efficiently and with minimal stress. I'll tell Bernard, of course, because he's officially the most understanding man on the planet and if he can't think of a way to get me out of this, then no one can. Then I'll mention it to my nearest and dearest on a strict need-to-know basis only, because this is surmountable. After all, people manage to wangle their way out of situations like this all the time, don't they?

Besides, it's just not possible. True, there's never a good time for an axe like this to fall, but the timing here really couldn't be much worse. In one month's time, Bernard and I are getting married; it's as simple as that.

So trying my best to channel Kate Middleton, I trip downstairs with the letter clutched in my fist to somehow break the news to my wedding-planner-in-chief. Which would be Mum. I find her in the kitchen, walloping the hell out of the Magimix, busy making the icing for my wedding cake.

'Where did you disappear off to? You're supposed to be here helping your dad and me,' she says crossly when she sees me coming into the kitchen. Bear in mind this is a woman who's got about two hundred pounds of lamb cutlets in the deep freeze. You don't mess with a woman with two hundred pounds of anything in the deep freeze.

'Yeah, I know,' I say in a wobbly voice I barely recognise as my own, 'but the thing is, Mum, something a bit, well, unexpected has just come up—'

'You're as bad as that oaf out the back garden. Now grab an apron and start making yourself useful. You can drain the rum marinade off the sultanas and dump them into the mixture. Barring your father hasn't already drunk the rum himself, that is. Which, to be honest with you, I wouldn't put past him.'

'Mum, you're not listening to me—'

'Jesus, Tess, you're worse than useless! What was the point in you taking time off work to help if all you're going to do is stand there and let me do everything? May I remind you, madam, that getting married at home was all your bright idea?' Then turning back to her Magimix, she mutters darkly, 'getting married to Bernard in the first place was all your bright idea too, let's not forget.'

Now normally that last sentence would automatically trigger The Conversation. The same bloody conversation I've been having with just about everyone ever since

Bernard and I first got engaged. But under the circumstances I let it slide and instead just shove the letter under Mum's nose, then wait the approximate two-second delay while she processes it.

But there's silence. A long, bowel-withering silence.

'Well, this has to be a joke,' she eventually says, all the blood suddenly draining from her face. 'Maybe something Monica and Stella would do to get a rise out of you before the hen night?'

Monica and Stella are my two best pals and although they both love a good giggle as much as we all do, there's no way in hell they'd ever contemplate doing something this cruel.

'It's not a joke. This isn't the girls messing. Look at the headed notepaper. This is legit. Believe me, it's about as legit as it gets.'

It says a lot about just how serious this is that Mum abandons her Magimix and slumps down wearily at the kitchen table, unable to say much else.

She doesn't need to though.

The crumpled look on her face tells me everything I need to know.

KATE

Your Daily Dish.ie
October 2014

TROUBLE IN PARADISE?

Here *at* Your Daily Dish *we're receiving troubling reports from the Castletown House residence regarding billionaire Globtech founder Damien King and his well-known socialite wife, Kate.*

The Gardai have said that following a 'complaint of a most serious nature', a court order was issued to Mrs Kate King at the property earlier today. A source close to Mrs King says that the order is in relation to a valuable painting, an end-period Rembrandt known as A Lady of Letters, *which we're told, is 'a source of contention between Damien and Kate King at the present time'.*

The painting is said to have been valued at upwards of €95 million. The Kings are well known to have a notable art collection, the jewel in the crown being A Lady of Letters. *Sources tell us that Mrs King 'is cooperating with the police in any way she can'. It's not yet known if charges are to follow or not.*

This of course has our heads spinning at Your Daily Dish. *Can our favourite celebrity couple really be warring over a painting? To such an extent that a court order was issued?*

Rumours have been rife for some time now that the couple have been living apart and are on the brink of separation. This troubling report would appear to confirm it.

Remember, you read it here first, on Your Daily Dish.

TESS

The present

'The main thing is not to panic,' says Bernard, my hubby-to-be, when I call to fill him in on what's just happened, my imminent heart attack, etc.

'Try *not* to panic?' I say, doing the exact polar opposite. 'Bernard, I've just been summoned for jury service, bloody *jury service* and you're telling me not to panic?'

I consult the now half-scrunched letter in my hand for about the thousandth time today. 'Here it is in cold, hard print. I've got to be at the Criminal Courts of Justice at 9 a.m. this coming Monday morning. So forgive me for panicking when this lands on me less than a month and counting before D-Day! Do you realise how much there's still left to do?'

It's a rhetorical question; of course Bernard hasn't the first clue what's left to do. After all, he's a forty-three-year-old heterosexual male. What the hell does he know about weddingy floral centrepieces or alternate menu choices for coeliac lacto-ovo vegetarians?

'Now I strongly suggest you stay calm dearest,' Bernard says patiently. 'All this panic is getting you nowhere. A nice cup of tea, that'll soon set you to rights.'

15

Bernard, it has to be said, thinks that there's no drama in this life that can't be instantly righted with a cup of Clipper gold blend.

'The thing you have to understand,' I sigh, regrouping and trying my best to keep cool, 'is that with a wedding like this, there's a whole clatter of stuff that you can only leave till these last, precious few weeks. So there's no way in hell I can handle something as huge as jury service right now. Besides, I've got my family and pals all roped into helping me out before the big day, how could I possibly just skive off to court and leave them to do all the heavy lifting for me?'

'Well, I'm sure they'd be most understanding, under the circumstances—'

'No, I can't do it, Bernard, it just isn't right. I won't do it to my friends and I certainly wouldn't put my family through that. I need to be here working around the clock along with everyone else, that's all there is to it. After all, we're talking our dream wedding here.'

'I suggest you just try to put this whole thing into perspective,' he says calmly. 'Remember, it's nothing personal. Being summoned for jury service can happen to any of us, at any time.'

'I know, but I've got my whole life ahead of me to deal with stuff like this! Why does it have to be right now? Landing on me out of a clear blue sky?'

'Such a pity you don't live in the UK,' Bernard muses calmly. 'Because over there, you know, you're allowed to turn down jury service twice and only on the third time are you obliged to serve.'

'But, sweetheart, I don't live in the UK. It's totally different here; if you're summoned, you've got to turn up, simple as that. And you know the nightmare I had at work trying to get time off – I can't have all that precious time eaten into with this crapology.'

'Now there's absolutely no need for neologism,' he chides gently, and it's all I can do to bite my tongue and ask him to stop using words I don't understand. 'The critical thing is to remember that this is how our judicial system works. That's how our democracy works.'

'I already know all of that, but the thing is, how am I supposed to get out of it?'

'In fact, did I ever tell you about the time I was summoned just a few months before I was due to take my doctorate?' he chats away, sounding perfectly relaxed about this, oblivious to the rising note of hysteria in my voice. 'I still had reams of research to do on the painting technique of the seventeenth-century Dutch Masters, with particular reference to Vermeer, which as you know is a highly contentious subject which needs a plethora of astute writing, not to mention the most forensic editing—'

'Eh, no offence, but can we just get back to the point?'

No rudeness intended in cutting across him, but when Bernard gets going on either Vermeer or Rembrandt, you could be on the phone all night.

'Sorry, sausage. But just remember that when it comes to court service, just because you've been summoned, it doesn't necessarily follow that you'll be selected.'

'What do you mean?'

'Well, both the Prosecution and Defence have the perfect right to turn down any proposed juror on the slightest pretext, you know.'

'So all I have to do is turn up at the courts, hang around for a bit and then maybe I'll just be discharged at the end

17

of the day?' I ask hopefully, for the first time since that bloody letter landed on me this morning, seeing a sudden glint of light in this nightmare. Could he possibly be right? Is that all there is to it? After all, if all this jury service malarkey takes no more than a single day out of my schedule, then maybe – just maybe – all is not lost.

'Better than that, sausage,' Bernard chats on. 'Fact is, there are a whole myriad of reasons why you can plead ineligibility to serve. So go online, check them all out and remember, at all costs, *nil desperandum.* Now I've really got to dash, I'm afraid. I've got a tutorial with my MA students at 2 p.m., so I'll call you later. That alright with you, dearest?'

'Of course it is,' I smile, for the first time all day starting to feel the tight constraint that's been around my chest actually start to loosen a little.

You see? This is why I love Bernard. This is why he and I make the perfect couple. This is why we *work*, no matter what anyone says. And believe me, in the run-up to this wedding, they've pretty much said it all. At stressed-out times like this, I can always rely on him to be the sober yang to my slightly more highly strung ying.

Even if I haven't the foggiest what his Latin reference meant.

*

Turns out Bernard is absolutely on the money. When I log onto the court's website, there's a whole section on who isn't eligible for jury service, not to mention all the reasons why you can be instantly disqualified the minute a Jury Selection Officer casts their eye on you. My eye greedily scrolls down the page, desperately trying to spot one that might just apply to me. Or if all else fails, one that I can plausibly fake and hopefully get away with.

Bernard, I know, would baulk at my doing anything that even remotely smacks of dishonesty, never having told an out-and-out lie in the whole course of his life. But then, I remind myself, Bernard doesn't have to organise catering for over fifty guests, get a marquee up, fully stock a bar, scrub and clean this house from top to bottom, then hound all our last-minute guests who've yet to RSVP. And that's just what I've got to do this week alone. So it's actually reasonably calm and quiet compared with the weeks that lie ahead, but don't get me started.

OK. So far the court's website is telling me that if you're in any way involved with the administration of justice, then you're automatically disqualified, simple as that. I scan quickly down the checklist to find out exactly who they mean, but given that I'm neither the President, the Attorney General, the Director of Public Prosecutions, a guard, a prison officer, a practicing barrister, a solicitor or a court officer, then that's feck all use to me.

My eye keeps speed-scrolling down, the words almost like a blur in front of me.

'*Those who have been convicted of a serious offence in Ireland, those who have ever been sentenced to a term of imprisonment of five years or more, those who, within the last ten years, have been sentenced to a term of imprisonment of at least three months and have served at least part of that sentence . . .*'

Silently cursing myself for being law-abiding all these years, I keep on reading, praying that I'll stumble on some handy little get-out-of-jail-free card that'll neatly extricate me from all of this shite.

19

'*Persons aged 65 and upwards . . . members of either the House of the Oireachtas (the Irish Parliament), members of the Council of State, the Comptroller and Auditor General . . . a person in Holy Orders, a minister of any religious denomination or community, members of monasteries and convents, aircraft pilots, full-time students and ships' masters . . .*'

Bugger, bugger, bugger, I think. The slow, sickening panic I've been holding at bay starting to rise again.

'*Those who provide an important community service, including practicing doctors, nurses, midwives, dentists, vets, chemists, etc . . .*'

Important community service? Yes, success! We might just have a winner on our hands here. Finally, this could actually mean all my problems are solved, I think, suddenly feeling calmer. And OK, so maybe working as a personal trainer in a gym mightn't necessarily be considered 'important community service', but plenty of my clients, not to mention my manager, would certainly disagree.

Well, this is it then, I decide firmly. I'm not officially summoned for jury service till next week, so cometh the hour, cometh the woman. I'll stride into the courts, be polite and professional, but by God, I'll plead my case. I work in a busy city centre health club, I'll tell them, and I've a long list of clients who are completely dependent on me.

And if that doesn't work, then I'll flash the engagement ring, say the wedding is less than a month away and, what the hell, if they'll only see reason here, I might even invite every single solicitor and barrister, as well as whoever's standing in the dock in handcuffs along to the afters.

Feck it, I think, firmly snapping my laptop shut, mind

made up. I'll name our first-born child after the judge if it'll give Bernard and I back our dream wedding day.

Because after what I've been through to get here, nothing is going to compromise that. No court case, no legal threats, absolutely nothing.

KATE

The Chronicle (weekend supplement)
January 2001

A SPECIAL REPORT by Maggie Kelly

There's nothing more headily infectious than being around a young couple, newly in love and with their whole lives ahead of them. So you can imagine my excitement at interviewing Globtech founder and scion of the famous King dynasty, Damien King, along with his beautiful young girlfriend, successful model Kate Lee.

We meet for afternoon tea at the Weston hotel and straight away I can sense that this really is a genuine love match. Damien is courteous, polite and so much taller and more handsome in the flesh than I'd ever have imagined, while Kate is even more stunningly gorgeous than in her photos and on her countless TV appearances – if that's even possible. She's just one of those rare natural beauties that it's impossible to peel your eyes off.

In the past she's been likened to the late Carolyn Bessette-Kennedy, but even that comparison fails to do her justice. Kate's super-tall, as you'd expect, with that famous waist-length, poker-straight blonde hair and cheek-bones you could feasibly grate cheese off. She jokes that she stands a shoeless inch taller than her boyfriend and he laughs this off, saying, 'You see? We're not even together a full year and already Kate's got me looking up to her!'

But there's something more than that. There's a glow about Kate, an inner radiance that no amount of clean living, Bikram yoga or daily juicing can give; in short, she seems a woman very much in love.

Over tea and clotted cream scones (which I notice Kate just picks delicately around the edges of), I ask the one question we're all dying to know the answer to.

'So how did you two lovebirds first meet?'

'Will you tell it, darling, or will I?' he asks.

'I'll certainly give it my best shot,' she smiles, taking a sip of Earl Grey tea. She speaks softly, so much so that I almost have to strain to hear her over all the hotel's chat and clatter in the background.

'Well, we first met about a year ago.'

'Eleven months, three weeks and four days to be exact,' Damien interrupts and she laughs him off.

'Back then I was working as a model in Paris, you see,' she tells me, 'and life was certainly hectic.'

Kate's selling herself short here of course, because we're all familiar with just how successful her modelling career has been to date. It's no exaggeration to say that she's probably been one of this country's best-known faces ever since she was first scouted as a teenager on a night out with friends in Dublin.

I ask her a bit about how she first started out modelling and she laughs, claiming she still remembers it vividly.

'Well there I was, all of seventeen years old, in a restaurant stuffing my face with pizza along with a few girlfriends,' she says, 'when next thing this older businessman-in-a-suit type approached our table and asked me for a quick word.'

'A modelling scout?' I guess.

'Turned out that yes, he was. He introduced himself, handed me a business card and made all sorts of wild promises about what would happen if I'd only call the agency he represented.'

'Now of course Kate is far too modest to say this,' Damien interrupts, gazing at her fondly. 'But, in fact, what this guy actually claimed was that his agency could make her a household name in next to no time.'

'Of course, I giggled about it with my pals afterwards,' Kate tells me, 'but I suppose part of me was intrigued by what he'd said, because I did indeed make the call the next day.'

Which as it happened turned out to be one of the more life-changing events in the life of Kate Lee. Within a matter of weeks after that first auspicious meeting, she'd landed not only the top agent in London, but also lucrative catwalk work with Chanel in Paris.

'It must have been dream come true stuff for you,' I say, 'but may I ask, weren't your family at all worried about you? A young teenager let loose in Paris on her own?'

'Turned out they were absolutely right to be as well,' she says with a slight grimace.

'Because she met someone quite unsuitable over there, didn't you, darling?' prompts Damien. 'Some kind of photographer.'

'Aurelian,' says Kate.

'Yes,' says Damien. 'I knew it was quite a girlie-sounding name.'

It's easy to picture Aurelian as an almost stereotypically Parisian fashion photographer, with a couldn't-really-care-less, shrug-it-away-and-light-a-Gauloise brand of sexiness. Kate tells me that about two years after they'd met she'd moved over to Paris full-time and not long after, by then virtually a household name with her career flying sky-high, they became engaged.

Which, it seems, is when all the trouble started.

'You see, the wedding was supposed to take place in Dublin,' she tells me, while Damien nods along, 'at my family's parish church. But, well you see . . . there was a bit of a glitch.'

'Yes?' I ask.

'The ceremony was just weeks away,' she goes on, 'and I flew over to Dublin to take care of some last-minute preparations with my mum. And I'm sorry to say that she and I rowed.'

'Which actually isn't such a difficult thing to do if you knew Kate's mother,' quips Damien, sotto voce, 'though of course I know you wouldn't dream of printing that.'

'It wasn't just any old heated disagreement either,' Kate goes on, 'this was a full-on humdinger with screeching, yelling, the whole works.'

'I won't stand by and watch my only daughter make the biggest mistake of her life with some photographer that we know nothing about!' says Damien, putting on a high falsetto voice.

Kate doesn't laugh along though, I notice, instead she quietly tells me that she just turned on her heel, headed straight back to the airport and caught a last-minute flight back to Paris and back to her fiancé Aurelian. Back to their top-floor shared apartment at Saint-Germain-des-Prés in the fashionable 6th arrondissement. Back, she'd doubtless hoped, to a sympathetic ear and a shoulder to cry on.

'Well, I was in for the shock of my life,' she goes on, describing how she'd burst in through the door, delighted to be home though not for a moment expecting Aurelian to be there. It was late afternoon and she knew for a fact he was due to be out on a fashion shoot at the Tuileries.

Prompted by Damien, she vividly describes throwing her wheelie bag on the hall floor, kicking off her shoes, about to go into the kitchen when, lo and behold, she heard voices coming from the bedroom.

'Anyway, let's just say that I discovered my fiancé was being unfaithful to me,' she says discreetly, trailing off there and leaving the story dangling.

'No, darling, the press will want a little more colour to the story,' Damien insists. 'Tell how you threw the bedroom door open – and well, there they were.'

'There's really no need,' says Kate demurely. 'I think anyone who reads this will be well able to draw their own conclusions.'

'Kate was horrified to see Aurelian in bed with another model who she'd worked with and who she knew very slightly,' says Damien, ignoring the warning hand Kate places on his arm. 'There they were, tucked up in bed together, sucking on cigarettes with a half-drunk bottle of champagne on the bedside table beside them, just to really hammer the point home. Must have been horrifying for you, you poor girl,' he adds, stroking her hand.

'So what happened next?' I ask, intrigued.

'Naturally she did what any woman would do,' says Damien. 'Got the hell out of there while he yelled all sorts of crap after her, you can only imagine. "Kate! *C'est ne signifie rien! Elle ne veut rien dire!*" '

Kate flushes slightly at the embellishment, and steps in to take over the story.

'What I actually did after that,' she tells me, 'was to jump into a cab and ask to go to Charles de Gaulle airport, mainly because I'd nowhere else to go and no one in Paris to turn to; which of course meant going back home, with my tail firmly between my legs.'

'Can't have been easy for you,' I say sympathetically.

'So Kate's mother had actually been on the money about Aurelian all along,' says Damien. 'You see, darling? Mother knows best. And I'd like to add for the record that her mum and I get along like a house on fire.'

'The problem was that when I arrived at the Air France ticket desk,' says Kate, 'I realised that I had absolutely no money on me. Not a red cent, nothing. Both my credit and debit cards were completely maxed out with pre-wedding buys, so of course they were of no use to me either.'

'And what did you do?'

'Well I hadn't a clue where to go and I suppose I was still in utter shock. So I gave up pleading with the ground hostess at the ticket desk, went and found a free seat in the middle of the concourse and instantly burst into tears. Mortifyingly embarrassing sobs too, I'm afraid. I made such a spectacle of myself that people started to notice and look my way.'

And one person in particular, it seems. Because there was a bar just adjacent to where Kate was sobbing her eyes out and as pure chance would have it, there had also been a huge Six Nations rugby game on earlier that day, Ireland versus France. The bar was jam-packed with supporters all

27

in high spirits, laying into the beers and whiling the time away before their return flight home.

'So there I was with a gang of guys from college,' says Damien, 'and we were in fantastic form because Ireland had just done the unthinkable and beaten France 22–10 at the Stade de France that afternoon. As you can imagine, there were more than a few pints of the black stuff involved.'

'And that's when you first spotted Kate?'

'Course I did, like just about every other red-blooded male there. You couldn't miss this knockout beauty bawling her eyes out in the middle of the airport concourse.'

Kate for her part says she barely even took notice of anyone around her, but all of a sudden she was aware of a guy hovering close by and looking worriedly down on her. Tall, classically good-looking, with dark hair and a light tan, dressed in an Irish rugby jersey and with the rugby supporter's obligatory pint of beer clamped to his hand.

'So, egged on by the lads, I walked right up to her and came out with probably one of the cheesiest pick-up lines of all time,' Damien grins.

'I realise this is probably a stupid question,' they say together, looking adoringly at one other, 'but is everything OK?'

It seems that Damien then sat down on a free plastic seat beside her and when Kate looked at him she tells me she had an overwhelming feeling that she could trust this guy. He had soft eyes, for starters, and she shyly confesses that she's always been a sucker for soft eyes. So she found herself telling him everything. He nodded, and listened to her tale of woe.

'But he said absolutely nothing.'

28

'Instead I just strode over to the ticket desk and paid for her return flight home—'

'—So of course I insisted that I'd have to reimburse him the minute we got back home, but he was having none of it.'

At this point, the pair of them almost overlap each other in their eagerness to get the story out.

'Anyway, I invited Kate to join my friends at the bar and they instantly took her under their wing. As you can imagine only too delighted that this stunningly beautiful, leggy blonde model had deigned to join us—'

'—Damien had even managed to wangle seats on the flight so we were beside each other the whole way home.'

'And when we'd landed safely—'

'—Ever the gentleman, he insisted on dropping me right to my parents' house – and he even managed to charm my mum over a mug of tea—'

'—Like I always say, get the mother onside and it's all plain sailing from there!'

But after I've switched off my tape recorder, Kate confides what really happened next. Befuddled and still punch-drunk from her emotional roller coaster of a day, it was only when her handsome saviour was leaving that she finally got around to asking him his full name.

'It's Damien King,' he apparently grinned at her. 'A lovely, warm, open smile too,' she adds in that soft voice. 'And I can't tell you, after the day from hell that I'd just been through, how grateful I was to meet such a gentle-man who looked after me and took care of me and who was . . . just so completely wonderful, really.'

Then came the clincher.

Instead of letting her pay him back for the ticket, Damien

apparently insisted that instead she let him take her out to dinner. Only it had to be the following night and that wasn't negotiable.

'Before she'd time to change her mind.'

'And he wouldn't take no for an answer.'

TESS

The present

Thursday night, dinner with the Pritchards. Did I tell you about my in-laws to be? Because not many people can say that they're genuinely fond of the family they're about to marry into, but I can. Deeply fond of them.

Honestly.

Bernard's parents, Desmond and Beatrice, are Anglo-Irish and now live in Donnybrook, the posh end of Donnybrook that is, in a once beautiful but now slightly dilapidated Victorian redbrick, surrounded by copper trees and with a banged-up Honda Civic sitting in their driveway on four blocks of cement. Untaxed, uninsured and ignored, much like the house itself.

True, their home could be beautiful if the Pritchards only tidied it up a bit, hoovered and maybe ran a duster over the place every now and then, but then that's all part and parcel of the Pritchard family charm. And we'll just skate over the wilderness that's their front garden, which right now is looking not unlike the set of *I'm A Celebrity . . . Get Me Out of Here!* In fact the one time my mother was here, her only comment was, 'well, we may not live in a house that grand but still, I think I'd rather die of shame than invite guests into my house if it was that filthy. The Pritchards may well act like they're posher than the Queen, but you'd want to see the state of their downstairs loo.'

You can tell everything you need to know about a person, according to Mum, by just a single glance at their bathroom. I tried in vain to convince her that she was missing the point, because that's the whole thing about the Pritchards; they seem to live their whole lives in chaotic squalor and it doesn't bother them in the slightest. It's all part and parcel of their whole 'take us as you find us' vibe.

Beatrice and Desmond, you see, not unlike Bernard himself, could best be classed as 'eccentric'. In an endearing way though, you can only admire them for all their warm-hearted, unaffected battiness. Desmond is a retired university professor (History of Art and Classics, just like Bernard himself). Meanwhile, his mum, Beatrice, used to work as a senior librarian and is now researching a non-fiction book, in her own words, 'all about Oliver Cromwell, politics and religion in the English Civil War, 1642–1651. Not your thing at all, my darling'.

In fact, I've a recurring nightmare that she invites me to her book club to discuss it and I am only hoping against hope that she doesn't give me an early copy to read then start grilling me on it.

I pull my car into the Pritchard's driveway, narrowly avoiding the same pothole that's been there ever since Bernard and I first started dating. There's a gentle thud on the roof of my car and I realise that it's Magic, the family's jet-black tomcat and officially the unfriendliest animal in the world, who's just jumped down from the branch of a tree to come and intimidate me.

'Hi, Magic,' I say, hopping out of the car and instinctively going to pet him, but he just squeals like I've actually done him physical harm and instead leaps up onto the bonnet of my car, tail pointing sharply upwards and hissing. Same as the big eejit does every single time he sees me.

'Come on, Magic,' I say soothingly, reaching out to placate him. 'Can't you and me be pals?'

He responds with a cross between a yell and a squawk that's so loud, next thing Beatrice is at the front door, still in her dressing gown and with a towel wrapped around her head. Almost as though I've arrived hours early for dinner and caught her off-guard, whereas actually I'm bang on time.

'What's that God-awful racket? Oh it's you, Tess dear, how lovely to see you. Now, Magic, shut up you silly puss, Tess is our guest and you'd better play nice.' Then she kisses me lightly and gratefully takes the bottle of wine I hand over.

I think it's worthy of note that it's only half six and as she air-kisses me, I can't help noticing that Beatrice already has a whiff of one G&T too many wafting from her. But then that's the Pritchards for you. No exaggeration, but in this house they generally start Happy Hour at mid-afternoon and keep on drinking till it's last man standing.

'Oh and just ignore Magic; I know we all do. The idiotic animal actually thinks he's a guard dog – do you know he'll only eat Pedigree Chum? And he'll only sleep outside in a little kennel that Bernard had to have made especially for him. Such a noodle.'

'He's . . . erm . . . certainly a little character alright,' I smile.

'And you've brought a little bottle of vino, how thoughtful of you. Come in and have an aperitif, Bernard's already here ahead of you. He's really so excited about the wedding now – as are we all. Not long to go now!'

I follow her inside to the gloom of their hallway, thinking that it's probably just as well that the entire house seems to get next to no natural light whatsoever; at least this way you're less likely to notice the thick layers of dust and cobwebs that coat just about every surface and square inch of the place.

I know my mother would flush scarlet in the face if anyone saw our house in this state, but that's the thing about the Pritchards, not only do they not care, I think they barely seem to even notice half the time.

Even if there are times when it does go just a *tiny* bit too far. On my very first visit here, Bernard and I were making small talk with the parents in the drawing room when Magic dragged in a dead mouse that he'd half-masticated and dumped it right at Beatrice's feet. And her reaction? To ignore it like it never happened and pour herself another stiff G&T.

'Tess, my sausage, is that you?' says Bernard, coming out of the kitchen with a sherry in one hand and a carving knife in the other.

'Hello, you,' I smile up at him as he bends down to give me a peck on the cheek.

'Had a good day?' he asks. 'Everything sorted about that dratted jury summons?'

'No, but don't worry, come Monday morning it will be,' I tell him confidently.

'Good, good, good,' he says absently, steering me past a big mound of books scattered all over the hall and on into the kitchen, where Beatrice is cremating what looks like it once started out in life as a rabbit.

Did I tell you about Bernard? Because he's just lovely and the total opposite of just about every eejit I'd dated right up till he and I met. With one messer in particular very much to the forefront of my mind at the minute, but we'll just skate over him like he never existed. Mainly because that particular chapter of my life is now buried deep in the back of my mind, padlocked and labelled 'Do not, on any account, enter'.

Trust me, you don't want to know.

Anyway, back to Bernard who's a big man, portly and greying, but with just the loveliest soft brown eyes. Gentle, kind eyes. He's also a full fifteen years older than me. He just turned forty-three last year and before he and I met, he quite literally hadn't dated since he was in college. And even that relationship petered out after just a few months.

In fact, half of me suspects that's the primary reason why Desmond and Beatrice were so welcoming to me right from day one. Up until Bernard and I started dating, I think they'd pretty much written off their only son as being neither gay nor straight, but in that grey hinterland in between. You know, a confirmed bachelor. One of those asexual people, who'd just rather have a nice cup of tea than dip a toe into the dating pond, purely to avoid all the emotional messiness involved.

His fellow college professors had long ago written him off as a young fogey in the William Hague mode and all the students he lectures had jokingly nicknamed him Billy Bunter because of his size, when, to everyone's astonishment, he suddenly started dating anew. True, he and I were a bit of an odd couple at the beginning, and attracted much head shaking and commenting behind our backs along the lines of, 'it'll never last'.

Even now, from the outside we look like a bit of a mismatch. There's Bernard, in his Clark Kent glasses wearing a crumpled linen suit, dandruff all over the collar and his tie on a bit skew-ways. Whereas here's me still in my work gear of a Lycra top, leggings, trainers and the warmest fleece I own – insurance against the cold of this house, which even in high summer never seems to get as much as a single ray of sunlight and is permanently freezing.

Even the way we met was a bit unusual and I'm only praying that his best man, a fellow professor, doesn't raise the subject in his wedding speech. Smash Fitness, you see, the gym where I work as an instructor, is on Nassau Street, slap bang in the middle of town and just across the road from City College, where Bernard lectures.

Anyway, cut to January two years ago and Bernard decided that he was developing a bit of a middle-aged spare tyre (and I hate to use the politically incorrect term 'porker', but in his case it was only the truth). In the spirit of New Year's resolutions, he decided that the only thing that would do him was to join a gym. And so gung-ho was he about his new fitness regime that he even booked a few full-on gut-burning sessions with a personal trainer.

Which is where I came in. But being brutally honest, this was no Hollywood 'meet cute'. I never really had that whole love-at-first-sight thunderbolt when I gave Bernard his first fitness assessment at the gym. Instead I took one look at this greying, overweight older man and if anything felt pity for the poor sod as I put him through a one-to-one boot camp class.

Boot camp at Smash Fitness, by the way, involves your

client doing a range of squats, lunges and press-ups, while the trainer yells all manner of motivational phrases in their face like, 'faster, harder, higher! Gimme ten more! Come on, burn it off . . . work through the pain!' We're actively encouraged to err on the savage side with our clients, as my boss operates under the perverse notion that the tougher and more insulting you are to people, the more likely they are to keep coming back.

It's not my way though. Personally, I prefer to encourage clients and cheerlead them towards their fitness goals, reminding them of how far they've come and how well they're doing and that's exactly the way I treated Bernard from the word go.

God love him though, he got so sweaty and red in the face when I first put him up on a treadmill, I really thought the guy might have a heart attack.

After a meagre ten minutes of what he claimed was medieval torture, he begged for mercy.

'I'm so terribly sorry,' he panted, gulping for air, 'but I'm afraid I've got pain in my hamstring muscles that haven't been used in decades.'

Typical Bernard. Unfailingly polite even when on the brink of an aneurysm. So just to make sure he got value from the full hour he'd paid for, I offered to take a look at his diet, to see what improvements could be made there. It's fairly standard practice at Smash Fitness to take clients off wheat, gluten, dairy, alcohol and sugar for a full six weeks and if clients can only stick to it, they'll soon start to look and feel unbelievably fantastic when they see visible results. Of course, Bernard nearly baulked at this when he realised that all his much-loved teatime sherries were now well and truly out, but I held firm.

Anyway, our session was finished and he was about to go his way and I mine, when he suddenly stopped me in my tracks.

'Tess,' he panted, still red-faced, sweaty and out of breath. 'I'm absolutely determined to do this correctly, you know, in for a penny, in for a pound and all that.'

'Good for you, you won't regret it,' I smiled, thinking how posh the English accent made him seem. The guy actually sounded a bit like Stephen Fry.

'The thing is, your website says that the gym offers an at-home service, where a trainer will call to your house with smoothies and then whisk you off for a brisk morning jog, isn't that correct?'

'Absolutely,' I said, delighted and relieved that I hadn't scared him off fitness for life. 'We can call to your home or to your workplace any time that suits you.'

'Then how's tomorrow morning for you?' he asked, taking off his specs and looking at me a little bit shyly.

'Well, normally we have a rota of personal trainers and I'm afraid I'm not scheduled for tomorrow morning.'

'Yes, that's all well and good, but the thing is some of the other trainers are quite brutal, almost to the point of being sadistic here, I find. So if it's quite alright, I think I'd really prefer it if it was you. In fact, I don't want it to be anyone else except you,' he added, the big brown eyes almost pleading with me.

What can I say? My heart went out to the poor guy and I found myself saying yes.

So the following morning I trooped around to his house at 7 a.m., with a kale, carrot and Brussels sprout smoothie, which, trust me, may look like a glass of mowed grass, but doesn't taste nearly as revolting as it sounds. It turned out

Bernard lived in exactly the sort of house I'd have pegged for him; no uber-cool penthouse bachelor pad for this guy. Instead his home was – and is still – a sturdy, well-built Victorian cottage right in the heart of Stoneybatter, otherwise known as the arty quarter of Dublin. With a crossbar bike in his hallway and piles of hardback books scattered all over every surface. The whole place was higgledy-piggledy, charmingly disorganised chaos, and it was only months afterwards when he took me to meet his parents, that I realised the apple hadn't fallen too far from the tree.

'Oh dear Lord, look at you,' he smiled, opening up the front door, all set to go in his tracksuit and trainers. 'You look so fit and fresh at this god-awful hour. How is that even possible? I'm afraid I'm one of those chaps who can barely string a coherent sentence together until I'm on my third pot of tea.'

'Follow the programme and you'll feel twenty years younger in no time,' I said firmly, and to be fair to Bernard, stick with the programme he did.

So gradually over time, he and I began to fall into a sort of routine. Twice a week I'd call over to him with smoothies at the crack of dawn, before dragging him out for a jog through the quiet of the early-morning streets. After a while, we grew so comfortable with each other that we even started joking and messing; I'd hammer on his front door and he'd answer still in his dressing gown, then try to cajole me inside for rashers, eggs and croissants. And from there, the conversation would go thusly: 'Are you having a laugh?' I'd playfully chide him. 'You're paying me to get fit, and we're going to do it right. So come on, trainers on and grab a warm, woolly fleece, we've a brisk two-mile jog ahead of us.'

'Oh God, the exquisite torture,' he'd mock-groan. 'Are you sure I can't tempt you with a lovely pot of Earl Grey tea? As a compromise, if I drink it with that wretched half-fat milk you insist on? And if I'm a good boy and cut out the blueberry muffin I always have whenever you're not around to goad me into good behaviour?'

'Bernard,' I'd grin back at him, 'what am I always telling you? Sugar is the Devil's food. I'm trying to detox you and here's you trying to put the equivalent of rat poison through your system!'

So this Tweedledum and Tweedledee carry-on went on for weeks; me using a combination of nagging and cheer-leading to try to wean him off complex carbs, starch and sugar; him only ever willing to jog all the way to the Queen of Tarts café in Temple Bar, so he could collapse through the door and order one of their famous chocolate pecan pies.

Then after I dropped him back at his house after one early-morning jog, to my utter astonishment, Bernard, still all sweaty and panting, asked me out. To go and see – get this – a screening of a French art house documentary about the Napoleonic Wars that was showing at the Lighthouse Cinema that weekend.

'You mean . . . on an actual date?' I blurted out, flab-bergasted. In a million years not seeing that one coming.

'Well . . . erm . . . it's just my way of saying thank you really,' he said, and I remember thinking how endearingly flustered he looked, whipping off his specs and absent-mindedly wiping them on his tracksuit top, the way he does whenever he's embarrassed. 'Thanks to you, Tess, I've lost a full two pounds this week, so I thought I'd celebrate with a large bucket of non-fat popcorn with absolutely no

40

hint of butter on it whatsoever. If you'd care to join me, that is?'

A date. An actual date. My first one since . . . well, since all of that. Initial reaction? To feel nervous and scared, with a tummy full of butterflies, the whole works. But then I thought: am I really going to let my past define my future? Isn't it time to let go and take a chance? And with who better than a gentleman like Bernard, who I knew in a million years would never dream of putting me through what I'd just come out of?

So to the movies I went.

The movie itself turned out to be a subtitled documentary all about the Napoleonic victory against the Prussians at the Battle of Jena, 1806. Bernard of course adored it and while I kind of wished Bradley Cooper or Matthew McConaughey would pop up on the scene to liven things up a bit, all in all, we'd a pleasant, relaxed, easy time together.

And so slowly, over the next few weeks, he and I morphed into a couple, in spite of a plethora of objections from both sets of our friends and from my family in particular. 'He's way too old for you,' they all chimed. 'A professor of Art History? Who likes to go on walking tours of the Alps and whose overriding passions in life are art, the history of art and absolutely anything to do with Napoleon? What the hell can the two of you possibly have in common?'

Most stinging of all came from my sister Gracie, who, the first time she met Bernard, immediately wrote him off as the most boring man on the planet and had absolutely no problem in telling me so.

'He's a rebound guy for you,' she told me out straight, 'and nothing more. He's the total antithesis of Paul; he's like the anti-Paul. That's the only reason you're bouncing

41

straight into this, you know. As long as you remember that, you won't get into trouble.' Nor has she changed her mind since, but then that's a whole other story.

And true, Bernard's core group of colleagues – mostly all confirmed bachelors working in academia – did intimidate me a bit at first, with all their shop talk about Kierkegaard's Theory of the Excluded Middle, and seventeenth-century Dutch art, but by then Bernard had really started to grow on me, so of course I soon started to see everything connected with his life through love goggles.

'You keep me young,' he'd often say to me, after a night out in a restaurant with my pals, or an evening at the multiplex seeing one of the slightly more commercial movies that would be a bit more to my taste. And for my part, I really fell for the fact he's so cultured and intelligent and passionate about what he does. I never went to college, and suddenly this man came along and opened my eyes up to a whole new world of opera, theatre and art exhibitions that I'd ordinarily never have gone within six feet of.

He's good to me, I'd tell all my family and pals. And after the emotional wringer I've just been through, I deserve someone like him. He's the equivalent of snuggling into a comfy pair of slippers after years spent in excruciating high heels that only ever made my feet bleed, if you'll pardon the tortured shoe metaphor. He's a man who calls when he says he will and who buys me flowers for no reason. Non-garage flowers too. And he's kind and polite and always gives money to homeless people when he sees them in the street.

OK, so maybe these aren't the sexiest qualities you look for in a life-partner, but in the long term, they work. Bernard and I *work*.

Besides, I've done the whole 'madly in love, this is Mr Right for the rest of both our lives' thing and where did that land me? Having to crawl back home at the grand old age of twenty-eight with my tail between my legs, that's where. Back to my old bedroom under Mum and Dad's roof, with Gracie in the room next door banging on the walls and yelling at me to turn the TV down. Back to months of humiliation and heartbreak and pain so searing it should nearly come with a safe word. That's where 'The One' landed me.

Long story and, I'm sorry, I'm not even going to go there.

So no matter what anyone else says or thinks, come what may, four weeks tomorrow, Bernard and I are getting married.

And jury service can just feck right off with itself.

KATE

More Sinned Against that Sinning,
Spring 2001

*After that first magical meeting at the departure concourse
at Charles de Gaulle airport, Kate and Damien had been
seeing each other for just over a year. And it was a very full-on
relationship too, even her mother had remarked on it.*

*Ever since that whole debacle in Paris, Kate's modelling
career had skyrocketed. So now she was travelling the world,
regularly flying cross-continent for photoshoots in one fabulous
location after another. She was effectively living out of a suitcase, and whenever she was back home in Dublin, it was far
easier for her just to stay with her parents, at the old family
home, at least until she had the time to buy her own place.*

*So in many ways, she almost used to think, Damien's court-
ship of her had been markedly old-fashioned and Victorian,
almost like something out of* The Rules *book.*

*Back then, they really were a couple to take notice of.
The papers couldn't get enough of them and in next to no
time it seemed like it was the Damien and Kate show. They
were everywhere: opening nights at the theatre, movie
premieres, days spent in corporate boxes at the races, even*

the high-society parties. You could hardly open a glossy magazine or Sunday supplement without seeing their good-looking, shining faces beaming back at you. Gossip columnists should almost have paid them royalties, Kate used to think, for the amount of column inches they generated out of the pair of them.

They'd barely been together three months when the press took it on themselves to start dropping 'gentle hints', and pretty soon gossipy little articles started appearing that Kate would blush to read:

*

'High-flying Globtech founder Damien and the glamorous lady on his arm, Kate Lee, were photographed at the opening night of La traviata at the Wexford Opera House last night. When questioned if he had any plans to make the lovely Kate the new Mrs King, Damien's enigmatic answer was, "just write that when you asked me that, I smiled."

'Meanwhile, Kate, one of our top models and the current face of Chanel, is rumoured to be on the verge of taking a small cameo role in the new James Bond movie, to be shot in and around the Caribbean next spring. But when asked whether she'd care to confirm or deny reports about a burgeoning film career, her only reply was a polite "no comment". When probed about whether she and Damien King were planning to tie the knot, her response was, "you know, I really think we'd better wind this up, it looks like the opera is about to start".

*

And so in a frighteningly short amount of time, a media couple was born. Because Kate and Damien were dazzling *together, one of those rare couples who somehow seemed greater than the sum of their parts.*

On the eve of her twenty-fifth birthday, unbeknownst to her, Damien had decided to surprise her with a holiday abroad, to stay at the Hotel Cipriani in Venice, if you don't mind. All pre-approved by Kate's beaming mother, who was only too delighted to accommodate this handsome, successful guy who came from such a moneyed background and who seemed supremely confident that he'd go on to make millions more under his own steam. Basically the stuff of any mother's dreams come true.

But then that was the thing about Damien, he had an almost lethal charisma about him. So much so that just about anyone who crossed his path would end up utterly bowled over by him. Kate had spotted it from very early on; how charming he was to absolutely everyone he met, without exception. From senior executives at his father's corporation, from whom he'd just borrowed heavily to set up Globtech, to the humblest busboy who came to clear the tables at the Michelin-starred restaurants he'd whisk Kate off to, almost bursting with pride to have this beauty on his arm. He'd smile directly at people, look everyone right in the eye and always, always remembered names. It was one of the things Kate really loved about him, his ability to walk with princes and paupers and to treat them both exactly the same.

When, out of the blue, that birthday trip to Venice came along, Kate was ecstatic. She knew the city, she'd once modelled here for a Victoria's Secret shoot, but as always on those work trips, her schedule barely left her time to get to and from the airport, never mind do a bit of sightseeing. Months before-hand, she'd mentioned to Damien casually in conversation

46

that she longed to see Piazza San Marco, to explore St Mark's Square, to sail along the Grand Canal and really spend time at the Doge's Palace.

And he'd remembered.

The whole trip had been magical from start to finish. From the moment they'd touched down at Marco Polo airport to step onto a speed boat that whizzed them directly to the Hotel Cipriani, Kate had almost felt like she was speeding through an oil painting.

But it was their last night that had been the most memorable of all. It was Kate's birthday and Damien had insisted on hiring a private chef to cook for them at the villa suite they'd been sharing. They'd eaten out so often and were both exhausted after doing the whole touristy thing, so Kate was delighted, welcoming the fact that it was a rare night in for both of them. Plus, it had just started to lash rain, the kind of Mediterranean rain that comes down in horizontal sheets, so a boat trip anywhere would have been a nightmare.

Dinner was served on their own private balcony overlooking a rain-soaked lagoon, but for some reason that evening Damien didn't quite seem like his usual affable, charming self. He was acting all jittery and edgy, and conversation between them didn't seem to flow as easily as it normally did. Every time Kate tried to chat about a fresco or sculpture they'd just seen, he'd just clam up, or else give her a curt, monosyllabic reply. So unlike the Damien she knew, who normally you couldn't shut up.

At one point, after yet another excruciatingly long drawn-out silence, she'd started to think he was about to dump her. Was that the reason for this private dinner? So she wouldn't burst into tears and make a show of him out in public?

47

Dinner came and went though, with ne'er a dumping in sight. Which immediately made Kate think – did he just want her to enjoy the last day of their holiday before ending it at the airport on the way home? Or would she just get the long, slow freeze-out that guys often did, where they just stopped calling, stopped phoning, where there was no contact at all and you were supposed to magically deduce that it was all over?

They both had a twitchy, restless night, but the following morning when Damien got up about 7 a.m. and abruptly walked out of the room without saying a word, Kate figured that it was all over. By ten in the morning, he still hadn't come back and she was wondering if he'd just abandoned her and was now already halfway on a flight to Rio just to get away from her, when suddenly her phone rang.

Damien. Telling her to go out onto the balcony and to stay on the phone. Puzzled, she did as she was told.

'I'm right down here in the garden,' he told her as she stepped outside, snuggled into her giant, oversized hotel dressing gown. She looked down, scanning the horizon – and sure enough she spotted him. Standing in a sea – no, an actual ocean – of white magnolias that had been carefully laid out all over the grass, three floors down beneath her. So stunning, they left her speechless.

'Read the flowers!' he yelled up at her.

In total shock, she did as she was told. They would have spelled out WILL YOU MARRY ME? Only the first M had blown away in the breeze, so what it actually said was WILL YOU ARRY ME? Apparently Damien's plan had been to spell it out for her in candles the previous night, only the thunderous weather put paid to that.

Rain or shine, day or night, it hardly mattered though. Kate's answer still would have been exactly the same.

48

Only one thing struck her as being slightly odd though. While she was excitedly phoning her parents and family to pass on the great news, Damien's first call had been to the press.

The Chronicle
April 2001

You could almost hear the sound of a million hearts – both male and female – being broken today as Globtech founder Damien King announced his engagement to one of the country's hottest and most successful models, the current face of Chanel, Kate Lee.

As scion of the famous King dynasty, it's expected that no expense will be spared and indeed that the couple's nuptials will make for the wedding of the year. Already the rumour mill has gone into overdrive and it's expected the loved-up pair will marry at the palatial home which the groom has recently purchased, Castletown House in County Wicklow, with a reception to follow for upwards of three hundred well-heeled guests.

When asked whether he could confirm or deny reports circulating that the King family were expecting former President Bill Clinton as guest of honour, the groom-to-be's cryptic response was "just write that when you asked me that, I smiled".*

---

* *An extract from* More Sinned Against than Sinning, The Unauthorised Biography of Kate King.

TESS

The present

And I'm still here, still sitting in the Pritchard's musty old dining room, dare I say it? Staring at the grandfather clock, and having a pretty hard time staying awake.

'No, no, what Immanuel Kant failed to grasp when he wrote about morality,' says Desmond, holding court at the head of the table, 'is that it all comes down to the individual. In an evolved society, morality is nothing more than a whim of the elective conscience.'

This, by the way, would constitute a reasonably normal topic of conversation in this house. Not for the Pritchards your common or garden gossipy small talk about the latest Netflix blockbuster or what's happening in the news, instead they roll out the conversational big guns right from the very first aperitif.

'I'm afraid I have to totally disagree with you there, Dad,' says Bernard, wolfing back his food and talking with his mouth full. 'Otherwise, what could Kant have possibly meant when he wrote "morality is not the doctrine of how we may make ourselves happy, but how we may make ourselves worthy of happiness"?'

'Well now, boys, in my opinion that theory has been the basis of all monotheistic religions for millennia now,' Beatrice chips in, reaching out for a bowl of roast potatoes and piling them up high onto Bernard's plate. And I swear to God, even though the groom-to-be practically begged me to help him lose half a stone before the wedding, he works his way through the lot of them in under a minute, shooting a guilty little look at me as if to say, 'yes I know, complex carbs are strictly off the menu, but as a guest under my mother's roof it would seem churlish to refuse'.

Beatrice seems to notice how hungrily Bernard is eating and I can see her glancing at him a bit worriedly, same as she always does every time we're invited here for dinner. But then I seem to walk into this trap every time we cross the Pritchard's front door – and it's the one and only tiny little niggle that I have in coming here.

According to Beatrice, you see, her only son was, physically speaking, a fine hunk of a man until I came along, but now, apparently, I won't be content till I've turned him into a skeletal shadow of his former self, living off nothing more than handfuls of nuts and seeds in between ice cold showers and five-mile jogs at the crack of dawn, that is.

Useless for me to protest the cold, hard reality, which is that when Bernard and I first met, he was overweight bordering on obese, with a BMI of 28.9. He pleaded with me to help him get in shape and that's exactly what I did, so he's now down to a reasonably healthy fourteen stone and with a cholesterol level that's not going to land him inside of an A&E department in the next few years.

But instead of acknowledging that Bernard is looking years younger and infinitely healthier, according to Beatrice I'm slowly starving the poor guy into an early grave and I

51

think that accounts for a large part of the reason she insists on us coming over for grub at least once a week. Once when she was a bit under the weather after a few G&Ts too many, I even heard her mutter to Desmond, 'at least this way I know the poor boy is getting a proper big feed every now and then'. She even slips him doggy bags to take home whenever she thinks I'm not looking.

Anyway, back to the dinner table, and on and on the three of them debate, cajole and shout over each other about their own personal theories on German philosophers, while I sit quietly staring through the gloomy half-light at yet another dusty pile of books scattered all over the floor, wishing to God I could contribute at least something to the conversation. Anything rather than sitting here mute, nodding along like I've the first clue what they're all talking about.

After a while though, kind-hearted Bernard seems to cop on that I haven't uttered as much as two words since we sat down – to cremated rabbit stew, by the way, with roast spuds soaked in oil and a bit of wilted cabbage on the side; the kind of food they serve in all those old men's clubs all along St Stephen's Green. I'm vegetarian but hate to be rude, so instead of actually eating it, I'm really just cutting up food then rearranging it, hoping no one will take any notice. Though to be perfectly honest, after a few stiff drinks I doubt if our host and hostess would pay the slightest bit of attention to me if I burst into a chorus of 'All the Single Ladies' and started twerking around the table.

'I'm afraid my dear Aged Ps,' Bernard chides gently from across the table, 'that we're being rather neglectful of our guest.'

'Begging your pardon, Tess dear,' says Desmond, who

basically looks like a computer-aged replica of Bernard himself, right down to the dandruff and the fact that clothes always look crumpled and slightly dishevelled on him, in Bernard's case no matter how many times I bloody well iron them.

'Oh, I'm terribly sorry, how rude of us,' says Beatrice a bit reluctantly. 'Then of course let's change the subject, to something that might interest Tess for a change.'

Silence. Then more silence, punctuated only by the ticking of the grandfather clock outside in the hall. Then Desmond pipes up, 'Oh, I know! Have you seen the Joshua Reynolds exhibition that's just opened at the Chester Beatty, Tess, dear? I read the most wonderful review, you know, apparently it's quite unmissable.'

'Ehh, no, I'm afraid I haven't as of yet,' I tell him, flushing scarlet, only too well aware that they're all looking at me now and that I'm the sole focus of attention.

'She's been terribly busy with all the wedding planning,' says Bernard loyally, bless him. 'Haven't you, sausage?'

'Things are getting pretty full-on alright,' I smile back, relieved that at least this is something I can talk about with confidence. Then I add uselessly, 'can't believe how fast the time is just whizzing by! I just keep making lists the whole time and yet the more I do, the more it seems there is to be done. No one had told me that planning a wedding is never-ending, really. But some lovely news, my pal Stella works in a hotel and only today she rang to say she's going to organise hiring all the cutlery, table linen, dinner plates and glasses that we need as a wedding gift for us. Isn't that amazing?'

'Terribly thoughtful of her,' Bernard smiles across the table at me.

I look hopefully over at my in-laws-to-be, praying one of them might want to keep up a bit of chat about the fact that we're getting married in just a few weeks' time, but no, no takers.

'And I've finalised the menu, you'll be delighted to hear,' I chat on. 'All very simple really; mozzarella salad to start, with spring lamb for our meat eaters and a wild mushroom risotto for our vegetarians, then chocolate mousse to follow and, of course, the wedding cake. I'm trying to keep it as straightforward as possible to keep the cost down. What do you think?' I ask.

No one answers though. Bernard's too busy stuffing his face with spuds while Beatrice just tops up her drink and stares into the middle distance, looking bored. Another long, protracted silence and I swear I can practically sense Desmond trying to inch the conversation onto something on a more cultural plane. Something that he and Beatrice are more in tune with, rather than hired dinner plates and menu plans.

A tad hurtful, but I let it pass.

'Oh I know what I wanted to ask,' Desmond says eventually. 'Tess dear, have you seen the Abbey theatre's new production of *The Threepenny Opera?* Are you a fan of Brecht and Weill? And the whole concept of the Alienation-Effect?'

I can sense Bernard smiling supportively across the table at me, but as ever on these occasions, I fail to shine.

'Well, emm, I'm afraid I've just been a bit busy with work and with all the wedding planning lately to get to the the-atre . . .' is all I can say by way of an answer, trailing off lamely.

Yet more silence, but as mortifying as it is to feel them mentally delegating me into the social slow lane, I remind myself that it's not exactly a barrel of laughs for poor

Bernard whenever he has to spend an evening at my family's house, either.

By contrast, whenever he comes to visit us there's precious little chat about arts and culture, instead he's forced to listen to my dad and my younger sister Gracie holding hot debates, which regularly spill over into out and out shouting matches, about whose team is doing best in the Premiership. Dad's a staunch Man. Utd man, Gracie is a lifelong Arsenal supporter, whereas the nearest thing Bernard's ever come to a football match is when he has to park his bike close to the training pitches around the back of City College.

To make matters worse, the very first time I brought him back to our house for dinner, I'd forgotten to fully brief the poor, unsuspecting guy. Which of course meant I never got the chance to explain that watching *Match of the Day* was sacrosanct viewing in our house.

'Alright if I turn the telly box off?' Bernard asked politely when we all gathered in our tiny sitting room after dinner, oblivious to the fact that Dad and Gracie were glued to the match and that the whole dinner had been scheduled so they wouldn't have to miss a single minute of it. 'Far easier to chat when the dratted thing is switched off, don't you think?'

The hot glare Dad gave him would have turned a lesser man to stone.

Nor are things any better for Bernard if he's forced to make polite conversation with my mum, who if she were ever to enter *Mastermind* could probably take 'great soap operas of our time' as her specialist subject. No kidding, the woman not only watches *Eastenders,* but avidly follows *Coronation Street* and *Red Rock*, as well as *Home and Away*. And even more astonishingly, she's actually able to keep fully up to speed on each and every one of them. Bernard, on the other hand, doesn't even own a TV so more often than not he just sits through evenings at our house with a look of painful resignation on his face.

'Imagine not owning a telly in this day and age,' Mum muttered after one of these excruciating family dinners. 'His house must look like it's just been burgled.'

Anyway, back to the Pritchards, and now Beatrice is looking over at me, like she's finally hit on some common ground that she and I can chat about.

'Oh, you know what, Tess? I've just thought of something you can most definitely help me with,' she says triumphantly from the top of the table. I smile hopefully back at her as she knocks back another gulpful of G&T, hoping against hope that this might be something I can contribute at least two words to.

'Tell me this, dear,' she goes on. 'I was in the library the other day and some schoolgirls came in, full of chatter and clatter and whatnot. They kept talking quite loudly about some sort of cultural phenomenon that I'm terribly afraid has completely passed me by. Pop culture, you know, far more your field than mine. But I found myself consumed with curiosity, so I thought, I know, I'll ask Tess.'

'Erm . . . ask me what?' I ask, silently praying I have something halfway intelligent to say here.

'What in God's name is a Kardashian?'

Now don't get me wrong, I'm genuinely fond of my in-laws to be, I really am. And I know for certain that Beatrice didn't mean to be patronising.

I'm sure it's just the way it sounded, that's all.

*

Hours later and with Bernard three sheets to the wind after a few sherries too many, he and I are bundled into my little car on our way back to his house, where I'm staying tonight. I instantly turn on the heater to try and thaw myself out a bit after the last few hours sitting in sub-zero temperatures. But then no member of the Pritchard family ever seems to feel the cold and I don't think they've switched their heating on since about 1997.

'Was that deadeningly boring for you, sausage?' Bernard yawns sleepily from the passenger seat.

'No! Not at all!' I say a bit overeagerly. 'Beatrice and Desmond are absolute dotes.'

'Good, good, good,' he yawns back at me and knowing that he'll probably be sound asleep inside of thirty seconds flat, I switch on the car radio. It's just midnight and there's a late-night chat show on, one of those programmes that's a big, shouty mess, where callers ring in to give out about water charges or else to gripe about whatever story is dominating the news that day. So I start to listen in, thinking if nothing else, at least it'll keep my mind awake.

'You know, I never liked that Kate King,' a woman is sniping over the phone to the show's host. 'If you ask me, Damien King is well rid of her. I've never come across greed like it! Hanging on to a painting that's worth nearly a hundred million euros, when I'm sure her husband has her more than well provided for in their separation? Wasting the Guards' time with that? Some people are shameless and in my opinion, I only hope she gets what's coming to her.'

I turn up the radio, hoping it doesn't wake Bernard, but he's snoozing peacefully away, completely oblivious. There's just something about Kate King that makes me sit up and pay attention. She's always in the news, she's one of those people who's forever looking out at you from news-stands and on the cover of glossy magazines. In fact it's impossible to sit in a waiting room anywhere in this country and idly flick through a copy of a social magazine without seeing her beautiful, sculpted and very definitely lifted face gazing haughtily back at you.

The woman's been a media darling for decades now, ever since she first started out as a model. Even more so since she managed to nab Damien King, one of the wealthiest men not just in this country, but in the world. So for years she wasn't just beautiful and famous, but the trophy wife of an actual billionaire, and apparently with no intention of *not* rubbing peoples' noses in their obscene wealth.

On paper, I think, eyes focused on the road ahead, there's never been any reason to dislike the woman and yet the weird thing is that everyone does. For years she was just too upfront about her glittering lifestyle, and it stuck in people's throats. In the worst throes of the recession, it was like the Kings were going out of their way to flaunt their obscene wealth in everyone's faces; the private planes, the statement homes, his fortieth birthday party that according to the papers cost over two hundred thousand, all while people who lived near the Castletown estate, not two miles from her front door, were having their homes repossessed.

Kate King is almost like a Marie Antoinette character of our age; you mightn't particularly like her and yet you still feel this irresistible pull to read all about her.

And like most of us, I vividly remember reading about her being in breach of a number of court orders about a year and a half ago now. Something to do with this painting, *A Lady of Letters*, or whatever it's called – a priceless

Rembrandt, apparently. The one Damien King was prepared to bring charges against his own wife to get back.

Or ex-wife, I think, correcting myself. Because if *Your Daily Dish* and *The Goss* and just about every other online journal I scan through these days are to be believed, Kate and Damien have been living separate lives for years now and are just biding their time apart till they can officially divorce.

I'm a bit behind with the news these days, what with all the wedding planning, but I know from my most gossipy pal Monica, who's obsessed with the Kings, that Damien has apparently shacked up with another woman, someone much younger. And did Monica mention something about this young one being an art historian?

I vividly remember charges being brought against Kate King over this painting she allegedly refuses to give back, and it being a huge story at the time. The press had a field day with it. It was everywhere, even made headlines on the TV news, that's how dominant the story was. Everyone was talking about it and from the sounds of it, they still are.

'You know, I heard that Kate King is refusing to leave that big Wicklow mansion they live in,' another caller chimes in, yet another woman all-too anxious to stick the knife into Kate King. 'She's holed up there without a stick of furniture in the place, and she still won't budge. Damien King will probably have to get another court order just to sandblast her out of there.'

'She'll get a right shock when he divorces her and she ends up in emergency accommodation somewhere,' another quips, a bit cruelly.

'Damien King bought that painting and he's saying

he's the rightful owner, so what makes that ridiculous woman think that she can just cling on to it like this?' says another.

Then a taxi driver calls in and thankfully his is the first reasonable voice I've heard on the show so far.

'Here's what I don't get,' he says as the host invites him to throw in his two cents worth. 'We all know Kate King has been charged over this, and we all know she's in breach of court orders and that this isn't going to end well for her. But what I don't understand is this: why doesn't she just give the shagging painting back to Damien King, if he wants it that badly? She's the ex-wife of a billionaire, so she can't be short of a few bob. Why is she bringing all this press attention and humiliation on top of herself when she could get out of it in the morning?'

'Because she wants the money, of course,' another caller on the line shouts over him. 'That's all she's ever been after, that's the only reason she even married him in the first place. Everyone knows that. That's a Rembrandt you know, worth €95 million. So wouldn't that set her up very nicely for life?'

'She's also trying to get back at Damien King too, never forget that,' says another. 'He's got a new girlfriend now and apparently they're engaged, that's what I heard. So if you ask me, Kate is clinging on to the painting for no other reason than to get back at him. He's dumped her, he's traded her in for a younger model, and that painting is the thing that he loves most in the world. So she's determined he'll never have it, because that's the vindictive type she is. Sure you'd know by the look of her.'

None of these people have ever even met Kate King,

I think. And yet they can be this vicious about a complete stranger, without hearing her side of the story first?

I glance over to Bernard wishing he were awake so we could have a proper gossip about it. Because there's a mystery here alright. Why would the woman invite all this trouble into her life and all of this negative press, when it could so easily be avoided?

It starts to rain now and as I switch on the windscreen wipers, my mind wanders back to another rainy night, oh, it must be about two years ago now. There I was, scurrying across the Ha'penny Bridge in bucketing rain, when I accidentally stumbled upon Kate King herself. But the woman I came across seemed absolutely nothing like the she-devil they're all so freely having a go at on the radio.

In fact, what I remember is a sad, lonely woman standing all alone on the bridge, soaking wet and with tears pouring down her face.

And so I switch off the radio.

Conflicted.

KATE

July 2001

With just a few weeks to go to the big day, as you can imagine for a wedding on such a titanic scale as this one, it had been panic stations. Kate and Damien's wedding was to be held at Castletown House, which had been gifted to Damien as a twenty-fifth birthday present and which could comfortably seat a guest list of three hundred with ample room to spare. Which was just as well given that the final, confirmed list of guests was rapidly escalating by the day.

Damien was not only an eldest son, but also the first of the King siblings to get married, so his family were determined to really push the boat out. The President was expected, along with no fewer than four other members of cabinet as well as the country's honorary consul to Monaco, where the Kings held a villa purely for 'tax status'.

A giant marquee was to be erected on the sprawling south lawn at Castletown House for the reception and local florists in County Wicklow were working on high overdrive to have everything ready in time. Not only that but Robbie Williams, Damien's favourite singer, had been booked to play at the reception.

Meanwhile, about a week before the wedding, Kate herself was just in the middle of a pre-nuptial panic attack over her wedding dress. She'd lost so much weight in the run-up to the big day that during her final fitting the dress almost threatened to drown her. The dress was utterly stunning in every sense; a close replica of the wedding dress worn by Princess Grace on her marriage to Prince Rainier, made of crushed cream silk taffeta, encrusted with delicate pearls and with a twelve-foot lace veil, held in place with a simple wreath of cream tea roses.

Next thing, out of the blue, Damien's father called her.

Instant panic stations. But then ever since she'd started dating Damien, Kate had only ever met his father on a handful of occasions. On every one of which he was dismissive of her almost to the point of rudeness. And never once had she been invited to call him by his first name, Ivan, so of course in her head she immediately gave him the nickname Ivan the Terrible.

'Mr King, is that you?' she said, answering her mobile in a froth of underskirts and taffeta at the designer showrooms where she was having her fitting. 'How are you?' Her tone was so respectful and over-polite that to hear her, you'd swear she was on the phone to a mortgage arrears company she owed a fortune to.

'Kate, there you are,' her father-in-law-to-be said gruffly while she strained so she could hear him properly. There was the deafening sound of engines roaring in the background, as if he were calling her from the airport.

'How are things with you, Mr King?' she asked nervously, not having the first clue what this could be about, and almost feeling like she might need to sit down to take this call. Ivan King terrified her, as he did most people.

But of course that was something she could never even discuss with Damien, who idolised his father and who wanted so badly to emulate him. In fact you could almost say that everything Damien did and every success he scored in business was done with the sole purpose of impressing his dad.

'I'm fit and well,' Ivan said gruffly, 'but then I'm always well. In fact, I've just touched down at Dublin airport and I'm on my way to see my solicitor in town. I'd like you to meet me there in one hour, please.'

There was no 'are you free?' or 'does that even suit you?' Just the presumption that she'd drop everything and rush to meet him. Which as it happened was exactly what Kate did, too terrified not to.

Exactly an hour later, with many rushed apologies to her designer, Kate found herself pulling up at McNally Ross solicitors just on the quays, right across the river from the Four Courts in the heart of the legal district. For about the fifth time, she tried calling Damien, to alert him to what was going on and to see if he had any idea what all this might be about. As bad luck would have it though, he was away in Brussels on business and his phone had been switched off all morning.

Ivan the Terrible was already in the solicitor's office ahead of her, waiting in the conference room, sitting at the head of the table as if he owned the place. Which, knowing him, he probably did. A grey-looking, bespectacled lawyer was introduced to Kate as a Mr Ross and Kate was invited to sit down in front of a legal document, with a pen strategically positioned right beside it.

'You're exactly seven minutes late,' said Ivan the T, who Kate knew to be notoriously punctual and highly intolerant of anyone who didn't meet his exacting standards. Mealtimes at the Kings' house were a bit like an army drill, according to Damien.

'I got here just as quickly as I could,' she said politely, determined not to feel intimidated. 'In fact, I rushed out on a designer friend of mine, just so—'

'But you're a model,' Ivan the T interrupted her. 'It's hardly life or death stuff we were interrupting, now was it? What were you doing anyway, strutting down a catwalk or something?'

'As a matter of fact, no, I was—'

'I'm afraid Mr King can only spare us a few moments,' the solicitor interrupted, 'before he has to leave for the airport again. His time is very precious and we must all respect that.'

And my time isn't precious? Kate thought crossly, but stayed tight lipped.

'So Miss Lee,' the solicitor went on, 'if you'd just be kind enough to turn your attention to the document in front of you, then we can proceed.'

'Oh now, you needn't look so worried,' said Ivan the T, waving his hand as if to dismiss Kate's concerns. 'This is absolutely nothing to concern you. All perfectly standard. We just need your signature on the dotted line, that's all. Then we can all get out of here.'

Kate began to read the document, but scanning down through it wasn't much help to her. It all seemed to be written in the most over-complicated legalese, littered with phrases like, 'the third party pertaining to the first part,' and 'hitherto forth and dated this third day of July, should the marriage come to be terminated . . .'

This is a pre-nup, she thought, horrified. So that's why

she'd been summoned here, with Damien safely out of the country: to sign a bloody pre-nup. Without her own lawyer present, without any warning or notice. She was about to become Damien's wife and now the King family just landed this on her and wanted her to sign her rights away?

Well, if they thought that she could just be bullied into putting pen to paper, then they had another thing coming. She had to talk this over with Damien, she just had to. Though instinctively she knew he'd probably laugh and tell her to rip the whole thing up, then fling it in the bin, where it rightly belonged.

'I'm so sorry to waste your valuable time, Mr King,' Kate said, standing up to her full height and pointedly shoving the document as far away from her as possible. 'But there's absolutely no way I'd dream of putting pen to paper on something like this. What you have to understand is that Damien and I love each other very much. We intend to spend the rest of our lives together and over my dead body would I ever consider discussing divorce before we're even married. And I'm afraid to tell you, nor would Damien.'

Later on that evening, Damien came back from Brussels and immediately called Kate. They'd been due to attend a movie premiere that night, a new release called *Gladiator* that was hotly tipped for Oscars, but as soon as Kate told him what had happened, he cancelled. Instead, he whisked her off for a cosy dinner, just the two of them, in l'Ecrivain, a Michelin-starred restaurant in the heart of town where he was a regular.

Still shaky from the whole experience, Kate told him everything and was beside herself with relief when he was just as dismissive of the whole thing as she knew he'd be.

'Oh, forget about it, I'm sure it's nothing,' he'd said,

topping up their glasses with a bottle of Cristal Champagne that he'd insisted on ordering. Kate never drank, it was her one and only golden rule, but she was still so shaken after that morning that she made an exception.

'Just the old man trying to protect family capital, that's all,' he went on. 'In fact he faxed me over the pre-nup this morning too. I've got it here in my briefcase. Never even glanced at the thing. Hadn't the time yet.'

'Damien! And you didn't think to call me? Just to give me a bit of warning that this was in the pipeline?'

'It's nothing! Trust me, this is just the way my dad is. Practically insists on a blood sample before he'll even hire a new employee, so you can imagine what he's like with a prospective daughter-in-law.'

'It was so scary in there today,' Kate said, allowing herself a tiny sip of champagne. 'I was caught completely off-guard, so I had no idea what else to do.'

'Sweetheart, by walking away from it you did the right thing. Besides, it's grotesque imagining you and I ever at each other's throats and screaming for a divorce. As if!'

Kate laughed and drank a tiny bit more.

An hour later, Damien was trying to convince her that this mightn't be such a bad idea after all and that the pre-nup meant so little, she might as well sign it.

'After all, sweetheart,' he said, reaching across the table to take her hands, 'you and I are never going to divorce anyway, are we? You're my perfect girl. Why would I ever want to divorce my perfect girl?'

'And I'd never divorce you in a million years,' she smiled back at him, randomly marvelling at just how handsome he looked in the candlelight.

'Well you know something?' Damien went on. 'Then

what possible difference can this make? It's just a signature on a piece of paper, that's all. It means absolutely nothing to me.'

Three glasses of champagne later when dessert was being cleared, he'd got her thinking it was actually all in her own best interests really. And Damien could be so persuasive when he wanted to be.

'Look at it this way,' he'd said, eyes glinting in the dim light. 'If you do sign, then in one fell stroke it proves two things to the old man: firstly, that you've absolutely no interest in the King family fortune and never had, and secondly, that you're marrying for love and nothing else. Plus it would certainly get you off on the right foot with the in-laws, wouldn't it?'

And by the time they called his driver around to take them home, light-headed from the champagne, Kate had already borrowed a biro from a passing waiter and signed on the dotted line.

TESS

The present

'I look like the Irish flag,' says Gracie, my baby sister and bridesmaid, shoehorning herself into the slinky little bottle green shift dress that she picked out for the big day months ago.

'Don't be ridiculous, you're gorgeous!' I say brightly, sticking my head around the fitting room door, so I can get a good look at her parading up and down in front of the mirrors outside.

'And it's too tight. Either I've put on weight or else it just doesn't bloody well fit properly.'

'You're as thin as a pin and it looks like a perfect fit to me.'

'Is it too late to get something else instead?' she whines, staring in the giant mirror ahead of her and fidgeting with the sleeves of the dress, almost as though they're itching her.

'You know right well it is,' I tell her firmly, going back into my fitting room. 'Besides, can I remind you that you're the one who insisted on wearing that dress in the first place? So in fairness, it's a little bit late to back out now.'

'I know, but what in the name of arse was I thinking?' Gracie insists. 'A bottle green dress against my head of carroty-red hair and freckly skin? By the time you throw in the white posy, I'll look like something off a St Paddy's Day float. You should have held me back, you should have ripped the bloody thing off my back when there was still time.'

'You're absolutely stunning, Gracie, love,' my mother coos over from a plush white armchair at a dressing table in front of a mirror, where she's sipping Prosecco – at half three in the afternoon by the way – while trying on fascinators and having an absolute ball for herself. 'A good spray tan will sort you out and wait till you see. You won't know yourself.'

'I promise you this much, Mum,' says Gracie, 'if I ever get married, I'll run away to the registry office just to spare you all this malarkey.'

'Don't be so ridiculous,' says Mum, balancing her glass precariously on the edge of the dressing table. 'And admit that deep down you really love dressing up. Besides, gay women have white weddings all the time these days, you know. Look at Ellen DeGeneres and your woman, what's her name, the tall blonde one that used to be on telly.'

'Not this gay woman, thanks all the same,' says Gracie.

The three of us are in The Bridal Room as it happens, which is this really exclusive shop outside Kildare town, about an hour from Dublin. It's boudoir luxurious in here, with plush velvet seating, deep pile cream carpets and, as you'd expect in a bridal showroom this posh, glasses of Prosecco on tap. It's my last fitting before the big day, hence my dragging Gracie and Mum all this way for the ride. And so far, in spite of all the behind the scenes trepidation about

70

this wedding from my side of the family, it's been fairly stress-free for all of us. So far, at least.

In fact I'd go so far as to say that this really is the joyous, happy, fun day out that I'd hoped for, and as an added bonus, I'm not having to listen to yet more long drawn-out lectures from my nearest and dearest about why Bernard and I will never work out and how I'm about to make the biggest mistake of my life, etc., etc.

I've been putting up with that for months now and I can't tell you how lovely it is to have a single day free of it. But then to a man, everyone around me has expressed doubts about Bernard, and the closer the big day gets, the more ominous those doubts seem to grow.

At this late stage, I'm basically sick to the gills of having to endure comments along the lines of, 'he's way too old for you!' 'You've absolutely nothing in common!' 'He's so bloody boring!' 'You're just doing this on the rebound!' And somehow the most stinging of all from my dad, 'ah pet, are you sure you're doing this for the right reason? You know what they say, marry in haste, repent at leisure. And I'm not just saying that because I'm having to shell out a fortune for the bleedin' thing either'.

To date, though, it's Gracie who's been the cheerleader-in-chief of all the doom-mongers; try as she might, she and Bernard just can't seem to connect on any level whatsoever. 'I feel like I'm about to lose my only sister,' she told me after a few drinks too many when we first got engaged. She was a bit pissed and I think she might have forgotten that she ever said it in the first place, but I certainly didn't.

It hurt then and it hurts even now to remember.

In fact Mum is the only one who doesn't seem to think that I'm heading for the divorce courts anytime soon. Not

71

that she 'gets' Bernard and all his constant references to obscure artists she's never heard of and exhibitions in galleries she's never so much as set foot in.

'I suppose he's solid and dependable,' is about the most lukewarm thing she's ever said to me in his praise, 'with a permanent, pensionable job and everything. So if nothing else, you'll always have a roof over your head. And I'll say this much for him, he's certainly not the type who'd ever cheat on you.'

Implication heard loud and clear and with that single sentence, Mum well and truly damned Bernard with faint praise. You may not exactly be marrying the love of your life, was her subtext, but I suppose you could do a whole lot worse.

And we all know exactly who she's referring to when she says 'a whole lot worse'.

Back to The Bridal Room though and maybe it's the Prosecco, maybe it's the fact that it's a beautiful, sunny spring-like day and we're all out of Dublin on a girlie jaunt, but right now the three of us are in great form, all my nerves and stress temporarily banished for the day as I focus on just having a lovely time with my nearest and dearest.

'Right then, are you all ready?' I call from inside the fitting room.

'Come on out, love, I have the camera ready,' Mum says.

'Take all the photos you want,' I yell back over the cubicle door, 'but whatever you do, just don't post them on Facebook or Twitter, will you? I want this to be a surprise for everyone on the big day.'

'Course I won't,' says Mum. 'Apart from Auntie Agnes, Brenda next door and Jill from the choir, I promise I won't show a single soul. Now come on out, we're all dying to see you.'

So I step out of the cubicle and swish my way up to a dais in the middle of the shop, then pirouette around so they can all get a really good look at the dress.

'Well?' I ask excitedly. 'What do you think?'

'Oh, my darling,' Mum says, welling up a bit. 'You're just . . . *beautiful*. The dress is even lovelier than I thought it would be. Now give me a nice big smile while I take a few snaps.'

'Absolutely stunning!' says the saleslady, bustling over to me with a pincushion to hand. 'It's like the dress was made for you!'

Said saleslady, by the way, is called Cindi 'with an i, not a y', as she pointed out to us, and she even looks a bit like a Cindi, with swishy, long blonde hair extensions and a big, bright smile. She's one of those bubbly effervescent women who almost seems to talk in exclamation marks and from day one she's been nothing but shiny, positive and upbeat through all my changes of mind and last-minute panic attacks over the dress.

'Do you think it works?' I ask nervously, though looking in the mirror, I'm actually cheeky enough to think that it does. It's the simplest dress you could imagine, just a plain white silk sheath, with spaghetti straps and a tiny fishtail swish to the ends, so it makes a little train as I walk around in it. No long veil for me. I decided against it at my very first fitting when I realised that against my pale, freckly skin, it made me look like a younger Miss Havisham.

So instead I'm just wearing a plain diamond clasp in my hair to hold it off my face. It's my 'something borrowed' from my pal Stella, who bought it in Claire's Accessories and wore it to her own wedding last year. I thought it would be particularly lucky because it was at this wedding that Bernard took me outside for a moonlit stroll when the dancing was in full swing, then out of the blue, proposed. Right down on bended knee and everything. Even though he ended up putting his back out, the poor dote. In fact, I spent my engagement night up in our hotel room holding an ice pack to his lumbar region, with him apologising profusely for our having to cut the night short.

Ahh, happy memories.

'Ooh, look at you, you're breathtaking,' coos Cindi.

'You're like a film star,' says Mum, with the camera focused firmly on me. 'Just stunning. Now keep smiling till I get a few more photos.'

'Have to hand it to you,' says Gracie with her arms folded, taking me in from head to toe. 'You certainly scrub up well. Looking good, babes.'

The three of them give an impromptu little round of applause and I giggle and twirl again feeling like a princess as Mum fires off another volley of camera shots.

'So who's the lucky guy then?' Cindi asks innocently, from where she's bent down on her hands and knees at my feet, making the tiniest little adjustments to the hem of the train.

But now, after a dream afternoon of laughter and messing and chat – there's total silence. Not a peep out of Mum or Gracie, absolutely nothing.

'Have you been engaged for long?' Cindi persists, to an even deeper silence this time. All I can hear is the tinny sound of Mendelssohn's Wedding March being piped over the sound system. And still not a word from either Mum or Gracie.

By now the silence is starting to get uncomfortable and I'm sure poor Cindi must be wondering why, after a whole afternoon of bright giggles and chatter, there's suddenly a pin-drop silence in the room. I swear I can almost see it writ large across her big, hopeful face . . . *did I just say the wrong thing?*

I look over to Mum, but she doesn't say a word about her son-in-law-to-be, instead she just stays firmly focused on her reflection in the mirror, this time with a giant dish-shaped hat on her head that's so ridiculously oversized it looks like you could pick up Sky Atlantic on it. Not a squeak out of Gracie either as she stares at herself in the mirror, shifting from this angle to that and pointedly saying nothing.

'He's called Bernard Pritchard,' I eventually tell Cindi, flushing scarlet red in the face and breaking this horrible silence, seeing as how it looks like no one else is going to. 'And he's lovely,' I can't resist throwing in. 'You'd like him, everyone does.'

Yet another unbearably long drawn-out pause and for a split second, Gracie and I lock eyes, me willing her to say something, anything, but she just glares into the mirror, now totally avoiding eye contact with me, the way she always does whenever she's struggling to keep her mouth shut. I swear I can physically sense steam coming out of her ears, cartoon-like, from the stress of having to bite back her tongue.

'So the groom's name is Bernard?' Cindi chats away, innocently skating over the surface tension that's almost pinging off the walls.

'Yes, yes that's right,' I answer automatically.

'Well I'm sure he and all your family get on like a house on fire.'

'He's a lecturer in City College,' Mum eventually chips in, while Gracie just stares blankly ahead, mouth firmly zipped.

'And he has a really good pension plan and everything,' Mum adds, to still total silence from Gracie.

Except this time the silence has somehow turned into something much, much angrier as Gracie and I stare each other down, me willing her to say something nice about her brother-in-law-to-be, her glowering right back at my reflection in the mirror, like she's determined not to blink first.

Lovely Cindi finally seems to sense that there are thunderclouds brewing between bridesmaid and bride-to-be, so she excuses herself and steps out of the room on the pretext of getting some more safety pins.

Which is when I seize my moment.

'Jesus, would it kill you, Gracie?' I ask her straight out.

'What are you talking about?' she asks blinking her blue eyes, faux innocent.

'You know exactly what I'm talking about,' I say, deliberately trying to keep the sharp, stinging hurt out of my voice.

'Now, now, girls,' says Mum from over at the dressing table. 'We've been having such a lovely day. There's absolutely no need for the pair of you to start into each other. There's a time and a place for conversations like this and that's certainly not here and now.'

'Mum, tell her!' says Gracie defensively. 'I never even opened my mouth and she's still having a go at me!'

'No, you didn't open your mouth,' I say, 'and that's exactly my point. For God's sake, Gracie, it's less than a month to go to the big day and yet when a total stranger asks you about the man I'm about to marry, you still can't find it in yourself to say a single good word about him?'

'Well what do you want me to do?' is her comeback. 'Be a complete hypocrite and pretend that I don't think you're about to make the biggest mistake of your life?'

'Come on now, girls, there really is no need for this,' Mum hisses warningly, ripping a fascinator off her head and turning round to face us both. 'Cindi might hear the pair of you squabbling and then what'll she think of us?'

'You're my only sister, Gracie,' I tell her, ignoring Mum, determined to say my piece. 'And what's more, you've agreed to be my bridesmaid. So is it too much to ask that you could be a little bit more enthusiastic about my wedding? God knows, I'm not asking you to be best friends with Bernard, you've made your misgivings about him clear enough—'

'And I'm sorry, I really am,' says Gracie, stepping down off the dais, where she'd been posing in her dress, and kicking off the high heels she'd been wobbling uncomfortably in. 'But I still stand by what I said.'

'I know you don't like him, but what I don't get is why you can't accept that I love him and I'm marrying him no matter what you might think!'

I'm red in the face and properly angry now. Hot tears are starting to sting at the corners of my eyes now that the gloves are well and truly off. The dull pain from the horrible comments and the thousand searing humiliations Bernard and I have had to put up with ever since we got engaged is suddenly fresh in my mind now, almost making me shake with white-hot anger. But then this particular row has been brewing between Gracie and me for a very long while, and no time like the present, etc.

'Yeah but you're marrying him for all the wrong reasons,' is Gracie's quick as gunfire reply. 'You know as well as I do that you're just getting married on the rebound from Paul. In fact this is such a textbook rebound case, it's almost a cliché.'

'That's not true and you know it isn't—'

But she just cuts across me.

'Well, I'm here aren't I, babes?' she says, stepping closer to me now, arms folded aggressively. 'I'm practically beaten into a dress that frankly makes me look anaemic with my pasty white skin – and all for you. Because you're my one and only sister and, believe it or not, I love you and I want to be there for you. Just don't expect me to dance cartwheels when you exchange your vows, because to be perfectly honest with you, I think in two years' time you'll be singing a very different tune. So there. Now I've said it. To your face.'

Silence in the room. Cold, stony silence. It's only now I notice that Cindi has already come bustling back in with a mouthful of pins, most likely having overheard the gist of our row. I'm actually shaking and even Mum is at a loss for words, which is not like her at all.

Thank God for Cindi though, who instantly clicks back into mindless-saleslady-patter mode, effortlessly gliding over the surface tension that's just beneath.

'I really am so happy you went with this style, Tess,' she says brightly, getting back to re-pinning the hem of my dress. 'You've certainly got the figure for it, and not many would have, you know. I don't think in all my years working here I've ever seen a dress suit a bride so well.'

I'll take a large bet that she says that to just about every bride who passes through these doors, but right now I'm just so grateful to her for changing the subject, that it doesn't bother me.

Still more silence.

'So have you been checking out the long-range fore-cast?' asks Cindi, aware of the dark undercurrent and seemingly determined to jolly us all out of it, bless her. 'Because you know there's a weather app that a lot of my brides find very accurate!'

'Erm, no,' I say in an unsteady voice. 'I haven't just yet, but I certainly will when it gets closer to the time.'

Another excruciating pause while Gracie stares furiously off into space and Cindi keeps steadfastly pinning the hem of my dress. Then Mum, bless her, comes to my rescue. She's drifted over towards a coffee table now so she can top up her glass of Prosecco and her eye falls on a news-paper that's lying there.

'Oh, now isn't that very interesting, girls,' she says, picking up the paper as something catches her attention.

'What's that?' says Cindi brightly.

'Kate King is in the papers again,' says Mum, sitting down on a sofa and leafing through the pages. 'On the front page and everything.'

'Really?' says Gracie, suddenly back to herself now that we're talking about something other than Bernard. 'But then, Kate King is never out of the papers, is she? Particularly these days with all this talk about court action and charges being pressed and some painting she and the ex are bickering over.'

'Oh yes, I heard about this!' says Cindi. 'My pal is a hairdresser who does a friend of Kate's hair and I heard it all from her first hand. Well, almost first hand.'

'Are they divorced yet?' asks Gracie.

'Legally separated and just biding their time apart till they can finalise it,' Cindi says knowledgeably, looking like she's delighted with the change of subject. 'And that's where all the trouble started, apparently. The Kings went for mediation ages ago and that broke down because Kate wants more money out of him, before she'll agree to a divorce. And even though Kate's been charged by the courts and everything, she's still sticking to her guns and is refusing to give back this particular painting that Damien says she's no right to. Insists it's her big insurance pay-out.'

'I love the way Kate does her hair,' says Mum, gazing dreamily at her photo in the paper. 'She always looks so fabulous, doesn't she? In spite of what she's going through.'

'She's had work done for definite.'

'Sure we'd all look fabulous if we'd had the amount of Botox and fillers that she's had.'

'And of course everyone knows Damien King wouldn't exactly be the world's most faithful husband, at least that's what I heard.'

'Well, maybe that's it then. Maybe that's why he wants rid of Kate?'

'Sure they were fifteen years married and they still didn't even have kids! Something seriously wrong there, mark my words—'

'Apparently he was desperate for a family and she'd been going for all these really expensive fertility treatments but none of them worked—'

'Oh, I read that too on *Your Daily Dish*—'

'And I'd say Kate was dying to get her hands on as many valuables as she could from that stately pile of theirs, before she got turfed out on her ear—'

'I'd love to know what went wrong there,' Cindi muses thoughtfully. 'When they first got together, they just seemed so . . . *happy*. So devoted to each other. I really thought they were a genuine love match.'

'And look at the two of them now, at each other's throats—'

I'm only half-listening to them all though. Instead, I slip out of the fitting room on the pretext of going to the ladies, to have a little lip-wobbling moment in private, where no one can see.

Feck Gracie anyway, I think, looking at my reflection in the mirror. To hell with what she said. I'm most definitely not getting married on the rebound and that's all there is to it.

In four weeks' time, I'll be Mrs Tess Pritchard. And Gracie and the whole lot of them can learn how to deal with it.

Just like I have.

KATE

Spring 2002

Eight months, two weeks and four days. That's exactly how long Kate had been married before she began to see a very different and slightly worrying side to Damien.

She could still remember it vividly. They had been due to have dinner that evening with a business contact of his, along with his wife. Not just any business contact though – Damien had so many, it was impossible to keep up with them all – this was a guy who'd flown in all the way from Missouri especially for the night and Damien was hoping to persuade him to come on board as a Globtech investor. Kate knew it was a huge deal for him and, as ever, the last thing she wanted to do was let him down.

About an hour before they were due to leave, she was still up in her bedroom at Castletown House, blow-drying her hair before changing into a slinky Armani cocktail dress she'd bought in Harvey Nichols earlier that day, a whispery slip of a thing that only someone as long and lean and elegant as her could possibly carry off. From two floors beneath her, she heard Damien coming home from work and moments later, he strode into the room and was straight over to her, locking his arms around her waist and nuzzling deep into her neck.

'Missed you,' he said, kissing at her ear. 'Did you miss me?'

'Stop messing,' Kate laughed, playfully pushing him away from her so she could concentrate on putting in her earrings. 'We only just saw each other this morning!'

'Far too long to be apart,' he said, gripping her even tighter. 'Nine hours stuck in the Globtech office without you? Completely ridiculous. Might have to start bringing you into work with me.'

He looked adoringly at her and a part of Kate glowed, still unable to believe that it really was possible for two human beings to really be this much in love, even after almost a year of marriage. Their life was completely perfect in every way and although she worried constantly about something going skew-ways, it never seemed to. Day after unbelievable day, she and Damien had remained as besotted with each other as they'd been since they first met. Everyone commented on it; friends teased them for still acting like newlyweds and even the gossip columns were constantly filled with stories about 'the loved up Mr and Mrs King'.

But then Kate was still naïve enough to find being in the full headlamps of Damien's attention endearing and romantic. The way he was so full-on and almost obsessive about her, insisting on being with her every night of the week and when they weren't together, calling and texting all the time. Wanting to know the tiniest detail about her day, wanting to tell her all about his.

'Oh that's so sweet . . . he's nuts about you!' all her girlfriends had said, not a little enviously.

'Keeping tabs on you, is he?' was her mother's only

comment, when Damien had taken to calling in to the family home at all hours before they were married, even if he knew Kate was out on a modelling shoot. He'd sit with her mother, charming her, buying expensive gifts for her, encouraging her to tell stories about what Kate had been like as a little girl. Never in her whole life had Kate dated anyone so unabashedly besotted with her and she found it intoxicating. Like standing out in full, glorious sunshine.

'So where are we meeting the Sandersons tonight?' she asked him, focused on her dressing table mirror and fiddling with the back of an earring that stubbornly refused to go in.

Damien pulled a face and locked his arms even tighter around Kate's waist, kissing the nape of her neck and playing with her long, fair hair. He was still in his work suit and smelt slightly sweaty and musky from a long day.

'Oh, sweetheart, does it matter?'

'You're messing up my hair.'

'So what? I like it messy. It's sexier.'

'Well shouldn't we get a move on before we're late? If we've got to drive into Dublin for this dinner, we need to get going.'

'Let's not bother,' he'd said after a pause, sliding his arms even lower down her thighs and pulling her even closer. 'Let's just have a night in, just the two of us. We've both had a busy week, so why not have this evening to ourselves?'

'But won't that be rude to the Sandersons?' Kate asked, turning around to face him now. 'They've flown in all this way and you've been saying all week how much you've got to discuss.'

'Oh, babe,' he said, rolling his eyes. 'I'm putting them up in the Merrion hotel. They'll be fine there, with a bit of room service. It was only a business dinner anyway, we can always do it some other time.'

'But they've travelled from Missouri just for this!'

'So?'

'But . . . I was actually looking forward to going out tonight . . .'

'Ooh, now, sweetheart, I can think of ways to keep you far more entertained here at home instead,' he'd said, unzipping her dress, pulling her face to his and kissing her as he gently caressed the small of her back.

Half an hour later, tangled up in bed together in a mess of limbs and discarded clothes and Egyptian cotton sheets, Damien reached out to the bedside table for his phone.

'Hi, can you put me through to the Sanderson's room, please? Thanks. Hi, Greg, that you? Damien here. Yeah, good to hear your voice too. Listen, bit of a problem this end, I'm afraid. There we were, so looking forward to seeing you for dinner tonight, only Kate's been in an awful car accident and I'm afraid she's a bit shaken.'

Kate sat up and looked across the bed at him, horrified.

'. . . OK to take a rain check on tonight?' he chatted on, improvising easily as he went. 'No, no, she wasn't hurt, thankfully, but she's completely rattled as you can imagine . . . yeah, the car is a complete write-off . . . no, not the Jag, the Beamer . . . brand new as well . . .'

Kate lay back against the pillows, astonished at how easily the lie just tripped off his tongue. He even embellished it with all sorts of crazy, elaborate details. Apparently she'd been driving along one of the twisty by-roads that led to Castletown when another car came flying round a dangerous bend, crashing into her front right headlight and sending her reeling off the road. A hit and run, apparently. And yes, the Guards had been called, and were confident they'd find the culprits. Teenage joyriders, more than likely. For good measure, he even threw in that he'd taken her to A&E, where she'd been treated for minor shock, then sent home to rest.

What was really chilling was that he was so persuasive, so utterly convincing. If I listen to him much longer, Kate thought, I'll eventually start to believe this myself.

'All sorted, babes, we're off the hook,' Damien said, hanging up the phone and cuddling her tightly into him. 'So it looks like it's just you and me tonight. Bliss.'

She pulled away and hauled herself up on her elbows so she could look him square in the face.

'You could have just said one of us had a tummy bug,' she said. 'There was no need for the three-act opera.'

'The bigger the fib, the more easily people will believe it,' he'd shrugged lightly.

Kate said nothing, just looked steadily back at him.

'What now?' he said. 'Did I say the wrong thing?'

'Nothing. I hadn't realised, that's all.'

'Realised what?'

'Just what a good liar you are.'

TESS

The present

Come the following Monday morning and it's D-Day. Otherwise known as the day I'm due to pitch up at the courts for jury service, then see how long it takes for me to wangle my way out of it.

But by God, am I ready for them or what. I'm briefed, prepped and primed to within an inch of my life so I can get out of this and get back to planning the wedding ASAP. I've done my research back to front and thanks to a lovely barrister called Jackie, who's a client of mine at the gym, I'm reasonably confident – and I'm saying this with fingers and toes crossed – that I might just have stumbled on one or two 'outs'.

'The thing to remember about jury service,' Jackie panted at me from a treadmill at Smash Fitness during one of her lunchtime training sessions last week, 'is that many are called, but few are chosen. For every nine hundred summons the courts send out, roughly only three hundred actually turn out to be eligible.'

'I'm liking that statistic,' I told her gratefully, 'and there's a whole list of reasons as to why you can plead that you're not up to serve. I figure my best shot is to go in armed with a letter from my boss to say I'm invaluable at work and can't possibly be spared the time off.'

'But is that true, strictly speaking?' she asked me a bit worriedly.

'Well . . . maybe I've exaggerated just the tiniest little bit,' I told her. 'But come on, I mean how many times in my life am I going to get married? The wedding is just weeks away. Being locked away from the world to sit in on some court case is out of the question. I can't do it, Jackie, it's just not a runner.'

'Then let me give you a bit of free legal advice,' she panted, slowing the treadmill down to a walking pace, so she could catch her breath. 'The thing about the courts is that you think it's all designed to intimidate you, but really nothing could be further from the truth. Admittedly, it can be terrifying actually stepping into court and having to plead your case in front of a judge, but it happens all the time. I see it every day in work.'

'Really?' I asked hopefully.

'Absolutely. So just go right in there and if the Jury Selection Officer won't release you and you do actually get selected, then you'll get to go to court and can tell the judge exactly what you've just told me. That you're getting married in a few weeks, and you just can't possibly give them the commitment that they need. If you're lucky, he or she may even dismiss you there and then. But if not, remember that you've always got a second ace up your sleeve. Because even if you are called to serve, a barrister from either the Defence or the Prosecution has the right to object to you, for some reason that you may not even be aware of.'

'Yeah but like what?' I asked her, feeling lighter about all this than I have done ever since that blasted letter arrived. After all my stressing and fretting and driving Bernard mad with it, this might not be as bad as I think it will be.

'The thing is that appearances can say an awful lot about us without our even knowing it,' she tells me, in between gulping from a bottle of water. 'I remember being in court one time and an opposing barrister objecting to a juror because they happened to be wearing the tiniest little Pioneer pin. You barely even noticed it. But it was a drunk and disorderly case, so they felt because this particular juror was teetotal, clearly they might be biased.'

'So you mean look the part of "woman you'd least like to be deciding the fate of a prisoner in the dock" and I might just be home and dry?'

'Can't hurt,' she shrugged back. 'Though you certainly didn't hear it from me.'

*

So it's 8.45 a.m. on Monday morning outside the Criminal Courts of Justice. And you want to see how I'm dressed, I look like I'm about to either mug you or else ask if you've any spare change for a hostel. I'm wearing the scraggiest pair of jeans that I own, with a knackered-looking parka jacket about three sizes too big that Gracie lent me for the day.

Ah, Gracie. Bless her, she came into my room this morning, still a bit shame-faced from our blow-out in The Bridal Room on Saturday and after a whole Sunday of completely blanking me, finally looked like she was ready to make peace.

'You still annoyed with me?' she asked, direct and to the point, in that sort of shorthand that sisters seem to have.

89

'Mmm . . . what? What did you say? What time is it?' I mumbled from under the duvet cover, still in that halfway house between sleep and wakefulness.

'I'm trying to tell you I'm sorry,' she said, plonking down on the edge of my bed. 'You know, for being a total arse at that bridal shop place. So there. I said it. So are we mates again?'

'Ehh . . . yeah . . . course we are,' I say, to be honest, still groggy from sleep and only half-taking this in.

'So . . . I'm really forgiven? You know, for ruining wedding-dress-fitting day, etc.?'

'Gracie,' I say, hauling myself up onto one elbow, so I can look her square in the face. 'You're my only sister. Of course you're forgiven.'

She winks and grins at me and just like that she and I are back to being OK again.

'Good, because I really need a lend of your cream jumper. There's a new girl in work I've my eye on and I want to dress to impress. You know yourself, my clothes look like, well they look like what they are, which is straight out of a second-hand shop. And the thing is, Tess, you always look so . . . *clean.*'

She's looking to borrow clothes. Which means it's Monday morning. Which can only mean one thing. Court.

Suddenly I'm wide awake.

'Ehh . . . sure Gracie,' I tell her. 'Take whatever you like.'

'Great, ta,' she says, heading straight for my wardrobe.

'But in return,' I add, just as she's starting to rip my wardrobe apart, 'there's something you can do for me.'

And that was to 'style' me in her own unique way, the brief being, 'make me look like the last person alive you'd ever want serving on a jury'.

So now here I am, dressed a la Gracie; with manky, unwashed hair sticking out sideways, that looks like I stuck two fingers into a plug socket before I left home, jeans with more holes in them than there is denim and a t-shirt that says, *See You All At My Intervention*. All in all, I'd confidently say that I'm looking like the least likely person you'd ever want deciding whether you're guilty or not guilty.

About an hour later, walking down Parkgate Street and stepping in out of the chilly April wind, I'm immediately taken aback at just how different the Criminal Courts of Justice are from what I'd expected. I'd thought it would be like something off the set of *The Good Wife*, or else *Law and Order*. You know, a huge, Palladian-style building, with imposingly tall columns and ice-cold marble floors, with police leading handcuffed criminals to and from court. The kind of place designed to intimidate you practically from the minute you step through the door, whether you're guilty or not.

But it's nothing like that at all in here. Turns out there are twenty-two courts housed together in this brand new building, eleven-storeys high, and as soon as you step inside, completely full of light and air. The foyer is huge, circular in shape with overhanging balconies looking down at us, where each courtroom is clearly marked.

Most surprising of all is that it's actually warm and welcoming in here, so yet again it seems I've been misinformed by watching too many legal dramas on telly. I could even be in the foyer of a five-star hotel, the layout is that luxurious looking. The only giveaway of where I really am is the sight of important-looking barristers swishing around in wigs and gowns, trailing wheelie bags behind them stuffed full of case notes as they clip briskly about their business.

The foyer is packed out even though it's just before nine in the morning, as if every juror was summoned to appear at the same time and on the same date. Which is actually good news for me; after all, the more people that they have to choose from, the more likely it is that I can skive out of here early. Just like at the airport though, there's a security check to clear first, where you half-undress, then put shoes, bag, jacket etc. into a bucket while you're screened.

I set off the alarm, so next thing a beefy-looking security guy who's all shoulders with hardly any neck pulls me aside to pat me down. There's no time to waste, so I nab my chance.

'Hi there,' I smile brightly, 'can you tell me who I need to speak to about being excused from jury service?'

'You want to be excused?' he says disinterestedly, patting down my back and shoulders.

'Yes, that's right. I have a letter from work explaining that I can't possibly be spared this week, you see. Or any week for the foreseeable future.'

'Ha! Good luck with that,' he snorts, making me stand like a starfish, while he pats down the sides of my arms and legs. For God's sake, what does he imagine I'm trying to smuggle in here anyway? A nail file for some prisoner to file off handcuffs? An illegal sandwich?

'I'm so sorry,' I tell him firmly, 'but it's actually really important that I speak to whoever is in charge here. I shouldn't even be here you see—'

'OK, you're clear to go,' he says, totally ignoring what I just said. 'Here's your security pass. You need to wear it around your neck at all times. Take a right turn at reception for the Jury Selection Office, then wait there till you're assigned a number. Next!'

'Thanks, but there's absolutely no need for the security tag,' I insist, handing it straight back to him. 'Like I say, I'll be out of here in no time, so it's just a waste really.'

'Madam,' he says a bit more sternly, 'you need to wear your pass at all times. Now can you move along, please?'

'Honestly, I really won't be needing it,' I say firmly.

'Ehh, here's a tip,' says a tallish guy about my own age, who's standing right behind me in the queue to reclaim coats, shoes etc. from the security buckets. 'It might be a whole lot easier if you just took the badge.'

I don't even answer him though. Instead I just sum up as much dignity as I possibly can given that I only have one shoe on and am still fumbling for the other one, and stomp off in the direction of the Jury Selection Office.

Where my luck doesn't improve. There's a long, snaking queue ahead of me, because apparently it's not enough to just turn up here, you've got to register too. When I eventually weave my way up to the top of it, turns out there's an older, hassled-looking lady with a pinched face sitting inside a little office with a glass window and a hatch who seems to be in sole charge around here. Her name badge says Bridget, so I call her by name, hoping against hope we get off on the right foot.

'Good morning, Bridget,' I beam through the tiny hatch, bending down so she'll hear me loud and clear. 'I'm Tess Taylor and I'm afraid I'm ineligible to serve today.'

'Summons papers, please,' she says briskly, glasses wobbling on the edge of her nose.

'I'm afraid I'm indispensable in work and I even have a letter from my boss to say that I can't possibly help you out. I'm needed back at my job, you see. The next few weeks are crazy for us.'

She does a brief, cursory scan of the letter I thrust at her through the hatch – the one I had to beg my boss for, then stand over him and practically dictate. Anyway, by the time he was finished writing it, you'd swear I was an open-heart surgeon with a list of quadruple cardiac bypasses to perform this week, and not a humble fitness instructor with a rota of spin classes, yogalates and piloxing, plus appointments with despairing clients; distraught because they ate too many takeaways at the weekend.

Bridget scans down through the letter while I hold my breath.

'Chilly morning, isn't it?' I ask lightly, in a wan attempt to win her over.

Silence.

'That's a gorgeous suit you're wearing. Reiss, is it? The colour really suits you.'

More silence.

'Sorry,' Bridget says flatly, 'but I'm afraid your field of employment doesn't come under the category of important community service.'

'But it *is* an important community service!' I insist, reddening in the face. 'I've a whole list of clients depending on me this week. People who really need me! And I'm sure everyone that turns up here says that to you, but trust me, no one else can do my job—'

'You work as a fitness instructor in a gym?' she asks disinterestedly, referring back down to the letter.

'Yeah . . . but I was promoted to Assistant Manager only recently,' I throw in for good measure.

'You're not a guard, you're not a pilot, you don't work

in the medical profession and you certainly don't work for the Director of Public Prosecutions either.'

'Well no, but you see I've a whole rota of clients this week who I can't possibly cancel on, it wouldn't be fair on them, you see—'

'Therefore you don't perform an essential civic duty. Take this number, and make your way through the door on the left. And move along, please, there's a long queue behind you,' she adds, busying herself stamping a form with a number on it.

'I'm sorry, Bridget,' I insist, panic starting to rise now, 'but I don't think you're really hearing me properly. The thing is I really can't be here today, or any day for the next few weeks. I have to leave. *Now*. Look, you've got plenty of other people here to choose a jury from, so why can't I just be excused? I'd be happy to come back in another month or so and give you all the time you need then, I just can't do this today. Please, Bridget, you have to help me!'

'Your juror assignation number is 487. Kindly proceed through the doors beside you and take a seat in holding area number two. Next!'

I'm aware of the line behind me inching forward impatiently, so I've no choice whatsoever now but to roll out the big guns.

'But you don't understand!' is my last-ditch attempt to get her to listen properly. 'I'm getting married in a few weeks' time and you've no idea how much I still have to do . . .'

'Honestly, some people seem to think the whole world revolves around them,' mutters a woman a few down from me in the queue, clearly audible from where I'm standing.

'There's always one who thinks they're the exception to

the rule, isn't there?' says an older man behind her, again, good and loud so the whole line can hear.

'I wouldn't mind, but I had to cancel a weeks' holiday in Lanzarote just because of this,' says the first woman. 'And you don't hear me moaning, do you?'

'It's our civil duty to turn up for jury service but to hear the way some people go on, you certainly wouldn't think it.'

'Miss? Can you step aside, please?' Bridget says impatiently through the hatch. 'There are people waiting behind you.'

'No offence, but I think you'd better do as she says,' comes a man's voice from directly behind me, making me jump, he's that close. I turn sharply around to see that same tall, dark-haired guy who was right behind me in the security queue earlier. 'In the interests of jury harmony, that is,' he adds dryly.

I turn to glare at this smart arse, but I don't think he even notices. Instead he just hands his summons over to Bridget and says, 'here to report for jury service.' Then catching my eye with a twinkle, he adds, 'And just to make your day nice and straightforward for you, Bridget, I'm actually eligible to serve.'

A smart arse *and* a lick arse, I think crossly, moving away.

The worst possible combination.

KATE

August 2005

So when did it all start to go wrong? Certainly articles like this one didn't help, Kate thought, casting a cold eye over the computer screen in front of her, wondering who in hell these so-called 'sources close to the couple', actually were:

The Goss.ie

KATE'S INNER TURMOIL

She's officially known as the woman who has it all but the question on everyone's lips is, when is she going to start producing little junior Kings to fill that enormous mansion she calls home?

'Damien and Kate have been married for over four years now,' says a source close to the couple. 'And although they're both longing for a child, it seems that nothing is happening.'

The Goss can now exclusively reveal that Kate has been seeking secret fertility treatments at a top clinic on London's Harley Street, at a staggering cost of £16K (roughly over €21K) per consultation.

'She and Damien are absolutely desperate for a family,' our source adds. *'So desperate that Kate is prepared to put herself through all of this. You've no idea the amount of medication she's been prescribed, just to bring this about, with luck. Most of their elite social circle have several kids by now, and all they want to do is be a part of that.*

'After all, what's the point of living in that fifteen-bedroomed mansion if you can't fill it with kids?'

What indeed, we wonder at The Goss.ie

All we can say is, watch this space.

*

Jesus, save me, Kate thought furiously, instantly slamming down her laptop so she didn't have to look at the offending article for a second longer.

If I ever get my hands on that 'source', then whoever they are, there'll be a bloody massacre.

TESS

The present

Sweet Mother of Divine. It's now 10.30 a.m., I've been at the courts for almost two hours and so far absolutely *nothing* has happened. We're all being kept in a 'jury holding area', which is a bit like one of those rooms you're made to wait in before a Ryanair flight, with uncomfortable bright-blue plastic chairs all latched together and an overhead TV that's showing breakfast TV on what feels like a continuous loop. To the point that if I have to watch one more 'spectacular makeover' or cookery demonstration, I really think I'll pan-fry my own liver.

There's still absolutely no sign of anything happening and so far I've had to cancel and reschedule three appointments I'd made for this afternoon, confidently thinking I'd be out of here in plenty of time and still manage to squeeze everything in. One was with the wedding florist, who did my pal Stella's wedding last year and who Stella swore by; as much for the fact that she's not a rip-off merchant as for the stunning flower arrangements she managed to weave on a very tight budget (tight little pink bud roses at Stella's wedding, so I'm going for the exact same flower, except in cream).

Another was with the marquee company, who I was meant to meet with to chat about where to position the tent in our tiny back garden, and on top of that, I had an appointment with Hannah from across the road, a trainee make-up artist who'd very kindly agreed to do a trial run on me today. All three of them are rightly pissed off with me for postponing at the last minute, but right now, they're nowhere near as fed up as I am.

Weirdest of all, though, is that I seem to be about the only person here who's spent the morning so far busily on the phone, cancelling, apologising and rearranging my schedule. It's waiting-room-quiet in here and I know everyone can hear me loud and clear on the phone, but no one else seems too remotely bothered by the excruciatingly long wait.

All around this packed room, people are settling into reading the paper, doing crosswords, drinking lukewarm, watery coffee from the one vending machine here that's actually working, flicking through iPads or, in the case of one sweet-faced elderly lady just beside me, scanning the sports pages for the racing results, then marking off in biro the horses she's picked for the 2.30 today at Aintree.

My phone rings, yet again. And the conversation goes thusly: 'Hello? Oh, Graham, thanks so much for ringing me back. I was just calling to finalise the music choice for my walk down the aisle . . . yeah, I know we were meant to be meeting up this afternoon, but I'm afraid I'm going to have to postpone, if that's OK with you . . . not my fault . . . I really am so sorry, but I'm actually in court as we speak . . . what? No! No I haven't done anything wrong . . . honestly! Are you kidding? I've never been up on a drink driving charge in my life . . . yeah

100

. . . oh, of course, I've put loads of thought into picking the right song . . . and I think I'd really like it to be "Here, There and Everywhere" by The Beatles. Would that work for you? Great, fantastic, thanks. OK, well, I'll call you when I get out of here, which should be soon, with any luck . . . fab. And we can rearrange? Great. Well, till then. Yeah, you too. Bye Graham . . . and thank you for your patience.'

I click off the call and just as I'm scrolling down through all the messages I've yet to return, I can't help noticing that the guy who was annoying me in the queue earlier is right opposite me, just two rows over, seemingly listening in to every word.

'Beatles fan, huh?' he says, looking right at me and whipping off earbuds that he'd had attached to his MacBook Air. It's only now that I've all this bloody time to kill that I get a good look at him. He's got thick, dark hair and one of those long, lean builds, an ectomorph type; basically the kind of body shape that never needs the services of a personal trainer. One of those people who can eat all the carbs they like, never set foot inside a gym and still stay skinny for life. Basically, the sort who'd put me out of business inside of a month.

'Who isn't?' I smile back, as politely as I can, given that I still have another eight phone calls to catch up on, just so I can stay on schedule.

'If you ask me,' he says, 'we're all born with the music to every single Beatles song ingrained into our DNA. With the sole exception of "Here, There and Everywhere" which, as everyone knows, is a song about an obsessive love. Now surely you can do better for your – and apologies, but I couldn't help overhearing – "big walk down the aisle"?'

101

'It's not about obsessive love,' I say, still focused on my phone, 'it's a beautiful, romantic song.'

'Not if you really listen to the lyrics properly, it isn't,' he persists, arms folded now, dark eyes scanning me up and down, like he's been bored out of his head all morning and is now itching for a debate about the merits or otherwise of a Beatles' song.

'I'm sorry,' I say distractedly as yet another text pings through on my phone, 'but I'm afraid I really don't know what you're talking about.'

'Well, it's a well-known fact that Paul McCartney wrote that cheesy song for Jane Asher, his then fiancée. And in the lyrics, he clearly says that he wants her to be everywhere that he is, for every minute of every day, to the end of time, or words to that effect.'

'So?' I say, totally distracted by the sheer number of text messages I've yet to reply to.

'Well, you might have got away with it in the sixties, but nowadays you'd be labelled an obsessive control freak for going on like that. If I went and wrote a song like that for a girlfriend, she'd probably take out a barring order against me. Anyway, when it came to love songs, the best one The Beatles ever recorded was "Something" by George Harrison. Far more weddingy, if you ask me. Not that it's any of my business.'

I look back at him, thinking, *no, actually it isn't any of your business and how would you know the first thing about my taste anyway?*

My phone rings yet again, so I make a curt 'sorry, got to take this' gesture and answer. It's Mum, bossily telling me to pick up two tins of cider on my way home, so Dad can have them when he's watching the match later on tonight. Then she makes me hold on while she consults her shopping list, just in case there's something else she might have forgotten.

'Go ahead,' this guy smirks, mock exasperatedly, catching my eye. 'Take your call. It seems there's no end to the demands on your time when you're busy bride-ing.'

'Thank you, yes, if you'll excuse me, I will.'

'But trust me about "Here, There and Everywhere". Rethink. You can do so much better.'

So you think my taste in music is a complete load of cheesy crap? I think a bit narkily, stressed out of my mind with everything I'm now so scarily behind on. *Then maybe you should stop listening in on other people's phone calls.*

Just at that moment though, Bridget swishes in authoritatively, stands at the top of the room and addresses us all. So I make my hushed goodbyes to Mum and only pray that this means good news.

'Good morning,' Bridget says bossily, with absolutely no apology for keeping us hanging around for this length of time. Without even the courtesy of an explanation, in fact. 'If I can ask you all to take a look up at the TV screens above you, please, we're just about ready to begin.'

The TV screens? I think, dumbfounded. What does she want us to do here exactly? Stand up and answer questions on the lemon meringue and poppy seed bake they demonstrated on *Good Morning Ireland* earlier?

'In a moment, we'll go over live to the courtroom,' Bridget carries on, 'and the jury selection will commence. If your number is called, please make your way through the door behind me, where you'll be taken up to court, either to be selected or not by the Defence or Prosecution.'

Well this is something, I think, suddenly hopeful again. Plan A hasn't worked – Bridget refused point blank to hear a word out of me – so now I'm on to plan B. Basically what my barrister client in the gym advised me to do in the event of all else failing; which involves me actually being selected, then standing in front of a judge, throwing myself on his or her mercy and pleading that I'm getting married in a few weeks' time. And if that doesn't work then it's on to the plan of last resort, which is that maybe the Defence or Prosecution will take one look at me and object to me serving on a jury. And with great good luck, I'll comfortably get out of here in under an hour tops; which means I could still make some of my appointments. Which means it's all still to play for.

Next thing, Bridget clicks on a remote control and all the TV screens behind her suddenly go over to a real, live courtroom, with a judge's bench, witness box, press gallery; the whole *Judge Judy*. And looming in front of the screen is a middle-aged woman, round-faced and smiley, her features visibly red and thread-veined, she's that close to the camera.

Even better, I think. Because unlike Bridget, this one actually looks approachable. Someone who I can negotiate with. A woman who'll listen to reason. With any luck, that is.

'Good morning and thank you all for presenting for jury service,' says Smiley-face. 'I'm Sandra Shields, the Court Registrar, and I'm speaking to you via a live link-up from court number seven. In a moment, I'll pull a random selection of numbers out of the box here beside me and if your number is called, please make yourself known to the Jury Selection Officer on duty. You'll then be led to the witness box here in court, to await selection.'

104

'I have a question, please!' I say shooting my hand upwards, only to be shushed back into silence by Bridget, not to mention the filthy glares I get from all around me.

'However, if your number isn't selected,' Sandra the Court Registrar goes on, smiling straight into the camera, 'this doesn't mean that you've automatically been released from jury service. In that case, we ask you to remain in the jury holding area until the next court is ready to randomly select another batch of jurors. Some of you may not be selected at all, in which case, you're required by law to remain in situ until 4 p.m. today, when you'll be released by the Jury Selection Officer. You'll then be required to present each and every day this week, until you've formally been released. If you are selected, please bear in mind that a case may run on for longer than a week, and you'll therefore have a legal obligation to follow through and serve.'

I do not believe this. So if my number doesn't get called, I still have to pitch up here day after day for the whole week ahead? And not only that, but if I *am* selected, I could end up on a case that might run on for over a week?

Not. Going. To. Happen.

Right then, I think quickly, as fresh panic starts to build up inside me like heartburn. This looks like the only card I've got left to play. The sooner I can get up in front of a judge to beg her to listen to me, the sooner I'm hopefully off the hook and hotfooting it out of here.

Pick my number, I will the smiley-faced one, like someone willing their lottery numbers to miraculously come up on a Saturday night, as she starts spinning round an octagon-shaped tombola.

For the love of God, please pick my number just so I can get to speak to a judge.

'Number 127,' she announces as an older man two rows across from me shoots his hand up, waving his number. Bridget ushers him through a set of double doors directly behind her, then immediately after, numbers 358, 421, 706 and 511 are called as another cluster of people from all corners of the waiting area are guided through the hallowed doors out of here.

Jammy bastards, is all I can think, jealously watching them weave their way to court.

Come on, come on, come on . . . I silently beg Smiley-face, as she shoves her hand back into the tombola and pulls out yet another clutch of numbers. Not one of them mine and what's worse, that eavesdropping guy who was having a pop at me earlier does get picked. He shrugs apologetically at me, but I'm sorry, I'm just too frazzled and stressed right now to even respond.

They've called nine people in total by now, I've counted. Which means just three more to go.

Come on, lucky number 487 . . .

'Number 792,' Smiley-face reads out, as the old lady beside me who was intent on picking racehorses earlier says, 'what number did she say?'

'792,' comes a grunt beside her, from behind a newspaper.

'Oh that's me!' She beams delightedly. 'My God, I feel like I'm about to win a prize here or something!'

She just folds over her paper and shuffles out the door and I start praying. To God, to Buddha, to Santa, to just about anyone up there who'll hear me. Palms sweating, heart pounding, I'm clutching my number to my chest as the last and final number is read out.

'And the last and final number for this round of jurors is . . .'

Come on, come on . . .

'Number 487.'

'Yeeeeesss!' I yell, jubilantly waving my number in the air. 'That's me,' I yell over the room to Bridget, picking up my bag and making my way to where she's standing. She doesn't even acknowledge me though, just waves me out through the magic doors behind her and out of here.

'To those of you whose numbers haven't yet been called,' she announces curtly to the room, 'please remain seated, as the next jury draw will take place in exactly thirty minutes time.'

I'm only half-listening though as I practically skip my way to the doors ahead of me. Then I whip out my mobile and fire off a text to Bernard:

HAVE BEEN SELECTED. WHICH MEANS AT LEAST I GET TO PLEAD MY CASE TO THE JUDGE. WITH ANY LUCK THEY'LL SEE REASON AND RELEASE ME. HOPE TO BE OUT OF HERE LUNCHTIME AT THE LATEST. TXXXX

'All mobile phones must remain off from this point onwards,' is Bridget's parting shot as I swish by her through the double doors and on into a smaller waiting area, but I'm barely listening. This is a sign from the Universe and for the first time all day, I really feel that if the judge is even a half-reasonable person, that everything might – just might – be well.

That dark-haired guy from earlier is right ahead of me as we all shuffle our way up a flight of stairs.

'So you've been selected then?' he says, slowing down to switch off his iPhone.

'That's right,' I tell him, 'which means with any luck they'll let me out of here in under an hour tops.'

'You think?' he says wryly, raising an eyebrow. 'Dunno if I'd go getting my hopes up, if I were you. That's not quite the way jury service works, you know.'

But I don't even bother racking my brains to come up with a smart answer. I even find it in myself to smile angelically back at him.

*

So now we're all being guided up yet another short flight of carpeted stairs and on through heavy oak double doors that look soundproofed, before we're led into a jury room, with a conference table and twelve seats dotted around it, boardroom-style. From there, we're then guided through another door and on into court number seven.

And yet again it seems all my years of binging on legal dramas have completely misinformed me. You'd expect an actual, proper, live courtroom to be scary and intimidating, calculated to make you go weak at the knees and confess all in front of a judge.

But this is absolutely nothing like that at all. It's ultra-modern in here, warm and airy, with nothing in the slightest bit daunting about it, in spite of the fact that it's a huge courtroom. For starters, it's busy and bustling, with barristers looking puffed-up with their own importance swishing in and out of the double doors at the back of the court, chatting amongst themselves and gearing up for the business of the day.

It's about half-full in here, with people who look like they're here for a family or friend's case to be heard sitting in benches, patiently waiting on the kick-off. Meanwhile Sandra, the Court Registrar, the blonde smiley lady I instantly recognise from onscreen a few minutes ago, comes over and addresses us all.

'We'll have Judge Simmonds presiding over us today,' she tells us all warmly. 'And don't worry, she'll talk you through the whole procedure. So if you've any questions, you can address the bench directly.'

I shoot my hand up.

'Sorry about this, but I'm afraid I really do need to speak to the judge,' I tell her, aware of eleven pairs of eyes burning a hole into my skull. 'For . . . erm . . . personal reasons.'

'You're absolutely entitled to do that,' smiles Sandra. 'But all in good time.'

'. . . And the best of luck with it,' a crisp woman's voice comes from directly behind me. I turn around to see a woman in her early forties, at a guess, dressed like she's just fallen out of bed, in flowery leggings that could almost be pyjamas and a giant oversized sweatshirt. I don't even have time to react to her though because next thing, there's a curt 'all rise!' from a discreet door behind the judge's bench and everyone stands as a hush descends.

'This court is now in session with myself, Judge Ingrid Simmonds presiding,' says the judge, striding purposely towards the top bench in her wig and gown and taking a seat. Everyone in court follows suit except we jurors, who are all standing pinned in a straight line at the very back of the jury box, with two empty rows of six seats directly ahead of us.

It's only now I get a look at Judge Simmonds, who yet again is nothing at all like I'd imagined. I'd expected some crusty old man to be presiding, who nodded off during testimonies and kept a bottle of gin handy under his desk. But Ingrid Simmonds turns out to be in her early-fifties, at a guess, with short, cropped salt and pepper hair and a brisk, efficient, no-nonsense manner about her. Like a head-mistress in school who won't tolerate messing on any account.

She turns to address the jury bench first.

'Ladies and gentlemen,' she says, 'we have a busy day ahead of us, so allow me to get directly to the point. When the Court Registrar calls out your name, step forward and present yourself to both the Prosecuting and Defending barristers. They may at this point object to you, in which case you'll be asked to stand down and return to the jury holding area.

'Please take no offence if there's an objection to you serving, as none is intended,' she goes on, smoothly and clearly, a woman well used to being in control.

Take offence? I think to myself. If they objected to me, I'd probably lead a conga line out of here.

The court stays quiet as our names are called out individually.

'Edith Mooney,'

'Yes! Present!' says the elderly lady who'd been so engrossed in the racing pages earlier.

'May I ask if you're over the age of sixty-five?' the judge asks.

'Seventy-four last birthday,' she says proudly.

'In that case I can excuse you by right of age if you wish, but it's your decision.'

'Oh no!' she beams back. 'I wouldn't want to miss this for the world . . . sure it's like the best free entertainment you can get! I hope it's a good juicy case, mind you, I don't want to be stuck here all day for a parking fine or something boring.'

'Any objections?' the judge asks a cluster of barristers milling around the front of the court. There don't appear to be any though, just a lot of head shaking.

'Then take a seat please,' the judge adds, moving swiftly along.

Another three jurors are called and no one seems to have any objection to them, so again they take their seats in the jury box. One is a fifty-something woman, power dressed in a suit I recognise as L.K. Bennett, one is a much older man about my dad's vintage and the third is a lady who looks at least seventy and who's hobbling around on a walking stick.

'Will Kearns,' says the Court Registrar, reading out another name on her list and it's that guy who was having a go at my musical taste earlier, slinging a manbag over his shoulders and ambling casually into his seat, like he hasn't a care in the world. So that's your name then, I think, Will Kearns. Good luck on jury service because I for one will certainly not be joining you.

'Tess Taylor,' and I almost jump as my name is read out.

'Permission to approach the bench, Your Honour,' I ask, delighted that at least TV taught me that small bit of useful legalese.

'Go right ahead,' smiles Sandra, waving me out of the jury box.

I stumble up two steps to where the judge is looking

beadily back down at me, aware that not only my fellow jurors, but now it seems the entire court have stopped whatever they're all doing to pay attention.

'I really am so sorry about this, Your Honour,' I say in a low voice, 'but I'm afraid I need to be excused. I really hope you understand, but you see I've an extraordinary set of circumstances going on in my life right now, so it's just not possible for me to be here today. Or any day at all, in fact.'

'What's the problem?' asks Judge Simmonds politely.

'Well you see I'm getting married. In less than a month, to be exact. And I'm having the wedding at home and you just have no idea how much work there's still to do.'

With that, I break off and start to fumble around my bag for all the back-up material I brought with me as proof: my to-do lists and yet more lists, a letter from our Parish Priest confirming the date of the wedding, the receipt for my wedding dress which flaps out and falls down onto the carpeted floor beneath. I even produce my mood board in all its cream and white simplicity, which Judge Simmonds looks distinctly uninterested in.

'In fact only this morning, Your Honour, I had to cancel three really important meetings with our musician and florist and make-up artist, just so I could be here today,' I tell her, getting red-faced and flustered as the words just spill out. 'We're having a marquee in our back garden and hand on heart, I had absolutely no idea just how much work would be involved, you see. I mean, look at this, here's a list of just what I've got to do this week alone—'

I'm just about to show her sample menus from the catering company's brochure, when Judge Simmonds waves me silent right in the middle of my spiel about gluten-free starters and vegetarian options for mains.

'Will the barrister for the Prosecution kindly inform the court how long this case is expected to take?' she asks brusquely.

A tall, imposing barrister stands up – and somehow he's familiar looking. It's only when he speaks in that incredibly distinctive, cut-glass accent though, that the penny drops.

'The Prosecution can confidently predict this to be an open-and-shut case, Your Honour,' he says, and I think, bloody hell, that's Oliver Daniels. *The* Oliver Daniels. I know next to nothing about law and less still about the courts, but every dog on the street has heard of Oliver Daniels. He's one of the most senior barristers we have in this country and he's forever in the papers and on the news spouting on about this case or that which he's just won.

And that's another thing about him. To date, he's never yet lost a case, not in thirty years practicing here. Even I know that much.

'Can you give me a rough time span, please?' asks the judge, peering down at him.

'I would confidently aim to have this wrapped up in two weeks or less, Your Honour,' he says in an accent that wouldn't sound out of place in the Pritchards' drawing room, with all those clipped, crisp consonants.

'What say the Defence?'

'We would agree, Your Honour,' says the opposing barrister, a forty-something woman with short brown spikey hair peeping out from under her wig. God love you, I think, suddenly feeling sympathetic towards her. Whatever this case is, the very fact that she's up against the mighty Oliver Daniels would be enough to make me throw in the towel and run screaming for the hills.

'And you say your wedding is a full month away?' asks Judge Simmonds, turning back to me.

'Yes, that's right, so you see it's completely impossible for me—'

'Nonsense. As you see, the case shouldn't last any longer than two weeks max, so you're cleared to serve. Unless either the Prosecution or Defence have any objections?'

None though, worst luck.

'Kindly return to the jury box, please,' says the judge briskly.

'*What?*' I say, looking at her dumbfounded. 'But no, I can't! You don't seem to understand!'

'Please step down and re-join the other jurors.'

'But . . . but . . . in the UK, you're allowed to be excused if you're getting married,' I insist, clutching frantically at straws.

'Sadly, that is not the case in this jurisdiction.'

'Please! You have to release me!'

'You are aware of the penalties imposed for failing to serve?' she says sternly, raising her voice just the tiniest bit, which I have to say is very intimidating and which completely shuts me up. Seconds later, Sandra gently links my arm and steers me into a seat in the back row of the jury box, as the judge clears her throat and addresses us.

'Next, you're all required to be sworn in, which the Court Registrar will do momentarily. First though, can the Registrar read out the details of the case you're about to hear, please?'

'Certainly, Your Honour,' says Sandra, slipping back to her desk which is directly in front of the judge, but graded down a level. Then she shuffles around a big sheaf of papers and stands up to address the court.

'Court number seven at the Criminal Courts of Justice is now in session, with Judge Ingrid Simmonds presiding.'

There's pin-drop silence in the court as everyone, barristers, solicitors and anyone lingering around the public benches, focuses on the bench.

'And the case you're about to hear is that of *King versus King.*'

KATE

The Chronicle
May 2006

KATE AND DAMIEN 'PROUD TO BE GODPARENTS'

This hot off the press and exclusive to readers of The
Chronicle; *the pitter-patter of tiny feet is soon to resonate
throughout the grand corridors of Castletown House at last.
But no, lest readers jump to the conclusion that Kate and
Damien are soon to expect a little addition to the King family,
let's put this straight for the record.*

*Mo Kennedy, wife of Globtech's high-flying CFO Joe
Kennedy, has just given birth to fraternal twins, to be called
Ella and Joshua. So who better to ask to be Godparents than
Damien and Kate King?*

The Chronicle *can exclusively reveal that the Christening
ceremony took place yesterday at St Patrick's Church in
Avoca, County Wicklow and the proud Godmother looked
utterly stunning in an elegant, cream lace Alice Temperley
suit, as she posed proudly for our cameraman holding her
brand-new Godson. Her husband Damien told reporters at
the scene how 'besotted' he was with his new Godchildren*

116

and how at two-months-old, they already have him wrapped around their little fingers.

When the couple were asked if they planned to start adding to their own family, Damien looked thoughtful and told us, 'we're working on it'. Kate meanwhile remained tight-lipped, as she bundled her Godson into a waiting car and climbed in after him.

'Any plans to become a mum yourself soon?' our reporter called after her.

'I think that's quite enough questions for now, thanks', was her reply, firmly slamming the car door shut behind her.

TESS

The present

Officially, you're not supposed to talk to anyone about the case you're sitting in on. Or 'the case you're presiding over' as Judge Simmonds keeps saying time and again. With apologies for littering this with all the legal references, but some of it is bound to rub off on me, M'Lud, my learned friend, etc., etc.

For all that I'm still mightily pissed off at being manacled to the King case, all in all, our first day actually turns out to be a complete doddle. Which I'd say comes as a huge relief to my fellow jurors, because looking around the jury box now, the majority of them have to be sixty plus. Apart from the Granny Brigade, there's that woman dressed in what could pass for PJs who looks about forty-something, a guy in his early-twenties who's wearing bright red jeans and a lot of man-bracelets and a much younger, fresh-faced girl who can only be about eighteen at most.

Poor kid, I think, looking over at her in her studenty parka jacket with a thick chunky jumper under it. She looks barely old enough to vote and here she is, snared into doing jury service. And then there's that guy Will, who I'd guess

118

is mid-thirties at most. But apart from us younger ones, the vast majority of the jury look like they're only able to listen to this for a few hours max, before it's time for them to toddle back to their nursing homes for a nice afternoon snooze.

'Firstly, I'd just like to roughly outline the format this case will take,' says Judge Simmonds, speaking imperiously to us from her high bench dominating the court. 'To begin with, you'll hear opening statements from both the Prosecution and Defence, and each side will clearly outline their case to you. The Prosecution will then present their case first and a number of witnesses may be called, which the Defence has a right to cross-examine. Once the Prosecution has concluded, then the Defence will present their case, again, with the right to call witnesses who may be cross-examined. Finally both sides will make brief summation speeches and then you'll be escorted into the jury room in order to deliberate and reach a verdict. If any of you have any questions at any time,' she adds, 'then all you need do is raise your hand and speak directly to me.'

'Oh yes, I have a question, please!' pipes up a voice from directly behind me. We all turn around to see that white-haired elderly lady who was sitting beside me in the jury holding area earlier, who I think is called Edith. The same one who was busily picking out winners from the racing pages of today's *Chronicle*.

'Yes?' says the judge.

'When do we get lunch? It's just I only had tea and toast for breakfast and my stomach is starting to rumble.'

Titters from around the court at that, which the judge silences with a quick bang of the gavel in front of her.

'Food breaks will of course be provided for you, you need have no worries on that account.'

The court settles down again and the morning starts with a few brief introductions from each of the barristers representing both sides, which takes no more than a half-hour tops.

The mighty Oliver Daniels is up first for the Prosecution and you could nearly hear a pin drop as he rises to his feet, instantly putting me in mind of Winston Churchill addressing a war cabinet. Although maybe that's just the sight of Oliver's brandy and port gut that sits on the desk in front of him all by itself, he's that morbidly overweight.

'Ladies and gentlemen of the jury,' he begins, taking care to make full-on eye contact with each and every one of us, the effect of which I have to say is utterly mesmerising. 'Firstly, on behalf of the Prosecution, may I thank you in advance for serving on this case.'

'Five grand a day in legal fees,' another old lady sitting beside me hisses to no one in particular. 'That's what he's costing Damien King apparently. It said so in the *Daily Star*.'

'I'm afraid I must ask members of the jury to remain silent,' says Judge Simmonds sternly, peering down at us from over her glasses.

'Oh, I'm so sorry, Your Honour, but you'll have a right job getting me to shut up,' she says by way of apology, to more titters from around the packed courtroom. 'This is just like a real-life drama, only much, much better.'

'Except that's precisely what it's not,' says the judge. 'May I remind the jury that this is no TV show you're about to witness. This is the stuff of real people's lives and the decision you'll be asked to make will have major consequences for both parties.'

It's unspoken, but her subtext is crystal-clear. Shut up yacking, this ain't no episode of *The Good Wife*.

'If I may resume, Your Honour,' Oliver Daniels booms to renewed hush around the room. 'Ladies and gentlemen, the matter before you here today is as straightforward as could be. My client, Mr Damien King of Castletown House in County Kildare, as you may be aware from the extensive press coverage, is sadly in the throes of a separation from his ex-wife, Mrs Katherine King. They've been living apart for some time now, until their divorce can be finalised. However, I'm sorry to say that as often happens in these cases – and in spite of an incredibly generous settlement in favour of his ex-wife – regrettably the matter became acrimonious.

'Then during the month of April 2014, when relations between both parties were irrevocably broken down, Mrs Katherine King took unlawful possession of a painting, an end-period Rembrandt, no less, and point blank refused then and refuses now to give it back to its rightful owner, my client. We the Prosecution will show that Mrs King has been served with no less than three court orders to return this painting and is in breach of every single one of them.

'Now I can assure each one of you that the last thing my client would ever have wished would be to resort to the courts to have his rightful property returned to him, but sadly that is what the matter has come to. The case against the Defendant is a grievously serious one; she is charged under section four of the Criminal Justice Act, for taking unlawful possession of what rightfully belongs to another, in this case, the King family trust. Throughout the police investigation and preliminary hearing, Mrs King was given every chance to simply return the painting and all charges against her would have been instantly dropped. Ladies and gentlemen of the jury, I have to tell you that the Defendant refused this offer, and so with deep regret on the part of my client, this is where we all find ourselves today.'

He gives us a moment to digest this and my eye wanders across the courtroom to where the Defendant's legal team are sitting, all busily scribbling away and whispering to each other.

'Oh my God,' says that young, studenty girl who's sitting just on my right. 'Don't tell me that's Kate King, sitting behind all those lawyers? She's so *thin*!'

And it's only then that I see her. She must have been sitting at the back of the court all this time, only I was so flustered I never even noticed her coming into court. Tall, ghostly pale and so painfully skinny that I just want to take her home and give her a super-sized feed of steak and spuds. Kate King is hollow-eyed, almost haunted looking, there's no other word for it. Even from here it's obvious that she's trembling a bit. Her blonde hair is neatly tied back and she's wearing an expensive-looking cream cashmere coat, that famous angular face white as snow as she sits ramrod straight and listens to the case being outlined against her.

It's really her, it's really her. The one and only Kate King.

'Now not for a moment am I asking the jury to magically become art historians overnight,' Oliver Daniels goes on, pulling my attention back to him. 'However, I will ask that you visualise the most priceless artefact you've ever seen in your life, multiply its value by about ten thousand and perhaps then you'll come close to just how much this particular portrait is worth.'

He pauses here for dramatic effect and it works. There are a lot of impressed nods from around the courtroom and up here in the jury box too. But then the one and only time I've ever seen a Rembrandt up close and personal was on the cover of an Art History book back in secondary school.

'My client Damien King,' says Oliver Daniels, 'as you'll see throughout this court case and as you may perhaps be aware of from his public profile, is a wealthy man. You may hear stories of lavish spending and excess and here I must ask you not to be in any way swayed by this. Remember, Mr King works hard for every penny and personally built up his company, Globtech, from scratch into the world leader that it is today. His fortune is clearly his to spend in any way he chooses. After all, it's no crime to be successful, now, is it?'

Clever ploy, I think, and out of the corner of my eye I can see a few more heads in the jury box beside me nodding along like they agree wholeheartedly. Everyone knows the King family are loaded and it's no harm to pre-warn us not to get too pissed off when we hear tales of parties that cost two hundred grand, enough jewellery to put Liz Taylor in the shade and racehorses that go on to become Grand National winners.

'However, into every life a little rain must fall,' Oliver sighs, 'and sadly such was the case with Damien King. We the Prosecution will show that throughout his fifteen-year marriage, not only was he a lavish and extortionately generous husband to the Defendant, but that when his marriage broke down, Mr King was equally generous to his now ex-wife, as befits a successful and wealthy businessman of his standing.'

Part of me is wondering how much Kate King walked away with – it had to be well into the high millions, surely. But Oliver Daniels's booming voice cuts across my meandering thoughts.

'However, may I remind the jury that you're not here to preside over a divorce case. Far from it. The Kings had in place a cast-iron pre-nuptial agreement prior to marrying and I can assure you that Katherine King has been amply provided for and well-looked after. Damien King, as you'll hear throughout the course of this case, is not an ungenerous man.'

And now my eye wanders over to the man himself, who's sitting directly behind Oliver Daniels and who keeps passing notes back and forth to him. But then it's hard not to stare at Damien King; he really is that good-looking. A total magnet for the eye. It's weird though, I've seen his photo look back at me from countless papers and magazines, so many times that I almost feel I know him, with that illusion of familiarity you get with well-known faces.

He must be tall, I figure, as even sitting down he's still head and shoulders above the whole team of barristers he's surrounded by. Classically dark good looks too, although he's greying slightly around the temples. And as you'd expect, he's dressed in an expensive-looking suit and has an air of authority about him, of confidence even. Like this whole case is purely a formality to be got through before he can get back to running the world, or whatever it is that his company does.

In total contrast to his ex-wife, who's sitting directly opposite the jury box with the nerves practically pinging from her. She's twitchy and uncomfortable-looking and her barrister keeps having to whisper in her ear, presumably to tell her to relax and sit still.

Not that I'd be relaxed facing the combined forces of Damien King and Oliver Daniels myself. In fact to look at both men, you can almost imagine them chummily sitting together over a boozy lunch in some five-star restaurant where a starter costs about thirty euros, laughing this whole case away in supreme confidence that they already have it in the bag.

'However, I very much regret to inform the jury,' Oliver booms on, sounding more and more theatrical the more he warms up, 'that during the course of her separation, Katherine King took it on herself to challenge this pre-nuptial agreement, claiming that in no way was it enough to sustain her in the manner to which she's become accustomed.

'Apparently,' he tosses at us, really twisting the knife in, 'her own penthouse apartment, a substantial monthly income plus all of the jewellery which had been lavished on her by her husband weren't enough to satisfy her. Mrs King deems a two thousand square foot apartment insufficient for her. Not prestigious enough for a soon-to-be divorcee without children. If you can believe that.'

At that, there's a ripple throughout the court and the judge has to shush us before Oliver can go on.

'Greed, you'll find, lies at the very heart of this case,' he says smoothly, eyeballing each and every one of us here in the box. 'Financial greed, plain and simple. On the brink of divorce, Mrs King has taken it on herself to lay claim to the jewel in the crown, as far as my client's assets are concerned, which of course is the Rembrandt painting, *A Lady of Letters*.

125

'Now I would urge the jury to remember that name. You'll be hearing a lot more about it as this court case progresses. The painting itself is currently missing and is not at Castletown House. A thorough police search of the property during the police investigation has confirmed that much. But Mrs Katherine King is aware of precisely where it's being kept, she has admitted in preliminary statements. And to this day, she is refusing to reveal its location, or indeed to return it to its rightful owner.

'Theft is a serious matter, ladies and gentlemen,' he goes on in that newsreadery voice, 'as is breaching no fewer than three court orders. By her own admission, the Defendant freely admits that she knows the precise location of the painting and we the Prosecution will contend that she is currently hoarding *A Lady of Letters* for herself, presumably to sell it on the open market as soon as she feasibly can. Oh, and just so you're all aware,' he tosses in lightly with his back turned to us, 'Christie's estimate is that the minimum reserve on a portrait of this importance would probably fetch upwards of one hundred million euros at today's prices.'

An impressed murmur around the court; which he instantly hushes with an imperious wrist wave.

'My client and I will prove beyond all reasonable doubt that this portrait is the rightful property of the King family trust and should be returned to them at once. And that, ladies and gentlemen of the jury, will present the case for the Prosecution.'

I actually feel like giving the man a round of applause. He's just so clear and firm and authoritative and everything he's saying makes perfect sense. I'm on the verge of thinking that it's game over for Kate King, when her barrister, the spikey brown-haired lady sitting beside her who looks a bit like a younger version of Margaret Mountford from *The Apprentice,* rises to her feet.

Silence as we all wonder what in hell she can possibly do to wriggle her way out of this one. And the answer, it seems, is not that much at all really.

'Ladies and gentlemen of the jury,' she says, weaving her way around her desk and walking calmly over to the jury box. 'Please let me introduce myself. My name is Hilda Cassidy and I'm here to represent Mrs Katherine King. Unlike my learned friend though, I have no desire to ramble on at length when there's absolutely no need to,' she adds, speaking slowly and simply and looking each one of us straight in the eye.

There's no sense of nervousness from this woman at all. In fact the exact opposite; if anything she has an air of cool confidence about her, though how anyone expected to spar with Oliver Daniels possibly could is beyond me.

'Now, ladies and gentlemen, you've heard a lot of fine rhetoric from the Prosecution, haven't you?' she goes on. 'He presents quite a case, I'm sure you'll all agree. You're possibly even sitting there wondering why my client doesn't just hand the painting back and have done with it. Am I right?'

Exactly what I was wondering, as it happens.

'My client Mrs King and I have just one thing to say to you at this point,' she says, and in spite of myself, I'm sitting forward now, all ears. Well, you never know, the scariness of Oliver Daniels's opening speech might just have swayed Kate King to change her mind, plead guilty, hand the shagging thing back and just have done with it.

Pin-drop silence and every eye in the court is directed her way.

'Just remember that none of this is how it looks,' Hilda shrugs. 'And in spite of the implications from my learned friend, my client has stolen nothing, has taken nothing and has done precisely nothing to merit her having to endure this. Under the clear and certain terms of her pre-nuptial agreement, Mrs King is entitled to keep all gifts given to her by her husband during the course of their marriage. And as *A Lady of Letters* was a birthday gift for her, this is clearly included under those terms.

'An innocent woman is sitting in this courtroom today, ladies and gentlemen. A lady who has done absolutely nothing wrong. And we the Defence won't rest until we prove it.'

And with that, she turns on her heel and goes back to her seat at the bench.

*

So my first day in court turns out not to be such a complete disaster after all. As soon as we've heard the opening arguments from opposing counsel, Judge Simmonds discharges us, telling us we don't have to be back till ten o'clock tomorrow morning, when the Prosecution will open their case.

Which, to be perfectly honest, a small part of me is actually looking forward to. But then watching Oliver Daniels in action is a bit like how I imagine watching Laurence Olivier live on stage must have been over half a century ago. That same sense of transcending your whereabouts, you're so completely mesmerised by the performance you're witnessing.

Another shock: leaving the court turns out to be a big eye-opener too. We were warned that there might be 'some media interest' in the case and sure enough the minute we step outside the building, there's a small cluster of photographers with lenses focused on the doors like trained snipers, waiting to snap either one of the Kings. Sure enough, I clock Damien King being ushered down the courtroom steps surrounded by what looks like a team of flunkeys, as a battery of flashes go off in his face. Meanwhile the rest of us slip past him, unnoticed and ignored.

Best of all though, because we're released so early, I still get to meet with our wedding singer, Graham, who's a tenor in the City College Choral Society. Bernard put me in touch with him ages ago so we could pick out some music for the actual church service, 'Here, There and Everywhere' by The Beatles for my walk down the aisle included. In spite of that interfering guy Will from jury service expressly warning me off it.

Mind you, I'd expected Graham to pitch hymns like 'Panis Angelicus' for the actual service, but this guy turned out to be more of a musical theatre aficionado, who kept suggesting arias from *Les Mis* and, God help me, *Cats*. If this fella gets his way, I'll be the first bride in history to walk down the aisle to 'Master of the House'.

And with time to spare, I even manage to squeeze in my postponed meeting with Hannah, the lovely trainee make-up artist from across the road who very kindly agreed to do a trial run on me before the big day. And OK, so her smoky eye make-up does actually make me look like a panda that's just been in a fight with another panda over the last of the bamboo shoots, but seeing as how she's prepared to do this for half nothing, I'm not really in much of a position to complain.

'Mother of God, Tess, what did you do to your eyes?' says Mum when I get back home later in the evening.

'Have you been crying? Or did someone in that courtroom give you a black eye?'

'No, Hannah across the road was practising on me.'

'You mean you let that nutter near your face? Hannah, who goes around with a tide line at her neck and streaky fake tan all down her legs? And don't get me started on those tattooed-on eyebrows of hers. They look like two caterpillars chasing each other across her face.'

'She's doing me a really good deal on the make-up,' I say, examining myself at the mirror in our TV room and trying to blot down the worst of it with a tissue.

'Are you mad? Tess, love, do you not think that's taking the idea of a budget wedding a bit too far? You've got to look at these photos for the rest of your life, you know.'

I shush her down though and instead veer the conversation towards what happened in court today. Her reaction speaks volumes; all deeply satisfying.

'You're kidding!' she says, mouth agape. And it says a lot for how excited Mum is about this that she actually live-pauses *Coronation Street*, so she can hear this news first hand.

'Talk about lucking out. The King case? I'd kill just to be a fly on the wall in that courtroom. Can you imagine all the gossip you're going to hear first hand? Like having a front row reserved seat at the best show in town. And you, you roaring eejit, you actually wanted to wriggle out of it? Madness. I've reared a total nutjob.'

'I still do want out,' I tell her, 'but the judge was having none of it. Besides, apparently this will only take eight days tops, so even when it's all over, it still gives me a few weeks before the wedding.'

'So what was she like, then? Kate King. Does she look

like she's had a facelift? I'll bet she has, you know. No one her age can possibly look like that without a bit of help from a scalpel.'

'Skinny. And trembly. And there's a lot more going on with this than meets the eye, if you ask me,' I say knowledgeably, feeling like a court reporter sitting on a massive scoop. But then there's just something alluring and seductive about knowing the ins and outs of a hot court case like this one before anyone else does.

'Hang on a minute,' says Gracie, coming into the TV room with a plate of beans on toast, picking up the remote control and immediately flicking over to *Game of Thrones*. 'Should you even be talking about this? Don't they warn you in court that you're not allowed to discuss the case, even with your nearest and dearest?'

'Well technically, yeah,' I tell her, 'but then what are they going to do? Come around here and bug the house?'

Besides, the list of things the judge told us we couldn't do would almost make you laugh. Apparently not only are we supposed to keep our mouths zipped tight, but we were warned by the Court Registrar not to read anything about this case in the papers, listen to it on the radio or even Google it online in case it's 'prejudicial to the outcome'.

'That's a joke!' I muttered to no one in particular when we were first told. 'We're not supposed to check it out online? In this day and age?'

'Apparently it's about making sure that we all come to the case with open minds,' says Will, the guy who I was a bit snippy with earlier on. 'But then I reckon they think we all live in caves without Wi-Fi or electricity and communicate with the outside world via carrier pigeon.'

I'm about to answer him, but just then my phone rings

again; my pal Monica wanting to arrange a girlie movie night this weekend.

'Back to bride-ing for you, I guess,' he says with a quick, tight smirk and the minute we were discharged for the day, he is gone.

KATE

December 2006

It was just coming up to Christmas when Kate discovered to her great joy that she was finally pregnant. She'd been feeling run-down and seemed to be tired all the time, so a trip to her GP and a quick test later confirmed the happy news. Damien, naturally, had been ecstatic.

'Because I plan on having a big family, babes, so you may as well be warned!' he'd joked, as they celebrated the news back at Castletown House. 'Two boys and two girls, to start with anyway.'

Kate was lying stretched out on a sofa and looked fondly over at him as he made an embarrassingly ridiculous fuss over her, putting cushions at her back and massaging the soles of her feet, etc. The whole works.

'Now don't you worry about a thing, sweetheart, I'm going to take such care of you, you won't believe it.'

She'd laughed and told him to stop treating her like an invalid, but just moments later, that wonderful, joyous mood between them shifted. She watched, unable to believe it as Damien picked up the phone and started to tell people the news. Her mum and his father, Ivan, she didn't mind so much, after all, they were both family. But she drew the line when his next call was to a journalist he knew and trusted at *The Goss*.

'Damien, you can't be serious!' she'd protested, sitting bolt upright and feeling an instant wave of nausea rising to her throat. 'We're not really supposed to tell anyone, let alone some gossip columnist. I've barely been pregnant for five minutes, suppose something goes wrong?'

'It won't,' he said, ignoring her. 'Because things don't go wrong for me. Ever.'

'This is crazy, you can't do this!'

He just waved her silent though and went ahead with the call anyway, while she looked on, dumbfounded. She heard him charming this journalist, joking and flirting, not actually telling her out straight, but hinting that Christmas had come a little early for the Kings and they were planning to fill the bedrooms at Castletown sooner rather than later.

Jesus, Kate thought furiously, he's almost writing out the copy for her. They'd rowed about it the minute he was off the phone, the first proper, humdinger of an argument they'd ever had.

'How do you think it'll feel for me,' she said furiously, 'to have to read about this in print? No one is supposed to know until I'm safely at the twelve-week mark. You're asking for trouble, Damien, and you're mortifying me while you're at it!'

'Sweetheart, that's just your hormones making you narky,'

'This is nothing to do with hormones, I'm genuinely angry, actually!'

'Then I gotta tell you, you're making a big deal over nothing,' he said, coming over to massage her shoulders, apparently still blithely cool about the whole thing. 'It'll just be a few throwaway hints in a few papers, nothing more. The press are going to write about us anyway, so we may as well be the ones that dictate what they write. Frankly, Katherine,' he added with a shrug, 'I can't see what you're getting so upset about.'

Katherine. He only ever called her that when he was really annoyed. She pushed him away, but he just shrugged and left the room, leaving her quietly seething on the sofa.

But then that was another slightly less palatable thing Kate was fast learning about her brand-new husband. Like the ultimate media junkie, it wasn't enough for the two of them to be out night after night, enjoying the highlife. Instead, Damien absolutely needed everyone to know about it too, to make sure he was talked about for his fabulous lifestyle as much as for his successes with Globtech.

Like a tree falling in the forest that makes no sound if there's no one there to hear it, it was as if nothing ever really happened in his life unless it had appeared in cold, hard print. Preferably with a nice, glossy photo to go along with it.

Like it or not, Kate reasoned as she tried her best to calm down, this was the man she loved. And after all, considering that she and Damien were happy in every other respect, this side of him seemed a relatively minor annoyance to have to put up with.

Even if just at this moment it certainly didn't bloody well feel like it.

*

As it turned out, Kate's forebodings had been right all along. It was the day before Christmas Eve and she and Damien were on a flight to Verbier to celebrate the holidays along with Mo, her husband and kids, and another group of friends. They would all be off skiing, of course, but Kate just planned to hide out in the hotel's luxury spa for a blissful week of rest and pampering.

She was just at the ten-week mark in her pregnancy by then and was feeling exhausted all the time. Even the smell of food made her nauseous and she looked, she knew, ghostly, no matter how much make-up she plastered on.

Then one hour into the flight, she felt a sharp stomach cramp so violent that she knew immediately that something was very wrong. A cold, panicky feeling swept over her and instinctively she glanced around for Damien, but he was right at the back of the business class cabin, of course, drinking champagne and chatting to Don and Michelle Mayhew, another couple in their group.

Suddenly Kate felt a dampness between her thighs and put her hand down to discover the seat was now soaked with blood. Heart palpitating, she rushed to the loo to find she was bleeding a frightening amount, so heavily, it was almost non-stop. Then weakness and more nausea. She locked herself into the tiny bathroom for so long, that a concerned flight attendant ended up tapping gently on the door and politely asking if she was OK. In what weak little voice she could muster, Kate just whispered to her through the door, 'My husband. Get my husband for me. Please. Hurry.'

Damien was there a moment later, and Kate managed to haul herself up to unlock the door and let him in. She didn't even need to tell him what had just happened though. The devastated look on her face said it all.

*

The following summer, Kate found herself pregnant again. This time though, she took absolutely no chances, swearing

136

Damien to secrecy so she wouldn't have to suffer a repeat of him leaking it to the media all over again. At least this way she'd be spared the mortifying humiliation of her miscarriage actually making it into the grubbier tabloid papers for all to see.

Mind you, it still didn't stop Damien from dropping the heaviest of heavy hints 'that my lovely wife and I might have some very interesting news for you soon', to most of their social circle. Pretty soon and to her annoyance, Kate found herself fending off calls and concerned texts from girlfriends asking if there was anything they could do for her.

There wasn't, as it happened. She knew their friends only meant to be kind, but still it left Kate cross and angry with Damien for doing exactly what she'd begged him not to. She cancelled every social do that she'd been due to attend and mostly stayed at home, resting and taking care of herself in the peace and tranquillity of Castletown, just as she should have done first time around.

As it happened, though, it was an incredibly busy time and she and Damien had a lot of engagements they were expected to go to during those first weeks; no less than three weddings, two of which were abroad, a charity auction and three black-tie balls.

'Don't you worry, sweetheart,' Damien had said to her, yanking himself into a dress suit and black tie for a gala do at the American ambassador's home later that evening. 'You just stay here and rest up. Everyone will understand.'

'But are you sure you'll be OK on your own?' she'd asked him worriedly, stretched out on their bed, sipping a herbal tea.

'Course,' he'd smiled, pulling on his dinner jacket and striding across the room to give her a quick kiss goodbye.

'Mind you,' he added from the door on his way out, 'if some hot babe starts making moves on me, then you'll only have yourself to blame.'

He was joking, just teasing. Of course he was.

Still, though, all that night Kate worried and didn't really sleep soundly till he eventually came home, which was hours and hours later; well past dawn.

*

Then, just as Kate was reaching the eleven-week mark and she was actually starting to feel the worst was behind her, disaster. Another miscarriage, this time so frightening that her housekeeper had to call an ambulance. Damien was away in Brussels on business and it was hours later before she even got to speak to him from her hospital room. He changed flights of course and immediately rushed home to be with her, but still, it was too late and by then, it was all over.

This time, the awful, aching emptiness inside Kate just wouldn't go away. She felt like a failure in every single way imaginable. And she knew Damien well enough by now to know exactly what he was thinking, as he looked down on her in her hospital bed, with drips and cannulas and God knows what else coming out of her.

Why was it that every other woman in the world could do this so effortlessly and just not her? He wanted a family, and so did she, so, so badly. But there was no denying the disappointment in his eyes. This was a man who had everything else in life handed to him on a plate. So why was this working out to be so bloody hard? Damien didn't do failure and the more this went on, the more Kate felt like she'd become exactly that.

Then followed more doctors, tests and still more bloody tests. When Kate suffered a third miscarriage after just a few weeks, her consultant decided to call in the big guns. IVF was mooted and both Kate and Damien agreed that maybe this was a route they should consider going down.

'It says here that IVF increases our chances of a multiple birth,' Damien read from one of the endless leaflets and booklets of information they'd been inundated with. 'I've always wanted to be the proud father of twins. Can you imagine? Three King men under the one roof – we'll have a dynasty!'

Kate had tried to smile, but kept her fears to herself. The chances, they'd been told, were frighteningly slim given her medical history. Even with this gruelling round of treatment, the success rate was still just below twenty per cent.

'What's hugely in your favour is that you're still young,' her consultant had told her; a buff, bearded sixty-something who spent more time chatting to Damien about rugby than he ever did about Kate's condition. 'But what's causing us a problem is that tilt in your uterus, particularly when you couple it with your history of endometriosis. So both conception and carrying a foetus to full-term are major issues here. IVF will boost your chances of conception, but after that, I'm afraid—'

He'd trailed off there, leaving Kate to imagine the very worst. Still, though, she steeled herself and so began an incredibly painful round of ovulation induction, intra-uterine insemination and something she never really fully grasped called pituitary gland suppression. All she knew is that the cocktail of drugs she was now on was enough to fill a pharmacy.

For someone like her that had barely taken as much as

a paracetamol in her whole life, she now found herself pumping her body with all sorts of stimulants and hardcore medication. Every single day she had to inject herself with a follicle stimulating hormone, followed by a heavy dose of something called Clomid. The combination of drugs made her feel sluggish and depressed and bloated her out so she could barely recognise her once slim frame.

'You may not be pregnant yet,' Damien had said, taking in her bulging tummy with a distinctly unimpressed up-and-down glance, 'but you sure as hell look it.'

More pregnancy tests – every single one negative. And to add to it, a frightening number of Kate's contemporaries – women who'd married around the same time she had – were now falling pregnant like ducks in a row. Falling pregnant easily and effortlessly, like it was the simplest thing in the world.

It seemed that not a month passed without Kate being invited to some baby shower or else, worse, a Christening. Babies, babies, babies. There was no escaping them. Kate frequently went to visit Mo and when she'd see how healthy and happy her gorgeous twins were, she'd hug them so tightly to her that they'd pull away from her complaining, 'Aunt Kate, you're hurting!'

There was an awful, hollow throbbing inside of her that was inescapable now and nothing seemed to fill it. Not even the ridiculous amounts of money she was spending these days. Never having been much of a spendthrift before, Kate had taken to shopping in a way that she wouldn't have dreamt of in the past.

She'd remembered the way Damien always glowed proudly at her when she was immaculately dressed and looking her best. And so she hit the designer stores; kitting herself out top-to-toe in straight-off–the-catwalk high fashion, that only someone as tall and thin as her could really pull off. It actually got to the stage where she and her girlfriends knew the staff at Harvey Nichols and Brown Thomas by name.

Kate would fill her walk-in wardrobe with hanger after hanger of exquisite dresses, most of which would never even be worn, but still, it was something to do to pass the long, lonely weeks when Damien was away on business. Plus it went a way towards sating that gnawing emptiness inside of her. These days she was buying stuff she barely needed. Shopping, spending, accumulating, collecting; anything just to take her mind off things.

Well I have to fill the time somehow, don't I, she figured. Seeing as how the entire medicine cabinet of drugs she was taking wasn't the slightest comfort to her at all.

In fact the only thing that eased that dull ache inside of her was the surreptitious glass of wine she'd taken to having late at night to soothe her sleep. When Damien and the house staff were already in bed and there was no one around to see.

TESS

The present

'Good God, Tess, what have you done to yourself?' says Bernard when he calls over to the house later on. 'You look like Coco the Clown.'

'Make-up malfunction.' I shrug as he bends down to kiss me in our tiny hallway. Filling the hall, as he always seems to do, he's just that big.

'You're not going to look like that on the big day, are you, sausage?' he asks worriedly. 'It's just . . . well perhaps a little avant-garde, wouldn't you say? Not that I wouldn't marry you if you turned up in a black refuse sack,' he adds hastily.

But then Bernard lives his whole life in permanent fear of being thought of as impolite. This is a man who'd eat a plate of regurgitated baby poo if you plonked it in front of him, rather than cause offence.

I steer him into the kitchen, away from Mum and Gracie and their telly marathon, stick the kettle on then fill him in on the day's events.

'You're working on the King case?' he asks, plonking down at the kitchen table, all ears. 'How extraordinary.'

'I know, it's like the case of the decade! Can you believe it? I thought I'd end up on a TV licence fraud case or something equally boring.'

'Because, you know, that family really do have the most astonishing collection,' says Bernard, drifting off a bit. 'A Vermeer, a Titian, a Goya, even a very rare Gainsborough portrait of the Duchess of Marlborough. But of course the jewel in the crown is the famous Rembrandt; the one that Kate King is insisting is hers.'

'She's in breach of three court orders, you know,' I say, pouring out two cups of tea and bringing them over to the table, careful to serve Bernard his just how he likes it – English breakfast, loose leaf and always, always in a good china cup and saucer – only too glad that Gracie isn't here so she can slag him off afterwards.

'What can you possibly mean, sausage?'

'Well I'm not really supposed to talk about it, but . . .' Feck it anyway, my will to yack is just too overwhelmingly huge. 'Oh Bernard, you should have heard Oliver Daniels in court today, he was just brimming over with confidence. They have a cast-iron case against Kate King, because they think the whole thing will be over in about eight days. And as for her defence lawyer, she was beyond useless! She barely even bothered to try. Just said "it's not how it looks", and that was it really.'

'Well, innocent until proven guilty, and all that.'

'It's bizarre though,' I say knowledgeably. 'I'm telling you, Bernard, I sat this close to Kate King herself and you should have seen her. The woman was a nervous wreck. All trembling and twitchy. She couldn't even look us in the eye.'

'Now, sausage, you know you're not really supposed to discuss the case outside of court.'

'Fine, then, let's talk about something else.' I shrug, inwardly cursing Bernard and his ethics for not even letting me chat about this at my own kitchen table.

'Jolly good idea,' he says, taking a sip of the tea with his little finger pointing upwards, a gesture which makes me doubly glad Gracie isn't around to see. I can just hear her and Dad now, slagging Bernard off for the tiniest little thing and referring to him as 'his ladyship' behind my back. In vain I've tried to plead that just because Bernard doesn't drink Heineken from the tin and follow the FA Premier League that doesn't make him either gay or a granny; but as my mother wisely says, when it comes to Dad and Gracie, you might as well be trying to reason with a pair of gorillas.

Silence. And I know I've piles of stuff to go through with Bernard about the wedding and everything, but all I can think about is the case.

'Well, can I at least tell you about the other jurors?' I ask hopefully.

'Best not to,' says Bernard, shaking his head.

'Shit. I can't even talk about that much?'

'Afraid not, sausage. And there really is no need for the expletive.'

'Sorry.'

An even lengthier pause before he pipes up again.

'Although I did meet them once, you know. Both of them.'

'The Kings?'

'Yes, absolutely. I was invited to a party at their mansion house in the country. Castletown, I think it's called.'

'Bernard! And you're only telling me this now?'

He ponders for a moment, then says, 'I'm just wondering

if it would be a breach of ethics for me to talk to you about it, with the case and everything . . .'

'Are you mad? Of course it wouldn't be!'

He weighs it up for a minute, then decides that on balance it's probably OK.

'They invited me to a party, essentially so they could show off *A Lady of Letters*. The whole Art History faculty was invited and I must say, their hospitality really was to be commended. Do you know, they served the most wonderful fork supper after a sumptuous drinks reception and even had specially chosen vintage wines to complement each course? I particularly remember a very rare Chablis, a 1962 if I recall—'

'Bernard, love, never mind about the 1962 Chablis,' I interrupt, knowing full well that once he starts talking about food and wine, there'll be no shutting him up. 'Tell me about the Kings at the party.'

'Well do you know it really was the most extraordinary thing. Kate King was there, naturally, but seemed terribly overwrought and stressed. At that time you see we had a visiting professor at City College who happened to be working very closely with Damien King; apparently she was helping him to gift a sizable donation. The plan was that he'd set up a King foundation so his art collection could tour internationally.'

'And?' I say, all ears.

'Well it seems Mrs King got a bee in her bonnet about this particular visiting professor, who was rather young and attractive, as I recall. And Mrs King seemed to assume that she was carrying on some kind of ding-dong with her husband.'

I'm on the edge of my seat now, but then I think I can

145

guess what's coming. And by the way 'ding-dong', would be Bernard-speak for having an affair. Anything remotely sexual he tends to coat over in nursery school language. When we're in bed together, it's not unlike being in bed with an Enid Blyton book. Pet names for everything: willies, boobs, the works.

'So what happened?'

'Well Kate King disappeared off for a bit while the rest of us were all having a perfectly lovely time of it. Then I distinctly remember she didn't appear for the supper, which seemed odd given that she was our hostess. Damien King said she had a migraine, but of course no one believed him, if anything the lady seemed to be three sheets to the wind. But right after supper, we were all asked to congregate around *A Lady of Letters* and in she came, practically spewing fire, the poor lady.'

'What did she say?'

'Oh, sausage, does it really matter? The fact is that her marriage has broken up now, the painting has disappeared and now she's in court accused of art theft. If anything, the poor lady deserves our sympathy.'

'Bernard! I really need to know what happened at that party, it might be important for the case.'

He looks troubled though and doesn't even bother helping himself to a chocolate Hobnob from the packet in front of him. Most unlike him.

'Now you know that wouldn't be ethical, Tess. All I will say without prejudice is that the talk of the party afterwards was that old truism.'

'Which one?'

'That hell hath no fury like a woman scorned.'

KATE

The Chronicle
15th November, 2007

LET THEM EAT CAKE!

Kate's blow-out birthday bash costs in excess of €200,000!

Last night at their palatial mansion, Castletown House in County Wicklow, Kate King hosted a lavish costume ball to celebrate her husband Damien's fortieth birthday. And we can exclusively reveal that the cream of Irish high society were all present and correct – all four hundred and fifty of them, to be precise.

The host and hostess looked utterly resplendent, as ever, dressed as Louis XVI and Marie Antoinette. Kate looked particularly breathtaking in a gold lame dress designed for her by Jenny Packham and said to be an exact replica of the gown worn by Grace Kelly in the costume ball scene of To Catch a Thief.

Property mogul Joe Kennedy and his beautiful wife Mo were among the assembled glitterati, with Mo utterly stunning in a red wig and elaborate costume, dressed as Elizabeth I.

The Cassidys, billionaire owners of Cassidy's Oil, also looked notably striking as Danny and Sandy from Grease and let's not forget Clive Fay, also from Globtech Ireland, and his wife Constance, who came as Jay Gatsby and Daisy Buchanan.

Other notables included the Minister for Finance, who came as a particularly terrifying Dracula. Although maybe he'd just come straight from Government buildings, it was hard to tell. Meanwhile His Excellency, the Honorary Consul to Monaco, chose to play it safe, dressed as Simon Cowell in a most uninspiring white Gap t-shirt, jeans and stacked Cuban heels. His wife on the other hand was a little more adventurous as Alice in Wonderland, complete with a toy white rabbit clamped to her arm for the night.

Kate, our glittering hostess, spared no expense in making this the party of the year with a Bollinger reception to greet guests, including a champagne fountain which flowed freely for the entire night, 'even when the room was empty' as one astonished guest later told us.

The evening began with guests lining up to greet the Kings, who were seated side-by-side on specially constructed golden thrones, French Empire-style. Then followed a seven-course banquet served on gold plates in the ballroom at Castletown House, which had been made to resemble an exact replica of the Hall of Mirrors at Versailles, right down to chandeliers and rococo ceilings specially imported for the party. After-dinner entertainment was kicked off by no one less than Bono himself, who'd agreed to give a special impromptu perform-ance at the party, as Damien King allegedly is a huge fan.

Meanwhile each guest was gifted a specially crafted goodie bag from 'good King Louis and Marie Antoinette', containing tiny gold tie pins for the gentlemen and skin care products from MAC for the ladies.

As Kate King posed for photographers on her throne, our reporter asked how she felt about spending so much on a party, when the rest of the country is in the throes of possibly the worst fiscal crisis since the Depression.

Was she, we wondered, at all concerned about hosting such a public and lavish celebration, given that many people not far from the Castletown estate were suffering evictions, seizure of assets and even bankruptcy?

'Please don't . . . this really isn't a night to talk about money,' was Kate's initial tight-lipped reply. However, we persisted, asking how she could possibly justify spending so vast a sum on just one night.

'Because it was what he wanted,' she blushed, looking adoringly at her husband, Damien. 'He works so hard for all this, you know. And besides, isn't he worth it?'

TESS

The present

I'm not joking; the next day in court is like having a front row seat at the Oliver Daniels one-man tour de force show.

'Three hundred grand a year, that's what I heard he earns,' hisses Jane beside me in the jury box, the woman who always looks so groomed and business-like, dressed head to toe in L.K. Bennett. I was yacking to her earlier and it turns out, at the age of sixty-two, she works for a start-up online recruitment agency set up by her son. She's smart and efficient and I already like her.

We were all given croissants and coffee in the jury room before the case kicked off at 10 a.m. this morning – the croissants were rubbery and the coffee all watery and luke-warm, of course, but still, a welcome gesture. Anyway, I got chatting to a few of our disparate gang and so far they seem lovely, with the notable exception of red-trouser guy, who I've discovered is called Ian and who's a used-car salesman.

No messing, his eyes actually glazed over when I told him that, no thanks, I wasn't in the market for a new car, so instead he targeted Jess, a forty-something mum of four; the same lady who turned up in what looked like PJs yesterday and who's in a baggy, oversized jumper today with what I'd swear is the dregs of mashed banana caked to the arm of it, almost like the poor thing came straight here from giving her kids brekkie and carting them off for the school run. Ian took her in with a quick up-and-down glance and was straight onto her like a limpet.

'So what do you drive?' he asked her, the man-bracelets rattling annoyingly.

'A ten-year-old knackered Mazda, that might as well have "taxi" written on the top of it,' she tells him, 'I spend that much time ferrying my kids around.'

'Yeah, but would you not consider changing it? I'd give you a fantastic deal, you know. I'd look after you.'

'Ian, I haven't slept in two years,' Jess replied sharply, 'and this is basically the first time in weeks that I've spent with a group of adults and without my toddler, my four-year-old and my two pre-teens screaming at each other in the background. Do you honestly think that changing my car is a priority in my life right now? The only thing I'd change the car for right now is a bus pass, so at least I'd have an excuse not to chauffeur my family around any more.'

Which instantly shuts Ian up. She caught me trying to hide a smile and gave me a quick wink as if to say, 'now that's how you deal with the Ians of this world'.

I got chatting to Beth too, who I've discovered is a first year student at UCD, studying English and History.

'So how are you fitting jury service around all your lectures?' I ask her, dying to know.

'It's brilliant,' she beams delightedly. 'Thanks to this, I

don't have to sit an exam I was due to have next week. Just as well, because I hadn't done a tap of work for it.'

Other than us though – and that guy Will who was slagging off my taste in music yesterday, and who arrives dead late and all out of breath this morning – the vast majority of our fellow jurors seem to be very much at the 'active retirement' stage of life and, to a man, are treating the case as a lovely piece of live entertainment, a pageant put on solely for their amusement.

Anyway, back to court. A lot of this morning's evidence is technical and therefore has the potential to be deeply boring, but for the fact that Oliver Daniels has a wizard-like way of spinning drama even out of the most ordinary, banal details.

First witness is Detective Sergeant Joe McHugh, a beefy, stocky fifty-something guy with absolutely no neck at all, just a head, then shoulders.

He's sworn in and Oliver Daniels is straight up onto his feet. 'Detective Sergeant,' he begins, 'would you care to outline for the court the events of July 26th, 2014?'

'Certainly,' says the copper, and he then goes to flip open the cover on his iPad to refer down to his notes.

'At precisely 11 a.m. on the morning in question, in the company of two junior detectives, I arrived at the home of Mr and Mrs King, Castletown House, County Wicklow.'

'And I'm sure the purpose of this visit wasn't a social call?'

'Indeed it was not. A court order had been obtained by Mr Damien King from the Circuit Civil Court issuing a demand that the painting under contention, *A Lady of Letters*, be summarily returned to Mr King, its rightful owner.'

'Objection!' says Hilda Cassidy, Kate's barrister, straight up on her feet, full of indignation. 'Your Honour, that is precisely what we the Defence are here to contest. That Mr King is not, in fact, the rightful owner at all.'

My eye wanders across the room to where Kate King is sitting demurely, dressed head to toe in black today, which only seems to accentuate how ghostly white her face is. She looks like a woman who hasn't eaten or slept in weeks, in stark contrast to her ex, who's right behind Oliver Daniels looking swarthy and suntanned and even a bit relaxed about all this.

'Sustained,' says the judge. 'Sergeant McHugh, I'd kindly remind you to pick your words a little more carefully.'

'Oh . . . emm . . . sorry about that, Your Honour,' says the sergeant, starting to sweat a little now, the stifling heat of the court clearly getting to him. But then it's packed out in here today, even the public benches are jammed and as far as I can see, it seems to be standing room only at the back.

'If you would be so good as to resume?' says Oliver politely.

'Certainly,' the sergeant says. 'We found Mrs King to be at home on the morning in question, so the court order was delivered forthwith and immediately.'

'And did you outline to Mrs King precisely what this court order meant?'

'I certainly did,' says the sergeant, getting red in the face. 'I personally took great care to explain to the Defendant that a court order meant that the painting was ordered by law to be returned immediately. And of course that failure to do so could result in prosecution.'

'And did Mrs King comply with this court order?'

153

'I'm afraid to say she did not. Sure isn't that why we're all sitting here?'

Titters around the court at that, which Judge Simmonds instantly silences.

'Can you tell us about the events of September 15th, in your own words?' Oliver prods, resuming questioning.

'Well, a second order was issued on September 15th and then a third on October 24th. I served them all on Mrs King myself and took considerable pains to point out the seriousness of repeatedly breaching such an order.'

'And did you search the property?'

'Absolutely. On both occasions myself and my team conducted a thorough search and I can confirm that the item in question was definitely not at Castletown House.'

'No further questions, Your Honour.'

A respectful bow from him and then Hilda is straight back up on her feet.

'Just a few short questions, Your Honour,' she says before turning to the witness box. 'Sergeant McHugh, were you aware that a pre-nuptial agreement was in place between Mr and Mrs King?'

'I may have read something about it in the paper, alright,' the sergeant nods. 'And my wife mentioned it too, but then she seems to know more about this case than I do myself, there's been so much in the media about it.'

'When the Defence get to open our case,' Hilda goes on, speaking plainly and simply, 'we'll obviously be going into a lot more detail on this. But the critical thing is that under the clear and certain terms of this pre-nuptial agreement, all gifts bestowed on Mrs King throughout her marriage became her lawful property. They were hers and no one else's.'

She pauses for a moment here, to really take in the jury and to make sure we're all paying proper attention.

'So my question is this, Sergeant. If someone called to your home and served a court order to you for something that was rightfully your property, say for instance a laptop or a valuable piece of jewellery, or something else that was of great value to you. Would you just hand it over without any argument?'

'Well . . . no, I suppose I wouldn't really,' the sergeant trails off.

'And if they were to serve you with a second court order, and even a third? Would you cave in to such bullying and intimidation, or would you hold firm and stand your ground?'

'I'm not certain how to answer that really,' says the sergeant, scarlet in the face now from the stuffiness in the room. 'It's a hypothetical situation really, isn't it?'

'No further questions, Your Honour.'

Now the hush around the courtroom earlier has turned to knowing nods and muttered comments.

'Ooh, it's getting nice and juicy now, isn't it,' whispers Edith excitedly from behind me.

'They should cut the bloody thing in two and give them half of it each so that we can all go home,' hisses an elderly man beside her, who I think is called Barney and who's sitting back, arms folded, just drinking it all in.

'We'll take a lunch recess there, back at 2 p.m., please,' says Judge Simmonds as the assembled court scatters to the four winds. However, for those of us on the jury, it seems that it's a slightly more official affair.

Instead of being allowed to disappear off to the nearest coffee shop and get an hour's headspace away from everyone else, we're all corralled onto a coach to whizz us off to a hotel not far from the court, a dingy-looking place called the Queen Street Arms that looks like it hasn't seen a lick of paint since the 1980s. A fifty-something court usher with bullet-grey hair so 'set' looking that it's almost like a helmet, introduces herself as Mona and tells us she'll be accompanying us for the remainder of the case.

'And I must at this point remind you that it's strictly forbidden to discuss the case amongst yourselves, until both sides have been heard and you're in the privacy of the jury room,' she says bossily. 'Nor are you permitted to check mobile phones or any electronic device for media coverage about the case. Posting on social media is also strictly forbidden.'

'Posting on social *what*?' says Ruth, a seventy-something lady who I've discovered is a tiny bit hard of hearing. She wears a hearing aid, which completely solves the problem, but sometimes forgets to turn it up fully.

'She means like Facebook and Twitter,' I tell her helpfully.

'What the hell is Twitter?'

Next thing, we're ushered into a private dining room with just the one dining table which seats exactly twelve, and it seems this is it. Like we're being kept in some sort of isolation booth, shut out from the world, not even allowed to intermingle – God forbid – with other people in a normal restaurant.

Not that I can imagine from the state of the place and the overwhelming stink of boiled cabbage that anyone with half a choice would actually elect to eat here. This is the kind of 'hotel' that you drive past praying it'll be turned into a car park someday and put out of its misery.

I'm last into the room and am angling for a seat beside either Beth, Jane or the sweet elderly lady with a walking stick who I've since discovered is called Minnie, but there's only one seat left: beside Will, as it happens.

'One hour for lunch and then, at exactly 13.55 hours, I'll escort you to the coach which will drive you back to court,' says Mona, crisply addressing the room. 'So I suggest if you need a bathroom break, you go at 13.50 sharp. Judge Simmonds must not be kept waiting.'

Will gives me a quick nod and clears the empty chair, which he'd slung his jacket and manbag over.

'Make room for the Beatles fan,' he says dryly as I pull into the seat beside him.

'Very funny.'

'So did you make all your appointments yesterday after-noon?' he asks, shoving a clumpful of coal-black hair out of his eyes. 'Sorry, but it was impossible not to overhear you. You were on the phone for ages and it certainly made for intriguing listening.'

I wince a bit as I remember just how waspish I was with him then, and seeing as how we're all locked in to this jury thing together, decide that I'd better make peace.

'You know, if I was a bit snippy with you yesterday,' I say tentatively, 'well, I really am sorry. I didn't mean to come across like that.'

'Hey, you're allowed,' he smiles. 'A bride's gotta do what a bride's gotta do.'

'The thing is,' I say, grabbing a bottle of water from the table in front of us, 'I just don't think I'm my best self when I'm stressed.'

'Why are you stressed?' he asks, folding his arms and looking keenly at me now. 'Engagements are meant to be a happy time in your life, aren't they? You know, marrying the love of your life and all that?'

My stomach does an involuntary flip at the 'love of your life' comment, but I let it pass.

'Oh God, how long have you got?' I say, with a grimace. 'You know, I think the whole trouble started when I decided that a great way to save money would be to have the wedding reception at home. I'm telling you, if I'd known then what was ahead of me and the sheer amount of hassle involved, I think I'd have just been a tiny speck on the horizon.'

'Just remember,' he says, dark eyes reading my face, 'all that matters is that you turn up to marry him and he turns up to marry you. Because everything else is nothing more than white noise. Believe me.'

'It's Will, isn't it?' I ask, even though I'm pretty certain it is.

'Yup. And you're Tess. And this starter is pure vomit, if you ask me.'

I smile at this because it's true; we've just been served prosciutto that's virtually one hundred per cent fat, on a bed of lettuce that looks like it first started wilting about two weeks ago. Just plonked down in front of us, without anyone being asked if they actually wanted it or not.

'But don't you really appreciate the amount of choice there is for us at this restaurant?' I say, playing with the prosciutto that I can't bring myself to even look at.

'Personally speaking, I was overwhelmed at the breadth of the menu we were offered.'

'Be interesting to see what they'd do if you came in and said you were a lactose-intolerant coeliac . . .'

'Who's vegetarian . . .'

'And vegan,' we both say together, as the starters are cleared away a bare three minutes after they were dumped down in front of us, boarding-school-style.

'In fact the grub here is so delicious,' says Will, tongue in cheek, 'it almost makes you wonder what we're in for as a main course. The Ebola special, perhaps?'

'And based on this delightful culinary experience, I'm wondering where they'll treat us to lunch tomorrow? Because I hear there's a wonderful greasy spoon on the M50 where they do a mean egg and chips, swimming in a bed of congealed fat.'

'Ah yes, I've heard about this,' Will plays along, 'although it could prove tricky to get a reservation. That place is Michelin-starred, I hear. And as you're discovering, jurors are only ever entertained at the very best restaurants.'

The main course arrives, again without anyone having a word of choice in the matter. Lamb shanks and soggy broccoli, in gravy with the skin already formed on top of it.

'Ahh, a rare delicacy,' says Will, playfully picking off the skin, his eyes glinting. 'It's our lucky day.'

'In fact it all looks so divine,' I tell him, 'I'm thinking of changing my mind and having my wedding reception here instead.'

'When is the big day?' he asks, shoving his plate away and facing me now.

'In just under four weeks,' I smile. 'Well, actually three weeks and four days, but who's counting?'

'And you mean to say you're having your reception

somewhere other than here at the Queen Street Arms? Let me guess, there's a two-year waiting list to get in here and somehow you didn't make the cut?'

'And also the fact that I didn't want our guests to feel overwhelmed or intimidated by the retro 1980s decor.'

'I take your point. This place would put you in mind of Versailles, really, wouldn't it?'

He nods towards the peeling wallpaper with the damp behind it showing through and we both grin, just as dessert is served – jelly and ice cream in a bowl with a wafer on top.

'You know someone should enter whoever designed the menu here into *Masterchef*,' says Will. 'I've been waiting on jelly and ice cream to be recognised as retro-chic and finally the Queen Street Arms have done it.'

'From now on let's call it the Ebola Arms, will we?'

'Certainly has a ring to it. Could catch on.'

We're given about three minutes to knock back lukewarm teas and coffees before being ushered onto the coach and back to court. But just as everyone is gathering up coats and scarves to ward off the chilly April air, Will stops me in my tracks.

'And by the way, Tess?'

'Yes?'

'Don't let all the stress get to you. Just keep remembering that this is supposed to be a very happy time for you, and you'll be fine.'

'Yeah, I will, thanks. Marriage really is the best, isn't it?'

'So I'm told.'

'Are you . . . ?'

'Am I what?'

'Married?'

A tiny pause while he looks at me with an expression that's unreadable.

'Divorced.'

KATE

The Goss.ie
17th December, 2007

KATE's €90K CHRISTMAS SPENDING SPREE!

Who else but Kate King could possibly manage to spend upwards of €90k Christmas shopping in a single day? The Goss.ie *can exclusively report that Kate, along with her best friend Mo Kennedy and a few other close friends, flew to London City Airport in her husband Damien's private Gulfstream jet, whereupon they transferred into a specially chartered helicopter which flew them directly onto the rooftop of Harrods. No humble taxis or pubic transport for these well-heeled ladies!*

Once Kate's party arrived at Harrods, well-placed sources say they shopped for hours, only pausing to revive themselves with a snipe of Dom Pérignon at the store's famous Champagne Bar. Kate allegedly sampled Harrods' own vintage Hostomme too and enjoyed it so much that she ordered three dozen crates of it to be delivered to her palatial residence at Castletown House, just in time for Christmas.

The ladies then spent the rest of the day shopping, with

tens of thousands reportedly being spent on Christmas gifts. Well ahead of the posse though was Kate herself, who managed to nab no fewer than six designer dresses from Harrods' couture hall in just under an hour, at a total cost of €20K. Then it was up to the gift department, where for the remainder of the day she reportedly blew another €40K on 'gifts for the staff at Castletown', as she later told us. These allegedly included a selection of TAG Heuer watches for the gentlemen and a whole assortment of Mulberry handbags for the ladies.

The shopping party continued on till well past the shop's official closing time. We're reliably informed that Kate and her entourage then wound up an undoubtedly hectic day with dinner at The Wolseley, before retiring for the night to the Presidential Suite at – where else? – the Mandarin Oriental hotel.

When The Goss *contacted Kate to ask what she was planning to buy her husband Damien for Christmas, her response was, 'well he's recently developed an interest in Baroque art. So I suppose a Caravaggio. Or a Rembrandt. Whatever'.*

*

'You've been following me around all day,' Kate pleaded to the reporter who'd recognised her and who hadn't let her out of his sight ever since he'd spotted her party first arriving in Harrods earlier that morning. 'We're just a few girlfriends having a private day out. Nothing more. Please understand I was speaking to you off the record. So you won't write about it, will you?'

But he went ahead and ran with the story anyway, embellishing freely as he went. Just like the bastards always did.

TESS

The present

By the following day the press pack outside the courts has swollen and just trying to weave my way inside is like an obstacle course. I bump into Minnie doing exactly the same thing, though God love her, she has to take the steps slowly on account of her walking stick, so I link her arm, help her up and together we just battle our way through them. No one bothers taking our picture of course: they're all saving themselves for either the Kings or else Oliver Daniels; grade-A paparazzi fodder.

'Makes me realise what life must be like for proper celebs,' Minnie smiles warmly as soon as we're safely inside the courts building.

'Makes me realise that I need to start wearing make-up before I leave the house.'

Edith is in the lift ahead of us, full of chat about how she's certain today is going to be a good one.

'We're due to hear all about the Kings' separation agreement,' she says knowledgeably. 'Oh ladies, I can't tell you how much I'm enjoying this case! I'm the envy of all my neighbours to have a front row seat here.'

I wave at Will as we're all ushered into the jury box and he gives half a wink back. He's in a deep-blue shirt today and it suits him, brings out his dark eyes, I think distractedly. Possibly might be a nice fella for my pal Monica, if she were up for a blind date?

But then that's the thing about being engaged and in a secure relationship. You feel this need to match up the rest of the world as well. I'd been trying my level best to pair off all my single pals with some of Bernard's colleagues, only most of them are 'confirmed bachelors'. And considerably older too. Or as Monica dismissively said of one of them, 'thanks, but no thanks. I point blank refuse to date anyone if they're within five years of getting the free bus pass'.

The whole morning in court goes by in a blur. As ever, all eyes are zipping back and forth like a Wimbledon centre court match between Damien and Kate King, assessing their faces, gauging their reactions to what's being said. Which can be summarised thus: him, stoic and unflappable, radiating confidence; her, head down, eyes staring at the palms of her hands, white as a ghost. She's dressed head to toe in black again today with just the hint of a white collar sticking out, blonde hair tied neatly back.

'Even when Kate King isn't all glammed up, she still looks fabulous,' I hiss to Jane, who's right beside me.

'Hmm, if you ask me, she looks like Goody Proctor from *The Crucible*,' Jane, our resident businesswoman who's always dressed to impress whispers back. 'Almost like she's trying a bit too hard to create the illusion of innocence.'

She can be a bit mistrustful, Jane, if you ask me.

In summary, it's not a good morning at all for Kate King. All Oliver Daniels is short of doing is pointing one of his pudgy fingers in her face and yelling, 'gold digger!' It's all out in the open; there are absolutely no secrets here.

Mind you, it's all done very cleverly and subtly. Over the course of the morning, Oliver slowly weaves together a picture of the young Kate before she met Damien, doing very nicely as a model, thanks very much, but with her sights set on far, far loftier goals. He describes how she essentially lived out of a suitcase before they met and yet quickly adapted to the highlife the minute she got the ring on her finger.

We're told tales of her spectacular excess that would almost make a Euromillions Lotto winner blush. Damien King's chief accountant is called as an expert witness and stuns us with some of the figures that Kate King managed to work her way through on an annual basis.

'So Mrs King's allowance was thirty *thousand* euros a month?' Oliver puts the question to him, taking great care to emphasise the 'thousand'.

'Yes, but only very rarely did she actually stay within that budget,' says our witness; a baldy, squinting middle-aged man who puts me in mind of a vole let out of its cage for the day. Then he hands around printed spreadsheets outlining what he refers to as 'just a small sample of Mrs King's monthly outgoings'. Every one of us in the jury box gets a copy, and it would nearly make your jaw drop. The figures that are being bandied around the court are staggering, unimaginable to the rest of us.

'Mrs King regularly spent in excess of five thousand euros a month on facials, microdermabrasion treatments and botox . . . her hairdressing bills frequently ran into thousands . . . in fact on more than one occasion Mrs King flew her personal hairdresser out to join her on holiday so he could tend to her tresses . . .'

166

'No local hairdresser she could have patronised?' Oliver interrupts.

'It appears that was never an option Mrs King would have considered.'

Hilda is straight up on her feet, objecting like mad and spitting fire.

'Your Honour, I can't just sit here and allow the Prosecution to paint such a negative picture of my client. There were good reasons why her expenditure was high and I'd just like to—'

'Credit card bills don't lie,' shrugged Oliver as the judge rules in his favour and allows him to continue this line of questioning.

'And since when is it a crime to spend money?' Hilda snaps back, full of indignation.

My eye automatically drifts towards Kate to see how she's reacting to all this, but again nothing. All she's doing is just staring straight ahead, completely dead-eyed.

Then a former butler who worked at Castletown House is called, takes the stand and is sworn in.

'A butler?' whispers Barney, our resident jury granddad, as I've nicknamed him in my head. 'What is this anyway, an episode of *Downton Abbey*?'

And Oliver Daniels's character assassination juggernaut just keeps trundling on. We get an in-depth description of Kate King's wardrobe, we're even shown pictures of it on a screen. No kidding, it's the approximate size of our whole house. There's one entire room for her casual wear, another for evening gowns, plus a third that's temperature controlled 'so her fur collection could be kept at optimum temperature'.

Disgruntled mutters from all around the court at that

and from the corner of my eye I can see a pack of journos in the press box madly scribbling away. No prizes for guessing what's going to take centre stage in the late editions and online. Because there's no room for doubt and it's just confirming what we knew all along; this is a woman who loved to spend her husband's money and spend big. Oliver even draws a veiled parallel between Kate King and Imelda Marcos, right down to her shoe room, which again we're shown pictures of and told that her collection exceeded several hundred.

And as for the lady herself? It's astonishing to witness really. Here she is having her good name torn to shreds for all the world to see. And her reaction? To sit quietly, stare blankly at the wall behind us, bite her lip and occasionally give the tiniest headshake. That's it. No attempt at denial, no urgent notes passed to or from her barrister trying to defend herself.

In fairness, Hilda Cassidy is trying her level best. Time and again she's on her feet to cross-question witnesses, but sadly, 'yes, this may seem like a lot of money to spend on clothes, but you must understand that Mrs King was a corporate wife and thus expected to look the part', just doesn't seem to cut it as a justification. I glance around the jury box and can almost read people's thoughts. We all read the papers and we know for ourselves just how much Kate King enjoyed spending her husband's money.

'You must understand that Mrs King would never have dreamt of running up such expenses of her own accord,' an exasperated Hilda says at one point when she's questioning the witness. 'At least not without actively being encouraged to do so by her then husband,' she adds, taking great care to address us.

'It's hard for us to get our heads around the colossal figures that are being bandied about here today,' she goes on, 'but all these expenses must be seen for what they were at the time: a very small percentage of Damien King's annual salary, including all his remunerations. Ladies and gentlemen of the jury, you've got to put all these expenses into proportion. After all, isn't a wife entitled to live in the manner her husband expects her to?'

It's a weak point though and it's as if she knows it. The dogs on the street know how much Kate liked to spend; it's been drip-fed to us by the media for years now. No question about it. This round just went to Oliver Daniels.

*

Lunch recess is called and that bossy woman with the iron-grey hair called Mona comes with us as we're bussed back to the Ebola Arms, then ushers us upstairs into the same dingy, cabbage-smelling dining room we were in yesterday.

'One hour for lunch, kindly be prepared to re-board the bus at 13.55 p.m. sharp!' she says, just as I manage to catch Will's eye. He does a mini Nazi salute behind her back and I can't help giggling. Anyway, this time I'm sitting in between Barney and an elderly lady called Mai, who has a perm so tight it looks like someone poured a tin of baked beans over her head, and who literally doesn't stop moaning from the very moment we sit down.

'Terrible food. I had indigestion all day yesterday. And you know my bowels wouldn't be the best anyway, so this is doing me no good at all.'

I glance away and see that Will's sitting about as far away from me as is possible. He's sandwiched in between Edith

169

and yet another older lady whose name I don't know, but who I've silently christened Lily of the Valley on account of the perfume she wears.

Poor Will looks like he's fighting a losing battle wedged between Mapp and Lucia. He's struggling to make conversation with them both, but I can't hear a word they're saying. The only other eye contact we share is when he holds up a forkful of gloopy beef casserole with so much stringy fat in it that it looks like a heart attack on a plate, and rolls his eyes over at me.

Meanwhile Ian with the jangly man-bracelets is deep in chat with Beth and although I can't hear what they're saying, the bored look on Beth's face is almost comical. Like the poor kid has a thought balloon coming out of her head saying, 'get me out of here, quick'.

I mime a fake throwing up gesture over at her, but then Mai reclaims me. 'I can't possibly finish this lunch, you know,' she says huffily, shoving her plate away. 'It'll set off one of my attacks.'

'Your attacks?' I ask innocently, but then I'd only been half-listening to her.

'IBS, lovie. I'm a martyr to it, I'm afraid. I find I'm either bloated, constipated or else running to the bathroom every ten minutes. Dreadfully uncomfortable. Not to mention embarrassing.'

I'd been picking at the vegetables on the side of my plate but shove it away now, appetite suddenly wilted to nothing.

'Did you say IBS?' says Barney from beside me, suddenly all interested in the conversation. 'Because I get terrible attacks of that from time to time too. Ever since I had my hip replaced, my bowels haven't been the same at all. I take these for it and it does ease the symptoms, a bit,' he adds, producing a box of pills from his pocket and placing it in front of him.

'And the farting is desperate. Mortifying,' says Mai.

'Don't talk to me. There are times when my wife says the farting is like a Zeppelin passing overhead.'

'You should try having four natural births one after the other,' Jess chips in from across the table. 'I'm telling you, my bladder control is shot to hell ever since. It can get embarrassing.'

'With me it's high blood pressure,' says Edith, opening up her handbag and whipping out a long strip of tablets. 'I've to take five of these pills, three times a day after meals. Otherwise you'd all be calling an ambulance to zip me off to the nearest A&E.'

'Ha! That's nothing,' says Lily of the Valley from the bottom of the table, 'I've had three rounds of chemo and sure look at me, I'm still here. Hard to kill off a bad thing!'

They all laugh and now the floodgates have opened, as everyone around the table over the age of sixty-five, which is most of them, spill all.

'Three solid months I was in hospital for tests and in the end all they did was put a coronary stent in. Beyond useless, the lot of them, if you ask me. Made no difference whatsoever.'

'Have you a pacemaker? I don't know myself since I got mine put in . . .'

'No, but I have had a knee replacement . . .'

'And I'm on a waiting list to get my piles sorted out . . .'

'I had a coronary bypass about two years ago and I haven't been the same since . . .'

'Anyone know the way to the bathroom?' says Mai, loudly

interrupting everyone else. 'Wouldn't you know it, that bloody casserole has given me an IBS attack.'

'Told you you shouldn't have eaten it, Mai – it looked lethal.'

'I'm sorry everyone,' says Mai, standing wobbly on her feet, 'but I need the ladies room. Now. And I'm afraid it's a number two, so you might need to ask the bus to wait for me. My bowels take ages to move.'

'Dessert,' says our waitress, plonking a bowl down in front of us, without even asking whether we wanted it or not. 'Nice slice of Black Forest gâteau. Enjoy.'

*

On our way back to the bus, Will ambles over to me.

'You do realise,' he says with a twisted smile, 'that between you, me, Jane, Beth, Jess and Ian, we lower the average age of this jury by about fifty years? In fact I might come in on a Zimmer frame tomorrow, just so I can fit in that bit better.'

'Don't let anyone hear you,' I say. 'Otherwise they'll be serving us all Complan for lunch next.'

'With a handy glass in front of each of us to put our teeth into while we're eating.'

'Not a bad idea. I'll bear that in mind.'

*

By the time we get back to the courtroom, it's completely packed out and feels even more stuffy and overheated than this morning. So much so that Jess begins to nod off a bit and I have to keep nudging her to stay awake.

'Sorry,' she hisses back at me. 'Bloody kids had me awake since 5 a.m.'

And I don't blame the poor woman either, the Prosecution's

character assassination of Kate King thunders on all afternoon and it's deeply, profoundly boring. Damien King's family lawyer is called as a witness and he spends a good two hours droning on about the pre-nup agreement that Kate signed before getting married.

'Legally and contractually binding in every way . . .' he says, as I throw my eyes frustratedly across to Ruth.

'And Mrs King entered into this willingly and without duress?' asks Oliver Daniels, fingers tucked into his black gown as he strides up and down across from the witness box.

'Absolutely. I was present myself and can confirm that she was more than happy to sign on the dotted line.'

'Mother of God, all that took two and a half hours,' hisses Ruth, who looks like she's about to nod off herself. 'I timed it. And he could have said it all in five minutes or less. As my grandchildren would say: "booooring".'

'That's lawyers for you,' I whisper back. 'If you ask me, they're trying to drag this out for as long as possible, just so they can bump up their fees.'

'And under the terms of this pre-nuptial agreement,' Oliver continues, 'can you outline the settlement to be conferred on Mrs King?'

That takes another full hour and to be perfectly honest it's an inordinately generous settlement, by anyone's reckoning; one hundred and fifty thousand euros a year, plus her own penthouse apartment? To me and to most people, that'd be akin to winning the lottery. This, I think, is certainly not going to play well with the man in the street. And although Hilda Cassidy's cross-questioning is effective, the damage has already been done.

'I can't and won't sit by and watch my client be portrayed as something that she isn't,' she insists at one point.

'All evidence to the contrary,' quips Oliver under his breath, but we can still hear him, as he doubtless meant us to.

'Your Honour, the settlement according to Mr and Mrs King's pre-nuptial agreement is beside the point here. What matters is that under the clear and certain terms of this agreement, Mrs King is entitled to keep any items gifted to her during the course of her marriage. Which include *A Lady of Letters.*'

'*A Lady of Letters* is the rightful property of the King family trust and therefore it is not in my client's power to gift it to Mrs King—'

'It was a personal gift, given to her on her birthday!' Hilda snaps back, as the judge calls for order.

'If cross-examination of the witness has concluded, the witness may now stand down,' says Judge Simmonds. 'Mr Daniels, have you quite finished?'

Then Oliver turns to face the jury box, the black gown swishing theatrically behind him.

'Just one more thing, Your Honour,' he booms. 'Ladies and gentlemen of the jury, I did warn you that this was a case of unprecedented greed and avarice. We the Prosecution contend that so embittered was Mrs King at what you and I would consider to be a fortune – and Mrs King perceived to be a paltry sum – that she took it on herself to seize the single most valuable asset from her ex-husband's consider-able portfolio. We contend that she helped herself to the one thing that she knew her husband loved most and which therefore would hurt him the most.

'Why else, ladies and gentlemen,' he thunders on, 'would Katherine King withhold *A Lady of Letters* from its rightful owner, knowing how much it means to him?'

He gives a theatrical pause and just lets that last sentence hang there, pausing for a moment to glance all around the court. Yet again all I can think is, wow. If this guy had decided to become an actor, doubtless he'd have at least one Oscar gracing his sideboard by now.

With that Judge Simmonds bangs the gavel and tells us that we'll take a recess, to resume again at 10 a.m. in the morning. So we all shuffle out of there, one thought firmly to the front of everyone's mind.

So far, it's game, set and match for Damien King.

KATE

April 2010

After yet another failed round of IVF, it was decided to take a break to wean Kate off the drugs and let her body recover for a bit.

'And you never know,' her consultant told her cheerfully, 'now that you're taking your focus off having a child, maybe you'll conceive naturally. I see it happening all the time.'

Slightly more of an obstacle, Kate had thought, when you only get to spend maybe one night a fortnight with your husband. Damien was working hard as Globtech stretched its tentacles over yet another continent and while he was outwardly affectionate and loving when they were together, it was the long, lonely nights when he was away that she worried herself sick. And missed him. And then went back to her vicious cycle of worrying and stressing some more.

Boredom and loneliness, she decided, were her problems. She could only socialise so much and there was quite literally nothing for her to do at home except rattle around her vast mansion. Housekeepers and a team of gardeners kept the place going, so what did that leave for her? Now that she'd eased back on all her medications, why not go back to work for a bit? Be independent again and start earning her own money?

'Sweetie, you're beautiful and you know we love your look,' her agent had briskly told her, 'but the fact is you're on the wrong side of thirty, pushing thirty-five. Have you seen this month's *Vogue*? Fashion is an ageist business as we know and what's in demand this particular season are models barely out of primary school. I've clients of fifteen who are working more than the rest put together.'

By then, Damien had a new fad on the go; yachting. Which of course meant more trips away to this regatta at Henley, or that sailing competition in Monaco. Kate gamely pitched up at whatever events he asked her to; immaculately dressed and hoping for nothing more than that he'd notice. But like a snake shedding its skin, Damien had cast off all his old pals from the 'Castletown set' as the papers billed them, and was now intent on carving out a whole new social circle for himself. A lot of which was predominantly younger; with an exceptionally high proportion of pretty twenty-something girls thrown into the mix too.

God knows Kate was trying her hardest to look well at all times and to present a perfect shop front to the world, but it was hard and getting harder when all her husband wanted was to 'go clubbing with Aurelia and Sasha. You can come if you really insist, Kate, though it'll probably be a late one, so maybe you'd be better off going back to the hotel?'

Kate did her best with his new set, but the fact was these girls intimidated her, with their perfect twenty-five-year-old dewy skin, fresh faces and boundless, youthful energy. So she went out to find the best cosmetic surgeon that money could buy and started pumping herself full of botox, fillers, collagen, you name it. It mightn't have made her look particularly fresher or younger, but still. It gave her a badly needed confidence boost, particularly whenever another young twenty-something was hanging around Damien just a little bit too closely for her liking.

And so after a while, Kate hit on a different project to occupy her and fill up her time some more. She'd decided to embark on a multi-million-euro renovation and restoration job at Castletown. No expense was to be spared; her one and only brief to the architect was to make this the kind of palatial house that her husband had always intended it to be.

But her silent brief was a little different.

Turn this into a home that Damien will never want to leave.

This was large-scale stuff. There was to be a home cinema, a snooker room, a wine cellar, an indoor pool, the list went on. Kate had always adored the house but now she was determined to turn it into her project, lovingly transforming it from a slightly run-down eighteenth-century manor house into the sumptuous palace that it was to become; basically the type of home that would put many five-star hotels into the shade.

She herself had wanted Castletown to have a tasteful, classical feel, but of course Damien insisted on adding on a giant subterranean car park to house his collection of Porsches, and of course his pride and joy, the Aston Martin Classic. The house boasted not just a gym, but also a 'wellness room', a plant room, superloos in every bathroom (which were just like any other loo, really, Kate thought, except that they cost €3,500 each and blasted your bum with warm air), and of course, 'smart' his 'n' hers dressing rooms, which catalogued their clothes and kept her furs at optimum temperature.

'Spend as much as you want, babes,' Damien had told Kate over the phone when he called her one night from a business conference in Buenos Aires. 'After all, it can only add to the value of my house.' Kate winced a little at the 'my' house comment, but it didn't deter her. For eighteen months while the work was carried out, she was tireless, showing up at the site every day, questioning every little detail. She wanted the place looking like the Mandarin Oriental by the time she'd finished with it and no trouble was too much.

Plus all this usefully served another function too. Whenever she met up with her girlfriends, not to mention all the other Globtech wives, and when their conversation inevitably turned to kids, at least this way, if nothing else, her project gave her something to talk about. A sort of 'baby' of her own, albeit one that was made of bricks and mortar. Her friends would proudly chat about what Santa was bringing to their ever growing broods for Christmas this year, and then one of them would almost certainly turn to her, cast a quick eye down at her tummy and ask the dreaded question, 'so what's new with you, darling?'

Now in return Kate could confidently talk about rising-damp treatment for the basement at Castletown, preservation orders and did the other ladies really think that Farrow & Ball really was the best paint out there?

Not quite the same thing as joining in with all the mummy chat. But still, it filled a burning gap in her life that somehow nothing else would.

And it was better than nothing. Marginally.

*

Kate could never put her finger on exactly when she first suspected that Damien was having an affair. No rumours reached her and certainly no 'concerned friends' ever took her aside to give her a heads-up.

But she knew. He was away from home so often by then and barely back for one night a week. And while he was still outwardly affectionate towards her, something had shifted. Kate wasn't his sole focus any more. That need he once had to be around her all the time had completely vanished. He no longer called her at all hours of the day and night 'just to hear the sound of your voice', and his 'work trips' away from home grew longer and longer.

Around this time, out of the blue, Damien abandoned all interest in yachting and suddenly developed a new passion for horse racing. Never having shown the slightest degree of interest in anything with four legs in his life before, now suddenly he was all about breeding thorough-breds, form sheets and winning the Derby at the Curragh. And in true Damien style, nothing was done in half measures. He had state-of-the-art stables built in the vast grounds at Castletown and soon began consulting the best trainer in the country as to which were the best horses for him to buy at Goffs horse sale.

He didn't buy just one though, he bought five, all bred to be champions, which was all Damien ever wanted to be surrounded by. Now his conversation was about nothing but which meeting to race his pride and joy, a two-year-old filly called Castletown Lass; just so there was absolutely no confusion about who her owner was.

Kate, meanwhile, was in a fug of drugs and moodiness brought on by a whole new cocktail of anti-anxiety meds she'd been prescribed, to help with the increasing edginess and insomnia she'd struggled with for so long. But massive fatigue was one of many side effects and she found it tough going to keep pace with the whirlwind social life that was as necessary to Damien as breathing. However, to her surprise, instead of being a bit miffed at her non-attendance to a lot of race meetings, suddenly he went completely the opposite way.

'You're exhausted, Kate,' he told her one morning when he was off for a weekend meeting at Ascot. Flying there by helicopter, the whole works. 'Why not stay here and just rest up for the weekend? No point in you coming with me if you're just going to drain yourself out, is there?'

'Are you sure?' she said, puzzled that he was barely even trying to persuade her to go.

'Course!' he said, throwing the last of his weekend clothes into an overnight bag. 'Much more important that you stay here and just chill out. Call you when I'm there. Promise.'

And just like that, he was gone. Later that afternoon, stretched out on the sofa in the TV room at home, Kate had flicked on the racing live from Ascot. The camera panned around the parade ring . . . and there he was. It was a long shot, but there was no mistaking Damien, looking tanned and relaxed and handsome with a tall, rangy young girl at his side, blonde and very pretty – not unlike a younger, healthier-looking version of Kate herself – she was dressed in jodhpurs and a woolly jumper and was clearly either a groom or a trainer.

It looked like Damien and she were getting on like a house on fire, laughing and chatting intently as she pointed out details about each horse that went by. Live on TV for all the world to see.

He said he'd call that night, but didn't. So Kate called

him and left message after message, desperately trying to keep the anxiety out of her voice. Then eventually she gave it up as a bad job.

I'm completely paranoid, she thought. All I saw was Damien having a laugh with an attractive woman, so why am I jumping to all sorts of crazy conclusions?

It was all the bloody drugs she was on that were making her so tetchy and mistrustful. That was all. She went up to bed and checked her phone one last time before switching off the light. Just past midnight.

And still no reply from Damien.

*

Vicky Dresden, that was her name. Twenty-six years old and a horse trainer, based at Cheltenham. But Damien had hired her to train his, by now impressive, stable of horses and so he'd relocated her to the nearby town of Avoca in the last few weeks. Very handy for them both, Kate had thought bitterly. It wasn't that Damien talked about her a lot, it was the fact he barely mentioned her at all, despite the fact he spent every bit of free time he had down at the stable yard with her.

Meanwhile Kate was meant to be at home resting and taking her medications, but found she couldn't sit still. Night after night Damien didn't come home and eventually, she cracked. Out of her mind with worry, she even drove to Avoca and parked discreetly outside the little cottage that she knew Vicky was renting.

But there was nothing. No sign of Damien's car, no closed curtains with the sound of music and giggles and romance wafting back out at her. Instead the house was in pitch darkness.

Jesus Christ, would you look at me, Kate thought, her heart hammering off her chest. Look at what I'm turning into. What was I going to do here anyway, hammer the front door down and accuse a total stranger of having an affair?

It was the drugs, she knew. The old Kate would never in a million years have behaved like such a paranoid, out of control nut-job. But still. When Damien eventually did saunter through the front door a full three days later, she was more than ready for him. On top of all her daily anti-anxiety meds, she'd even taken half a Valium, just to help keep her nice and calm.

'Good trip?' she asked lightly as Damien brushed the side of her cheek, before loosening his collar and tie and crashing out in front of the TV.

'Oh you know, work. I love Paris, but you know how these trips are. Completely exhausting, I never get a minute to myself.'

He put his feet up on the coffee table, then picked up the remote control, flicking channels until he came across a Golf Classic tournament being screened live.

'I thought you would have called me,' she said evenly, coming around to face him. 'You used to call me all the time when you were away. Day and night. And if you couldn't get through, you'd leave long, romantic messages for me. But these days? Nothing.'

'Yeah, you know I tried, but the Wi-Fi signal was crap. Besides, there really wasn't time. And honey, do you mind moving? You're blocking the TV.'

'So that's it?' she snapped. 'That's all I get after three days away? "You're blocking the TV".'

That caught his attention and he turned to really look at her then.

'What's got into you? What's with the attitude?'

'I tell you what's with the attitude, Damien! You disappear for days, I barely get a lousy text message from you and then . . . then . . .'

She broke off though. Days of pent-up frustration and worry and anger choking her to tears.

'Hey, hey, what's this?' he said, getting up and putting his arms around her to calm her down. 'What's really going on here?'

'It's . . . you,' she gulped. 'It's us . . . it's everything . . .'

'What? Tell me?' His tone was gentle, he sounded concerned.

'It's that . . . I'm here on my own in this ridiculously big house all day every day and you're never around and I'm bored and lonely and I just . . . I can't get the thought out of my head that there's something going on between you and . . . Vicky.'

There. She'd said it. There was almost a relief in voicing her greatest worry out loud. She looked up at Damien, but his face remained blank. Unreadable.

'Just tell me I'm being nuts,' she pleaded. 'Tell me this is all nonsense and that there's nothing going on between you, because I've been going out of my mind here . . . this sudden passion for horse racing, the fact that you spend far more time with her than you do with me . . .'

'Sweetheart,' he said, rubbing her back to soothe her. 'I want you to listen to me very carefully because I'll only say it once. There is nothing going on between me, Vicky or any other woman I've been in contact with. And yes, right now, you're acting like a crazy lady.'

'But I've just been so worried! You've no idea what it's like here for me, all alone in this house, feeling like crap all the time, and you're not even answering my phone calls!'

'It's those bloody drugs,' he sighed. 'They're making you do things you never normally would. So drop it, babes. You're my perfect girl, don't you know that by now? So why would I want to be with anyone else?'

He looked her in the eye as he said it and for a blessed minute, Kate actually felt a wave of relief. He was so utterly convincing, it was impossible not to believe him.

Damien went back to watching the golf and that, as far as he was concerned, was that. But later that night, as Kate lay alone in bed, she remembered what an award-winning liar Damien could be. How he was at his smoothest and most reassuring when he was spinning complete fiction.

She'd seen it before. She had first-hand experience of it. And suddenly she shivered.

TESS

The present

The richest irony of all is that we're not supposed to chat about the case outside of court. And yet everywhere I go, everyone else is doing exactly that – without exception. This really has captured the public imagination like nothing else, mainly because it's got all the key ingredients going for it: bottomless wealth, power, sex, celebrity and greed. Basically, the kind of story that ends up being turned into a made-for-TV movie.

The court reporters have done their job well and, by the time we're all leaving the building, news of the day's events in court already seems to be everywhere, for all the world to see, and to cast judgment on.

On the way home on the bus, I keep overhearing other passengers buzzing about it.

'If you ask me there's no shame in Kate King,' mutters a girl opposite me to her pal, while I tune in, all ears. 'Money. That's the only reason she even married Damien in the first place. Sure everyone knows that. Love match, my arse.

'And the brazen cheek of her to sit there in court and claim that one hundred and fifty grand a year isn't enough for her? I hope they send her down for theft and throw away the key.'

Nor do I get any respite from it when I get home. No sooner is my key in the front door than Mum bustles out from the TV room to meet me.

'Unbelievable!' she says. 'It's been all over the news. Do you know, I never liked that Kate King one bit and now I'm delighted that the whole world gets to see what a self-centred, greedy woman she is. No wonder Damien King wants rid of her.'

Mum, it has to be said, has never forgiven Kate King for doing a five-page magazine spread on her husband Damien's fortieth birthday party, which apparently cost two hundred grand. It was the timing more than anything that annoyed her; the story appeared in the papers the very same day my dad was made redundant from his job, which was installing house alarms for a local company.

'Mum, you know I'm not really supposed to talk about the case—' but I'm wasting my breath. She keeps it up all the way through dinner and even Gracie chimes in.

'Never liked her . . .'

'I never understood what he could possibly have seen in her. I mean not only is Damien King loaded, but he's gorgeous-looking too. He could have had anyone he wanted. Hollywood movie stars, *anyone*. And she's such a cold fish,' Mum went on. 'Even when she was modelling, there were other far prettier girls than her knocking around. She's too thin, for starters, and that bony, snooty face of hers . . . how would anyone ever find that attractive? It says online that she just sat there totally unemotional in court. Is that true, Tess?'

'Mum, I told you, I'm not supposed to—'

'Ahh shut up then, you're worse than useless. I'd say

Damien won't know himself once he's free of her. I'd say she must have drained him dry over the years.'

'Three hundred pairs of shoes?' says Gracie, in disbelief. 'And her own personal nail bar in her bedroom? Eighteen months in the Mountjoy women's prison, that's what that woman needs. That'll sort her out quickly enough—'

'It's like the Heather Mills and Paul McCartney case all over again, if you ask me—'

Mum, Gracie and I are having a TV dinner of micro-waved cannelloni and veg, the kind Mum only ever bothers with when she's been glued to the telly all evening. And it's just the three of us around the table: Dad's out helping a mate of his to paint a house this evening. He's been doing a lot of handy, part-time bits and pieces like that lately and thankfully it's keeping him going, cash-wise.

But while the other two horse into their grub, I just play with mine, then shove it away, uneaten. And all the time there's just one thought going round and round my head, like it's on a loop: Damien King is a billionaire. He could probably afford ten Rembrandts if he wanted them. So what kind of a man would put his ex-wife through this, no matter how acrimonious things were between them? And if Kate King knew this court case would come about and that she'd be vilified from right, left and centre – why didn't she just hand the painting back to him in the first place and have done with it?

Dinner is interrupted by a phone call on my mobile. It's the wedding florist, looking for final budget approval; her third time ringing today.

And to my shame I'd completely forgotten all about her.

*

I arrive at court so early the next morning that there's even time to wander over to a coffee shop across the road for a take-out. It's one of those cluttery, packed places that offer bacon butties along with free Wi-Fi at this time of day, so it's obviously a popular spot around here. And sure enough, there's a few hacks in here from the press box that I recognise.

Two youngish guys to be exact, clustered together at a table by the window, looking for all the world like a pair of hipsters (hairy beards, low-slung jeans, the whole Williamsburg vibe). I can practically feel their eyes boring into me and all I can think is . . . shit. They've copped on to exactly who I am. I'm just inching my way forward in the queue and sure enough, next thing there's a discreet tap on my shoulder.

'Hi there,' says the hairier one of them, looking at me earnestly. 'Look, I hope you don't mind my approaching you like this, but the thing is, I write for *The Chronicle*—'

'You really shouldn't be speaking to me,' I hiss at him, hoping no one else in the queue overhears.

'Hey, I just wanted a minute of your time,' he says insistently, making no attempt to move. 'Obviously you can't talk to me just now, but if you'd like to make a few quid for yourself when the case is all over, we'd be more than happy to buy your story.'

'Can you just leave me alone?' I tell him firmly, inching down the queue to get away from him.

'We'd pay really well for something as big as this, you know,' Beardy persists, clearly not taking no for an answer. 'And I hear you're getting married soon. Few extra quid might just come in handy.'

'Please! I really don't want to speak to you, now or anytime.'

189

'Actually we were just leaving,' comes a familiar voice from just behind me. I turn around and in an instant flush of relief see that it's Will. 'Weren't we, Tess?'

'Erm . . . yes! Yes, we were,' I say.

'Tell you what then,' says this journo guy scratching his beard, completely undeterred. 'Here's my business card. If you ever fancied chatting to me when all this is over – off the record, of course – we'd never quote your name, but we'd really love to hear from you.'

'You do realise we could report you for this?' says Will, clamping a protective arm onto my shoulder.

'Yeah sure, man. But this would all be totally hush hush, you know—'

'Come on then, Tess,' Will interrupts, 'I reckon we can find somewhere else to have coffee. In peace this time.'

'Hey, take it easy!' says Beardy. 'I was only trying to—'

'I think I know exactly what you were trying to do,' says Will, steering me towards the door and out of there.

We step outside into the warm spring sunshine, my head still reeling from the barefaced neck of that guy.

'You OK?' Will asks, looking at me concerned.

'Yeah, absolutely,' I say. 'It's just hard to remember how visible we all are up there in that jury box. And scary to think the press know exactly who we are and that we can be got to so easily. Jesus, Will, they even knew about my wedding!'

'Shower of vultures. Whatever you do, don't speak to them and if you're approached again, report it to Moany Mona.'

'That what we're calling her now? Moany Mona?'

'You've got to admit, it's got a ring to it,' he says, with a tiny half-smile.

'Thanks, Will. That's sound advice.'

'Come on then,' he says, the dark eyes scanning up and down the quays to see where else is open. 'We've still got half an hour before kick-off and I reckon the very least I owe you is a coffee.'

He leads the way to a hotel further down the road, where they're serving tea, coffee and croissants in the lounge area. It's lovely in here too, all plush sofas in that nude mink colour you see everywhere, with a gorgeous smell of freshly brewed coffee to greet us as we come through the door.

'Fancy in here, isn't it?' I say approvingly as we both order Americanos and grab a table. Will plonking down on the seat opposite, so he's facing me.

'A vast improvement on the Ebola Arms anyway.'

'Ahh, don't be so quick to knock the Ebola Arms,' I tell him playfully. 'I'm still thinking of changing my wedding reception to have it there, I'll have you know.'

'So who's the lucky guy then?' Will asks.

'He's called Bernard. He's an Art History Lecturer at City College.'

'Fancy job,' he nods, sitting back. 'So go on then, flesh out the picture. What's this Bernard like?'

'He's a dote,' I say firmly. 'And I'm a lucky girl. Even if—'

'Even if . . . what?' he asks, instantly picking up on it.

'Well, let's just say even if not everyone thinks so,' I trail off lamely.

'Ahh,' says Will. 'Now I'm beginning to understand that whole "stressed bride" thing you've got going on. Let me guess: your in-laws-to-be are giving you a hard time?'

'That I could handle,' I say, rolling my eyes. 'But this is even worse.'

'Go on,' he says, his eyes busily scanning my face.

'Well most of the trouble is coming from within my own family.'

'So now it gets interesting,' he says, leaning forward and tossing the breakfast menu aside. 'Well, if you want to talk about it, I'm a pretty good listener. Or so I've been told.'

I sit back against the cushy, plush seat and exhale, taking a moment to formulate my thoughts.

'Oh God, where to start?'

'Wherever you like.'

'Well the thing is,' I begin tentatively, 'Bernard and I have always been a bit of an odd couple, which really doesn't bother either of us, even if, on the surface, we do come across as a mismatch.'

'Opposites attract and all that, I suppose.'

'Absolutely. But that's not really the issue as far as my family are concerned.'

'So what is?' he says, listening attentively.

But I clam up here, almost hoping a waiter will come along to interrupt us with our coffees. No such luck though. Will is still waiting on an answer, completely focused on me. There's a pause as I take a moment to really look back at him. He seems like a nice guy, the sort that I possibly could even open up to, albeit that I barely even know him. But I can't go there. It's still too soon, too raw, too much. Not now, not yet, maybe not ever. For God's sake, I hardly even talk to Bernard about this and when I do, he'll give me a hug and come out with something like 'we all have a history, dearest'.

'Let's just say my family think I'm getting married totally on the rebound. That the only reason I'm doing this is because Bernard is the complete antithesis of . . . well. Of another – situation – a very complicated situation that I'd just come out of.'

Sorry Will, I think, but that's all you're going to get. And to be honest, I'm amazed you even managed to get that much out of me.

'Ahh,' he says after a long pause, taking it all in. 'Now I think I understand. So the real question is, what was it that you'd just come out of?'

Our coffees arrive, so thankfully we're off that acutely painful subject and instead start tussling over who gets to pay the bill. Will beats me to it though, shoving a fiver into the waitress's hand as I grab the opportunity to veer the conversation another way.

'Anyway, that's more than enough about me,' I say, taking a sip of coffee. 'How about you?'

'You're trying to change the subject,' he says lightly.

'Will,' I say, looking right at him, 'trust me, you'd be doing me the greatest kindness right now if we could just chat about something – about anything – else.'

He reads my face quickly, then nods.

'Of course,' he says. 'So what would you like to talk about?'

'Well . . . what is it that you do for work?'

And now that I come to think of it, it's actually very difficult to second-guess what it is that he does for a living. He doesn't strike me as someone who works in an office, that's for certain. The casual gear, the trainers, the manbag – not working at all and on the dole is my best guess. I'm cursing myself for asking the question in the first place and hoping I didn't mortify him if he is 'between jobs'. Then I catch him smiling back at me.

'Go on, give up, Tess, you'll never guess,' he says, sitting back in the chair and stretching his long legs out in front of him. 'No one ever does.'

'What is it then?'

'I'm a writer, as it happens.'

'Wow. You mean like a journalist?'

'No, I mean like an author.'

'What sort of books?'

'Crime fiction mostly,' he shrugs.

I flush a bit, half-wondering if I could in fact be sitting beside the equivalent of James Patterson or Ian Rankin and I didn't realise. What was his last name again? I rack my brains wondering, then it strikes me. Kearns, I think that was it. And yet the name Will Kearns still doesn't ring a bell. So I figure he's probably a self-published author, one I've yet to hear of and can only hope he'll forgive me for not having read any of his books.

'So are you on a deadline at the moment?' I ask him, more for something to say than anything else, really.

'I'm always on a deadline. The world of crime fiction moves so fast you wouldn't believe it.'

'Must come in handy sitting in on a case like this one. At least you can say you're here in the name of research.'

'I'd love to be able to claim that, except that we're not allowed to talk about the case, are we?'

'Oh don't talk to me,' I groan, rolling my eyes. 'That stupid rule is actually driving me nuts.'

'Me too,' he grins back. 'It's like the jurors on this case are probably the only twelve people in the country *not* talking about it.'

'And you wouldn't want to cross Mona. God knows what she'd do to you if you were found flaunting rules.'

'Judge Simmonds must not on any account be kept

waiting!' he trills in a high falsetto that's actually such an accurate impression of her, I laugh.

Then a pause, and this time the silence sits uneasily. Almost as though we're both itching to swap theories about the case, but officially can't. At least not until we get into the jury room when we've heard both sides. Deeply frustrating, believe me.

'So what *are* we allowed to talk about?' I eventually ask.

'Well, you never told me what *you* did for a living,' he says. 'That seems like a pretty safe subject to me. The jury police can't possibly object.'

'I'm a personal trainer over at Smash Fitness,' I smile. 'And I recently got promoted to Assistant Manager; which basically means I do double the work for the exact same money. I love it though. It's a terrific club to work in, always busy and . . . well, I suppose I'm one of those annoying people who can't wait to get to work in the morning, really.'

'Lucky you.'

'Never wanted to do anything else, really. Back in school, the only thing I was ever any good at was sports.'

Then a long silence.

'Erm . . . have you something against personal trainers?' I eventually ask, only half in jest. 'Don't worry if you do, because I get that a lot.'

'No, quite the opposite,' he says, the eyes twinkling back at me.

'How do you mean?'

'It's just that I'm a marathon runner myself,' he says, absent-mindedly playing with a sachet of sugar.

'Seriously?'

'Yup.'

'Wooo . . . impressive,' I whistle. 'And I mean that very

sincerely, by the way. I'm barely able to get through a 10k run, so I take my hat off to anyone who can manage a full twenty-six miles.'

He takes a sip of coffee and shakes his head. 'Well this certainly is a first,' he says. 'Usually whenever I talk running with anyone, they just glaze over and write me off as some kind of a fitness nut slash glutton for punishment.'

'Who counts calories to the point of obsession . . .'

'And who looks on carbs as the work of Satan . . .'

'Who doesn't smoke or drink alcohol . . .'

'And goes to bed at nine in the evening . . .'

'So you can be up at 5 a.m. to haul yourself into a tracksuit and start pounding the pavement. I can fully sympathise,' I nod along. 'I get that myself all the time.'

'Really?' he says, the eyes glinting.

'Yup. Generally the very minute I tell people what it is that I do, they act like a gym is some kind of religious cult that I'm planning to suck them into. Then they'll either start talking fad diets and how they're planning to lose two stone in a month, or else they'll look at me accusingly like I'm silently judging them. Almost mentally weighing them up to see if they're carrying a few extra pounds – as if!'

'And I wouldn't mind, but contrary to rumour, most marathon runners actually eat like horses. Whereas people assume we live off handfuls of nuts and seeds and nothing more. You can't run a race like that without serious carb-loading beforehand.'

'Me and all! Just because it's my job to keep clients on the straight and narrow doesn't mean I don't enjoy a decent bag of chipper chips every now and then.'

'In fact on that note . . .' says Will casually eyeing up a breakfast buffet table beside us, laden down with the most divine-looking cronuts and Danish pastries. 'What do you think?'

'Let's go for it.'

'We may as well.'

'Might even stuff a croissant into my handbag for later on.'

'And when we get to the Ebola Arms, I might just end up nicking it off you.'

*

Minutes before the 10 a.m. kick-off, we finish our coffees and head back to the courts together, strolling side-by-side down the quays. Just then my phone rings. Bernard.

'Oops, sorry, I have to take this,' I say apologetically.

'Work away,' says Will, keeping pace beside me.

'Hi there,' I say, answering the call.

'Hello, my sausage,' Bernard yawns down the phone, but then he's never been much of a morning person. 'Just making sure that you hadn't forgotten about tonight?'

'Emm . . .' I say playing for time, all the while thinking, forgotten what? Tonight? What's happening tonight?

'It's that lecture I was telling you all about, remember?'

It's noisy on the street though with the last of the rush hour traffic still lining the quays, so I have to put him on speakerphone so I can really hear what he's saying properly.

'Tess? Are you still there?'

'Yeah, just a bit hard to hear you, but that's much better now. What were you saying? Something about a lecture?'

'That's right, on the third Revolutionary War and the Battle of Austerlitz?' His voice rings out loud and clear across the pavement.

I catch Will's eye and sense just the tiniest hint of a grin.

'Oh right. Yes, the Napoleonic Wars,' I say, my memory well and truly jogged. Then Will politely takes a step ahead of me so as not to eavesdrop.

'With particular reference to the Third Coalition?' Bernard chats on excitedly. 'You hadn't forgotten, had you, sausage? I've been looking forward to it for so long.'

'No, no of course not.'

'Now it's well over three hours long, so we might need to eat beforehand.'

'Wow, three hours,' I say with about as much enthusiasm as I can muster and even though Will is half a pace ahead of me now, I could swear I see him trying not to crack a grin.

'And you know the best bit of all?' says Bernard. 'I've just found out that it's possible to do a walking tour around the site of the battle itself! Can you think of a better way to spend our honeymoon?'

At that point, I have to cut him short and get off the phone, because we've just arrived at the court steps and have to go through the usual waltz of trying to dodge the hardy press hacks who are present and correct, as always. Including that hairy-looking idiot who had the neck to approach me in the coffee shop earlier.

'Bernard, I'm afraid I really have to go—'

'Alright, sausage, see you later, and I hope you're as excited as I am.'

I click to end the call as Will turns back to me, grinning cheekily.

'So that's Bernard then?'

'That's him alright.'

'And you've got a three hour long lecture on the Battle of Austerlitz to look forward to? Wow, lucky you,' he smiles.

I throw him a filthy look.

'Forgive me, I couldn't help overhearing,' he shrugs. 'And all I can say is, sooner you than me.'

I pull a face at him, shoving my phone back into my bag and tripping up the steps.

'The things we do for love, eh?' he says, following hot on my heels.

'Oh don't you fecking start,' I groan, as we both keep our heads down and weave our way into court.

KATE

Castletown House, April 12th, 2014
Her birthday party

All that money for you, Kate thought, staring dully at the painting that now hung in pride of place on her drawing room wall, and I'm not even certain that I like you.

It was a Rembrandt of course – only the best would do for Damien – but the canvas was just so depressingly dark, which of course would have been typical of the mid-seventeenth-century period when it was painted. There was almost a coldness about *A Lady of Letters*, as the girl in the painting sat at her desk utterly focused on writing, quill and paper in hand, with just one solitary, thin reed of sun slanting through the diamond paned window behind her. It threw the only scrap of light in the whole painting onto the page in front of her, illuminating the letter she was writing, but not her face.

Cornelia Stoffels, apparently that was her name, according to Kate's research. She looked young too, maybe twenty? It was hard to tell, given how shadowy the painting was, not to mention the heavy period costume she wore, pure seventeenth century with its white puffy sleeves and long white skirt billowing out from underneath the desk. Meanwhile *A Lady of Letters* just sat poised and scribbling away, almost with an urgency to her.

I'll say this much for you, Kate thought, locking eyes with the painting's subject this time. You look fresh, simple and unaffected, free of all the jewellery, white powder and rouge that ladies of your background and class at the time would have plastered themselves in.

Fresh, simple and unaffected. Just like a certain someone else who would probably turn up at the party tonight, she thought, a sudden feeling of nausea clenching at her stomach.

Oh God, was she really going to go through with this? If Damien had the cheek to bring that little madam here – to Castletown House – under his wife's very own roof, did she have the strength to do as she'd been planning? Did Damien really feel that confident that he could get away with something like this? If he really was prepared to humiliate Kate that far, was she equally prepared to shame him right back?

Correction. Shame both of them.

Damien had strayed before, of that she was certain, though he'd always been far too discreet and way too good a liar for her to ever really catch him out. But this time it was very different; Kate could sense it. This was more than just some little obsession of his that would blaze bright for a short time, then just fizzle itself out, as had happened in the past. This was serious, this was the real thing. This was happening, and possibly under her own roof too.

Tonight. In just under two hours' time, to be exact.

Her stomach clenched again and Kate felt like a bag of jittery nerves, totally on edge just thinking about what lay ahead. To get some fresh air, she paced over to one of the giant, sixteen-pane sash windows that overlooked Castletown's elegantly manicured gardens and as she did, her eye fell on the grandfather clock ticking discreetly in the corner of her vast drawing room.

Almost six o'clock, she thought, glancing up at the time. And her guests were due to arrive at seven-thirty. She still had to shower, get dressed and made up, but . . . could she chance having a little drink now, just to calm her nerves?

Her eye fell longingly on the elegant bar table that staff had set up all along the side of the room, as she weighed up the pros and cons; then quickly decided that of course she could. A small one. To steady her. Given what lay ahead tonight, who the hell would blame her?

From the corner of her eye she spotted a bottle of Hendrick's gin, which seemed to be almost winking at her. Moving quickly towards where the spirits were stacked at the far end of the bar table, she helped herself to a good-sized G&T, took a gulp, then waited that precious few minutes' delay till it took blissful effect.

Better. This definitely made her feel better. This was a good idea. And if any of the staff burst in on top of her, she could always pretend it was only water. She raised her glass in a silent toast to *A Lady of Letters* and helped herself to another large gulp.

Apparently you come with a curse, she thought, staring at the gloomy canvas that even in a room this vast, still seemed to dominate it. Ever since Damien had bought the painting – ostensibly as her birthday present, if you could believe that – Kate herself had discreetly been investigating it. And from the little she'd managed to glean so far, she sensed that *A Lady of Letters* had an awful lot more secrets to give up than Damien could ever possibly have envisaged when he flashed his chequebook and handed over such a ridiculous amount of money for something he knew next to nothing about.

But then, that was Damien for you. Fifteen long years of marriage had taught Kate that that was the whole essence of the man. For him it was all about acquiring the impossible and no sooner had he done it than he'd grow bored and move on. Time was when Kate herself had once been a prize acquisition for him, and just look how quickly the sheen had worn off her. This painting was another so-called impossible treasure and you could be guaranteed he'd have forgotten all about it in under a month.

No, Kate thought. The whole reason he hounded down this painting, outbidding five underbidders to get his paws on it, was to impress one person and one person only. And that certainly wasn't his wife.

Just the fresh reminder of her rival and the fact that she could seriously have the gall to show her face here tonight set Kate's nerves on edge again, as she knocked back the last mouthful of G&T; which weirdly seemed to have absolutely no effect on her. None whatsoever.

Will I just chance having another tiny one, she wondered, fiddling with the now empty stem glass in her hand. She listened out and heard the downstairs doorbell ringing before her housekeeper bustled down the back hallway to answer it. Probably the caterers arriving, and bang on time too.

She glanced around the drawing room, which had always been her favourite part of Castletown, and in a house boasting over a dozen reception rooms, that was really saying something. She looked up at the Louise Kennedy crystal chandeliers that glittered from the ceiling, the rich tapestries that hung on the walls, the luxurious deep pile cream cashmere carpet and the vintage china collection safely secured in elegant display cases on either side of the fireplace that she'd once taken such pride in sourcing.

How much longer, she thought, before my time here is up? How long do I have before I'm cast aside and someone else moves in to take my place? Into her beautiful house that she'd put together from scratch, all those years ago? Her home, which had her stamp in every single room.

And where she'd once been so happy.

Kate's mouth went dry at that thought and her eyes started to well up. Now she definitely needed a drink. She listened out in case any of the staff were lingering in the hall outside, but there wasn't a single sound. She had the whole room to herself for the moment so moving quickly, she helped herself to another small G&T. Well, smallish.

Bugger it anyway, she thought, whatever it took to get her through the night.

She could so clearly envisage the whole evening ahead; this very room packed to the gills with Damien's corporate colleagues, mostly mega-high rollers who she knew he was going all out to impress. Then of course there'd be their mutual 'friends', although few enough of them deserved that title now, and somehow Kate predicted fewer still in her future.

She could just imagine Damien ting ting-ing on a crystal glass for silence, as guests lowered their champagne flutes and stopped nibbling at the foie gras to give him their full attention. But then that was Damien for you. Whenever he spoke, people listened. The man had a voice that could nearly power Sellafield.

He'd make a short witty little speech, of course. You could always rely on Damien to make a decent speech, and it would all be done so elegantly, so smoothly, that from the outside none of their well-heeled guests would ever suppose the real reason behind all this.

In fact this bloody party tonight had absolutely nothing to do with the fact that it had been Kate's birthday just a few days ago, and this was allegedly her loving husband throwing a soirée for their 'closest friends' to show off the priceless gift he'd just lavished on her. And those inverted commas around 'closest friends' were there for a bloody good reason. Damien had long since stopped caring about birthdays and anniversaries. So this – her so-called birthday gift, this ridiculously extravagant acquisition – certainly wasn't intended for Kate's benefit.

And if that little madam did have the brazen neck to turn up here tonight? Then God alone help her.

Just then the clock in the drawing room struck six. Time for Kate to start getting ready or else her guests would be in on top of her. She took one last glance up at *A Lady of Letters* and sighed.

Well, congratulations. You've barely been under my roof for twenty-four hours, and already your curse seems to be functioning beautifully.

TESS

The present

Court number seven is in session and almost like he's doing it deliberately to throw us all, this morning Oliver Daniels completely changes tack. Instead of breaking down Kate King's character and taking pains to show her as little more than a money obsessed spendthrift who's out to siphon off everything she can from the dregs of her marriage, today he's going out of his way to paint a picture of the most likely reason why she acts this way.

Deeply confusing, believe me.

Kate herself slides into court and as usual every eye in the room automatically veers towards her, all set for the daily fashion parade. She's dressed in a cold icy-grey trouser suit this morning, hair immaculately knotted into a neat chignon at the nape of her neck and with make-up so flawlessly applied, you'd swear she'd stopped off to have it done professionally on her way into court. She makes absolutely no eye contact with anyone, not even with her own barrister, just slips into her seat, looking pencil thin and even more strained than usual.

Damien King, on the other hand, swishes into court

surrounded by flanks of barristers and junior counsels, full of good-humoured chat and bonhomie, even waving to the back row of the public gallery, automatically assuming they're all there to support him.

'He'd remind you of a star football player stepping out to play in a testimonial match, wouldn't he?' says Barney to the right side of me, and it's hard not to agree. Next thing, Judge Simmonds strides in to an instant hush around the court, calls us to order and initiates the day's proceedings, inviting the Prosecution to take the floor.

'Ladies and gentlemen of the jury,' says Oliver, pudgy fingers and thumbs tucked into his swishy black gown. 'You've heard a great deal about Mrs King's primary motivation for withholding *A Lady of Letters* from my client.'

'And I was really enjoying all that too,' Edith stage whispers over to me while the Defence vigorously objects. 'I was telling the girls at Bingo last night all about it and they couldn't believe my luck in being here. Mad jealous, they were. Some of them said they'd even try to get a seat in the public gallery if they could, just to cheer me on. Wasn't that nice of them now?'

'Edith, you'll get us thrown out of here for yacking,' I hiss back, but Judge Simmonds is straight onto me.

'I must request silence in court at all times,' she says, sounding exactly like an exasperated schoolteacher dealing with a bunch of recalcitrant kids. 'And that includes from the jury box,' she adds, glaring hotly at me.

We all settle down as Oliver continues.

'Now we must ask whether there may be other reasons why Mrs King has behaved as she has,' he says, directly addressing the jury box. 'And once we've done that, then

I think you'll find everything else will fall neatly into place for you.'

Is Kate King about to take the stand herself, I wonder, automatically finding myself sitting forward, all ears; because that would certainly make for an interesting day.

'We know beyond all doubt that the Defence is in possession of the painting in question,' Oliver goes on, 'refusing to divulge its whereabouts, in spite of a lengthy police investigation. Not to mention no fewer than three separate court orders, all of which she's chosen to ignore.'

'Sorry, but I've got to object to that,' says Hilda, springing to her feet. 'Your Honour, we've been over this already, or maybe my learned friend has forgotten? Why would my client give back what's her own rightful property?'

'Be careful, Mr Daniels,' the judge cautions Oliver and after a discreet cough, he resumes.

'However, the Prosecution now feel it incumbent to paint a picture to the jury of Mrs King's mental state in the run-up to her marriage collapse,' he says, to a plethora of more objections from Hilda.

'And why is this even necessary, Your Honour?' she asks the bench indignantly.

'Our aim,' Oliver replies smoothly, 'is to illustrate not just a motivation, but to provide a possible understanding for Mrs King's refusal to give back the disputed painting.'

Judge Simmonds pauses for a moment, then tells him to proceed.

'But tread cautiously,' she adds.

Again, my eyes automatically drift towards Kate King and yet again, she gives absolutely nothing away. Just stares down at her elegantly manicured hands folded neatly in her lap, studying her palms and fingernails.

'So for our first witness of the day, the Prosecution calls Dr Michael Shaw.'

There's a frisson around the court, but then Michael Shaw is a very well-known and noted psychiatrist. He's always on the news giving insights and psychological profiles on cases just like this one, and even has a popular column in one of the papers called 'Mind Yourself'.

He takes the stand, all bearded and bespectacled, is sworn in and without a minute's hesitation, Oliver's on the offensive.

'Dr Shaw, Mrs Katherine King is obviously not a patient of yours, but you've been summoned here today to throw a little light on a matter that's been troubling me.'

The good doctor nods as Oliver presses on.

'During a thorough search of the property at Castletown House, a whole cocktail of medications were discovered on Mrs King's bedside table, including Alprazolam, Bromezapam and Nitrazepam. When questioned about these during the course of the police investigation, Mrs King freely admitted that they were hers and had indeed been prescribed to her.'

I look across to Hilda who's frantically whispering to Kate, who in turn, looks blank and unreadable. Oliver then goes on to list a whole other clatter of prescription drugs with names ending in what sounds like '-azepam'.

'My question to you is this, doctor,' he goes on. 'Can you outline to the court the primary reasons why any patient would have need of all those drugs?'

Dr Shaw doesn't even hesitate.

'Typically the medication you list would be used to treat panic attacks, insomnia and generalised anxiety disorder.'

'Can you outline the symptoms of those ailments, please? In your own words.'

'Conditions of that sort may take many shapes and forms with various different patients,' says Dr Shaw authoritatively. 'There can often be a variety of symptoms. Physical ones, such as shortness of breath, dizziness, loss of appetite, hyperventilation and heart palpitations.'

'And what,' says Oliver, sounding like he's actually gone and rehearsed this in front of a mirror, 'of the psychological symptoms?'

'These frequently include a great fear of losing control, and I'm very much afraid that's the case with the vast majority of patients.'

'Any other symptoms you'd care to add?'

'Often a feeling of unreality or of being detached from your surroundings is also common.'

'So would it be fair to say,' says Oliver benignly, 'that someone suffering from this type of anxiety very often aren't aware of what they're saying or doing?'

'Yes,' nods Dr Shaw. 'Yes, I most definitely would. The side effects can include a patient often feeling a complete unaccountability for their actions,' are Dr Shaw's last words.

'So there you have it,' Oliver concludes. 'We can safely assume that patients suffering from such disorders simply don't know what they're doing. Would you agree? A yes or no answer will suffice.'

'Yes. Yes, I would.'

'No further questions, Your Honour.'

*

At lunch in the Ebola Arms this time, I'm sandwiched in between Ruth, who can be selectively deaf if her hearing aid isn't on right, and Minnie. And the pair of

210

them seem to have decided that it's all over bar the shouting.

'Not that Kate King is my favourite person or anything,' Ruth half-shouts, I think mainly just so she can hear herself. 'But to be perfectly honest, now it looks like the woman just isn't in her right mind.'

'Lots of people have panic attacks,' Beth says stoutly from the other end of the table. 'That doesn't mean anything. My mum takes sedatives for them, she's absolutely fine.'

'That may be,' says Ian beside her with a rattle of his man-bracelets, shoving lunch away and instead opening a packet of crisps that he's had the foresight to bring in with him. 'But I'll bet your mum doesn't go around hoarding priceless paintings that aren't hers.'

'Well I don't know about the rest of you,' says Jane curtly, 'but I was shocked by the sheer amount of medication Kate King is on. Enough to open a small pharmacy with.'

'Oh I absolutely agree with you there,' says Minnie in between mouthfuls of soup so gloopy I actually have to eat mine with a fork. 'If you ask me, Kate King hadn't a clue what she was doing, more than likely. Her brain is probably just a bit befuddled. Sure I'm the same myself if I forget to take my blood pressure tablets.'

'Still and all though,' says Barney from across the table. 'That painting doesn't belong to her. Fair is fair. She has absolutely no right to it, in my opinion. The only reason she even wants it in the first place is to get back at your man, moneybags King.'

'What are you saying over there?' demands Ruth. 'Speak up, would you?'

Barney checks over his shoulder to see if Mona's here, as we all automatically do these days. She'd eat the face off us if she thought we were chatting about the case, and continues to live under the delusion that we're the only twelve people in the country not talking about it. Luckily though, she's out of the room, so Barney goes for it.

'Kate King, let me tell you,' he goes on prodding the air with his soup spoon, 'was disgusted with her settlement, so she decided to help herself to the single most valuable asset her ex owned. It's as simple as that and you mark my words, our jury deliberations will take no time at all.'

'Oh I hope not!' says Edith disappointedly. 'I'm really enjoying all of this.'

'Ehh . . . sorry to interrupt,' says Will politely from the far end of the table. 'But shouldn't we at least wait till we've heard Kate's side of the story? Innocent until proven guilty, and all that. We still haven't heard from her Defence yet; they've barely even warmed up. Should certainly be interesting as soon as they get going.'

'Ahh, don't annoy me, son,' says a lady beside him who I think is called Daphne and who I've only ever had one conversation with, about how she mislaid her bus pass and had to pay the full fare on her way to court. 'She's guilty as sin and out to bleed the poor fella for every last drop.'

'I bet Will's only sticking up for Kate King because he fancies her!' says Minnie with a laugh that's more like a cackle really. I throw him a sympathetic glance and he just shrugs back at me.

Then Ruth pipes up, 'Sorry, everyone, but if you ask me, this bread roll is like a bullet. Anyone mind if I whip out my teeth?'

*

Mona has a job herding us all up to get back onto the bus because no sooner does she start barking at us, 'lunch is over, time to move!' than all the elderlies take that as their cue to make a dash – or rather a hobble – to the loo.

'The bus will leave here in precisely four minutes' time,' sniffs Mona, unimpressed. 'So kindly don't take too long on your bathroom break.'

'Gives me just enough time to finish this delightful dessert then,' Will smiles benignly back at her, the only one of us still sitting at the table and actually eating.

Meanwhile I'm gathering up my coat and bag, while Mona thunders off in the direction of the bathroom, no doubt to bark at everyone in there. 'Fair play to you,' I say to him, pulling my coat over my shoulders, 'you were the only one of us who could face that bowl of . . . whatever gloop it is.'

'Oh come on, semolina? Who could resist? Last time I was served a bowl of this,' he adds, slopping a spoonful of it back into the bowl, 'was back in boarding school. Ahh, memories.'

'Three minutes and counting!' we can hear Mona barking from the corridor outside where the loos are.

'In fact throw in a few house masters parading over us, with a double maths exam scheduled for the afternoon and this is like an action replay of my misspent youth,' he says, pushing the bowl away and getting up to leave.

'Day care, I'd have compared it to.' I smile as we walk out of the dining room together, down the stairs and out into the warm sunshine, where the jury bus is waiting for us. 'For me this whole experience is the nearest I've come to being in an old folk's home, ever since my gran passed away.'

Next thing, Mona marches out of the hotel, herding Barney, Minnie and Edith ahead of her, almost like they're hostages.

'Quick as you can, please,' she barks, 'Judge Simmonds doesn't like to be kept waiting!'

'Sweet Jesus,' mutters Barney, clambering up onto the coach just ahead of me. 'The Gestapo had nothing on that one.'

'After you,' says Will, taking my hand and helping me up the steps. 'And whatever you do, don't forget your Zimmer frame.'

'*Shh*, or they'll hear you!'

*

It's stuffy and airless back in court this afternoon. As usual, it's packed to the rafters and because it's such a warm day, the whole atmosphere feels close to stifling. There's a dense mugginess that's actually making it hard to breathe.

'Jesus, Tess,' Jess hisses to me, as we take our seats in the jury box, under the full gaze of the press box and public gallery. 'I'm going to find it very hard to stay awake. Do me a favour and give me a good dig in the ribs if I start to nod off.'

'Kids have you awake at the crack of dawn again?' I ask her sympathetically.

'How did you guess?' she yawns. '5 a.m. again this morning. I could have strangled them.'

'Oh, you poor thing.'

'Do you have kids?' she asks.

'No.'

'Want one of mine?'

Judge Simmonds bangs us all to order and even Oliver

Daniels himself seems red-faced and sweaty, like the stifling heat is getting to him too. I glance around and notice that the only person who looks as unflappably cool as he always does is Damien King himself.

And speak of the devil.

'Ladies and gentlemen of the jury, I now call my next witness. Mr Damien King.'

It's like a sudden shot of adrenaline has sent us all fizzing and in a second we all go from soporific drowsiness to full-on high alert. Radiating confidence and urbane sophistication, Damien steps from the bench where he'd been sitting with his legal team, nods briefly at the judge and without making the slightest eye contact with his ex-wife, takes the oath and strides up to take the stand.

KATE

Castletown House, April 12th, 2014
Her birthday party

'Looking fabulous as always, Kate, my darling!' cooed Samantha Sullivan, weaving her way through the packed throng in the drawing room to air kiss her on each cheek, Mediterranean-style. 'Is your dress Prada? Yes, I thought I recognised it. From the prêt-á-porter collection, am I right?'

'You're absolutely right,' Kate chimed automatically, randomly thinking of how much Samantha had always reminded her of a parrot.

'You know I was almost going to buy it myself only it was just a tiny bit too big on me. But then that's the problem with being a size zero, the petite sizes always sell out so quickly, don't they?'

Typical Samantha, Kate thought. Giving a compliment with one hand, while trumping it with an even juicier one for herself the next minute. Outwardly though, she nodded politely, then murmured some lame excuse about having to greet more guests who'd just arrived, purely to get away from her.

If it comes to a split between Damien and me, she thought, then he was more than bloody welcome to Samantha Sullivan and her ilk. But then she stopped herself short and quickly recalibrated that thought. *When* it came to a split between her and Damien, more like it. Because this really was it, this was The End.

She could tell when he'd strayed in the past; it would all be done very discreetly of course, with nothing to ever embarrass her on her own doorstep. Still, though, she'd always know.

One sign was that he'd suddenly start being a whole lot nicer and more attentive to her at home. Another was that he'd go out and buy her the most ridiculously lavish gift imaginable. But nothing topped this. €95 million for a Rembrandt portrait? This was serious, this was in a whole different league.

Another drink, she thought, suddenly realising that her glass was empty already. Weird, she must be on her fourth G&T by now – or was it her fifth? – yet not one of them seemed to be having as much as the slightest effect on her. She started to weave her way through the ridiculously crowded room towards the bar, eyes firmly glued to the door on the lookout for one particular guest to make her entrance.

Somehow she managed to elegantly dodge one friend after another, all clamouring to grab her, with a polite wave of her hand and quick, hostessy smile, mouthing 'back in just a moment!' Next thing though Grace Clifford and that god-awful husband of hers, George, collared her, standing right in her path and stopping her dead in her tracks.

'There you are, Kate, darling!' said Grace, trying to force her mouth into a smile, which was a considerable achievement, given the amount of collagen her lips were puffed out with. 'Happy Birthday! We left a little something for you on the hall table on our way in. Nightmare buying you a gift; what do you get for the woman who has everything?'

Lots, Kate thought. A faithful husband who knows how to keep his mickey in his trousers would be a very good start. But until then, a very large gin would have to do. Now. She eyed the bar hungrily and twitched to get moving, but somehow there was just no getting away from this pair.

'A flying lesson!' said George, almost sloshing over the glass of champagne in his hand, he looked that excited about it. 'So what do you think? Thrilled to bits, I'll bet!'

'Yes . . . and thank you, very generous of you,' Kate replied automatically, with about as much enthusiasm as she could muster. A flying lesson? For someone like her who needed a double strength Xanax before she could even get as far as the airport terminal? Did these people even *know* her?

'Out in Weston aerodrome,' George spluttered on, purple-faced from the heat of the crowded room and from the booze he was freely knocking back. Which reminded Kate, where were all the wait-staff who were meant to be circulating and topping up people's glasses? If she could just nab one of them, she'd be fine.

She glanced anxiously over her shoulder while George warbled on about the merits of flying a single engine Cessna against the advantages of his own private Gulfstream jet, a fiftieth birthday present to himself, from himself. Classic mid-life stuff, not unlike the vast majority of the men here tonight. But then you'd only have to take a look at George to know that he was clearly going through male menopause; the wide open-necked shirt, the trousers so tight you could practically see what he was thinking. Utterly vomitus stuff.

'You alright, Kate?' George asked, sensing his hostess was distracted. 'You seem jittery tonight. Not like you at all. Everything tickety-boo?'

'Yes absolutely, but erm . . . if you'll excuse me, just some more guests I haven't said hello to yet,' said Kate, gladly making her escape, not least from the kind of man who'd freely use a phrase like 'tickety-boo'.

Out of the corner of her eye, she spotted a waitress laden down with a heavy tray of champagne flutes over at the far end of the room, but to weave her way over to her, Kate would have to walk right past Serena McFadden who'd brought her sister Fay along with her. The Wisteria sisters, as the pair of them were rightly nicknamed; on account of how skilled they were in the dark art of social climbing. To be avoided, avoided, avoided even at the best of times, and just as an aside Kate thought, how were the pair of them even invited in the first place?

Jesus, what did she have to do to get a drink around here? She kept her head down, not the easiest thing to do when you're six feet tall, and somehow wove her way through the packed room all the way to the bar table, smiling while guests nabbed her, then lying through her teeth claiming she'd be 'back in a sec, just have to see to something urgent in the kitchen'.

Not a single bloody waiter free to serve her, so with shaky hands, she reached across the table and just helped herself to another G&T. A very large one this time; God knows she certainly could do with it. She gulped back a lovely, long sip before someone else came to accost her and again, took another minute to survey the room.

Did some of them already know, she wondered, fresh anxiety clutching at her chest. Did they already suspect that things weren't as they should be in the King household? Did Sylvia know? George and Grace? Even Rebecca and Sam? Long-time friends. People Kate and Damien had shared holidays with. Friends who'd been invited here to the Kings' palatial home of Castletown House for every major celebration going; Christmases, birthday parties, Easter weekends, Halloween fancy dress parties, you name it. Well, every possible celebration that didn't involve children, obviously, which was a whole other story.

Hard to imagine, Kate thought, nervously gulping back her drink before someone else approached her, that parties like this had once been her whole raison d'être. But then Damien lived to entertain and for 'entertain', you might just as well read, 'show off on a titanic scale'. He and she had once been seen as a golden couple, centre of the glitterati; a myth that the press and public still – unbelievably – continued to swallow. All of course drip-fed by Damien's expert PR team and even on occasion, by Damien himself. And there was even a time when Kate had been more than willing to go along with that fantasy.

With a pang of sadness, she thought of their tight-knit social circle. There were people in this room who she'd been fool enough to trust, who she'd actually come to think of as real friends. And yet from here on in, it was only a matter of time before the whole house of cards imploded dramatically.

Once the news broke – and God knows how much longer it could be contained for – then it would all be over bar

220

the shouting. Her little circle would be split right down the middle and like it or not, people would choose sides – his side, more than likely. They always did in cases like this, didn't they? Life would go on pretty much as normal for the wealthier, more successful partner, whereas for Kate, it would be the long, slow freeze-out. No one needed to even tell her how it worked, she thought dully. She already knew.

Friends she'd counted on and been loyal to over the years would just gradually stop returning her phone calls until it became almost embarrassing. She knew the drill well enough. Then she'd bump into them somewhere like David Marshall's trendy hairdressers in Dublin and they'd be full of excuses as to why they never phoned: 'Ooh, I'm so sorry, but the thing is we've been renovating the house, haven't been in touch with anyone.' Or 'You must be fit to kill me for not returning your calls, but the thing is, we've been away in Dubai for weeks now, we're literally just back!'

Kate had heard it all. Had come out with it all before, in many cases. But of course, when the social guillotine fell, she'd know only too well what was really going on behind the oh-so-polite subtext. She'd been forced into the same corner herself many times over the past few years when couples they knew had drifted apart. Damien, of course, would always keep in with whichever partner was the most valuable to him in business, but then that was Damien for you.

Just about the only thing going for her was that she moved in a discreet and rarefied world where everyone was perfectly charming and friendly to your face; it was behind your back when the knives really sank in. God, Kate thought, if even just one person here were to take her aside tonight and confide in her what everyone else was probably gossiping about, then far from bursting into tears, she'd probably hug them. Because in one fell stroke they'd just have proved what they really were: a true blue friend.

Then a more sickening thought. Had any of them already seen Damien out in public with . . . but Kate consciously broke her destructive thought pattern here. Mainly because she still couldn't bring herself to articulate the name. And yet she'd be expected to this evening, wouldn't she? She'd be expected to smile as she greeted her rival, offer her a drink and make sure the canapés kept coming in her guest's direction. Like so many wives here had done before her. It was how you behaved in their civilised little world, it was expected, this was the norm.

Well sod that for a lark, she thought, slowly starting to become coldly furious with the help of another sizable gulp of gin. So Damien just assumed that she'd put up and shut up tonight? That she'd act the part of the perfect hostess, for no other reason than that was the done thing?

Over her dead body, she thought, fresh energy fuelling her resolve. After all, Damien was the one who had the barefaced cheek to bring this under her own roof – in front of all their mutual friends, for Christ's sake. He's the one who wanted this to be a night to remember. Well, Kate certainly planned on making it one.

'Wonderful party and may I thank you so much for your lavish hospitality,' said a voice behind Kate, making her jump. She turned around to see a forty-something, grossly over-weight man with a bloated face and about three chins who instantly reminded her of Billy Bunter from her childhood comics.

'Oh, thank you, that's very kind,' she said automatically, not having the first clue who this could be.

'I'm Bernard Pritchard, by the way,' he said, going to shake her hand. 'I'm an Art History Lecturer at City College and your husband very kindly asked me along—'

'Would you excuse me, please?' said Kate, abruptly cutting across him. 'Something I need to see to downstairs.'

The stranger nodded politely as she glided away from him. All she needed to do were hear the words 'City College' and, could listen to no more. She'd almost made it as far as the door, when she walked right into Mo Kennedy, wife of Damien's CFO at Globtech, and the closest thing that Kate had to a best friend out of their entire circle.

'Mo, thank Christ you're here,' Kate said, hugging her warmly.

'Wouldn't have missed it for the world,' said Mo, her suntanned face smiling broadly, like she always did. But then Mo was one of the few in their circle who was so genuinely happy and content with her own marriage and family, you'd almost have sworn Prozac was involved.

'It's good to see a friendly face,' Kate replied. Oh God, did she just slur that last sentence a bit? And if she did, had Mo noticed?

'Are you OK?' Mo asked, looking at her a bit worriedly.

Shit. She did notice, but then Mo was the type not to miss a trick.

'Absolutely fine,' Kate lied.

'Don't give me that bullshit, you're as white as a ghost,' Mo told her straight. 'Something up? Is it because you've got about three hundred of the great and the good here tonight and you're expected to entertain them all? Can't

223

say I blame you. All these people! Bloody hell, even the Wisteria sisters, who let them in?'

You're one of the good ones, Kate thought, looking at her fondly. And when it comes to a split, I only pray to God you'll take my side.

'So come on then,' said Mo, 'what do you think of the painting? It was a birthday gift for you, wasn't it?'

'I think it's . . . overwhelming really,' Kate answered automatically. 'What about you, do you like it?'

'Honestly?' said Mo.

'The truth and nothing but.'

Why not? It would certainly be a rarity these days for someone in her life to be straight with her.

'Well of course I know it's beyond price and everything and that it's probably heresy of me to say so, but quite truthfully? It's just all a bit too dark and gloomy for me. There's almost something spooky about the woman in the portrait, isn't there? And what's all this you said about *A Lady of Letters* coming with a curse? Is that really true?'

Is it true? You don't know the half of it.

'Course I'm no art expert,' Mo chatted away as Kate's eyes went back to anxiously wandering over the room, scanning, scanning, scanning. Was she here yet? Had she somehow arrived without Kate seeing her?

'But I don't think I'd want to have something like this in my house,' Mo went on. 'It just gives me a really weird feeling, like something awful is about to happen. I hope you don't mind my saying that, do you?'

'Not at all,' Kate said, before adding, 'and as it happens, I think you're absolutely right.'

She broke off from saying any more though, because that's when she first spotted her. She must have been here for a good while too, only the room was so crowded that Kate never noticed. But she bloody well noticed now. This girl stood out, your eye couldn't help but be drawn to her.

And that's what she looked like really, a girl and no more. All of twenty-fucking-seven. Approximately half the average age of pretty much everyone else in the room. Instinctively Kate scanned her rival up and down, taking in everything.

She looked fresh-faced and glowing as usual, dressed down in a simple white shift dress and flat ballet pumps with a huge mane of unruly red curls falling loose about her shoulders. Next to no make-up on and not even a scrap of jewellery, in stark contrast to every other woman here, who'd gone all out to impress and who between the lot of them were probably wearing the combined Harry Winston spring/summer collection.

She was standing over by the huge bay window, deep in conversation with Damien and a group of colleagues from Globtech. Damien looked as tall and handsome as ever in black tie, his dark hair gleaming, his black eyes shining proudly every time he looked at her.

You used to look at me that way once, Kate thought, taking in the whole scene with a stab to her chest that physically pained her. A long, long time ago now. She could see him introducing her to everyone, hand proprietorially positioned right on the small of her back. He looked like he was mid-story, doubtless about how he'd managed to acquire the portrait in the first place. But to see him now, gesturing proudly towards it, you'd almost swear he'd painted the bloody thing himself.

'Please don't tell me that's her?' said Mo, following her gaze.

225

'Who do you mean?'

'For God's sake, Kate, this is me you're talking to. You don't have to put on an act with me, like you do with most of the piranha bowl you've assembled here tonight. Believe it or not, I'm actually on your side. I'm talking about the girl you can't stop staring at who's over there beside Damien. Please don't tell me he had the brass neck to bring her here tonight?'

Tell her what you're planning. You can do it. Besides, Mo is on your side. You might as well have someone who's in your corner out there telling the story, instead of the alternative.

'Yes. That's her. That's Harper Jones,' Kate managed to get out, though the strain of it meant that she immediately knocked back the rest of her drink, barely caring how it looked.

Harper fucking Jones, she thought, immediately turning back to the bar to refresh her drink, waving her now empty glass in the barman's direction and madly trying to catch his eye.

A visiting Art History lecturer over from the States, and a global expert on Rembrandt, to really add insult to injury. Working in the Art History department at City College. The official story of how they'd met was that Damien had been interested in donating some of the Kings' art collection to the National Gallery, and he got in touch with her to ask her advice.

And he just forked out over €95 million for the privilege, she thought bitterly. To put that into context, Henry VIII didn't pay that much to nail Anne Boleyn. And that's €95 million over at Christie's, by the way. There was naturally huge media interest in the sale, although Damien was a silent bidder and specifically asked to remain anonymous. 'So this can be a surprise for my lovely wife.'

Such a lie. Such an elegant load of bollocks. Camouflage for what was really going on, and nothing more.

'Harper Jones, what a ridiculous name,' said Mo and Kate almost wanted to hug her for that alone. 'And I'm sorry, but I just don't get it,' she added indignantly, 'how could one woman possibly do that to another? To walk into your home, when God knows what's going on behind your back? And how can Damien do that to you, after everything you've been through? On your birthday? Kate, love, how are you taking this so calmly? If it were me, I think I'd be spewing fire! Are you really going to take this lying down?'

'Just give me time,' said Kate, wondering why the hell the barman was taking so long. Impatiently, she reached across the bar and just helped herself to another G&T, barely even bothering with the tonic this time.

Then Mo's hand fell on hers.

'Maybe it would be an idea to go easy on the sauce? You need your wits about you to navigate your way through tonight. God knows, I certainly would.'

'Cheers,' said Kate, pointedly not putting the glass down and clinking glasses with her. A moment later, one of the wait-staff sidled up beside her and whispered, 'I just heard Mr King say he'll be making his speech very shortly.'

'Thank you,' said Kate politely, 'in that case, will you tell him I'm just slipping upstairs to powder my nose first.'

'Want me to come with you?' said Mo worriedly. 'We could stay up there for the evening, if you wanted. We could even get the hell out of here, so you don't have to put up with this.'

'That's kind of you, but no. There's just . . . something up there that I need. Back in a moment. And Mo?' she added, over her shoulder. 'Don't you worry. If Damien and madam over there think that I'm going to take this lying down tonight, they've got another thing coming.'

'Then to quote Bette Davis,' said Mo under her breath, 'fasten your seatbelts. It's going to be a bumpy night.'

TESS

The present

You can hear a pin drop up here in court number seven. Everyone is on the edge of their seats, the press box included. It seems the only person not completely riveted by what Damien King is about to come out with is his ex-wife. She's sitting not six feet away from him but unlike the rest of us, is looking absolutely anywhere except at him.

'Mr King,' Oliver begins, clearing his throat. 'May I take you back to events between July and October of 2014. Would you care to tell the court in your own words exactly what happened?'

'Certainly,' says Damien, looking about as unruffled by his surroundings as it's possible to be. He sounds relaxed and in total control, like this is barely knocking a feather out of him. And it's worth noting that his voice is deep and husky. Quite sexy, now I come to think about it.

'As you know, my company had acquired the painting in question, *A Lady of Letters*,' he goes on to explain, 'and at the time you refer to, it was temporarily being displayed at my home at Castletown House.'

A few pleased nods from around the court at that, as Oliver picks up the reins.

'And then?' he prompts.

'Well, during the period you refer to, my ex-wife and I had regrettably recently separated and I had moved out of the marital home, Castletown House. Katherine remained there, however, and is still there. For the present.'

'Go on,' Oliver prompts him.

'Well during the months you mention, I had reason to return to the house, in order to collect some of my own property. Naturally, given how valuable *A Lady of Letters* is, I was anxious to remove it and place it in the safekeeping of the King family trust.'

'But when you arrived to take away the painting in question, what did you discover?'

'I arrived at Castletown along with some removals men, only to discover that *A Lady of Letters* had completely disappeared. And given that the family trust had just paid a vast sum of money for the Rembrandt, you can imagine my distress.'

'So you naturally assumed that a burglary had taken place?'

'Of course. And yet none of the security alarms had been activated, which instantly roused my suspicions. I called the police, then dug about a little further and quickly realised myself that the painting had in fact been taken by my estranged wife.'

'How did you discover this?'

'By Katherine's own defiant admission,' says Damien, almost sounding reluctant to answer. 'Of course, far be it from me to sound ungentlemanly, but it was at this point she decided the painting in question was her rightful

230

property and wouldn't return it. She calmly insisted that it was in a perfectly safe place, but absolutely refused to reveal where this was.'

'She refused to reveal its location?'

'Regrettably, yes,' Damien says, sounding genuinely sorrowful about this. 'And on a number of occasions, too. The last thing I ever wanted to do was to involve the police and to start issuing court orders, but unfortunately, after negotiations with Katherine broke down, that was the only route left open to me.'

'So to clarify, you wanted it returned because, as its rightful owner, you possibly wished to display the painting in your new home?' Oliver leads him, and I'd almost swear the two of them have rehearsed this part.

'I only wish that were the case,' Damien smiles. Actually smiles. 'Because believe me, if that were the case, I'd have given it to Katherine willingly, and with a whole heart. However, the painting was purchased in the name of the King family trust and as it's a work of some note, our intention was always to make sure that it could be viewed by the general public at any time. The last thing I would ever want to do,' he adds, with a quick, tight smile in the direction of the jury box, 'would be to hoard it to myself under lock and key.'

Oh God, this guy's good, I think. So persuasive. So utterly convincing. The whole package.

'So what were your plans for the painting?' prods Oliver.

'Quite simply, we intended to use it in a forthcoming exhibition based on the life of Rembrandt that would tour the USA. An A-list tour too; one that would take in galleries such as the Met in New York, the National Gallery in Washington and the San Francisco Museum of Modern Art.'

'A noble aim indeed,' Oliver nods, satisfied.

'And at this point there's something I'd like to add, if I may,' Damien goes, respectfully turning to address us up here in the jury box.

'Please do,' says Oliver, waving his chubby hand in our direction and if I was a bit suspicious before, then now I'm totally convinced.

They've practised this whole verbal tennis match between them.

'I'd just like to take this opportunity to express my utmost apologies to each and every one of you,' says Damien, looking up to the jury with utter sincerity written all over him. 'Because I feel very strongly that a case like this should never have come to court in the first place. This is a simple, straightforward matter of misappropriated property, which should be returned to its rightful owner. Which as we've stated time and again, clearly is the King family trust.'

I glance around and can visibly sense his words working their magic on the faces around me. The guy really is that persuasive.

'And I'd just like to add something else, if I may?' he adds.

'Please,' says Oliver, with another wave of his hand.

'It's heartbreaking to have to discuss this in a court of law,' Damien says, 'because I loved my ex-wife and continue to love her to this day. All I ever wanted to be was a kind, considerate and indeed generous husband. Throughout our long and happy years of marriage I'd gladly have gifted her anything she'd set her heart on. I wanted and continue to want nothing but the best for Katherine. Were it up to me, she'd be more than welcome to the painting. She could even use it as a dartboard, if that made her happy.'

A few titters at that, before he goes on.

'But sadly, *A Lady of Letters* isn't mine to give, and never was.'

Bloody hell, I think. He's so utterly convincing that I can hear Mai beside me whispering, 'You see? None of this was his fault. All her doing. Told you so.'

'The only thing he ever did wrong was to love that greedy, self-centred woman,' hisses Jane, who I swear to God looks almost on the verge of tears. A lot of us in the jury box are even looking at Damien King sympathetically now. Meanwhile from across the floor, Kate is blankly eyeing the wall behind him, barely reacting to a single line he's saying.

'Greed,' Barney chips in, shaking his head. 'Sure you can see it written all over her face. You only have to take one look at her.'

'So the King family trust bought the painting and presented it to your ex-wife on her birthday, isn't that correct?' says Oliver.

'Absolutely,' says Damien, again turning to speak to us in the jury box. 'But then I'd have done anything to make Katherine happy. Just to see the smile on her face. The only hitch was that it was never intended to become a personal possession of hers. As I've already stated for the record, *A Lady of Letters* belongs to everyone and not just to one single individual. If it did, then none of us would even be here.'

Oh dear God, it's like Minnie, Edith, Ruth and just about every pensioner I'm surrounded by is *melting* at that. The only one of us in the jury box who doesn't look like he's being swayed by such a compelling argument, I notice, is Will. Instead he's sitting back, copiously taking notes and otherwise looking completely unmoved.

233

'I want Katherine to be happy,' Damien says calmly. 'At whatever cost and whatever it takes. Except, regrettably, when it comes to *A Lady of Letters*. Because it's just not in my power to give. My ex-wife is a wonderful woman,' he adds, 'and I know that were she quite herself, there's no way she'd have resorted to behaving in this manner.'

'No further questions, Your Honour.'

'The Defence may take now cross-question the witness,' says Judge Simmonds, glancing down at her watch. 'But I must add that you'd be well advised to be as brief as possible. Be warned that I'll be adjourning for the weekend very shortly.'

Hilda Cassidy rises to her feet, her eyes flashing.

'It's been a long day for everyone,' she says in that clear, unwavering voice. 'So before we adjourn, I have just one short question, Your Honour.'

'You may address the witness and pose your question,' says Judge Simmonds, eyes still glued to her watch.

'Mr King,' says Hilda coolly, taking full advantage of the tiny parcel of time that's available to her. 'You've stated under oath that you very much loved your ex-wife, and still do, and that you'd do anything in your power to make her happy. Isn't that correct?'

'Absolutely,' says Damien, looking so laid back that you'd swear he was about to order a pint of Guinness in a minute, to really get the weekend started.

'Well, it's very puzzling,' says Hilda, shaking her head, 'because the Defence have a key witness who will personally testify under oath to the fact that you gifted Katherine King this painting, as a birthday present. And as you know, under the terms of her pre-nuptial agreement, she's

234

legally entitled to keep gifts. Yet now, in this spectacular about-turn, you claim that the painting belongs to your family trust.'

'And so it does,' says Damien smoothly.

'So let me get this straight. In April 2014, the painting is my client's, and yet just a few months later, you seem to have completely changed your mind.'

'That's actually not the case at all—' Damien tries to say, but Hilda barrels over him.

'Which begs the question, what can have brought about this change of heart? You have a new partner, don't you, Mr King?'

'Objection!' says Oliver, so sharply that every eye in court swivels towards him. 'And how precisely is this relevant, Your Honour?' he thunders on, approaching the judge's bench. 'This case is about the rightful owner of a painting, and to drag my client's private life into it is unfair, unwise and frankly a waste of time.'

'I'll allow the question,' says Judge Simmonds. 'But be careful,' she adds with a peering look down at Hilda.

For a moment, Damien looks flummoxed, but he still answers the question anyway.

'Yes, that's correct, I have a new partner. It's not a secret.'

'It certainly isn't,' says Hilda. 'So could your sudden change of mind possibly have anything to do with the fact that your partner is an art historian and an expert on the seventeenth-century Dutch Masters, notably Rembrandt? And that she is in fact hotly tipped to be appointed curator of this exhibition in the USA that you've just described to us?'

A shock ripples through the court at that, as the judge calls us to order.

'I'll instruct the Defence not to pursue this line of questioning,' she says, 'as clearly, it can only ever be speculation. And I think we'll adjourn right there for the weekend. Till then I would charge the jury to forget that last question and we'll resume this hearing at 10 a.m. sharp on Monday.'

'Ah no,' groans Minnie disappointedly from beside me. 'I would have loved to have heard how Damien King tried to wriggle his way out of that one.'

I know exactly how she feels too. It's unfortunate that Hilda didn't get to continue questioning him, but as far as the press are concerned it makes absolutely no difference. Whether it's expunged from the record or not, it's out there now and you can be sure that Damien only wanting the painting for the new girlfriend will be the dominant story wherever you look this weekend.

Which, essentially, is the first point that Team Kate has actually managed to score.

KATE

Castletown House, April 12th, 2014
Her birthday party

None of her distinguished guests realised it, but Kate had already made up her mind exactly how she was going to fight her corner tonight. The only hitch being that she knew there wasn't a hope in hell of her going through with it without the tiniest bit of medicinal help.

A Lexotan, she decided, the welcome thought striking her while chatting to Mo earlier. Lexotan was a sedative her doctor had prescribed a while back, just to help calm her nerves when she felt anxious. Not quite as good as a stiff drink, but for now it would just have to bloody well do. She knew for definite there was a strip of them left somewhere upstairs in her room.

Somehow she shook off Mo, made her way through the crowd of guests to the grand staircase and if she did stumble just a bit on her heels as she made her way upstairs, then all she could do was pray no one noticed.

Thank God though she got as far as her bedroom without being accosted any further. But then that was the worst thing about a night like this; everyone wanted a piece of you, people didn't seem to realise when you needed to do a Greta Garbo and just be alone. She closed the door firmly behind her and the cool of the room came as a blessed relief after the intense heat of one hundred and fifty assembled guests downstairs.

Strange thing was that although she felt woozy, she still wasn't out and out drunk, at least not that much, at least not yet. Nerves and adrenaline had kept her in overdrive all evening and now suddenly she knew she had to lie down.

Perching on the edge of the giant, four-poster bed, she kicked off her shoes, cursing herself for not having the foresight to have brought a drink up here with her so she could at least have savoured it in peace; anything rather than having to endure all the frowning and hissed tut-tuts from guests, who'd seen how aggressively she was knocking back the G&Ts earlier.

Downstairs she felt like her every move was being watched, but it was quiet and soothing and cool up here, even if the noise, the chat and the background music still drifted up. Everyone had turned up tonight, and by that she really did mean everyone. Even a few handpicked and carefully chosen press hacks were here, all of whom had been pre-vetted by Damien first, of course, to make sure they were fully 'on side' and could be guaranteed to write about the whole evening in the most glittering and effusive way imaginable.

Well, good, Kate thought. They came here for a story and by Christ were they about to get one.

She wondered how many of their guests had already noticed, how many knew that her days here at Castletown House were numbered. Doubtless the chatterers downstairs were already writing her off as a soon-to-be 'first wife'. And even at that much, she'd failed miserably.

It mattered not that she'd been the perfect wife in every other respect for the past fifteen years; that she'd wined and dined everyone Damien had wanted her to, that she'd entertained lavishly, never failing to look ornamental and to shine at his side just as he wanted her to, so they could act the part of Mr and Mrs Perfect Couple.

'You're my perfect girl,' he used to say to her, back in the day. 'Always stay my perfect girl.'

But in their cloistered little circle, first wives had only one real role to carry out and that was to provide children – the more the better. Particularly for a man like Damien who was almost monarchical in his ambitions and who'd openly wanted as many heirs and spares running around who could be groomed to one day take over Globtech for him.

The cold, hard fact though was that after fifteen years he and Kate were childless and there were no words to describe the dull, aching pain that caused her; day in, day out. It had almost got to the stage where she couldn't even pass by a baby's buggy on the street without feeling a familiar, sharp, tugging pain right to her solar plexus.

These days Kate was even avoiding some of her girl-friends, mainly because all their chatter ever seemed to resolve around was kids. There was always one pal who was organising either a Christening, a Confirmation or else humbly bragging about how 'little Sophie had just been cast as the lead in her school play'. Kate would listen politely, commenting when she was expected to, then escape to the bathroom for her own private lip-wobbling moment as soon as she feasibly could.

With the sole exception of Mo, who'd always been a bit more sensitive than the others, it was as though this was all the women in her circle could talk about. Didn't they realise what she'd already been through? Didn't they know how empty and useless and stupid all their talk made her feel?

Which of course meant the stage was practically set for someone like Harper Jones, all of twenty-seven years of age and doubtless with ovaries like Sten guns. She'd probably be pregnant before the year was out. Certainly if Damien had his way, which he invariably did. Then he could conveniently elbow Kate to one side, while claiming he was only doing the right thing in standing by his oh-so-young girlfriend and their unborn child. Thereby managing the difficult feat of getting exactly what he wanted, under the guise of being the good guy just trying to do his best, while still managing to curry popular favour from all sides.

Vintage Damien, in other words.

In fact his PR team were probably planning that far ahead already. Nothing would surprise Kate. Not any more.

Suddenly she clearly heard more ringing at the doorbell, more noise and more of a kerfuffle as yet more bloody guests arrived.

'Where's my wife? Has anyone seen her?' she heard Damien's voice filter up as far as her bedroom door, instantly making her stomach clench.

'I don't know, Mr King. I'm so sorry, but I haven't seen her since the party started,' Elena, their housekeeper answered. 'I thought she was in the drawing room with you.'

'Well can you just find her, please?' came the impatient reply. 'She's needed. Now.'

Kate's stomach flipped at the realisation that she couldn't

hide up here for very much longer. Suddenly she felt shaky, nauseous and weak with nerves. Where were those bloody Lexotan tablets she'd come up here for, anyway? She pulled open a drawer on the bedside table to check if they were there, but no, nothing. So in one quick move she was up and padding barefoot through the dressing room and on into the bathroom she shared with Damien. Or rather, that she used to share with him. Right now Kate was hard pressed to remember the last time they'd actually slept together as man and wife.

She fumbled about in the bathroom cabinet, accidentally spilling over a whole open bottle of paracetamol, which bounced off the marble floor then scattered everywhere.

Shit. Must be drunker than I thought.

Normally she'd have been on her hands and knees scrabbling about to pick them up, but right now she was beyond caring. Instead she kept on rummaging around and quickly found what she'd been looking for. She unscrewed the cap and knocked back a single Lexotan, splashing a gulp of tap water into her mouth to wash it down. Then she thought, what the hell, why not have a second one? God knows if she was going to go ahead with this, then she'd need all the medicinal help she could get. Just to take the edge off, that was all.

She was just about to replace the bottle when from the master bedroom door there was a loud knocking before someone just barged straight in. And only one person in this house ever did that.

'Katherine! Oh for God's sake, what the hell do you think you're doing?'

Damien, suddenly standing right in front of her, taking it all in. The pills rolling around the floor, while she stood there with a bottle of sedatives clamped to her hand. Says everything, she thought from out of nowhere, that he won't even call me Kate any more; almost like he just wanted to put the maximum distance between them.

'I had a headache,' she began to improvise weakly. 'I just needed something to get me through the rest of the evening . . .' But it was too late. He was straight over to her, grabbing her wrist, snatching the bottle from her and scanning the label.

'Lexotan, Katherine? Seriously? With half the board of Globtech downstairs? And you're slurring your words too, how many drinks have you had?

'Don't be ridiculous, I've just had one or two – no more than anyone else here.'

'The US ambassador has just arrived with his wife and you're up here pill-popping and hiding away like some basket-case recluse? Get your fucking act together,' he hissed at her, 'if it's not too much to ask.'

'Well would you blame me?' she retorted, the words halfway out of her mouth before she could rethink what she was about to say. 'Given tonight's guest list?'

Then silence, while he coldly scanned her face. A hot, angry silence.

'I've no idea what you're talking about,' he said after a pause.

'Yes, you bloody well do.'

'Katherine, you're clearly drunk and you need to—'

'So it's OK for you to invite your girlfriend here tonight, but not for me to have a drink? I'm just expected to stand by and say nothing? Is that it?'

'What exactly do you mean by that?' he said coldly, a façade of politeness in place now that they seemed to be on the brink of something this momentous. But then she and Damien rarely communicated at all these days. If she wanted to know what was going on in his life, generally she had to read about it in the papers.

Another pause, one that seemed to throb between them, before Kate could bring herself to answer.

Do you even want to know, she asked herself before opening her mouth. Do you really want to say what you're about to? Because this was a potential game-changer, she was on the brink of saying something that would alter everything. Her whole life, her home, everything she'd known for the past fifteen years was now about to evaporate right in front of her eyes.

Fuck it anyway, she thought. I choose honesty.

'I know all about you and Harper Jones,' she eventually said in a voice that barely sounded like her own. 'I know that's the whole reason for this evening. And I know that's why you bought that painting, for her and certainly not me. It's damn all to do with the fact that it was my birthday or anything like it. I know what you're up to, Damien, and I know what you're planning. So don't even bother to deny it.'

She was just trying to figure out what percentage of her really did want him to deny it, when he spoke.

'Now I want you to listen to me very carefully, Katherine, because I'll only say this once.'

'Alright then.'

Deny it. Go on, I almost dare you.

'You're in absolutely no condition to be seen, let alone to act the hostess this evening,' he said, while she just looked blankly back at him, her brain not quite able to catch up with what he was saying.

'Just take a look at yourself,' he went on, roughly yanking her head towards the bathroom mirror. 'You're pathetic, do you know that? Stay up here, go to bed and on no account show your face downstairs again. You're in no fit state to attract any more attention to yourself than is absolutely necessary. Got it? Good.'

And he was gone, closing the bathroom door behind him.

Kate couldn't move, couldn't think, couldn't do anything except recognise that she was in raw, numb shock. But just then from the bedroom outside, she suddenly heard Mo's worried voice.

'Oh, hi, Damien,' she was saying. 'I've been looking everywhere for Kate . . . is she in here?'

'Ah Mo, there you are,' said Damien, instantly back to being all charming again now that they were no longer alone. 'Yes, my lovely wife is just in the bathroom. But unfortunately she's not feeling too well, so I think she may have to sit out the rest of the evening. Such a shame, but you know how it is whenever she gets one of her migraines—'

'Migraines?' Kate could clearly hear Mo saying indignantly from the other side of the bathroom door. 'Are you kidding me? Kate's never had a migraine in her life.'

God bless you for that, Mo. Good on you.

Mo waited till Damien had gone, then tapped softly on the bathroom door.

'OK if I come in?'

Kate said nothing and next thing Mo's vibrant, suntanned face was peeking through the door, where Kate was perched on the edge of the bath, ghostly pale as she concentrated on breathing deeply and waiting for the dizziness to pass.

'Jesus Christ, Kate,' was all Mo said, taking her in from head to foot. 'I'd heard rumours that things were bad. But I never imagined it had come to this.'

*

Mo tried her best to dissuade her, but Kate had insisted on coming back downstairs, claiming she felt a bit better now and only hoping Mo would buy into the lie. The drawing room was like a furnace by then so she asked one of the wait-staff to open as many windows as possible. Not that it seemed to make the slightest bit of difference, the air was still stifling.

'You alright, Kate? You look so flushed.'

'Kate! There you are, sweetie, where have you been? You're missing out on all the fun!' she was dimly aware of Samantha Sullivan saying to her, before even more tinny, disjointed voices started coming at her from just about every direction.

'Damien looks like he's gearing up to make one of his speeches, better batten down the hatches . . . and charge your glass, as they say!'

'Not a bad idea, this could go on for quite some time.'

Good humoured, joshing remarks flew at Kate as she weaved her way through the crowd to nab a spot right at the very back of the room, where she could be sure Damien wouldn't notice her. Just in the nick of time to hear him ping a knife off one of her good crystal glasses, while an obedient and almost seraphic hush fell on the throng.

'Good evening, friends, Romans, countrymen,' he began to a polite titter from the room, looking relaxed and calm, seemingly the only person here not to feel the intense heat. 'You're all so welcome here tonight and I hope you'll indulge

245

me when I extend a particularly warm welcome to the US ambassador, His Excellency Dr Patrick Roberts. And of course to his fragrant wife, Flora, who we're especially delighted to have here tonight.'

More applause for the ambassador, resplendent in white tie and tails with the fragrant Flora standing beside him. She looked more or less like a bargain-basement Camilla Parker-Bowles, Kate thought woozily, with her flicked back, over-bleached blonde hair, double strand pearls and an Asprey handbag. All she was short of was scissors to cut the ceremonial ribbon on whatever hospital wing she was just about to open.

All eyes automatically veered towards them both . . . well, all eyes except Kate's. Instead she just stood inside the door busily scanning around the room before her eyes lit on what she'd been looking for. And sure enough there she was, Harper Jones; standing not two feet from Damien with her eyes sparkling, gazing adoringly up at him as he warbled on welcoming this dignitary and that in descending order of importance, almost like he'd rehearsed it. Which knowing Damien, he probably had.

Kate's blood ran cold just at the sight of her and Damien so close together, so open about what was going on. Then a rush of blood to her head almost startled her in its ferocity and in that moment, she knew she couldn't contain herself any longer.

'Now, I know you're all anxious to get back to the bar – not looking at anyone in particular, Eamonn Norris!' Damien was saying as sycophantic laughter trickled around the room. 'So with no further ado, let me introduce you to the newest addition to the King collection . . . *A Lady of Letters!*'

More applause and even a few cheers, which Damien shushed with a faux-modest wave of his hand.

'I'm sure by now you've all had quite enough of me warbling on, so instead, I've got a little surprise for you all. And if you'll be good enough, please allow me to introduce you to someone infinitely more qualified to tell you a little more about the painting than I ever possibly could. Ladies and gentlemen, please give a very warm welcome to the Emeritus Scholar and Visiting Lecturer in Art History at City College, Dublin . . . the very lovely Miss Harper Jones.'

He turned to Harper just then and without even knowing it, he seemed to beam. His whole face just lit up, like he couldn't hide how he felt and didn't even bother trying. Just like he used to whenever he looked at Kate, once upon a time.

Kate felt sick. And just at that moment, from out of nowhere she heard a small, unsteady voice she scarcely recognised as her own.

'Actually, it's my turn to say a few words.'

Confused silence from around the room and Kate was aware of all eyes on her.

'Excuse me?' said Damien, completely wrong-footed, which was something that rarely happened to him and was almost comical to watch on the rare occasions when it did.

'If no one has any objection, that is,' she said, aware that she might have garbled that sentence just the tiniest bit, but hoping no one noticed. 'After all, this is supposedly my birthday party. Or had you forgotten, Damien?'

'Sweetie, is this really wise?' came a voice from Kate's right as a hand clamped down on her shoulder. Kate turned to see Mo looking worriedly back at her, but she just brushed her away and worked her way through the room all the way up to where Damien was standing right in front of the portrait. His smile was practiced and warm, but the eyes were flinty and Kate knew only too well what must be going through his mind. As far as he was concerned, she was a loose cannon tonight, liable to say or do anything.

Kate turned to face the room, flushed in the face now that she was the sole focus of attention.

'You know, darling,' Damien said. 'I think our guests would far rather hear from an expert like Harper, don't you? How about we just let her speak instead?' His tone was all lightness and concern but his grip on Kate's slender arm was hard as a rock, almost bruising her.

'Sorry,' she said, shrugging him off, 'but I've bloody well kept silent for long enough and tonight all that changes.'

She cleared her throat, trying to ignore that her knees were actually shaking, cartoon-style. A lightning-quick glance around the room made her feel even worse. Because apart from Mo there wasn't one single friendly face here that she could count on. It was like standing slap bang in the middle of a whole petri dish full of tension.

'Ladies and gentlemen,' she began, with just the slightest wobble at the back of her throat. 'You came here tonight to . . .' but she broke off here, aware that Harper Jones had angled herself to the forefront of the room and was now standing just a few feet away from her, eyes almost out on stilts to hear what she came out with next. She looked so fresh and youthful and just the very sight of her filled Kate with a hot, bubbling rage that almost made her feel like throwing up.

'You all came here to hear about . . .' she began again, trying her best to concentrate, but the trouble was that the whole room seemed to be getting blurry and even guests in the front row were zooming in and out of focus, now that the Lexotan pills had finally started to take effect. Mo had somehow worked her way up to the front and looked like she might come and steer her away at any second. Anything to save Kate from herself.

'You came here to see *A Lady of Letters*,' Kate managed to get out, the dizziness getting almost unbearable now. 'Well, for a start, it's cursed, did you all know that?'

An excited ripple went around the room, which only spurred her on.

'Yes!' she said. 'Because I've started doing a bit of research into it and I can tell you, there's an awful lot more to this painting than my loving husband ever thought. Wherever she goes, all manner of misery follows. And guess what, everyone? It seems that curse isn't just fiction. Because whether you believe it or not, there's an even more un-believable drama unfolding right under your noses here this evening—'

'You know, I think maybe our guests have had enough speechifying for now,' Damien interrupted, moving towards her to steer her away, but Kate backed away from him, stumbling over on her heels and tripping on the hem of her floor-length dress as she did. She managed to grip the fireplace behind to steady herself as a worried murmur swept through the room, but she'd come this far. She was damned if she was about to shut up now.

'No! I'm afraid I still have more to say,' she told the room defiantly, to pin-drop silence. 'You see, Damien here wants you all to think *A Lady of Letters* was bought for me, but in actual fact nothing could be further from the truth. In fact, the only reason why he went to so much trouble, not to mention such considerable expense, to acquire this god-awful and frankly depressing painting was so that he could—'

'Thank you so much for that, Katherine, but you know, I really think that's enough for now,' Damien said sternly, this time locking both his arms around her shoulders and physically hauling her away. Almost manhandling her, at least that's how it must have looked to everyone.

'I wasn't finished!' Kate yelled as he half-pulled her as far as the door, 'and if it's entertainment you all came here for, then let me tell you about my husband and a certain lady who had the brass neck to turn up here tonight . . . that's her right there, in the white dress, Harper fucking Jones herself. So much for the wife always being the last to know!'

It was too late though. All Kate could focus on now was the room spinning around her, as what seemed like a thousand sets of eyes followed her as Damien lifted – or rather yanked – her out of the room.

'She's just a little tired, that's all, nothing to worry about,' she could hear him reassuring everyone as her eyelids started to close over in spite of herself, almost like she'd just been given a strong anaesthetic.

'Are you quite alright, Mrs King?' said a voice from right beside her. 'Is there anything I can do to help?'

Kate's eyelids flicked as she recognised the guy who'd spoken to her earlier, the one who worked at City College and who'd reminded her of Billy Bunter. Bernard something, she vaguely remembered.

'That's kind of you, Bernard, but there's really no need, thanks,' said Damien. 'It's been a long day for my wife and she just needs a little lie down, don't you, darling?'

'I do not need a fucking lie down, I'm trying my best to

tell everyone what's going on here, under my roof!' she tried to yell. 'Why won't you let me finish, you bastard?'

Now she was aware of cameras going off in her face as the press hacks there lapped up the sideshow, but by now Damien had manoeuvred her out into the hallway and practically dumped her on Elena, the housekeeper.

'See to it that Mrs King gets safely to her room for the rest of the night. And make bloody sure that she stays there.'

TESS

The present

Saturday night and it's a joint dinner for both my family and the Pritchards. Not my idea, I hasten to add; it was Bernard who felt it would be a good idea to get everyone together before the wedding, 'just to break the ice a little before kick-off'.

Of course I've been a guest many times before in Beatrice and Desmond Pritchard's house and Bernard – in fairness to him – regularly endures dinner with Mum, Dad, Gracie and I, as often as he can stick it out. But given that the two families have never all sat around a table together, I reluctantly agreed that this was probably for the best.

'Although, to be honest,' I make the mistake of saying to Gracie as she helps zip me into an LBD when we're getting ready for the big night, 'I doubt very much we'll all end up one big happy family, like something out of a Dolmio ad.'

'Just promise me Bernard isn't going to spend the whole night droning on about the Dutch Masters,' she says, and I just about catch her eyes roll in the mirror in front of us.

'No, because Bernard doesn't drone,' I tell her firmly. 'Bernard is lovely. And what's more, he's going to be your brother-in-law, so you'd better get used to him.'

'Doing my best here,' she shrugs. 'But you're the one who always comes back from dinner at the Pritchards' complaining that you were bored out of your skull.'

'Now that is just not true—'

'You and your selective memory, yes it bloody is. Only last week you said Ma Pritchard spent half the night rabbiting on about ancient Greek and Roman civilization, and the other half having a go at you because you never went to college.'

Shit. I knew it was a mistake retelling that to Gracie in minute detail. However, in the interests of diplomacy, I keep my mouth shut so as not to add flames to the fire.

First row of the night kicks off before we've even left our house.

'Ah, here,' groans Dad, looking red-faced and practically beaten into the one suit we managed to find that still vaguely fits him. 'Not only am I missing Juventus versus Real Madrid tonight, but now I have to wear a bleeding tie as well? Are you joking me with this, Tess?'

'Now you just keep your mouth zipped tight during dinner,' Mum cautions him, dusting down a jacket that he hasn't worn since my granny's funeral, all of ten years ago. 'And whatever you do, don't whip out your phone while we're all eating so you can check the score.'

'At least we'd better get a decent feed out of this,' mutters Dad.

I don't open my mouth, but to be perfectly honest he'll be lucky. Thing is, at Bernard's insistence we're all 'dining at my club', as he puts it, this evening. Which admittedly does sound posh and special-occasiony; until you see the state of the club, that is.

It's called the Royal Celtic and it's situated right bang at the top of St Stephen's Green, in the heart of the city centre, which is all fine and dandy until you actually get inside the place and you see the sad state of disrepair it's fallen into. It's one of those old men's clubs in an enormous Georgian townhouse, with the most ridiculous admission policy whereby you can only join if you're nominated by three other members. And that's before you have to give them a blood sample just to get through the front door.

Bernard, like his dad, Desmond, before him, is a fully paid up member of the club and inordinately proud of it. He's taken me here a few times before and at one point even suggested we have our wedding reception here, but I held firm. One look at the mouldy old dining room with the peeling walls and the overwhelming stink of damp would be enough to send most of our guests running. And don't get me started on the food, because it's like the menu here decided it liked the look of the 1980s so much, it may as well stay rooted there.

The Pritchards and Taylors all arrange to meet in the dining room and things don't get off to the most auspicious start. I make the introductions with a knot in my stomach and am trying my best to steer the subject on to something safe, like the weather, when next thing, my dad's off.

'So . . . ehh . . . what team do you follow?' he asks Desmond, who just looks back at him blankly.

'Team?' asks Desmond, all at sea.

'In the Premiership?' Dad prods, ignoring the warning look from me.

'More of a cricket man myself, I'm afraid.'

254

'Cricket? Sure that's the only game where you can hear the score and still not know who's won.'

'Must say, I'm a big fan,' says Desmond.

'Well, right you are so,' says Dad disinterestedly, going back to looking uncomfortable in the suit and staring wistfully out the window.

God Almighty, I think, the tight knot of tension inside my stomach starting to solidify now. Would it even be possible for our two families to look any more different from each other? There's Mum sitting bolt upright in her 'good' suit from M&S, looking desperately stiff with her pin-neat perm, while beside her sits Beatrice, with matted, waist length grey hair that looks like it hasn't seen a comb in ten years. In sharp contrast to Mum, Beatrice is dressed as she always is, in a long flowing black kaftan that makes her look a bit like a fortune teller.

Meanwhile Gracie is sitting across the table from me wearing a denim mini with torn opaque tights as her little act of rebellion, while to my right, poor old Bernard tries his best to make stilted small talk with Dad. And none of us are getting on well.

Underscoring all this, there's loud dance music seeping in from the bar in the building next door, like there's a proper party in full swing there with a live DJ and everything. You can clearly hear Beyonce's 'Single Ladies' throbbing through the walls loud and clear. Unlike the club dining room, which is completely silent apart from the ticking of a grandfather clock and the dull murmur of chat drifting our way from the only other people here; an elderly couple who have to be in their eighties if they're a day, sitting over by the window. Given their age profile, they'd be right at home on jury service, I find myself thinking.

'I think we'll have a little drinkie for everyone to break the ice!' says Bernard, cheerily grabbing a passing waiter and ordering aperitifs all round.

'Very nice in here, isn't it?' Mum says to no one in particular as I silently bless her for at least making an effort.

'Except they're rather slow with the drinkies, I find,' says Beatrice impatiently. 'I'm absolutely gagging for a good stiff G&T. What's your tipple?'

'I don't drink, I'm afraid,' says Mum. 'A nice strong cuppa tea would do me grand.'

Another long pause and this time I can actually see Gracie itching to bop along to Beyonce with the party crowd next door.

'Oh, I know! I must tell you about the show we saw at the theatre last night,' Desmond pipes up, breaking the silence.

'What show was that?' I ask him politely.

'We went to see *DruidShakespeare*. Absolutely wonderful, wasn't it, Bea?'

'Completely breathtaking,' Beatrice nods, helping herself to a G&T from the tray our waiter brings and immediately knocking back a huge gulpful. 'Have you seen it?' she asks Mum.

'Oh . . . erm . . . I'm afraid not, no,' says Mum awkwardly.

'Well you really ought to. It's a combination of Richard II, Henry IV parts one and two, and then just when you think it can't get better, Henry V. All in a single day! Can you imagine?'

'Sounds like it's an absolute must see,' says Bernard enthusiastically.

'How long does it go on for?' asks Gracie.

'Six and a half hours with two intervals,' says Desmond. 'But to be perfectly honest, I came out just wishing it had been longer.'

'We really must try to get tickets, sausage,' says Bernard and all I can do is hope none of the Pritchards caught Gracie mouthing over the table, 'sooner you than me'.

'Are you a regular theatregoer?' Desmond asks Dad.

'Ehh, not really, no. Last show I saw was Brendan O'Carroll doing *For the Love of Mrs Brown* at the 3 Arena. Now that was a great night out, wasn't it, love?'

'Ahh now that was magic,' says Mum, suddenly lighting up. 'But then we love Mrs Brown!'

'Sure who doesn't?' Dad grins.

But instead of this leading on to easy, relaxed conversation, there's mystified silence from the Pritchards.

'I'm told it's about a man who dresses up as a Dublin matriarch,' Bernard explains helpfully.

'Oh, I'm terribly sorry,' says Beatrice. 'But I'm afraid we don't own a TV.'

A shocked look on Mum's face and then more silence, apart from the discreet ticking of the clock in the background and the *thuf thuf* muffled noise of the party seeping in from next door.

We order and, as ever, the menu is like a flashback to the eighties. Melon balls, lasagne and what sounds like nothing more than a slice of Viennetta for dessert. By then though, Beatrice is already onto her third G&T and if she'd actually set out tonight with the sole intention of mortifying the Taylor family, then frankly she couldn't be doing a better job. Starting with Dad then working her way on to Gracie and myself, knocking us all down one-by-one like pins in a bowling alley.

'So tell me all about yourself, Jack,' she says to Dad, as our main course is served.

'Call me Jacko, love, everyone else does.'

'Jacko, then. So what is it you do for a living?'

Embarrassed looks from Mum and I to each other.

'I'm actually in between jobs right now,' says Dad after a pause. 'So I'm working freelance at the minute.'

'Doing what exactly?' Beatrice persists.

'Bit of painting and decorating. Tell you what, I'd do a nice job on this place if they ever wanted,' he adds, taking in the peeling paint on the dining room ceiling.

'And what did you do before that?' Beatrice prods.

More awkward silence.

'I was working for an alarm installation company.'

'Isn't that a rather good job? Why did you leave?'

'Because I was made redundant,' says Dad, getting red in the face now, though I can't tell if that's because he's embarrassed or because the collar and tie are choking him.

Then it's Gracie's turn.

'And what about you,' Beatrice says, turning to her. 'What do you do?'

'I work in a call centre,' says Gracie.

'Oh, really? And I assume at your age that you're some sort of a manager there? Or perhaps an executive?'

'No, I'm a customer service representative,' says Gracie, 'which basically means I answer the phones.'

'Oh,' says Beatrice, distinctly unimpressed and fast losing interest. 'And is that what you always wanted to do?'

'Well put it this way,' says Gracie, a slight edge creeping into her voice now, 'you never hear kids in playgrounds saying "when I grow up, I want to work in a call centre", now do you?'

'Does it at least pay well?' asks Desmond.

'I'm twenty-five years of age and I still live at home,' is Gracie's terse reply, as she shoves her dessert plate as far away from her as possible. 'So what do you think?'

Meanwhile I'm sitting across the table from her, willing her to tell them that she's only doing this job till she saves up enough to move to Canada, where she's hoping to work as a graphic designer, basically her dream job. I want her to say that she's even got her visa and accommodation in Toronto sorted out and that all she needs now is cash, but it's too late. Beatrice has already dismissed her and moved on.

'And neither of your daughters went to college?' she says to Mum this time. 'I must say, I really do find that mystifying. But then the Pritchard family place a very high premium on education and always have.'

'Lucky that you can afford it then,' says Dad, as a throbbing vein starts to bulge out of his forehead. Which with him, is never a good sign. Last time it happened was when he was hauled up for a tax audit. 'Not all of us have that luxury, just so you know.'

Dinner goes from bad to bowel-witheringly mortifying. Edited highlights include Desmond and Beatrice talking at length about their upcoming summer walking tour of the ancient Roman ruins at Cerro da Vila, while Mum chats about the great deal she got on Groupon for a week's holiday in Sneem, County Kerry.

'The weather will probably be shite,' shrugs Dad.

'But at least we speak the language,' says Mum. 'And the food won't be a problem.'

'And it's cheap. And I can still keep up with the League.'

In the midst of stiff competition, though, the award for

the single worst moment of the whole miserable evening has to go to Bernard himself.

'Oh, I forgot to tell you all a lovely bit of news,' Mum says to the table at large as coffee is being served.

'And what's that?' asks Beatrice, waving for the waiter to come and refill her glass.

'You know how my ladies from the local amateur musical society are all coming to the wedding? Well, they were wondering if they could sing a bit of a medley at the afters?'

'That's a fantastic idea!' I smile. 'Of course they can sing. We'd be thrilled to have them perform, wouldn't we, Bernard?'

Now at this point, in the interests of diplomacy, all my husband-to-be has to do is smile brightly and come out with something along the lines of, 'yes, that sounds wonderful, thank you!'

That's all that's needed here, that's all it would take. That little.

Instead though, Bernard looks worried, bites his lip, then after a pause says, 'and may I ask what it is that they're proposing to sing?'

'Oh you'll love this,' Mum beams proudly, 'a fifteen-minute medley of ABBA's greatest hits including "Dancing Queen", Tess's very favourite song. They've been rehearsing it specially and everything. Now isn't that a lovely surprise?'

I give Mum a peck on the cheek, thank her and only then become aware that Bernard is saying absolutely nothing. Just fiddling with his cufflinks and looking uncomfortable.

'Bernard?' I prompt. 'Isn't that thoughtful of Mum's pals?'

'Oh, sausage,' he says, looking guiltily at me. 'Is that really the kind of function we want?'

More silence and this time it's my turn to look dumb-founded.

'And what's wrong with a bit of ABBA at a wedding?' Dad says, loyally sticking up for Mum.

'Well obviously nothing, per se,' says Bernard, as if he's not even aware that he's on the brink of causing offence. 'But perhaps it's just not quite suitable, that's my concern. After all, we're hoping that this will be a classy affair. Lots of my colleagues from the faculty will be there, you know, and we don't want to create the wrong impression, now do we, sausage?'

'You're saying there's something wrong with ABBA?' Dad insists, with just the tiniest hint of aggression in his voice now.

'No, I'm merely suggesting that this mightn't be the most appropriate venue for an amateur musical group to perform. That's all.'

'So a wedding isn't an appropriate venue? Where is then, according to you? A funeral parlour?'

'Well now you're just being facetious,' says Bernard, sounding a bit pompous, which is a side of him that I've never seen before and which is starting to set off alarm bells in my head.

'Just because my family never went to college,' says Dad on the defensive now, 'doesn't mean we don't know how to enjoy ourselves, now does it?'

'I'm afraid to say that last comment can only indicate a rather large chip on your shoulder,' is Bernard's cool reply.

'And *your* last comment can only indicate that you're acting like a patronising git.'

By the time coffee is being cleared away I've given up. Can't take any more of this; can't and won't. So I excuse myself from the table, slip downstairs to the ladies and am just splashing cold water on my face to relieve the tension when Gracie bursts in.

'Jesus, Tess,' she says immediately coming straight over to me where I'm standing over the sink. 'For the love of God, just tell me what you see in that insensitive, up-his-own-arse gobshite. Just tell me that much and then I'll keep my mouth shut for the rest of this miserable night.'

I freeze. And I try to fumble around my head for all the standard phrases I normally use whenever she's having a pop at Bernard. That he's lovely and gentle and warm-hearted, etc.

But right now, I can't. Nothing will come to me.

I haven't a single word to say in his defence.

*

The only good thing that can be said about the whole dismal evening is that it winds up early, about 10 p.m., with me cross and upset at Bernard and him utterly unable to understand why.

He bundles the Pritchards into a taxi and I do the same with Mum and Dad, with everyone still bristling. Gracie stays by my side so when the parents have been safely dispatched, there's just her, Bernard and me left on the pavement as both taxis zoom off.

'Bernard, did you really have to?' I say to him, not caring that we've got Gracie as an audience, with her arms folded and her face tight as she stands supportively beside me.

'Did I really have to what?' he asks, genuinely not having a clue.

'You really offended Mum and Dad back there! She's gone home very upset, you know.'

'Sausage, you know what? You're tired and emotional . . .'

'No, I'm not!'

'And I really don't think the side of the road is an apt place for this conversation. Let's get you a taxi and get you home safely, then we'll talk in the morning when you're feeling a little more like yourself again.'

He flags down a cab, which obediently pulls up on the kerb beside us. Then Gracie interrupts.

'Sod this anyway,' she says. 'I'm going for a late drink. You coming, Tess?'

'Goodness, that's certainly not a good idea,' Bernard says to me, gripping me by the elbow. 'Now, Tess, I really think you ought to do as I suggest and take the cab home. There's a good girl.'

'Actually I *am* going for a drink,' I tell him firmly, shoving off his grip. 'And I think you should too, Bernard. We need to talk.'

'Then let's talk tomorrow, when you're feeling quite alright again—'

'No, let's talk now. Right now, in fact. Because this won't wait a moment longer.'

'Tess, it's late and you're tired and emotional. Do be sensible and just come home.'

I can't think of anything smart enough to retort, so instead I just glare at him as a gang of women who look like they're in the middle of a hen night bash past us, singing the chorus from 'You've Got the Love' by Florence and the Machine.

'Sausage,' says Bernard, just a tad threateningly. 'If you're not going to get into this taxi now, then I most certainly will.'

'Fine, then be my guest.'

'Fine, then I'll call you in the morning.'

'Good luck trying to get me to answer the phone,' I say, aware of how childish and petulant it sounds, but at this point, beyond caring.

It hardly seems to matter though. Because for such a big man, Bernard can move pretty niftily when there's a row he wants to get away from. In one quick move he's into the taxi and zooming away, leaving me on the pavement silently gnashing my teeth.

'If you ask me, it's the eighth wonder of the world,' says Gracie dryly, 'how a catch like him wasn't snapped up years ago.'

She links my arm supportively and leads me into the bar next door to the Royal Celtic Club that was belting out all that music earlier on. I'm still too shell-shocked to even question where we're going, so I just follow where I'm led.

'Make a sentence out of the following words,' she says as the doorman waves us inside. 'Alcohol. We need. Right now.'

Turns out it's a basement bar that's packed to the brim with wall-to-wall Saturday night revellers, all having a laugh and kicking the night off in style. In other words, the perfect antidote to the stiff, formal, damp-smelling club next door, and basically the kind of place that the Pritchards would run screaming from. Plus the average age in here is about thirty, so immediately I feel the hard knot of tension that's been inside me all evening start to lift. This, I think, is exactly what I need to expunge from my memory the last two hours of my life.

'You do realise that your fiancé just used the phrase, "there's a good girl" to you?' says Gracie as we wedge our way up to the bar. 'And you call yourself a card-carrying feminist?'

'Don't remind me,' I groan, slumping against the bar with my head in my hands. Just then, two girls beside us get up from barstools to leave, so we nab the free seats while we can.

'You know something?' I say to her as she's ordering drinks for us both. 'All I wanted tonight was for everyone to get along. So was that too much to ask? Was I aiming too high?'

'Look,' she says evenly, 'I'm sure the Pritchards are lovely people. And as soon as I get a vodka and tonic into me, I'm sure I'll probably admit that there's no harm in Bernard either, for all that he's the most boring fart I ever met. But Jaysus, Tess, you just don't fit in with them, any more than Bernard does with us. So what will it take for you to see that he's not the one for you?'

Our drinks arrive but I stay silent. Mainly because Gracie has a point and I know it. Of course I know that Bernard and I are a bit of a mis-match, that's been obvious from day one.

'It's a mis-match that works though,' I say, knocking back a massive mouthful of the vodka before muttering deep into the glass. 'At least, I used to think so. Sort of. Most of the time.'

'Couple more where these came from,' says Gracie, waving her drink under my nose, 'and you'll be singing a very different tune, babes. Because right now, you know what you're starting to sound like?'

'What?' I say dully.

'Like someone who's really trying to convince herself more than anyone else.'

*

It's well past eleven now and this bar is actually turning out to be quite the hot spot. A fortieth birthday party is in full swing over at another table and there's about a dozen guys wearing t-shirts that read, 'Happy Birthday, Kevin!' who all seem to be having a rare old night of it. They're laughing and singing along to the music and it's hard not to get swept up in all of that infectious fun.

Mind you, it could also be the fact that I'm now on to my third vodka that's making me chillax so much, or was it my fourth? I still can't bring myself to dwell on the earlier part of the night, so in this lovely boozy haze, I'm parking it for now. Like Scarlett O'Hara, I'll think about that tomorrow.

Gracie, in the meantime, has scored. Well, admittedly I'm a bit woozy so I mightn't be the best judge, but at least I think she has. She's still sitting on the barstool beside me but for the last half hour has been chatting away to a performance artist called Elaine, who seems in absolutely no rush to get away.

Mind you, Gracie always says it's way easier for a gay woman to get lucky in a straight bar, mainly because in gay bars it's mostly all about sex and one-night flings. There's a notable one here in Dublin called the Priscilla bar and Gracie never fails to score in there on a Saturday night. But as she's been saying for a while now, 'I'm twenty-five. Twenty-five and never having had a girlfriend that stuck around for longer than three months is pathetic in gay-land. I want a proper long-term relationship.'

'I wish there was a Priscilla bar for straight people,' I often used to moan at her back in my single days.

'Oh, get over yourself. Every bar is a Priscilla bar for straight people.'

I'm feeling nicely anaesthetised by now and am half-wondering if I should leave Gracie and Elaine to themselves and slip off home, when next thing I'm aware of a guy standing directly behind me.

'Well of all the gin joints in all the towns in all the world,' says a familiar voice and I turn around in astonishment to see Will. All tall and lean and dark, and clad in one of those bright-red 'Happy Birthday, Kevin!' t-shirts, as he queues up to buy a round.

'I don't believe this!' I say, genuinely glad to see him. 'It's so weird to see you outside of the courts.'

'You wouldn't want to say that too loud,' he grins, 'or people might get the wrong idea and think I'm the one in the dock.'

I introduce him to Gracie and her performance artist pal and everyone shakes hands, but then Gracie and Elaine quickly settle back to their cosy one-on-one chat, so it's just Will and I alone.

'Are you here for the fortieth?' I ask.

'How did you guess?' he says with a tiny smile.

'And is the birthday boy enjoying the night?'

'Oh, Kevin's having a blast,' says Will, leaning casually up against the bar and looking in no rush to go anywhere. 'Mind you, we had planned to do the Stations of the Cross tonight, but I think that's gone by the wayside.'

'You planned to do what?'

'You know, where you pick fourteen bars and have one drink in each of them, then see who's last man standing. This is only our fifth but I've a feeling we're holed up here for the rest of the night.'

'Certainly sounds an awful lot more fun than my evening was.'

He looks at me keenly now and suddenly I'm aware of just how much I've had to drink. The wooziness I felt earlier has turned to full-on dizziness and the room is actually starting to spin around a bit.

'So what happened to you?' he asks, genuinely sounding concerned. 'Tell me.'

I look at him for a second, wavering then decide, why not? So I tell him everything, describing the whole god-awful, miserable night from start to finish. And he listens too, leaning in to really hear me because it's so noisy in here.

'So that's the reason why you find me propped up at the bar on a Saturday night, just in case you were wondering. My wedding is less than four weeks away, myself and the groom are at each other's throats, he just insulted my parents so now our two families are at loggerheads—'

'Montagues and Capulets,' Will nods. 'Say no more. I get it.'

'And on top of all that, I've to be in fecking court for at least the next week.'

'But surely that's a bright spot in your day,' he says wryly. 'You mean you don't leap out of bed first thing every morning like I do?'

'You know what I mean, Will. I could just really do without it right now. No matter how interesting the case might be. I need to be home fixing things, trying to make it all right before the big day.'

He pauses for a minute and just looks at me. Like he's got something on his mind and isn't quite sure whether to say it or not.

'What?' I ask.

'What do you mean "what"?'

'You're looking at me funny.'

'Look, here's the thing,' he eventually says. 'Remember I told you I was divorced?'

'Yes, of course I do.'

'Well, my ex and I were perfectly happy before we got married, or at least I thought we were. But somewhere along the way, it all became more about the big day than about two people who couldn't wait to spend the rest of their lives together.'

Because of 'She Looks So Perfect' by 5 Seconds Of Summer belting out in the background, I find I'm leaning forward on the barstool, straining in to listen to him.

'Then somewhere in the run-up to the wedding I started having doubts,' he goes on. 'And what's more I think my ex did too. She and I weren't getting along and it had got to the stage where all we talked about was the wedding. You know, guest lists and centrepieces and all sorts of meaningless crap. Very little was said about what would come after.

'Then, on the morning of the wedding, I woke up in my hotel room after a sleepless night, got up, looked out the window and just saw sheets of rain pelting down, with flashes of thunder, the whole works. Real hurricane weather. So for me, of course, that felt like the Universe screaming at me "don't do it!". I did seriously think about knocking on my fiancée's door – the whole bridal party were all staying in the same hotel – and telling her how I felt, that I was having second thoughts. But of course in the end I couldn't bring myself to let her down like that. It just seemed so unnecessarily cruel.'

'I'm so sorry, Will . . . I don't know what to say.'

'So I got married out of cowardice really. That was the only reason why I went through with it. And of course we spent the next eighteen months of our lives bickering and arguing over anything and everything. But you know what, Tess?'

'What?'

'Our divorce was so painful and protracted that I remember thinking, if I'd only had the guts to man up that morning, knock on my ex's door and tell her how I really felt, we'd have been so much better off. Both of us. Yes it would have been mortifying and painful in the short term, but a drop in the ocean compared with what we did end up going through.'

'You poor thing,' I say, shaking my head. 'That's unthinkable.'

'So the moral of the story is, if you're having doubts, remember this: you'll never get another chance to voice them. It's like they say in the marriage service, speak now or forever hold your peace. Because, Tess, this is for the rest of your life. And the rest of your life is just way too precious for you to compromise.'

KATE

Castletown House, April 14th, 2014

Monday morning after the infamous party and Kate woke up to total silence, apart from the distant hum of a hoover two floors beneath her. She had no memory of going to bed the previous night and yet here she was in her nightie, with her shoes kicked off and abandoned on the floor beside her. She felt groggy too, as if she'd been given an even stronger sedative than the one she'd taken the night of the party to really knock her out.

Drowsily she hauled herself up onto one elbow and fumbled around on the bedside table for her mobile phone. She checked the date and saw that yes indeed, it really was Monday morning. Jesus. Had she really lost most of Sunday? From the deepest fug at the very back of her mind, she grasped around trying to assess just how bad the night of the party had been. How much of a show did she make of herself? On a scale of one to mortified, where did she lie about now?

Suddenly shaky, she slumped back onto the pillows and waited on a wave of nausea to pass. But she must have taken a lot more tablets than she was used to and pretty

271

soon she was out cold as a deep, drugged sleep enveloped her.

Up until her phone ringing, that was. Mo checking up on her to see how she was.

'Kate? It's ten thirty, don't tell me I woke you?'

'Morning or night?'

'Oh God, you're even worse than I thought. Right then, just stay put, I'm coming to get you.'

That woke her up alright.

'No, there's really no need . . .' she muttered lamely into the phone, but Mo was having none of it.

'Get up, have a shower and be ready for me in half an hour. And Kate?'

'What?' she said dully.

'If you don't do as I say, then I'll do it for you. And you'd be well advised not to push me on this. I'm the mother of twins. Believe me, I know all about coercion and brute force.'

*

'So how about you start at the beginning and tell me what in the name of arse is really going on?' said Mo, stirring the cappuccino in front of her, then sticking the spoon into her mouth to lick the froth off. 'And remember, whatever's said at this table, stays at this table.'

Kate shot her a warm look of gratitude, knowing that Mo was one of the few people in her life who really meant it. The very last thing she'd wanted to do this miserable morning was to haul herself out of the house, out into daylight to face the world again. But Mo had insisted, point-blank refusing to take no for an answer. True to her word, she'd even gone as far as hoisting her out of bed and shoving her into the shower.

'You smell like you haven't even washed since the party,' she'd said bossily, and Kate didn't bother arguing, as she was only telling the truth. 'Now you know you've got to get out there and face the world sometime or other,' Mo went on, 'and the sooner the better, if you ask me. Besides, this is going to be the talk of our whole set, whether you like it or not. So if all the bitches are going to gossip, then the least we can do is give them a decent bit of ammunition. I'm dragging you out for brekkie and I won't take no for an answer. I'll be right there beside you, just like a wing-woman, and if anyone dares say boo to you, then they'll have me to answer to.'

So without having any say whatsoever in the matter, Kate found herself being lugged out of the sanctuary of Castletown House by an over-energetic Mo, then plonked down into the passenger seat of her four-wheel-drive Jeep.

During the whole drive to Avoca village, Kate just wanted to bolt for the hills. Even the sight of her pale, bony-looking face in the car mirror, still blotchy from all the crying, made her wish she could just open the car door at the traffic lights and make a run for it. In total contrast to Mo, who sat beside her at the wheel, looking all tanned and healthy and glowing, as somehow she always did.

Twenty minutes later, Kate found herself in the plush, marble-floored conservatory of the Avoca Fern House Café, just a five-mile drive from Castletown. Ghostly white and still shaky from Saturday night, she was perched at a table for two right by the window in full view of the whole room. There was a double strength Americano and a plate of scrambled eggs on the table in front of her that Mo had insisted she order, the very sight of which was making her still-fragile stomach want to heave.

As the waiter fussed over them, Kate looked anxiously over her shoulder to her left and right. Because everyone she knew seemed to gravitate here for coffee on a Monday morning after the school run; neighbours, friends, plus a lot of women in the Kings' social circle who'd been there on Saturday night. They were sure to be found here around this time, and Kate was anxious to know just how fast word had spread.

Sure enough, there was that awful Sophie Fitzmaurice with two other girlfriends Kate didn't recognise at a table tucked into the far corner, deep in chat. All three dressed in the standard yummy mummy Monday morning uniform of yoga pants, Converse trainers and tight Lycra tracksuit tops that somehow still managed to highlight the contours of their carefully toned arms.

Sophie had of course been a guest at the house on Saturday night; she'd been there to witness the whole humiliating debacle first hand. She immediately spotted Kate, and gave her a polite wave and a too-bright smile, before settling into a cosy huddle of gossip with her mates at the table. Not too difficult to guess what their topic of conversation was either. Half of Kate almost wished she were brave enough to stride over there and say, 'you want to hear it straight from the horse's mouth, ladies? Well here I am, so come on! Why not take your chance and ask me anything?'

'Just try to tune them out,' Mo said, following Kate's gaze. 'They're going to talk anyway, so I suggest you let the bitches get on with it.'

'I'm just sick at the thought of facing everyone who was

there,' Kate groaned weakly, while Mo looked on, warm and concerned. 'It's physically turning my stomach.'

'Then forget about the whole bloody lot of them,' said Mo firmly, 'and talk to me. How were things between you and Damien yesterday?'

At that, Kate slumped back into the cushioned chair she was sitting on and gazed out over the lush County Wicklow gardens in the far distance, badly wishing that it was eleven at night instead of eleven in the morning, so she could reasonably order a G&T and get away with it. It was certainly the only way she'd got through yesterday, with the help of lovely gin and lots of it.

'He was cold with me,' she eventually said. 'So cold, you've no idea. But then you know what he's like; Damien doesn't do outward shows of emotions, certainly not any more. He came into my room first thing yesterday morning and couldn't have been any more business-like about the whole thing.'

It was as if Kate had been one of the hired help at the party, she thought to herself. Like she was one of the wait-staff who'd let him down and who could take it as read that she was fired, without the actual words ever needing to be uttered. As far as Damien was concerned, her contract with him had come to its natural end and now it was purely a question of what and when her payoff would be.

'Did he give any reaction about what – well, you know – about what you'd said that night?'

'I only wish he had,' said Kate, leaning forward to take a sip of coffee from the china cup in front of her and sure enough, the instant wave of caffeine did seem to magically perk her up a little. 'Instead, though, he couldn't have been more dismissive of me,' she went on. 'All he said was that the housekeeper would pack up some things he needed immediately and that he'd move into the Dublin townhouse till more solid arrangements can be made.'

'Those were his exact words?'

'He said he'd speak to his PR manager to see what could be done to minimise this in the press . . . and then that was it. Three minutes, Mo. That's all it took. Three minutes to wind up the last fifteen years of our lives.'

Kate wasn't exaggerating either. She'd had Sky News on TV in the background and she'd actually timed him. Then after he'd left, she spent the rest of the day holed up in her room, curled up in a tight little foetal ball over by the huge bay window, waiting on the dull throbbing ache inside her to pass.

She'd gazed out over the Castletown lawns where one of their trainers was leading a thoroughbred stallion that had once been Damien's pride and joy on a brisk cross-country gallop. Horse breeding was a passion of his not so long ago, as he'd seen it as a passport into the upper echelons he so badly wanted to be a part of. This was the same Damien, by the way, who could barely tell one end of a horse from another. And yet again, that fad came, burned brightly, then faded to nothing the minute he got bored with the whole idea.

So now it's my turn, Kate thought. Discarded and cast aside because my husband is now bored of me. I might as well be Katherine of fucking Aragon. The way Damien saw it, he'd given her fifteen years of his life – the highlife – and in return she'd given him absolutely nothing. Well, only a childless marriage and whopping monthly credit card bills.

'Did you ask him about your woman? Harper what's-her-name?' Mo asked, taking another sip of her cappuccino.

'The weird thing is there's a small part of me that doesn't even blame her,' Kate sighed.

'This is the girl who broke up your marriage and you don't blame her? Kate, what's got into you? In your shoes, I think I'd have overturned tables the other night!'

'She just happened to be in the right place at the right time; like I was myself all those years ago. It's Damien I'm really angry with. That he brought it right to the door of my own home, for everyone to see. That's how little he cares, Mo. He could humiliate me in public like that and still not give a shit.'

'And you're absolutely certain that it's serious between them?'

Kate nodded, 'One hundred per cent.'

'Because, Kate, this is your whole future here. Don't for God's sake jeopardise it just because he's infatuated with a pretty young thing. There's so much at stake here. You don't need me to tell you.'

'Look, I'm certain, Mo, OK?'

Kate hadn't meant to snap, not when Mo was being so kind, but somehow that's the way it came out.

There was a squeal from the table directly behind her and Kate turned her head just in time to see Serena Lynch join a table of other yoga-clad yummy mummies, all full of excited chatter to see each other again, even though they'd probably only met at the school gates not half an hour ago.

Serena Lynch, everyone knew, had been through exactly the same thing not so long ago. Apparently her husband, who Kate knew very slightly, had treated her to a fortieth birthday present of a trip on the Orient Express. Where he told her that not only was their marriage over, but that he was leaving her for a twenty-nine-year-old stand-up comedian by the name of Simon. Apparently his reason for the extravagant trip was so he could 'break the news to her in style'.

And of course not forgetting the apocryphal tale of Claire Toomey, another of the Globtech wives who herself had once been a high flying Director of Operations at their Middle East division, but who packed it all in as soon as her third child came along a few years back. Claire, who quite openly went around warning anyone who'd listen that she knew instinctively that there was something going on when 'my husband just started being too nice to me'. Apparently the clincher had been the day he picked up his socks from the back of the radiator, then volunteered to go and collect the kids from football practice. So she managed to hack into his email account – the idiot had used the family dog's name as a password – and there was the proof of his affair for her to see, in glorious Technicolor.

'Nude selfies, the whole works,' she'd said.

Over the years Kate must have heard a dozen stories, all with real human pain and heartache behind each and every one.

And now it's my go. My turn to be the one to keep the rumour mill in overdrive. My turn for all the pity and the pain.

She liked to think that just about every woman in her circle who'd been through the same thing would support her, reassure her, maybe even give her a shoulder to cry on. It just didn't lessen the unimaginable, searing sting of it, that was all.

'Come on, Kate,' Mo said, cutting across her thoughts. 'Talk to me.'

Kate took a sip of the coffee in front of her, which seemed to help. Not as much as a stiff G&T, or better yet, one of her Lexotan pills, but she could always have one the minute she got home, without Mo or anyone else around to judge her.

Come to think of it, with Damien now officially moved out, who was to stop her from drinking herself into a stupor all day? In fact, that was probably the most comforting, reassuring thought she'd had all morning. So, spurred on by that she began to open up a bit.

'You know he's strayed before,' she said, and Mo nodded. 'More than once. But never, ever anything like this.'

'You know that for certain?'

Kate nodded. 'Thing about Damien is that he likes to think he's unreadable,' she said in a meek little voice so unlike her own. 'It's something he prides himself on in business. None of which is helped by the fact that he is and always was an excellent liar.'

'So I've noticed,' said Mo wryly, but then her husband Joe was the CFO of Globtech, so if anyone knew his modus operandi inside out, it was Mo.

'Plus he's had every opportunity to play away from home. Not when we were first married, of course, but over the last few years it got so I could almost sense it, to the extent that the sheer worry alone was nearly pushing me over the edge. And whenever I'd confront him on it, there'd always be a perfectly plausible excuse, usually work-related.'

'Well he does travel an awful lot,' said Mo, which was true. For the past few years Damien seemed to spend as much time out of the country as he did at home, to the extent where his accountant had almost persuaded him to

279

declare himself a tax exile. Globtech was one of those spidery corporations with tentacles everywhere. You name it, from Buenos Aires to Beijing, they had more world-wide operations on the go than Starbucks.

'Then just under a year ago—' Kate began to say, but broke off as a raw, visceral memory from Saturday night suddenly shot up to the surface, sharp as broken glass.

Jesus, she thought, suddenly feeling she needed to be sick, right here, right now, at the table if need be. It couldn't be true, could it? Had she actually seen what she'd seen? She certainly thought she'd noticed something on the night, but she must have been so out of her mind with booze that she'd just buried it away. But now here it was in the cold light of day, clear as crystal, waiting for her.

Her very worst nightmare come true.

'Kate?' Mo said, looking worriedly over at her. 'What's wrong? You've gone white as a sheet.'

'I think that – on Saturday – at least I thought I noticed—' but she broke off here, unsure whether she could make it all the way to the end of her sentence. Would Mo even believe it? For Christ's sake, she was having enough difficulty wrapping her head around it herself.

'You think you noticed what?'

But at that Kate bottled. Not here. Not now. Not in public. It was too humiliating, too painful. She didn't think she could even tell Mo, who was being so lovely to her and who she implicitly knew she could trust with anything. Just at the thought of what she'd witnessed, her hand began to tremble involuntarily when she reached for the coffee cup in front of her and suddenly all she wanted was a drink. Now. She needed one, she couldn't possibly get through today without one. Or two. Or ten.

She had to get out of here, to get home. To be safe and to hide away, even from well-meaning friends and acquaintances. And to drink herself into a gentle sleep till all of this just magically went away.

TESS

The present

Sunday morning and after a sleepless night during which I dreamt vividly that the wedding marquee blew away and we ended up having the entire reception at Pizza Hut in the Nutgrove shopping centre, unsurprisingly I wake up wrecked, red-eyed and with a pounding headache. I listen out for a bit but there's total silence in the house, which means Gracie, Mum and Dad are all still out for the count. I can only hope they are enjoying their Sunday morning snooze after what they all had to suffer through last night.

I know there's only one thing for it whenever I feel this shite, so I give myself a healthy dose of the same advice I give to all my clients at the gym whenever they've overdone it the night before. Mind you, generally it's far easier to dole out this advice than to actually follow it myself.

I haul myself out of bed and somehow manage to root out leggings and a fleece from the back of my wardrobe. I even manage to lace myself into a pair of trainers, stumble my bleary-eyed way out the door and into the car. Because in the fragile state I'm in after last night, deep down I know that there's only one thing that'll sort me out properly.

Last night. Jagged memories of Bernard and his family and that awful club of his keep coming to me in shards. But I shove them to the back of my mind, knowing that a good endorphin rush is by far my best hope of dealing with everything later on. Much later on, preferably when I'm dosed up with coffee and am able to think straight.

Till then though, there's only one place where I'll be able to run in peace and park all thought of what happened. In fact just about the only place where I can clear my head without Mum, Dad or, God forbid, Gracie chipping in their two cents worth.

From our house it's just a ten-minute drive to Dun Laoghaire pier and given that it's still only eight in the morning, I know there's not a chance of my meeting another soul here. Which couldn't be better. I park right by the end of the pier, clamp my iPod on, lace my trainers up tighter and get moving.

Apart from the odd early-morning dog walker, I've got the whole pier to myself and already the crisp fresh air and the sight of the morning sun dappling on the water's edge is starting to work its magic. I hit the shuffle button on the iPod and start to run, slowly at first but gradually building up a gentle – a very gentle – momentum.

'Uptown Funk' by Mark Ronson comes on first, then a bit of Foo Fighters, and by the time my playlist hits 'Happy' by Pharrell Williams the fug from last night is finally starting to lift a bit. But then it's just impossible to wallow on a morning like this, when I'm surrounded by water, in peace and solitude and with the fresh sea breeze full in my face.

I'm just getting into my stride when in the distance I notice another runner coming towards me, head to toe in black Lycra with a black baseball hat pulled down low over her face. It's only as the figure gets closer that I see it's a woman, tall and stick-thin, with blonde hair tied back into a ponytail. She slows her pace down to a walk, panting for breath as if she's at the end of a long run.

Without really looking at her I nod a quick good morning; jogger code for 'aren't we the hardy souls out at this hour, when normal people are settling down to the Sunday supplements and a fry-up'.

But next thing, she stops right in front of me. I wonder if she's in trouble, has maybe lost her car keys or something, so I switch the iPod off and turn to face her. And that's when I realise that I actually know this woman. That most of the country knows her, in fact.

Because it's Kate King.

'I recognise you,' she says, speaking softly. 'You're . . . you're who I think you are, aren't you?'

I nod back, utterly shocked. *Jesus, what are the odds?* Only in an overgrown village like Dublin could something like this happen. I stand rooted to the spot, unable to think of a single thing to say back to her.

'Thought so,' she says, taking my silence as a tacit yes. 'I've spent the last week looking across a courtroom at you.'

'We shouldn't speak to each other,' I eventually find voice enough to say, the thought of what Moany Mona would do if she found out at the forefront of my mind. We were all given a stern lecture by her the other day about 'jury contamination' and warned that something like this – even a chance encounter that's pure coincidence – could result in the case being thrown out of court and a new jury having to be sworn in. Whereupon the whole palaver has to start all over again, right from scratch.

'I need to go,' I say. 'Now. In case we're spotted.'

284

'I understand,' says Kate quietly. 'And I promise I won't tell if you don't.'

'No fear of that. Doubt anyone would believe me anyway.'

'I come here every Sunday for a run and I never thought I'd meet anyone. I thought it would be private,' she says, almost like she's talking to herself.

'Me too.'

We look at each other for a moment, or rather Kate looks down at me she's so tall. And I swear I can almost see the thought written across her ghostly white face.

My good name, my reputation and my whole future lie in this girl's hands.

'I'd better get going,' I say, and she nods in understanding. 'So I suppose . . . all I can do is wish you good luck.'

'And thank you for your discretion,' she says, humbly and sincerely, a million miles from the Kate King that the media portray. 'I am grateful to you, honestly.'

I'm just about to plug into my music again and get back into my stride when she stops me.

'I'm sorry and I know I shouldn't . . .' she says simply, 'but I can't not say this before you go.'

'Say what?'

'That it's not what you think, you know. Absolutely none of this is what you think.'

*

On my way back home I stop off to buy a stack load of the Sunday papers, which as you'd expect are full of the King case and very little else. I'm flicking through them at our kitchen table trying to find something to read that's nothing to do with the case when Gracie half-staggers in,

285

hair like a bird's nest and with the dregs of last night's mascara smeared under her eyes.

'Coffee's just made,' I tell her. A grunt is the only answer I get back though.

'Good night?' I ask chirpily, feeling brighter after my run.

'Better than yours anyway,' she says, helping herself to a mug of strong coffee. 'Christ, I need this. So, any word from the boring fart himself?'

Shit. I never even checked my phone to see if Bernard was in touch. I scramble out of the chair and go to the kitchen counter where I'd left it charging last night. Says a lot that all Gracie has to do is refer to 'the boring fart' and I instantly know who she's talking about.

'Nothing,' I say, totally surprised as I check the phone. 'No missed calls, no texts, not a single thing.'

'Then it's just as well you don't seem all that bothered.'

A pause while she sticks toast into the toaster.

'By the way, who was that bloke you introduced me to in the bar last night?'

'Oh, you mean Will.'

'Yeah, him. How do you know him?'

'Well, ehh, he's sort of working on the King case too.'

'You mean, like a juror?'

'Well . . . yeah. Why do you ask anyway?'

'Oh, nothing. There's just something really familiar about him, that's all. It was driving me nuts all night trying to think where I knew his face from.'

KATE

Castletown House, June 2014

'Katherine?'

'Damien?'

Kate's heart instantly twisted in her ribcage. But then this was the first informal contact she'd had from him ever since their three-minute conversation the morning after that bloody party when he'd told her he was leaving. Then he'd left Castletown House so fast, you could barely see him for dust. His mind was made up and that, as far as he was concerned, was that.

'Are you driving?' Damien asked briskly.

'Erm, yes, actually,' Kate stammered.

'Then pull the car over.'

Jesus, she thought, her heart racing as her stomach shrivelled. What the hell could this be about? She'd already been inundated with letters from solicitors over the past few weeks but as far as she was concerned, they may as well all have been written in Sanskrit.

But then that's how Damien liked to do things; once you were axed, he barely even bothered giving you the time of day. He was exactly the same in business, was famous for it. Damien even had a habit of changing his mobile phone number once every six months to guard against ex-employees (or, far more likely ex-girlfriends) who'd dare bother him.

So it had been naïve of Kate to assume she'd be treated any differently. To date, any and all communication between them had been via all those formal, official-looking letters which she'd been strongly advised to pass on to her own solicitor, but so far had done absolutely nothing about.

These past few weeks, a good day for Kate was one where she actually managed to drag herself out of bed and as far as the shower. The only reason she was even behind the wheel of her car right now was because she needed to get to the local off licence to stock up. Pointless asking Elena the housekeeper or any of the few staff left at the house to go for her, mainly because all she'd get were more raised eyebrows and frankly she'd had enough of that lately.

Already she'd taken to hiding empty bottles around her bedroom, with the intention of getting rid of them later on, when Elena was out and not around to judge her. And already she'd been caught out. Mortifyingly too. Elena had been hoovering her walk-in wardrobe when she accidently knocked over a pair of riding boots and discovered two bottles of Hendrick's gin, neatly stuffed inside either boot.

'Mrs King, this is no good for you,' Elena had sniffed in her broken English, while Kate pretended to be far too absorbed in reading a text off her phone to take in what was being said.

'Is too much alcohol. You never use to drink like this and is very, very bad for you. No good hiding away here, need to face your problem. Need to be strong. Mr King very strong man, very powerful and you must be like a

288

tiger to face him. Not like this, weak and sick and so white. Like ghost. Need to stop drinking and eat good food instead.'

She knew Elena only meant well and was speaking out of compassion, but still. The minute she was out of the room, Kate helped herself to yet another large G&T. Anything to help propel her through yet another hour. Because that was how she was living these days; from minute to minute, hour to hour, day and night almost blending into one.

'My legal team are anxious to set up a meeting with you at your earliest possible convenience,' Damien said, pulling her back to the phone call. 'They've been trying to reach you for quite some time but it seems all of their communication is ignored.'

'Is that so,' Kate answered flatly, thinking, well, that's what all this is about then. Legals. Separations. All of the things that she'd so successfully been hiding away from for the past few weeks. As if by keeping her head in the sand for long enough, it might all just go away of its own accord.

'So it might be an idea to reply to them one of these fine days?' Damien added curtly, but Kate said nothing. Just stared out the car window onto the vast rolling parkland that bordered Castletown House.

How much longer have I got here, she wondered. This home that I've loved so much and put so much of myself into . . . how long before they arrive with a removals van to turf me out? After that, it's only a matter of time before he moves into my home with . . . she broke off here though. She still found it hard to articulate the name without her stomach clenching so tight it almost made her nauseous.

'But as you can imagine, that wasn't my primary reason

289

for calling you,' Damien went on. And this time, Kate switched off the engine, instinct telling her there was worse – a lot worse – to come.

A drink. Suddenly she needed a drink so badly that she broke into a cold, clammy sweat. And who cared that it was only eleven in the morning? Disapproving looks from Elena aside, who was even going to notice?

'What now?' she managed to ask in a tiny, quivery voice.

'There's something else you should know before you read about it in the papers or online,' he said, but this time sounding a million miles from the confident, self-assured Damien she knew so well. Kate automatically clenched the palms of her hands to the steering wheel, suddenly remembering what it was she'd noticed the night of her birthday and now dreading that the worst was still to come.

'And that is . . . ?'

'It's Harper,' he eventually said. And in a flash of clarity that cut through her muggy, hungover haze, Kate knew exactly what this call was all about.

Suddenly she had to focus very hard on breathing.

'The thing is, Harper and I are expecting a baby,' Damien went on.

I knew it, Kate thought, frozen in shock with the phone clamped to her hand. I bloody well knew it. The pointed way that Harper refused all alcohol at the party, and waved away the blue cheese canapés. Even the catering staff had commented on it. Kate had somehow absorbed it all and, remembering back to her own early days of pregnancy, suddenly put two and two together.

'So you see the sooner you and I can tie up all our loose ends,' Damien went on in a voice cool as metal, 'the sooner she and I can make it official.'

290

'Make what official?' Kate asked numbly, feeling a bit like someone who'd just severed a limb; not in pain yet, but in the full expectation of it to come.

'Well, our engagement, of course. Like I told you, she and I are together now. And we plan on staying together. I'm finally going to be a father, Kate. I thought you'd be happy for me. And I just thought it more respectful to tell you in person. Before you see it in the press.'

*

For the rest of that whole day, Kate didn't drink one single drop. Just stopped, cold turkey. She didn't even bother going to the off licence, instead she turned her Jeep around and headed straight back to the house. And she sent out for reinforcements, phoning Mo and begging her to call around, saying she needed to see her urgently.

Later on that evening the pair of them were holed up in the library at Castletown, mounds of legal letters and papers piled in front of them, accumulated over the past few weeks and up until then, totally ignored.

'Jesus,' said Mo, shaking her head as she scanned down through yet another letter from the McNally Ross legal firm. 'This is unthinkable. According to this beaut here, once you're divorced you're entitled to a monthly payout alright, but it really is a pittance. What they're offering would barely keep you with enough left over to get your hair done.'

Kate looked up from the letters she'd been scanning through. 'And this one here,' she said, tapping her biro off it, 'claims that under the terms of the pre-nup I signed, I'm not entitled to any shares from Globtech either.'

'This one's even better! According to this, you don't even

get to keep Castletown House. This beautiful house, that you've put your heart and soul into restoring? Apparently it all belongs to the King family trust and it reverts right back to them. Christ Almighty, babe, this shower could come and turf you out before the ink is even wet on your divorce papers.'

'Apparently I'm being offered an apartment in Grand Canal Quay in town,' Kate said, her eyes quickly darting up and down the page in front of her. 'It belongs to Globtech but it says here Damien is willing to sign it over to me. Providing I accept this offer now and don't challenge it through the courts.'

The thought that she was expected to just walk out the door of her own home to make room for Damien and Harper Jones made Kate long for a drink, so badly, she started trembling.

This is just a craving. And it will pass.

She was very proud of herself for resisting and making do with a sip of coffee instead.

'I don't believe it, wait till you hear this!' said Mo, reading from another document in front of her. 'If you'd had one child during the marriage, you'd be entitled to ten grand a month, and it goes up in increments the bigger your family. You'd even get more of a payout for a boy than a girl, if you can believe that. Bloody hell, Kate, who do the Kings think they are anyway? The Tudors in sixteenth-century England?'

'Not too far off.'

'What possessed you to sign that bloody pre-nup in the first place? Because unless your lawyers can come up with some master-stroke, under this thing you're entitled to nothing!'

Kate sighed, shoving the letter she'd been trying to make head or tail of away from her and rubbing her tired eyes.

'Oh God, Mo, it's the old story. I was in love. I was young and I was very stupid. You know how it is when you're in love in your twenties. You think it's going to last for ever and that other couples might break up but that it'll never, ever happen to you.'

'Well you're certainly in for a short, sharp shock with the money they're offering you.'

'I don't care about the money, Mo,' she said firmly. 'It's all anyone thinks I care about and it's actually the last thing I'm interested in. After all, I supported myself for years before I met Damien and I'll do it again if it comes to it.'

'Do you mean you'd have to go back to modelling?'

At that Kate almost snorted.

'That's a laugh, I'm almost forty years of age! In modelling terms, that's practically prehistoric. I'd be doing well to be offered catalogue work. I'd go from being the face of Chanel to the face of Stannah Stairlifts.'

'Oh, come off it, love, you're still gorgeous and you know it.'

'But there's lots I could do to start earning again. I could maybe go and work for a charity, if they'd only have me—'

'Well there are two things that you've got to do right now,' Mo interrupted 'As a matter of urgency.'

'What's that?'

'Number one, we hire you the toughest lawyer going. Believe me, you're going to need a Rottweiler to take on the might of the King dynasty.'

'And the second thing?'

'No harm to sandbag yourself with a bit of insurance just in case this pre-nup does actually hold up in court.'

'What do you mean?'

'Kate, you say money means nothing to you, but that's because right now, you have access to it. You've still got credit cards and a joint bank account. Trust me though, you'll sing a very different tune in a few years' time if Damien has his way. Which he inevitably will.'

'So what are you suggesting?' Kate asked, genuinely puzzled.

'Well you're here,' said Mo, gesturing around her, 'and, for the moment at least, you've got Castletown House all to yourself. So there's only one thing you can do really.'

'Which is?

She looked across the table at Kate with a dangerous glint in her eye.

'Stockpile.'

TESS

The present

Monday morning and the first people I bump into in the jury room are Jane and Edith, both chatting excitedly about the day ahead.

'So difficult not to read anything about the case in the papers over the weekend, wasn't it?' says Edith. 'It seems we really are the talk of the town!'

'Apparently today we'll be hearing from the Defence,' Jane says authoritatively. 'I was in a queue at the court cafeteria and I overheard one of Hilda Cassidy's junior counsels say so.'

'Ooh I hope not!' says Edith. 'Because that means it'll all be over soon and this is such fun, I really don't want it to end.'

'Come to think of it,' says an exhausted-looking Jess as she comes in, peeling a big, warm fleece jacket off her and helping herself to a watery-looking coffee, 'I'll be sorry when this finishes up too. You've no idea how much I'm enjoying getting a break from the kids and having adult company for seven hours a day.'

'Are all jurors present and correct?' says Moany Mona

295

at exactly one minute to 10 a.m., like we're kids in a play-ground being called into class. 'Mobiles switched off? Ready to go?'

I glance around to see Will just coming in, looking out of breath as if he ran up all the stairs to get here in time.

Mona clicks her tongue impatiently at the sight of him barely shaving our call time, but says nothing. I catch his eye and he does a quick mime of wiping heavy sweat off his forehead. Next thing, we're ushered into court number seven to start the day.

∗

The Defence opens and I for one am beside myself to see what Kate King's team have come up with to try to resuscitate her flailing case. First witness of the day turns out to be a Law Lecturer at UCD called Professor Douglas Proudfoot who's quizzed frontways and sideways about the pre-nup that was signed before the Kings got married, all those years ago.

'May I draw your attention to paragraph seven, clause six, Professor?' asks Hilda Cassidy, taking care to hand around copies of the pre-nup to each and every one of us up here in the jury box, which of course leads to much fumbling and rooting around handbags for reading glasses, etc.

'Sorry to hold you up, love,' says Minnie to Hilda, getting flustered now because she can't find her bag. 'But I'm afraid I can't see a single thing without my specs.'

I'm sitting right beside her and am aware of a few titters from around the court as I scramble around on the floor beneath her looking for it, then finally produce a giant Lidl bag stuffed full of fresh fruit and yogurt.

296

'Oh yes, Tess, have a look in there for me, there's a good girl,' says Minnie. 'I stopped off on my way here this morning to get a few groceries and I know I definitely had my glasses with me when I was in the supermarket.'

'Whenever you're ready,' says Judge Simmonds, with just a touch of impatience creeping into her voice, while I'm rummaging through Minnie's shopping and accidentally send an apple, two plums, a tin of cat food and a copy of *TV Guide* magazine rolling across the floor of the jury box.

Beth and I dive to pick everything up for her, as the titters from the public benches now turn into full-on giggles. Totally unperturbed, Minnie goes on to explain, 'Sorry about this, everyone. But the food in the hotel we're taken to for lunch is dire, Your Honour. Complete stodge and nothing else. So I figure, either bring in your own grub or else starve.'

'I'll definitely second that!' says Barney defiantly.

'Me and all!' Ruth half-shouts. 'Can something be done about it, Your Honour? You must have a bit of sway around here, couldn't you sort this out for us?'

'I really must request silence from the jury box—' Judge Simmonds starts to say, but Minnie cuts across her.

'Don't worry, I brought along a few bits and pieces of healthy fresh fruit for us all instead, just to keep us going. Anyone fancy a nice yogurt for lunch today? I even got the fancy low fat stuff, the one that's supposed to lower your cholesterol.'

'Ahh here. Are we not a bit long in the tooth to be dealing with cholesterol-reducing yogurt?' says Barney suspiciously.

'How about a nice red apple, then? Or would it hurt your teeth?' Minnie asks him worriedly.

'Please! I will have order in this court and that includes

from members of the jury!' says Judge Simmonds. It's the first time we've actually seen her lose her cool to date and I have to say, it's very impressive.

Meanwhile I manage to find Minnie's glasses and she gets an amused round of applause from the press box when she finally puts them on. Hilda gives her an exasperated eye roll and I have to nudge Minnie gently in the ribs to stop her talking before we're yanked out of here.

'If the side show has quite finished,' says the judge, 'then we'll resume.'

'As I was saying,' says Hilda, 'I'd really like to draw your attention to paragraph seven, clause six in the pre-nuptial agreement, which was signed by my client and which came into effect on July 29th, 2001. Would you care to read it aloud to the court, please?' she asks the learned professor, who's been standing patiently in the box all this time, like the rest of us looking slightly bemused by Minnie and her antics.

'Certainly,' he says, before rambling off a whole sequence of legal jargon, not a word of which I can fully grasp and judging by the bewildered looks from the jury box around me, nor does anyone else. And it's not a short, quick summation either. It goes on for a full two hours, with Oliver Daniels up on his feet and objecting just about every chance he gets. I'm trying my best to concentrate, but it's hard not to let my thoughts wander, and Beth beside me is heavy-lidded and looking bored out of her mind.

Only Will looks interested, I notice. He's sitting directly behind me in the back row, arms folded, leaning forward and drinking in every word the professor is saying.

'Thank you so much for enlightening us,' says Hilda, 'now could you possibly summarise everything you've said in layman's terms? For the benefit of those without legal degrees, you understand.'

'Of course,' says the Professor. 'Essentially this legally binding agreement means that Katherine King willingly and without duress agreed that should her marriage come to an end, she'd effectively walk away from it with precisely what she had walking into it.'

'And are there any possible exceptions to this edict?'

'With the possible exception of items gifted to her by her husband during the course of their marriage. As outlined in paragraph twenty-eight on page nine, subsection five.'

'Would you care to give us some examples of what these items might constitute?'

The professor takes off his glasses, wipes them in a tissue he produces from his pocket and thinks about this for a bit.

'With a contract like this, jewellery for instance would be one. Generally speaking, personal items of clothing too. Expensive handbags and furs. That sort of thing.'

'Now I'd like you to look at this document very closely, Professor,' says Hilda, 'if you'd be so kind. And tell me, would this in your opinion include birthday gifts?'

A tense pause while the professor scans through the document, then puts his glasses back on, decision made.

'Well?' says Hilda.

'Yes would be my answer. Birthday gifts do appear to be included.'

'No further questions, Your Honour.'

Lunch is called and I'm last out of the jury box because I'm wedged right up at the very edge. So I stay sitting while the court clears and give a bit of time to the more elderly jurors so they can shuffle out of here. I glance over to the other side of the court where Kate King is deep in conversation with Hilda. And for the first time since this whole court case started, I could swear I see her smiling.

*

Will falls into step with me as we're ushered, or rather cattle-prodded by Mona, onto the coach at lunch recess.

'Strange coincidence bumping into you like that on Saturday night,' he mutters so Mona won't overhear him, then come and haul the pair of us away in handcuffs for fraternizing outside of court. Which I wouldn't for a minute put past her, by the way.

'You too,' I answer automatically, clambering up the steps of the bus.

'Hope you got everything sorted? With your whole . . . you know, situation?' he adds tactfully.

I pull into a window seat and he takes the one beside me.

'Sorted? Don't make me laugh,' I groan, resting my head on the seat back and staring blankly out the window. 'Things are so far from sorted, I can't tell you.'

'You mean you and your fiancé didn't kiss and make up yesterday? I was sure you'd skip in here this morning, full of the joys.'

'Then I'm sorry to disappoint you.'

'Well you know what they say,' he says, looking at me closely now. 'If you're having man trouble, no one better than another man to talk to about it.'

'Ooh, what's all this then?' Edith butts in from the seat opposite us – Edith, in sharp contrast to poor old half-deaf Ruth, could probably hear the grass grow in her sleep – 'Did I hear something about man trouble?'

'It's nothing, nothing at all,' I tell her. 'Just a bit of a problem I had over the weekend, that's all.'

'Ooh, then you have to fill me in, love! I'm not half-bad at that sort of thing, for an aul' one. Or so my grand-daughters tell me. I've six of them, you know, and you remind me of them so much, Tess. They're all lovely young girls, who waste precious time on complete eejits that they meet online. Wherever that is,' she adds with an un-impressed sniff. 'Online. Some fancy nightclub in town, I suppose.'

'Online means on a computer, you eejit,' says Daphne who's tucked into the window seat beside Edith, earwigging along.

'How can you meet someone on a computer?' Mai asks innocently from the row in front of us.

'You sign up for all these dating websites,' Beth chips in helpfully. 'And you just type in your profile and what you're looking for, and the computer finds a match for you.'

'And are you on one of these thingy sites, Beth, love?' Mai asks.

'Yeah, it's called Tinder. Basically you're matched up with guys in your area and if you like their photo, you swipe to the right. If not, you swipe left. Then if someone whose photo you liked likes you back, then you've a match. Everyone I know is on it.'

'I was even on it myself for a while,' Ian lobs in from the far window seat. 'Until my wife found out, that is.' He snorts laughing at this, while the rest of us just look at him.

'Well in my day,' says Mai, shaking her head, 'you never had to swipe anything to find a fella for yourself.'

'There's even one for the over-sixties too, I heard,' Jess chips in from behind us. 'My parents are separated and

Mum met a lovely man through that site. We're all mad about him.'

'Please, dear God, don't let them start talking about catfishing,' Will mutters to me. 'I don't think I'm up to explaining that one to the Granny Brigade.'

'But sure where's the romance in that?' insists Edith. 'You might as well be out shopping for your vegetables.'

'So tell us what happened between you and your fella at the weekend, Tess,' says Mai, getting back to that again. 'Did you have a row?' she adds hopefully, like she's dying for me to say that yes actually we did and now the whole wedding is off.

'You know, ladies, I don't mean to be rude,' says Will tactfully, 'but maybe it's something Tess doesn't really want to get into here and now.'

'Ahh, go on, Tess,' says Daphne, leaning in from her window seat so she can really eyeball me properly. 'I was bored out of my mind in court this morning, be nice to have a good juicy relationship dilemma to talk about over lunch. Certainly make a change from us all whinging about the food.'

'Is he cheating on you?' Edith asks me sternly. 'Because if he is, you take my advice and show him the door immediately. Now, love, before it's too late.'

'Do you know, I've a lovely grandson who you'd be perfect for,' says Mai. 'He has a great job and everything. Doing very well for himself.'

'Where's he working?' says Barney, who's sitting right beside her.

'Woodie's DIY. A gorgeous fella and very handy if you ever want a few shelves knocked up. Does my garden for me every week without me having to nag him into it. You could do a whole lot worse for yourself, Tess. You mark my words.'

I give Will a glance as much as to say, now look what we've started.

'Ladies, you know, maybe we should talk about something else?' he says, but no, not a single one of the old biddy brigade is prepared to drop it. Even Jess has joined in now.

'So what did your fella do to you anyway?' she asks, point blank ignoring Will and refusing to drop this. 'Is he having cold feet about the wedding?'

By now I'm aware that all eyes on the bus have swivelled around to me and I'm starting to feel a hot flush creeping up my cheeks.

'Well, it was just . . .' I begin, half wanting to get it off my chest and half not wanting to have to share my private life with a coach load of pensioners who look like they're out on a day trip, and the rest of the jury, who I barely even know.

'Yes, pet?' says Daphne expectantly.

'You can tell us.'

'You can trust us . . . sure we won't say a word!'

'OK then,' I sigh, knowing that there's not a chance the biddies will drop this till they get what they want. And also, given that it's now Monday lunchtime and I still haven't had a peep out of Bernard – the longest we've ever gone without speaking – truth be told, I could actually do with some impartial advice here.

'Well, in a nutshell, Bernard wasn't very nice to my family the other night,' I tell them, as their beady eyes continue to give me their full attention. Even Will seems to be listening closely too, I notice.

'That's his name then? Bernard?' Minnie sniffs. 'Never liked that name. Reminds me too much of Dunnes Stores.'

'Yes, that's his name,' I say. 'And he was unbelievably rude to my mother too. He said things that really upset her and the worst part is he doesn't even seem to realise how hurtful he was being.'

Shocked silence from the Greek chorus around me, while they all digest what I've said.

'Well now, I have to say, I'm not liking the sound of this one bit,' Jess says darkly after a very long pause. 'If a man doesn't get on with your mum, it's a recipe for disaster. You just mark my words. The day I knew my husband was the one for me was the day he changed the spark plugs in my mother's car without her even having to ask. She told me he was the nicest fella I'd ever brought home. And that's when I knew.'

'Couldn't agree with you more,' Daphne chips in, 'my youngest daughter married a fella that I never had any time for. I tried to warn her before the wedding, but you know how it is with young girls in love. You might as well be talking to a toilet seat. And lo and behold they separated last year and now he's giving her a desperate time over access rights to the kids.'

'Shocking carry on,' says Barney, shaking his head sympathetically.

'I tried to tell her before the wedding, you know. I said, "no good will come of this. You marry a fella who's still living in a student bedsit at the age of thirty-five and you're only asking for trouble". But would she listen? No.'

'If he doesn't get on with your family now,' says Edith sagely, 'can you imagine what it's going to be like *after* you're married? Mother always knows best.'

'You're right, Edith love,' Daphne adds, 'if they left picking a husband up to all the mammies in the world, there'd be no need for divorce, now would there?'

'Bring back arranged marriages, that's what I say,' says Jess. 'I think I'll insist on it myself when my kids are all old enough to get married.'

I throw a panicky look to Will which he correctly interprets as time for a change of subject now that they're all on a roll.

'So you said you'd brought a few bits of fruit and yogurt for everyone, Minnie?' says Will cheerfully. 'Fantastic idea. How about I bring in a picnic lunch for us all tomorrow?'

'Oh yes, I'd completely forgotten about that,' says Daphne delightedly. 'Very kind of you, Minnie. I don't suppose you brought along any Fig Rolls for us? Nothing like a nice Fig Roll. Lovely and soft on my teeth.'

*

The afternoon court session starts bang on time and now it's over to Oliver to question Professor Proudfoot on the ins and outs of the King family trust, which the Prosecution insist are the rightful owners of the painting. For two hours. That's two full hours, non-stop, and to be perfectly honest I'm still none the wiser after. Oliver's questions are meandering and full of legal technicalities, and the professor's answers might as well be in Greek, for all the sense they make to a layperson.

I glance behind me and just catch Will's eye. He gives a tiny shoulder shrug as much as to say, no, me neither. And as the afternoon air in court is stale and stuffy, it's a right job keeping Edith beside me from dropping off. I'm having to check on her every few minutes just to make sure her eyes are still open. In fact, I half feel like dosing her lunch-time cuppa with Berocca from now on, just to keep her wide-awake and fully alert.

As soon as Oliver is finished waffling on, Hilda Cassidy is straight up on her feet to call another witness.

'The Defence now calls Mrs Mo Kennedy,' she announces, as we all look to see who's coming in.

This time a forty-something woman steps into the witness box, looking tanned and relaxed, and dressed in a vivid turquoise suit that only someone with her dark eyes and exotic colouring could possibly get away with, I find myself thinking. There's a vibrancy about this woman and a fresh energy zings through the whole court as she says the oath and takes the stand.

'Mrs Kennedy,' says Hilda, already up on her feet and addressing her directly. 'How long have you known my client, Mrs King?'

'Ooh, Mrs King and I go back about eleven years or so,' Mo says, sounding strong and confident. Sure of herself, in stark contrast to a lot of other witnesses we've collectively yawned our way through.

'My husband works with Damien,' Mo adds, 'so Kate and I first became friendly not long before she was married.'

'Would you describe your relationship as close?'

'Very close. Kate's even Godmother to my sons. I would go so far as to describe her as my best friend.'

I just about detect Kate opposite giving Mo the tiniest little half-smile, but like the rest of us I'm still at a total loss to know why her pal has been called in to testify.

'And you were present in Castletown House on the night in April 2014 that Damien King hosted a party to unveil *A Lady of Letters*?'

'Yes, I was there with my husband. It would be normal for us to attend all of Damien and Kate's parties.'

'Can you describe to us in detail the reason why this particular party was thrown in the first place?'

'I can think of three reasons actually,' says Mo, making direct eye contact with each of us in the jury box and looking utterly unfazed by her surroundings. A likeable woman, I find myself thinking. She's grounded and seems loyal. The sort of person that if you were Kate King and you moved in those terrifyingly exalted circles, you'd probably want in your corner.

'In your opinion, Mrs Kennedy,' Hilda calmly goes on, 'what exactly were these reasons? Will you elaborate for the court?'

'Well given that Damien had just shelled out an absolute fortune for *A Lady of Letters*, naturally he wanted to show it off to all and sundry,' says Mo, to a few suppressed mutters from the public benches at the back. 'I don't think Damien has much of an eye for art, but he certainly enjoys flashing the cash under everyone's noses. He went through a similar obsession with racehorses not so long ago and was forever hosting parties in corporate boxes at just about every major race meeting going. Not that any of us know much about thoroughbreds,' she adds, 'but we certainly enjoyed the free day out.'

A few more titters at that, including Minnie and Edith beside me in the jury box. Once again Judge Simmonds has to call the court to order.

'Any other reasons for this party that you'd care to tell us about?' says Hilda lightly.

'Well, yes actually,' says Mo, standing up tall and proud.

'Go on, please, Mrs Kennedy.'

Instinctively my eye swivels over to Kate King where she's sitting composed and serene right opposite us. And it's just a flicker, but I could swear that there's a complicit glance exchanged between the two women.

'Well you see by then, Damien had embarked on an affair with a visiting art historian who was over from the US,' says Mo, loudly and clearly, to an instant flurry of murmurs around the court. 'Of course it's out there in the public domain now, but at the time, this was news to all of us. Her name is Harper Jones and apparently she wanted to curate an exhibition that would reside in the States. Up until then, there had only been rumours, nothing more. But as it transpired,' Mo goes on, getting more and more indignant by the second, 'Damien had actually invited her to Castletown that night. Under Kate's – I mean, under his wife's own roof, can you believe that?'

Oliver huffs and puffs at this and immediately rises to his feet to object and make a fuss. He's overruled though and Hilda asks her to continue.

'So in my opinion,' Mo goes on calmly, 'a secondary reason why Damien forked out so much for that ugly looking painting was purely with a view to impressing her. And it worked beautifully, didn't it? They've been together ever since, haven't they? And proud parents to a beautiful baby boy to boot. Little Damien Junior.'

A ripple of whispers around the court as Oliver rises to his feet, puffing and red-faced. 'I must strenuously object to that last comment, Your Honour, and request that it be struck from the record. After all, may I remind you that we're not here to preside over divorce proceedings. The state of my client's marriage hardly seems relevant.'

'I would argue that it's supremely relevant, Your

308

Honour,' says Hilda firmly, squaring up to him, immediately putting me in mind of two bears in a pit battling it out.

'I'll allow it,' says Judge Simmonds after deliberating for a moment, 'but you'd better pick your questions more carefully,' she warns Hilda, who nods her thanks and gets back to the witness box.

'And what of the primary reason for Mr King's throwing this party?' Hilda asks Mo. 'Can you tell us about that?'

'I'd be delighted to,' says Mo, with a defiant glance across the floor at Damien King. 'Because it had been Kate's birthday just a few days beforehand, and Damien – I mean Mr King – had just gifted the Rembrandt to Kate, so this party was both to ostensibly celebrate that and to unveil the painting. This was a birthday party and the painting was her birthday present. At least, that's what Damien told everyone.'

'You're quite certain that this was a birthday gift?'

'I'm a first-hand witness to it. As is my husband. Damien came up to us on the night and told us so.'

'Can you remember his exact words?'

'Clearly,' she says, without a trace of hesitation. 'And I'm under oath, so I'm here to tell the whole truth. He showed us the painting and pointedly asked, "so what do you think of my little birthday gift to Kate?"'

'No further questions, Your Honour.'

My eye swivels towards Damien who's poker-faced now and giving not a hint of emotion away. And Kate, right opposite us, looks over at her friend and actually smiles. The first smile on record for her ever since this case started.

*

Maybe it's the suffocating heat of the courtroom and maybe it's just because it's been such a long day, but we're all exhausted by the time Mona comes to release us from the jury room for the day. It's a relief to finally get out of court and back into the fresh spring breeze. The press are all gathered on the steps outside as always, this time waiting on Mo Kennedy to appear, which she does, to a volley of cameras going off in her face. She nods, smiles, says absolutely nothing and hops into a waiting car to zoom her off.

Meanwhile the pensioner posse from the jury box are all scattering to the four winds, variously claiming that they want to be home in time to feed the cat/watch *Coronation Street*, or in Barney's case to take his grandkids off to see the new Lego movie. So it's just Will and I left at the top of the court steps.

'Well then, till tomorrow, I guess,' he says, clutching his manbag and making to leave. 'I'll stop off early to buy a picnic hamper for the old biddy brigade,' he adds. 'Yogurt, Fig Rolls, hard boiled eggs. I know the drill by now. Nothing that's hard on their teeth.'

'They should be paying you and I carers' allowance you know,' I smile back.

'Hope you don't mind my saying,' says Will, focusing over my shoulder now, 'but there's a guy over there who's staring at you.'

I turn around and sure enough, there he is, standing right behind the bank of photographers at the bottom of the steps and holding a big bunch of carnations. Bernard. Looking uncomfortable and red-faced, like he cycled all the way here so he could meet me in time.

'My fiancé,' I say to Will, instinctively making to leave. 'I better go.'

'Well, I'll see you tomorrow then.'

'No! Come and meet him,' I say, grabbing his arm and nudging him down the court steps.

'It's OK,' he says, stepping back. 'You two probably need some privacy.'

'Oh. OK then. You sure?'

'Positive.'

'Well, have a lovely evening, then.'

'And I'll see you bright and early. Oh and Tess?'

'Yes?' I say, turning back to him.

'I'll tell you one thing.'

'What's that?'

'It seems lovers' quarrels are swift to heal,' he says with a quick shrug, before pulling up his jacket collar and ambling off in the opposite direction.

KATE

The present

The ladies' loos at the Criminal Courts of Justice certainly weren't up to much, but for the moment, Kate thought, they served their purpose. By now she'd fallen into a habit of slipping in here immediately after the case had wound up each evening, partly to collect her thoughts in peace and quiet, but mainly to let the crowds outside disperse a bit before she made her way out of there. She knew by sight some of the press hacks who hung around the steps of the court and their comments to her were becoming more and more offensively personal with each passing day.

'Kate! How does it feel to have to face the man in court who threw you over for a younger woman?' was one particular beaut that was shouted at her yesterday.

Jesus! Did these people think that she wasn't human? Didn't they know how much all their barbed little stabs got to her?

'Over here, Kate!' another one had yelled at her. 'Can you comment on the fact that should you lose this case, your costs could be well in excess of one million euros?'

And then there was the one that turned her blood cold and kept her up for half the night last night.

'Kate! Comments have been made in the press that your reputation is in shreds since this court case started, do you have anything to say in your own defence? And can you tell us, how do you plan to rebuild your life when it's all over?'

How indeed? Kate stood in front of the ladies' room mirror, splashed a bit of cold water on her temples and for the first time in weeks, really had a good look at herself. At the dark circles under her eyes, at just how thin and pasty she looked. How much more of this torture could she take on a day-to-day basis anyway? And what about when it was all over? She'd either be vindicated or ruined, and right now her whole future was on a knife-edge.

Then Kate thought of the jurors, those same twelve faces that she knew by heart by now, from seeing them day in day out. And that young girl who she'd met out running yesterday. She was a pretty young thing, who was looking more and more stressed and confused by the day. There were a few other younger faces on the jury too, including a younger guy, dark-haired and broody-looking who seemed to be following every twist and turn of the case intently, but apart from that the average age of the rest of them seemed to be sixty-five plus.

Was that a good thing or a bad thing, she wondered? What conclusions were they all drawing so far? The thought almost made her weak at the knees. So to distract herself and to kill time till the press pack outside had peeled off for the evening, she fished her phone out of her bag and switched it back on again.

Five missed calls. All from the same person too. And a whole series of texts asking her to call back urgently, just as soon as she was out of court.

As soon as she saw who it was, a split second later she was redialling the number with shaky hands, as her whole body involuntarily began to tremble.

'Well?' was all she could ask in a weak little voice. 'Do you have news for me?'

*

About half an hour later, Kate figured the coast was clear and that she could leave in peace. Her tactic had worked too. As she stepped outside the court to a waiting taxi, there was just one lone photographer loitering at the bottom of the steps. He immediately trained his lens on her, scarcely able to believe his luck. Sure enough, he fired off a volley of shots right into her face as she ducked and dived to get away from him and into the safety of the waiting taxi.

'Just one question, Kate,' he asked as she clambered into the car. 'By any normal person's standards, you hardly need money this badly, now do you?'

Shocked at the directness of the question, she turned to face him.

'So why did you let this go to court, Kate? Why not just give back the painting? That's what no one can understand. What's it really all about anyway?'

*

'And you've actually spoken to him?

'Yes, just before I called you. He's been trying to reach you too, but your phone was switched off while you were in court.'

'Is he certain?'

'It seems he's as certain as it's possible to be.'

'That's all well and good, Kate, but is he prepared to go into court and tell judge and jury what you've just told me?'

'Obviously you'll need to speak to him first,' Kate said. 'But yes, is the answer. Yes, I think he just might.'

Hilda sighed and waved towards the leather chair opposite her desk for Kate to sit down. They were holed up in her office on King Street, close to the courts, probably the one place where the two women could talk with any degree of privacy these days. And this was a conversation that needed to be held in private.

'You look dreadful, Kate, this case is really taking it out of you,' said Hilda briskly, taking in her client from head to foot. 'You need to go home and try to get as much sleep as you can. Please take my advice; you're no use to anyone unless you're good and rested.'

'Plenty of time to rest when it's all over. Right now, you and I have mountains to move.'

'Can I get you a sherry?' Hilda asked, going to her drinks cabinet and pouring herself a small one.

'No, thank you,' said Kate quietly. 'I don't drink any more.'

Hilda took her drink and sat down in the armchair behind her desk.

'You know, this may not be the game-changer that you think it is,' she said, 'and that's my concern. Because I needn't tell you that we're on a knife-edge here. No sooner do I score a point, than bloody Oliver Daniels scores one right back. You heard Professor Proudfoot's testimony earlier today. The King family trust have a tight stranglehold on that painting.'

'But Mo testified that it was a gift.'

'Yes, but that can easily be discounted as hearsay. And that jury is unreadable. Things really could go either way for us. I need to be fully upfront with you about that.'

'I'm well aware of that,' nodded Kate, 'and that's why I think we've got to do this. I want the truth to come out. For better or for worse.'

Hilda sighed and leaned forward.

'Kate, you're exhausted and who could blame you? But it's my job to tell you that you're not thinking clearly.'

Kate shook her head, but Hilda wasn't finished.

'If we do play this card, then you know how it's going to read. You know how unfavourably it could play not just with judge and jury but with your whole reputation.'

Kate stayed defiant.

'It needs to come to light,' she said. 'And if I'm in any way criticised, then I'll just have to take it. God knows, I've certainly taken worse.'

'Criticised?' said Hilda. 'Kate, you'll be vilified for this and you know it.'

Kate took a moment to collect her thoughts and watched Hilda sip at the sherry from the glass in front of her. She felt numb, punch-drunk with day after day of nothing but accusations and snide comments being thrown at her from all corners of the court. And that was before she went back home to Castletown – while it was still her home – and switched on the TV to hear even more vile comments and abusive remarks about the case, mostly directed at her.

'I can't be pilloried any more than I already have been,' she said simply.

It was only the truth too. Last night in bed she'd accidentally tuned into a news panel show and of course the sole topic of conversation was the King case. She'd switched it off in disgust, but still couldn't sleep for the rest of the night. Then on the way into court this morning, her taxi driver had one of those early-morning phone-in chat shows playing in the background, with the case as the chief topic running through it.

Kate had listened in to about as much as she could stomach, correctly gauged that the balance of public opinion seemed to be squarely on Damien's side and immediately asked the driver to switch it off. Listening to a taxi driver ranting on about water charges and roadworks was infinitely preferable to hearing her good name and reputation dragged through the mud any day.

'Kate, we've talked this over already,' said Hilda, hands clasped in front of her, leaning forward across her desk. 'And you and I both know the subsequent price you may have to pay if we do call this witness. We agreed that if this could be substantiated, that we'd only use it as a last resort and nothing else. If it really looked like we were going to lose.'

'I know that,' said Kate quietly. 'And I know you're just doing your job by reminding me. But the thing is, I'm in the position of someone who's been stabbed in the back a thousand times. What possible difference can one more knife wound make?'

'And it'll hit you financially too, you do realise that?'

'Oh God, here we go with the money again,' Kate sighed.

'It's all anyone ever thinks I was after, and it's the last thing I'm interested in.'

Hilda took another sip of sherry.

'If you're sure then?' she asked.

'I'm sure.'

TESS

The present

'It was terribly thoughtless of me, sausage.'

'Don't forget insensitive.'

'And insensitive.'

'And just plain . . . dopey,' I say, grasping around for a suitable adjective.

'Well now, I wouldn't quite go that far.'

'Oh really? Because I would.'

'Tess, I have a first-class honours degree, a Master's degree, a PhD and a total number of sixteen letters after my name. I don't really think that "dopey" is an appropriate sobriquet in this instance. Now do you?'

'I thought this was supposed to be an apology?'

'And so it is. But please understand that I really want our wedding day to be a classy affair. Elegant and understated.'

'Bernard, I want all those things too, but I also want everyone to enjoy themselves and have fun. Particularly our families. Don't you? Even if they do have widely different ideas of how things should be done.'

He stops to think about this for a moment and whips off his glasses. It's never a good sign when Bernard takes off his glasses. Always means he's got something difficult to say but doesn't know how.

We're back in the sitting room at Bernard's higgledy-piggledy little cottage in Stoneybatter, which he insists on referring to as his study. I'm just lacing up my trainers gearing up for a run, while Bernard – who's supposed to be coming with me – just flops into the armchair opposite, fingers steepled and deep in thought.

'Sausage, need I remind you that your mother wanted to have an amateur musical society sing some sort of ABBA medley at our reception?' he eventually says. And 'ABBA medley' is uttered in such contemptuous tones, you'd swear Mum's pals wanted to get up and sing some Nazi war anthems from 1943. He breaks off here though, clocking the deeply unimpressed look on my face.

'And I suppose I just reacted without thinking really,' he adds. 'For which I am of course terribly sorry to have caused any offence.'

'Thank you,' I say. 'Apology accepted and let's say no more about it. Now come on, get into your tracksuit, we've a two mile run ahead of us before it gets dark.'

'Oh God, must we?' he groans, slumping even further back into the chair. 'Can't we just stay in, order a Chinese and read our books instead?'

Bernard's idea of the most perfect night on earth is a takeaway order of beef in black bean sauce, with a full tub of Haagen-Dazs to follow, and a book on the Battle of Waterloo perched on his knee.

'Come on, it's good for your soul,' I smile down at him, trying to pull him up by the hand so we can get moving.

'Besides, then you'll feel you'll really have earned your dinner later on.'

'Oh bugger it anyway,' he mutters. 'At this point I'd actually elect to listen to your mother's friends murdering ghastly ABBA songs rather than go out running.'

'Oh now come on, I thought we were past that? You've already apologised, so why are you bringing it up again?'

Then I eye him up suspiciously.

'This isn't just a tactic to make me forget about taking you running? Because I might as well warn you, it won't work.'

'But we still haven't made a final decision about what to do, have we?' he says petulantly, making no attempt whatsoever to put on runners. 'And while I'm awfully sorry to have caused offence, the fact remains that we've yet to decide whether we let the am-drammers hijack the wedding reception or not.'

'Well . . . of course they're going to sing,' I say, confused now as to where this might all be leading. 'Mum says they've been practising like mad and it would be really rude of us to call a halt to it now. You know that!'

He folds his arms stubbornly, most unlike him.

'If you really insist then. But for God's sake, for no longer than five minutes, max.'

'OK then, in the spirit of compromise, I'll tell her.'

'Although I just can't quite believe your mother really means to put our guests through this,' he grumbles. 'I mean really, Tess, an ABBA medley. In front of the Provost of City College. Do come on.'

'And so what if she does?' I say, determined to have this out once and for all. 'Bernard, you have to understand that's who my family are. We're not high-brow like the

Pritchards. We don't go to galleries and opening nights and obscure art exhibitions by artists that no one has heard of. I'm sorry, love, but that's just not the sort of people we are.'

'Oh, now I really must protest there,' he interrupts. 'The exhibition of David Teniers the Younger that you and I went to last week really was a wonderful night out. There's no possible way that anyone wouldn't enjoy it. He was a supremely gifted and often overlooked Flemish Baroque painter, who I always felt was subsequently overshadowed by Rubens.'

'You know, I think we're just veering a little bit off the point here—'

'Sausage,' he says slowly, as though the thought is only just occurring to him. 'You did enjoy coming to see the David Teniers with me, didn't you?'

I waver for a moment.

'Well, to be perfectly honest . . . I have had more fun nights out,' I say, then hastily tack on, 'not that the paintings weren't, you know, beautiful in their own way, but well sometimes it's lovely to go to a movie or a gig or something just a little bit . . . lighter.'

'You used to love coming to exhibitions with me,' he says, sounding a bit sad now. 'At least that's what you always said.'

I have to bite my lip a bit at that, when I see the hurt look on his big round face. Because it's true, back in the early days of our 'courtship', as Bernard insists on calling it, he'd drag me off to every gallery and lecture going. Still does. And even if I were bored out of my tree, I'd still smile and be enthusiastic and thank him for a lovely evening.

At the start it was because I'd just met the first genuinely kind-hearted man I'd come across in years. Back then, Bernard could have dragged me off to see six hours of some obscure art house movie in Mandarin with subtitles and I'd happily have gone along with him and said nice things about it afterwards, even if it had been a struggle to stay awake.

And now – well, it's habit more than anything else really. Habit and the fact that he's such a gentle soul, the last thing I'd ever want to do is hurt him. It would be a bit like kicking a baby hippo.

An immediate follow-on worry. This argument started out about something as trivial and insignificant as my mother's pals just wanting to let their hair down and have a laugh and a bit of a sing-song at our wedding. And now it suddenly seems to have morphed into something a whole lot bigger.

'Tess?' says Bernard looking confused and a bit lost. 'You do enjoy doing all these things with me, don't you? You and I do have lots in common? Don't tell me you've just been acting a part all this time?'

It's probably a bad sign that I have to think before answering. My phone beeps on the coffee table beside me and my eye gravitates towards it. It's the bridal showrooms in Kildare, where I'm due to have a final fitting this weekend. I waver for a minute, mind racing. Should I be totally honest with the man I'm about to marry? Or else is this the moment to keep my mouth shut and forever hold my peace?

Then something Will said about the rest of my life being way too precious to compromise comes back to me.

'We're very different people, Bernard,' I say as he looks

worriedly back at me. 'And most of the time that's fine, just so long as we agree to differ on certain things.'

On a vast number of things, I might just as easily have said, but baby steps and all that.

'Oh thank goodness, sausage,' says Bernard, looking gratefully back at me. 'For a moment there I thought you were going to tell me you were having cold feet. You looked so terribly conflicted.'

*

Hours later we're cooped up in Bernard's too-small bed, one he bought years ago when he figured he'd be single for the rest of his life, so this would just do him fine. An homage to his boarding school days, I figure. Nor did he see any reason to replace it when I came along, in spite of the fact we're crammed up against each other like two sardines.

The general plan is that I'll move in here after we're married, and I've been dropping subtle hints about upgrading the furniture and maybe giving the place a bit of a declutter, but so far it's all fallen on deaf ears. Like his parents, Bernard barely seems to notice the dust, the piles of books that are scattered all over the place and the fact that his bedroom carpet looks like it's been there since circa 1972.

In fact every time I come here I physically find it hard not to twitch to get a duster and a bit of Mr Sheen so I can give the place a proper blitz. The one time I did try to tidy up, Bernard almost had a fit and claimed that he couldn't find either his glasses or his original recording of *Death in Venice* by Benjamin Britten, featuring Gustav von Aschenbach, for two weeks afterwards.

So I gave it up as a bad job. After all, it's his home and for now I have to pick my battles, but I know that'll be an 'interesting' discussion we'll have to have, post-wedding.

Right now he's stuck into a biography of the Duke of Wellington so I snuggle up beside him, feeling drowsy and come to think of it, a bit frisky after the Chinese he insisted on ordering in earlier. I put my head on his chest and gently slide my hand under the stripy flannel pyjamas he always wears in bed. Then I playfully try to close his book and kiss him lightly instead.

'Put the book away,' I whisper suggestively, 'and let's have some fun.'

'Oh not now, sausage, I just want to finish this chapter. I'm at the Battle of Assaye in India and it's simply impossible to put down.'

I lean back against the pillow, look up at the ceiling and sigh.

BERNARD

Six weeks ago

Mornings were becoming by far the best part of Bernard Pritchard's day. Not that evenings didn't have their good points too, particularly when Tess came around and they had a perfectly enjoyable time together. And especially when he could talk her out of going for a brisk two mile run before what she'd laughably refer to as 'dinner', but which anyone with two eyes in their head could only possibly ever call a 'mound of grass'.

Kale was featuring strongly these days and Bernard had come to dread the very sight of it, appearing as it so regularly did, on his plate. Not to mention the astonishing variety of 'healthy, protein-filled treats', as Tess referred to the mountain of chia and pumpkin seeds which all his food seemed to come smothered in these days.

Tess would invariably tell Bernard that not only was it good for him, but that he was looking so much slimmer and fitter these days. To poor old Bernard though, while he gamely put up with it – after all, that was what one did when on the verge of matrimony – as far as he was concerned he might as well have been eating handfuls of revolting, starchy birdseed. It stuck in his teeth and made him run to the bathroom far more frequently than a grown man ought to.

Night after night this ghastly diet left him with nothing more than an unpleasant rumbling in his stomach, which frequently kept him awake in bed.

For weeks though, he did nothing, said nothing . . . and then hit on a plan. A perfect solution to his problems and a neat way of both keeping Tess happy and him properly nourished, fully restored back to his usual state of equanimity with the world.

At the college, he'd heard tell of a wonderful place where a lot of his students took summer jobs and where, they reliably informed him, you could get not just the best but arguably the cheapest breakfast in town. Egg muffins, sausage and egg, double sausage and egg if he was feeling particularly indulgent, pancakes quite literally swimming in syrup, hash browns and a wonderfully aromatic full-fat latte to follow. All terribly cheap and cheerful of course, but as far as Bernard was concerned, the food here tasted every bit as good as a Michelin-starred five-course dinner at Patrick Guilbaud's.

Why, he wondered for the hundredth time as he locked his bike to the gates at City College and walked the short distance to the bottom of Grafton Street, had he never stumbled on a find like this before? A few minutes later he was queuing up to place his order and to hear those wonderful words which had become such an integral part of his day by now.

'Welcome to McDonald's. How can I help you today, sir?'

*

One lovely, leisurely hour later, when he'd read *The Irish Times* from cover to cover and even got a sizable bit of the crossword done, Bernard strolled through the warm, spring sunshine back to the Art History department at the college, completely happy and at peace with the world again.

Which was more than could be said for the Art History department, where there appeared to be some sort of commotion going on.

'Bernard, you're late!' hissed his colleague Jasper Adams, Senior Professor of Seventeenth-Century Art History and a relatively recent addition to the college staff. He'd arrived at City College just about a year ago fresh from UCD, and he and Bernard had immediately bonded.

Jasper was in his early-fifties, as an astonishing amount of Bernard's friends seemed to be, and he'd recently joined the Royal Celtic Club on St Stephen's Green, where he and Bernard often retired to after work for a tipple on their way home. Home to Jasper of course referring to the house he continued to share with his mother, who he described as his 'best friend' and who he occasionally went on walking tours of the Cotswolds with.

'Where on earth have you been?' said Jasper. 'I've been looking everywhere for you. I even tried the gym,' he added, saying 'gym' in exactly the same tone of voice that he might use to say 'brothel'.

'Well my first lecture isn't till 10 a.m. this morning,' said Bernard, double-checking his watch. 'So I just stopped off for a quick spot of brekkie on the way here. Line the old tummy for the day ahead, you know. What's up?'

'There was a *woman* in here,' said Jasper, almost as though he was saying, 'there was an alien from Mars in here'.

But then the Art History department tended to be a tiny oasis at the college where the usual gender balance guidelines didn't appear to be working. The department was stuffed with visiting professors, adjunct professors, postdoctoral fellows and tutors, and in spite of much protesting from on high, every single one of them was male.

Of course no one counted the students who'd occasionally breeze in and out, as and when it suited them. Art History was considered to be a relatively dossy subject, so it tended to be a popular choice with students who were far more interested in hanging out at the Uni Bar rather than applying themselves to the study of Velázquez and Goya.

'Goodness,' says Bernard, 'who was she?'

'Well that's just the most annoying thing of all,' said Jasper, carefully removing his tweed jacket and placing it on the back of a chair. 'Because it seems that I can't tell you.'

'Nonsense, of course you can tell me.'

'I'm afraid you don't understand. You see this particular woman is a barrister involved in some kind of case that involves the rightful provenance of a painting.'

'And what did she want?'

'An expert witness – if required, naturally – at a forthcoming hearing, that's due to start in a few weeks. In an actual court of law. Can you believe it?'

'How very interesting,' said Bernard, wishing now that he'd skipped his carb-fest brekkie and come straight to work instead so as not to miss out on all the drama. 'Which painting are we talking about? And who's the artist?'

'Can't say, I'm afraid,' said Jasper moodily, as if he'd

really love nothing more than to tell his friend everything and that the cost of holding his tongue was very dear indeed.

'But of course you can.'

'Afraid not. Ethics and all that, you know. I've been told that I may possibly be called as an expert witness and that on no account am I to discuss the matter with anyone. Not even you, Bernard. I gave her my solemn word.'

'How very frustrating.'

'You've no idea. What's killing me is that it's such a damn good case too.'

'I wonder why they asked you and not me?' said Bernard, a little petulantly. He'd have adored being part of something as exciting as that, although he was loath to admit as much to Jasper.

'Ahh, now that much I am at liberty to divulge,' said Jasper brightening. 'You see, the new owner of the painting in question came to me roughly about a year ago when I was still working at UCD, merely seeking more information about it, nothing more. Purely investigative work, which I was delighted to do. The lady in question was most persuasive and alluring, very alluring indeed.'

'And I presume that's the reason you've been approached a second time?'

'It seems so. But other than that, I can't possibly tell you any more.'

And yet you made sure to tell me this much, Bernard thought crossly.

'What you and I really need,' Jasper went on, 'is to slip off to the club so I can tell you everything over dinner and a nice crisp bottle of Sauvignon Blanc. You'd love this story, it's just your sort of thing.'

'But if you gave your word to this lady,' said Bernard

firmly, 'then naturally you can't on any account go back on it. But as soon as this case is all over, then I may just hold you to that dinner at the club. So you can tell me the whole story in all its glory, without fear of breaking any code of honour.'

'Then that's a definite date,' said Jasper. 'I very much look forward to getting this off my chest at the Royal Celtic. Just you and I. And Mother too, of course.'

TESS

The present

I didn't sleep well and only managed to hoist myself out of bed this morning by a sheer miracle of will, so much so that I am almost late for court. I leave Bernard, who's sound asleep and snoring like a freight train, in bed, with his book still propped up on his chest and grab a lightning-quick bath (no choice there, Bernard refuses to get a shower installed claiming that he is and always will be a bath man), with my mind racing. All manner of thoughts keep swirling around but there's just one that I keep coming back to: I'm getting married in a few weeks' time.

So aside from the thousand and one things that are still left to be done, aside from the court case and aside from all the distractions that are going on in my life right now, when I think of the wedding one thought lodges itself firmly in my brain and now that it's stuck there, there's no budging it.

Why aren't I feeling happy?

*

I finally get to court and do the usual early-morning dodge-dance past the posse of photographers outside, including

332

the beardy-looking hipster who had the brass nerve to approach me last week, wanting me to tell my story after all this is done and dusted. The jurors have their own entrance into the court and it's weird, normally I can't help bumping into at least two or three of the others on my way in, but this morning there's no one about.

Bracing myself for a dressing-down from Moany Mona for daring to be late, I knock on the door of the jury room all set to see everyone lined up and ready to be ushered into court while Mona barks our names out one-by-one, army cadet-style. But when I do get inside, to my astonishment I find one and all sitting around the huge conference table, which is now laid out with an impressive buffet of croissants, bagels, cream cheese, doughnuts and a giant-sized fresh fruit platter, there's a gorgeous smell of coffee too, and they're all helping themselves.

'Ahh, there you are, Tess, love!' says Edith, waving brightly. 'Sorry for starting brekkie without you, but we couldn't help it. Everything just looked way too delicious.'

'You have to taste this cronut thingy!' Minnie says, or at least tries to say with her mouth half full. 'Apparently it's made up of half a croissant and half a doughnut. Now isn't that just the most wonderful idea! Whoever would have thought?'

'But . . . are we not all due in court this morning? And where's Mona?' I say to no one in particular.

'Now whatever you do, don't get distracted by the large pig that's flying past the window,' says Will, suddenly materialising by my side and as ever, towering over me. Looking sharp today too, in a grey v-necked jumped that I know by the look of, is pure cashmere.

'Oh, hi there,' I say, swivelling around to see him.

'You missed all the drama,' he says, smirking a bit at the incredulous look on my face.

'So what happened? Fill me in.'

'Ah, Tess, it was hilarious,' says Beth delightedly, with a mug of coffee in one hand and a half-eaten banana in the other. 'What kept you anyway?'

'And by the way, Will, thank you so much for this very unexpected treat,' Daphne interrupts her. 'Perfect grub for me, you know. Nice and easy on my tummy ulcer.'

'What? What are you saying over there?' says Ruth, half-shouting as she always does.

'I said THE FOOD IS LOVELY AND GENTLE ON THE AUL' TUMMY ULCER,' Daphne shouts back as Ruth adjusts a tiny, very high-tech-looking hearing aid embedded in her ear, a bit like one of the CIA.

'There, that's it, I can hear you perfectly now,' says Ruth, 'I knew I left the house this morning without switching this bloody thing on properly. There was I thinking you were all being a lot quieter than usual.'

'So is there no court session happening this morning?' I ask the room.

'Ahh, you should have got here on time, Tess, love,' says Minnie, coming over to me and handing me a delicious-smelling, fresh chocolate croissant, whether I want it or not. 'You missed out on all the fun.'

'*Fun*? In here?'

'It seems that the Defence have asked for a short recess this morning,' says Will, the only one not milling into the breakfast buffet. Instead he's standing apart from the others, coffee clamped to one hand and looking thoughtful.

'And did they say why?'

'Apparently they've got a last-minute witness that they want to call,' he shrugs.

'And this bit of extra time is to allow them to prep that witness, is my guess,' Barney chips in knowledgably, like he and the judge had a cosy chat about it, just the two of them. 'You know, the very same thing happened in *Kinsella versus Kane* back in 1997. It's entirely allowable, you know. A judge can request a recess at any time and for any reason.'

Since this court case started, Barney, I've noticed, is taking a keen interest in the law and although we're not supposed to read about this case, he's been making up for it by reading about just about every other one that he feasibly can. In fact, he's becoming a bit of a court statistic bore. So much so that if you end up sitting beside him at lunch, it's very much considered the short straw.

'So where's Mona?' I ask, amazed at this latest development, not to mention the light-hearted holiday atmosphere in here. Like the headmistress has just given us an unexpected and most welcome free class.

'Well that's the best bit of all,' says Edith joyously. 'Miracle of miracles, my prayers were answered. For the moment at least, we're rid of the old bitch.'

She looks around the room, seemingly surprised that we're all staring at her, aghast. But then Edith is normally so sweet and docile; hearing her swear is a bit like hearing the Queen drop an F-bomb during her Christmas Day broadcast.

'What are you all looking at me for?' she asks. 'Am I wrong? Sure that witch would drive anyone to strong drink.'

'Hear, hear!' says Jess, high-fiving her.

'It seems she's left us here for at least the next hour,

while we wait till the judge reconvenes us,' Will explains to me.

'Then Will very kindly ran across to the coffee shop over the road and came back with all these treats for us,' says Jane briskly. 'Incredibly thoughtful of you by the way, Will.'

'My pleasure,' he smiles, giving her a little mock bow. 'Anything to fill us all up so we can avoid lunch at the Ebola Arms.'

'Tess pet, if you're not eating that chocolate croissant,' Daphne interrupts, 'then can I have it? Feck the blood sugar levels anyway, I want the chocolate.'

'Course Tess isn't eating it,' says Mai nudging her, 'isn't she getting married in a few weeks' time? She's probably on a starvation diet till then, so she can fit into her wedding dress. Am I right, Tess, love?'

I don't say anything though, just hand over the chocolate croissant to a delighted Daphne, who wolfs it back in about ten seconds. Honestly, I think from out of nowhere, for someone who spends so much time complaining about her IBS and her tummy ulcers, there's certainly nothing wrong with this one's appetite.

'I heard that fella of yours was waiting outside the court for you yesterday,' says Edith kindly.

'Oh yes, with a big bunch of flowers and everything! Will told us.'

'And they say romance is dead.'

'Bet you had great fun making up your lovers' tiff last night!' Ruth chips in with a raucous cackle.

'No wonder she's late into court this morning!' says Minnie.

'Thanks so much for that,' I mutter to Will, who's still hovering close by, coffee cup in hand.

'I'm sorry,' he says, turning slightly away from the others so only I can hear. 'I cracked under questioning. You've no idea what this lot are like when they're trying to wean a bit of gossip out of you. If you ask me, they should use more pensioners in police interrogation rooms. It seems that they have ways and means of tripping you up.'

'Hmm.'

'So just to change the subject,' his eyes twinkling down at me, 'I got the hell out of here and came back with break-fast. Did the trick very nicely, as you see.'

'The things you'll do for a subject change, Will Kearns.'

'So is everything OK?' he says. He's one of those people who focuses on you so fully when he's asking you a question that it's almost unnerving.

'How do you mean?' I ask a bit defensively.

'Things back on track?'

'Erm . . .'

'With lover boy? Husband to be? The guy you're going to spend the rest of your life with?'

But I'm distracted just then as my phone rings. Turns out it's the wedding caterer, probably wanting to confirm an appointment we'd made to meet up after court today. I go to click the phone off, then notice that there's about another five text messages which have come through and which I hadn't seen. From the florist, the hairdresser, The Bridal Room and God knows who else. To be honest I give up scrolling down through them after a minute or two.

'You still haven't answered my question,' says Will gently.

Mainly because I can't. I grasp around, trying to find the right words to describe how stressed and conflicted I'm feeling not just right now, but all morning too. And if I'm being really honest, from even further back than that.

I want to explain that just a few weeks ago, I was so wrapped up in planning this wedding and with getting every tiny detail just perfect, because weddings are deceitful like that, you think that the last thing you'll ever end up as is some kind of Bridezilla who's obsessed with corsages and wedding cars and updos, and yet there's something about the whole three-ring circus that just seems to suck you in.

And now – it's hard to put my finger on – it's like I'm actually starting to see beyond the big day and into the future. My whole future. With Bernard. Who's a kind, good man that I'm desperately fond of and who I wouldn't hurt for all the world. And I'm trapped. Completely and utterly trapped.

'Tess?' says Will, looking a little worried now. 'You've gone very quiet on me, is everything alright? Because if it's some basic relationship advice that you need here, just take a look around you. It's like you're surrounded by a whole roomful of agony aunts.'

I know Will means well, but right now I can't think of a single thing to say to him. Too confused, too muddled, too sick with worry.

So I just say nothing and hope he'll draw his own conclusions.

*

Soon – way sooner than any of us hoped – Mona is back into the jury room, barking at us and lining us up to go back to court.

'Judge Simmonds is ready to resume the hearing,' she says sternly, before giving the jury room a lightning-quick up and down glance, taking in all the discarded coffee cups and empty cake boxes. 'And after court,' she adds sniffily, 'whoever is responsible for the mess in here had better stay behind to clear it all up. Most unfair to have to ask the cleaning staff to take care of it.'

'Don't worry, I'll do it,' Will says to her in a tone that's so overly polite I'd almost swear he's taking the piss. 'And if you'd like to help yourself to a few of the leftovers while we're in court, Mona, then of course please feel free. I can highly recommend the chocolate croissants. Nothing like a sugar hit to elevate the mood, I always find.'

'Might put a smile on her face for once,' whispers Daphne to Edith as the two of them giggle like a pair of bold primary school kids.

'Well all I can say is there better be a very good reason for this hold up.' I can hear Mai grumbling while we all line up. 'I've to get to the chiropodist after court today and I don't want to be late. My bunions are giving me awful trouble altogether.'

Turns out we don't have long to wait. Back in court there's a palpable air of excitement and Hilda Cassidy is buzzing around her bench clutching documents and looking far from her usual unruffled self. Kate King is sitting behind her as always, this time dressed in an elegant pale-blue coat that hangs so beautifully on her even from this distance I can tell it must have cost well over the four figure mark.

Meanwhile, on the opposite side of the court, Damien King and Oliver Daniels are deep in animated chat, surrounded by junior counsels in their wigs, gowns and tab collars, all listening intently and occasionally jabbing a hopeful finger up to fight for airspace.

All eyes are on us as Mona practically shoves us through

the double doors that lead into court from the jury room. I take a seat beside Will, this time in the back row, to be honest grateful for the chance of a few hours' distraction from the tangled emotional lather I'm in right now.

A bare moment later, Judge Simmonds is swishing in with her black gown billowing behind her and declaring that we're 'in session'. Wasting no time whatsoever, Hilda is straight up on her feet and addressing the bench.

'Your Honour, thank you so much for the brief recess. The Defence would now like to call a new witness.'

'Well you've certainly kept us waiting long enough,' says Judge Simmonds, deeply unimpressed. 'So for the sake of your client, I only hope that this new witness of yours provides worthwhile testimony.'

'I'm quite certain you'll find he will,' says Hilda confidently. 'The Defence now calls Dr Jasper Adams.'

I freeze in my seat. I know that name. Jasper Adams is a colleague of Bernard's. I've never actually met him, but Bernard is always quoting him and saying things like 'Jasper recommended we try this vintage wine/antiquarian book store/walking tour of Brontë country'.

My mind races. So does this mean that I'm compromised as a juror now? We were given a stiff lecture from Mona all about jury contamination before the case started and I wonder . . . could this possibly be something that might cause trouble for everyone else down the line? I look around, white in the face and feeling a bit panicky.

'What's up with you?' whispers Will from beside me.

'I know this witness,' I hiss back. 'That is, I don't actually know him, but Bernard works with him.'

'In that case you need to tell the judge. Now,' he says firmly, raising his hand without any hesitation. There's a kerfuffle and a bit of a commotion as Sandra the Court Registrar spots what's going on and immediately comes over to us. I lean forward and explain the situation to her, aware that every eye in the court is on me and that there's a lot of murmured conjecture around about what this could possibly be. Sandra listens, nods, then waddles straight up the steps to the judge's bench where the two of them have a hurried, whispered consultation.

'We'll take another brief ten minute recess,' sighs Judge Simmonds, banging her hammer down like an auctioneer as Sandra makes her way back down the steps to where I'm sitting with clenched knuckles in the jury box.

'Can you follow me, please?' she asks.

'Poor old, Tess,' I can hear Edith saying as I'm led out of the box. 'I knew there was something wrong with her when she didn't eat any of that delicious food just now.'

'And she came in white as a sheet this morning,' says Jess. 'If one of my kids looked like that, I'd whip them off to see a doctor immediately.'

'Trouble in paradise, if you ask me.'

'Oh definitely man trouble,' says Jane assuredly. 'I can spot it a mile off. Same with my own daughters, you know. If there's something up with either of them, the first sign is when they go off their grub.'

Last thing I'm aware of as I'm being led out of court is Kate King's pale, white face looking back at mine. And I don't think I've ever seen a woman look so worried.

*

A moment later, I'm being led down a long corridor with Sandra at my side as Judge Simmonds swishes on ahead of us. We take a lift to a higher floor, then down another

341

corridor before the judge stops abruptly at the door to her chambers, which turns out to be a tiny, private office with her name neatly printed on the door. Feeling like a school-girl caught smoking down at the bike sheds who's about to be hauled over the coals by the headmistress, I follow her inside as Sandra closes the door firmly behind us.

So now it's just me and Judge Simmonds, completely alone.

'Am I right in assuming you know the witness in question?' she asks, turning to face me, wasting no time in getting to the point.

I explain the situation to her while she listens intently, arms folded.

'But you've never actually met this person, Jasper Adams? Your knowledge of him is purely second hand?'

'Well . . . no, I've never met him,' I tell her, 'but still. I thought it only right to let you know.'

She nods curtly and strides back to open the door, where Sandra is standing patiently outside, like a sentry on guard duty.

'Would you kindly ask Oliver Daniels and Hilda Cassidy to come in here, please?' she asks. Sandra nods and imme-diately bustles off to do as she's told.

Then when it's just the two of us alone again, the judge walks over to the window just behind her desk, taking her wig off and pausing for a moment to look down onto the view of the car park below.

'I should tell you that it's my duty to inform both Prosecution and Defence counsel of this development,' she says. 'Because if either side have an issue with the matter – which might easily be the case – then we cannot proceed as planned. If any juror has a connection to a witness, then both sides have the right to insist on starting the case afresh.'

'So you mean . . .'

'It means a whole new jury will have to be sworn in from scratch,' Judge Simmonds says, still focused on the view down below her office window. 'You'll be dismissed as of now and no longer required to serve on this case.'

I take a moment to digest what she's telling me. That this huge court case, all this press interest, not to mention all the sacrifices that I've made myself just to turn up here every day, could all be for nothing.

'I can't tell you how sorry I am,' I say, and it's only when the words are out that I know I really mean it too. 'I hadn't realised it was such a big deal. I just thought I should be as honest with you as possible.'

'I understand,' Judge Simmonds says a bit more gently now as she turns back to face me. 'And for what it's worth, you certainly didn't do an easy thing in coming forward like this. But you did do the right thing.'

I'm asked to wait outside while Oliver and Hilda bustle importantly past me into Judge Simmonds' chambers, so I take a seat in the corridor, with my mind racing.

Two weeks ago, something like this would have been the answer to my prayers. So why am I sitting here with a knot of tension in my stomach, praying both counsels can agree that this doesn't really matter? That this is nothing more than a minor blip and that the case can continue as before?

KATE

'What on earth can be taking them so long?' said Kate to one of Hilda's junior counsels, an eager-looking thirty-something guy with a head so bald it looked exactly like a boiled egg from where she'd been sitting behind him.

'My guess is that the juror in question wants off the case,' he answered curtly, barely looking up from the mound of papers and legal files that were scattered all across the court bench.

Kate froze in her seat.

'But why? I mean, why now, when we're almost finished?'

'Could be for any reason. Conflict of interest for one. Though more likely it's because of jury contamination. You wouldn't know who could have tried to get to her. People's behaviour during a case like this would really amaze you.'

With a shudder, Kate thought back to her lonely run on the pier just the previous morning. How she'd accidentally bumped into that young, pretty girl from the jury, who was out doing exactly the same thing. Had she panicked, was that it? Had she realised that having just

344

come into contact with Kate – however accidentally – that she'd now have to report it all back to the judge? And worst of all, was there a chance that she'd quote Kate on what had been said?

What did I say anyway? Kate thought, racking her brains to remember back to that early-morning run.

This isn't what you think. None of this is what you think.

Yes, that was it. They'd been her exact words. And now they could potentially hang her. She glanced over to the other side of the court where Damien was being ushered outside by a cohort of barristers, all vying to pitch their theories of what this recess could potentially spell for them. He had his back to her, but as sheer bad luck would have it, at that moment he happened to turn his head just a quarter inch, so now their eyes met.

All this for a bloody painting, she tried her best to telegraph to him across the packed courtroom. *One that you probably wouldn't have even noticed was missing, if she hadn't been there to point it out to you.*

TESS

The present

I don't know if this is a good sign or a bad sign, but a few minutes ago, both Hilda and Oliver strode out of Judge Simmonds' office where they'd both been cooped up and walked right past me without as much as a single word; either to me, or to each other. I'm not entirely certain what to do now, so I sit, wait, fidget and worry, in that order. Then a minute later, the office door opens and Judge Simmonds herself is on the move.

'Well then,' she says to me, looking as intimidating as ever now that her wig is back on. 'I've discussed the matter at some length with both the Prosecution and Defence.'

'Yes?' I say weakly, fully expecting her to order me to pack up my bag, publicly apologise to everyone – from my fellow jurors, to the people that line up for free seats in the public gallery every day – then crawl out of here with my tail between my legs.

'And both sides are in agreement that as you've never actually met, spoken to or indeed had any contact whatsoever with this new witness,' she says, 'and that your knowledge of him is entirely second hand, they're happy for the case to go ahead, as planned.'

'You mean . . . we're OK then?' I half-stammer. 'We're back on track?'

'So it would appear.'

'Oh . . . well that's great to hear. Erm . . . thank you, and sorry if I caused you any trouble.'

'Well, come on then,' she says, beckoning me to follow her as she quick-marches down the corridor. So I do as I'm told, trailing a step or two behind her, she's walking so fast. We turn down another corridor in silence and all I can think is that not so long ago, I'd have been wailing and gnashing my teeth at still being shackled to this case, when a convenient little exit route had just appeared out of nowhere, like Alice in Wonderland's low door in the wall.

Weirdly though, that's not how it feels at all. The exact opposite in fact. Because right now I actually can't wait to get back to court, back to the jury room, back to see this all through to the final furlong. Being perfectly honest, I'm actually relieved that I haven't been turfed out and that I'll live to serve another day.

'So how are your wedding plans coming along?' Judge Simmonds asks me out of nowhere, as we both wait for the lift to take us back downstairs to court.

'I'm sorry?'

'The day you were summoned for service, I believe you mentioned that your wedding was imminent?'

'I can't believe you remember that,' I tell her, flabber-gasted.

'It's kind of my job to remember things,' she says, with just a hint of a tiny smile. 'Plus you did produce all manner of folders, files and I distinctly recall a mood board, showing how vital it was that you be excused from the case.'

I redden a bit at the thought of how inanely and desperately I'd acted back then. Then the lift arrives and we both step inside.

'Everything on track for the big day?' she asks politely.

'Ehh . . . well kind of,' is all I can come out with though. *You mean apart from a very reluctant bride, who's having serious knots in her stomach every time she thinks about her whole future? Oh yeah, other than that, we're all systems go.*

We arrive at our floor and the lift door obediently pings open.

'Glad you were called to serve then?' Judge Simmonds says, turning to face me before she steps out.

'More than that.'

'Do you know, it's quite extraordinary,' she says with a twinkle, clipping out of the lift as I trail after her. 'I've yet to meet an unwilling juror who regretted serving, by the time the case is about to come to a conclusion. Never fails to astonish me.'

*

'You did the right thing,' says Will.

'Certainly feels that way,' I tell him, stooping down to pick up the remains of a half-eaten cream cheese bagel. 'Although I have to say, I was terrified that Judge Simmonds would think I was only coming forward to try to wriggle out of the case. Yet again.'

'You're not though, are you?'

'Are you kidding me? Now? When things have just got interesting?'

We're in the jury room by the way, as he and I have offered to wait behind and clear up after this morning's impromptu breakfast picnic, while the others were all bussed over to the Ebola Arms for lunch. Lunch, which Judge Simmonds called practically the very minute that court reconvened. All to disappointed groans from the courtroom and even a muttered 'is this a court of law or a bloody holiday camp?' from the public benches, clearly audible throughout the whole court, as it was no doubt meant to be.

Will and I work on in silence for a bit, making sure every last morsel of breakfast has been cleared away. Anything rather than invoke the wrath of Moany Mona.

'Tell you something,' he says, scooping up fistfuls of crumbs and the bottom end of a breakfast roll. 'For a gang of pensioners who constantly complain about how hard it is to get something to eat that they actually like, they certainly are able to put their grub away, aren't they?'

I smile, but don't say anything, just concentrate on clearing away empty coffee cups.

'You're miles away,' he eventually says, stopping what he's doing.

'Am I?'

'Don't pretend with me. You know you are.'

'Sorry, Will,' I say, turning to face him. 'It's just that there's a lot going on right now. A lot of big decisions that I feel I'm being forced into making. You know what? At least in this case we get to decide on a verdict—'

'If we ever get to decide on a verdict—'

'But in my private life, I feel like I almost don't have any control any more. That with the wedding so close, I'm on this roller coaster and I've got no choice except just to roll with it.'

'"I am in blood stepp'd in so far . . ."'

'Sorry?'

'Nothing. Just a quote from *Macbeth*.'

'And for whatever reason, everything has come together at once and no one is giving me even the smallest chink of time to think things over.'

A pause while Will takes a minute to digest this.

'Remember, if you ever want to talk,' he eventually says, 'then I'll be there for you.'

'Thanks,' is all I can say back as I haul another stuffed black bin liner over to the door, ready to be cleared away. 'You're probably the only person in my life not putting any pressure on me right now'.

'Then long may that continue.'

'I really appreciate the support, you know.'

'By the way,' he says as we both get back to work. 'There's something you never told me.'

'Oh yeah? What was that?'

'Now it's none of my business, but . . .'

'Will, for feck's sake, we're stuck here on jury service together. As far as I'm concerned, you and I have no boundaries. Go on, ask me anything.'

'You know when I met you at the bar the other night,' he says, putting down a handful of empty coffee cups. 'It's just you seemed so upset and angry.'

'Understatement of the year,' I say, stomach clenching again just remembering back to that god-awful night.

'In that case,' he says, the dark eyes almost boring into mine, 'I hope that whatever you and the fiancé argued about was nothing too serious?'

I'm over at the window and take a moment to look down onto the street just below.

'It was about ABBA!' I say.

'Ah,' he says thoughtfully, before picking up the last of the rubbish and heading out the door.

*

'In my humble opinion,' says Barney knowledgeably, as we're all obediently lined up for this afternoon's court call. 'The Prosecution will spend a large part of the afternoon ahead throwing up every objection that they possibly can to this new witness, what's his name. The very exact same thing happened in *Kinsella versus Hamilton* in 2003, you know. I was reading up on it only last night. Although now I come to think of it, it might have been 2004. You wouldn't want to quote me on it.'

'Oh, don't you worry,' says Ian dryly. 'There's no fear of that.'

Turns out that Barney's not too far off the mark. Given all the delays we had this morning, this session is mercifully short and it's mostly taken up with Oliver Daniels trawling up just about every objection that he can possibly raise to Jasper Adams being called as a late witness. Insufficient time for the Prosecution to adequately prepare their cross-questions seems to be the general thrust of it. And as Barney accurately predicted, he spends for ever throwing up one case history after another where a late witness wasn't permitted.

'May God forgive me,' groans Daphne, who's sitting on one side of me while Will's on the other. 'And I really hope Barney can't hear this, but it chokes me to have to admit that aul' windbag was actually right.'

'Whatever you say, say nothing,' hisses Edith, who's sitting on the other side of Daphne. 'Otherwise we'll never hear the end of this.'

This goes on for, I kid you not, an hour. Then a good ninety minutes in, Hilda is up on her feet, firing back with case after case where late witnesses were absolutely allowed, listing them off in full. Names, dates, case histories, the whole works.

And dear God, but it's boring. More boring than being stuck in school on a sunny day, for a double maths class. So boring, in fact, that to my right, Will has started playing noughts and crosses on the freebie notepads in front of us, while Daphne is engrossed in writing out her shopping list. Cat food and Domestos bleach featuring strongly, I can't help but notice.

Everyone looks tired and fed up. Damien King is staring out into the middle distance like he's dreaming of the golf course he'll doubtless be rambling around the minute he's out of here. All the junior counsels look like they need matchsticks to prop their eyes fully open. The press are all openly yawning, and over at the public benches – which still have queues to get into them every day – people are getting up out of seats and drifting in and out of court. Anything just to escape the tedium.

The only person who looks keyed up and tense, I notice, is Kate King herself, who's constantly whispering to Hilda, passing her notes as she perches tensely on the edge of the bench.

I try my best to concentrate, but keep finding myself drifting off. So instead, I surreptitiously join Will in a few games of noughts and crosses, as he carefully hides the notepad under the table so we're not seen.

And once or twice, I even manage to beat him.

Then, just after 5 p.m., to relieved smiles from the Defence, Judge Simmonds says the magic words, 'I've listened to your arguments and I'm overruling all objections. We'll take a recess till Friday, then Jasper Adams may take the stand and the Defence may open with questions. I'm adjourning the court till then. With thanks to you all for your patience today.'

And like that, she's gone. As the jurors are guided out through the side door, it's hard not to be aware of a frisson of excited whispers running like an electric current all the way from the press box to the public benches.

What the hell can Jasper Adams possibly have to say that Kate King is so anxious we all hear?

KATE

The Chronicle
1st January, 2015

We've received confirmed reports from a spokeswoman for Mr Damien King that his fiancée, Ms Harper Jones, has been safely delivered of a baby boy, at 9.07 a.m. today. Ms Jones gave birth at the exclusive Mount Sinai Hospital in the Guggenheim Pavilion, on Manhattan's Upper East Side. Mr King was reportedly at his fiancée's side throughout the birth.

When contacted directly by The Chronicle, *Mr King said he was 'the happiest man on earth today. It's like a long-held dream finally coming true for me'. Both mother and son are said to be in perfect health.*

The baby is to be named Damien Henry Charles King and known as Damien King the Second. And even though he's just a few hours old, his name has already been placed on a waiting list to attend Eton College, his father's alma mater.

The Chronicle made several attempts to contact Kate King, *estranged wife of the proud father, for a comment, however all efforts to date have been unsuccessful.*

TESS

The present

'Tess Taylor, where in the name of God ARE you?' Mum screeches into my voicemail. 'You're about as much use to me as a chocolate teapot, so you are. It's now after 5 p.m. and if you don't walk through this front door inside the next half hour, then I won't be held responsible. Do you realise what still has to be done before Saturday night? This house needs to be dusted and hoovered from top to bottom, and all that's before you get started on the menu. Because let me tell you, you're on your own there, missy. You're the one who insisted that we host this shindig and if you think your sister and I are going to make slaves of ourselves, while you swan around the criminal courts with the likes of Kate King, then you've another thing coming . . .'

Ahh, my mother. The only woman in the northern hemisphere who can make a one-act radio play out of a humble voicemail message. I'm just heading out of the jury room having been discharged for the day and immediately click onto the next message, but sadly it's not all that much better.

'Tess?' comes Gracie's voice this time. 'You still sitting in court wondering whether or not you'll send Kate King to a maximum-security prison? Because the Mothership is having a total meltdown over this bloody party on Saturday night. A word to the wise; you'd want to get back here as soon as you can, for a bit of crisis aversion. You have been warned.'

*

Oh Christ, I think, my stomach instantly shrivelling to the size of a walnut. Saturday night. You see, instead of doing the whole Hen Night/Stag thing, Bernard and I decided that wouldn't it be better if we just had everyone around to our house for a joint party? A 'sten night', they're apparently called, or so I read in a bridal magazine. Back when I used to read bridal magazines.

But with everything else that's been going on lately, I'd completely put it to the back of my mind. I continue to scroll through all my texts and missed calls, groaning inwardly, the way you do when there's just so much still to do, and so little time.

As we're leaving, Moany Mona gives us a stern warning that the press pack outside court is bigger than ever today, so while everyone else has to run the gauntlet out through the main doors, this time the jurors are guided out through a discreet emergency exit handily situated just at the side of the building, where no one can spot us. There's the usual chatting and waving goodbye, and in Minnie's case, trying to cadge a lift off Barney who I'm secretly thinking she might just have her eye on.

'See you, Tess, love,' says Edith warmly, tottering down the stone steps on her way to the bus stop.

'Makes a nice change to be finished early for once, doesn't it?' says Daphne, following after her, 'means I can be home in time for *Agatha Christie's Marple*.'

I smile and wave goodbye, then get back to the rest of my messages. And dear God, but there must be dozens of them, from the wedding singer who sounds like he's having a complete hissy-fit, to the caterer who left some garbled gobbledygook of a voicemail, the gist of which seems to involve some cousin on Bernard's side who's now decided at the last minute that she's lacto-vegetarian.

Jesus, give me strength, I think, actually breaking out into a cold, panicky sweat. Tightness in my chest, shortness of breath, the whole works. I'm not certain that I can deal with all this right now, so instead I switch off the phone, shove it back into the depths of my bag and take a minute to stand on the court steps and just breathe.

One thing is certain. I can't go home. Not yet and certainly not now. I just can't bring myself to face this, not when my mind is in overdrive and there's just so much pressure coming at me from every single imaginable direction. And yet I know it's just not fair to leave Mum and Gracie sweating over the mess I've single-handedly created over Saturday night and all the attached brouhaha. So, although it's the last thing I want to do, this girl better haul herself back to the house, and fast. Even if the thought of what's waiting for me back there is making my knees start to feel wobbly.

I look around and see Will behind me, doing exactly the same thing as I was; checking his phone, catching up on the day's messages. Then he pulls on a very cool-looking leather jacket and ambles over to say goodbye.

'The curse of modern technology,' he says dryly. 'Sometimes I hate it so much that I'm accessible twenty-four seven, it's almost a relief to be in court with the phone switched off.'

'You read my mind,' I say, pulling a face at him.

'You look . . . strange,' he says.

'Strange?'

'Pressured. Like all this is getting to you.'

'Oh Christ, Will, you have no idea.'

'You off home? Wedding stuff to get back to?'

'Please. For the love of God, I'm actually *begging* you. Can we just . . . not use that word?'

Then suddenly I'm feeling dizzy as a strange, unfamiliar whooshing noise gushes through my ears.

'Jesus, Tess, you've gone white as a sheet,' he says, quickly gripping my arm by the elbow.

'It's nothing, I'm fine,' I say, trying to laugh it off, but it's no use. Suddenly my stomach is sick to the gills and heaving and I know that I've got to get to a bathroom inside of about thirty seconds flat or else I'm in big trouble.

'You look terrible, are you OK?' I can hear Will's voice coming in and out of focus as I frantically look around for somewhere that might be open where I could make a dash for the loo. A pub, a coffee shop, anything.

My stomach does another sickening heave and I try to gulp it back. Then another wave of violent nausea and this time it's too late. There's no stopping me. There's a public bin on the street right outside SPAR stuffed to the brim with empty cans and McDonald's cartons. I bend over it and a second later, I'm throwing up, too sick to my stomach to even care how it looks.

'There you go, that's it, just get it all up,' Will says gently, holding back my hair, though how he's enduring the stench is beyond me.

I stop for a minute, trying to gauge whether or not I need to be sick for a second time, as my eyes start to get fuzzy and a load of spots shower their way down my eyelids.

'All gone?' he asks.

I can't talk though, so I just nod.

'OK, let's get you a cab and I'll take you home. Where do you live?'

'No! Please. Not home if you don't mind,' I say, a fresh wave of queasiness hitting me just at the very thought of home. 'I can't . . . at least, not yet.'

He looks at me quizzically, the dark eyes trying to read my face.

'Very long story,' is all I can offer by way of explanation.

'In that case, let's get you to a bathroom,' he says, casting his eye up and down the street to see what's on offer. 'Come on, I'll come with you. And then maybe a glass of water.'

He glances around to see that the coffee shop across the road has closed up for the day by now.

'Limited choices, it would seem,' he says.

'Oh God, Will, I think I need to sit down. Now.'

'In that case, I'll tell you what,' he says, 'I just live ten minutes away. Why don't you come over there? Just till you feel better.'

'Oh . . . well . . .'

'Tess, you just puked into a bin on the street. What other choice do you have?'

*

Turns out Will lives right in the heart of Charlotte Quay Dock, a.k.a. probably the coolest, priciest part of the whole city. He thoughtfully rolls the taxi windows down as we drive through the traffic and the fresh air soon starts to make me feel a bit more myself again.

359

'How do you feel now?' he asks worriedly.

'Bit better, I think. At least, it's passing. Look, I'm so sorry, I don't know what came over me, I'm mortified—'

'Hey, none of that now! I've done worse myself,' he says with a tiny smile. 'And you know what they say. Better out than in.'

By the time we get to where he lives, the worst of the nausea has passed. I'm still a bit jittery, but at least I don't think I'll be sick again. Hopefully. Will insists on paying the driver as I clamber out of the cab, taking in the whole place.

And oh dear God, it's so achingly cool here, you wouldn't believe it. The apartment block where Will lives perfectly overlooks the Grand Canal basin, right beside the Bord Gáis Energy Theatre, where I often go to see musicals with my mates and where we're always saying we'd love to live, EuroMillions lottery numbers willing, etc.

Will unlocks the communal hall door and a minute later I'm following him into a marble-floored lift. It's deliciously cool in here and just being in off the street is making me perk up a bit. I'm a bit surprised when he uses a special key to get the lift going, and seconds later we're up at the very top floor.

'Fancy,' I say, but he says nothing, just nods at me to follow him, which I do, all the way down a very private-looking corridor to an apartment with a single word plaque on the door: 'Penthouse'.

'Ah, Will, the penthouse? Are you secretly a billionaire tech entrepreneur by day, or something?'

'A humble place, but my own,' he says, unlocking the front door as I follow him inside. And I have to stop myself from involuntarily gasping out loud. Because this isn't just your common or garden bachelor pad, this place is actually *breathtaking*.

We step into a huge open plan living room, where there's a sunken area in the centre of the floor with comfy-looking leather sofas dotted around, all pointing to the flat screen telly on the wall. The whole apartment is kitted out in blonde wood floors and furniture that's predominantly brown leather, the exact colour of espresso, with interesting-looking paintings covering most of the wall space. It's tasteful, so exquisitely classy that you'd swear an interior designer only signed off the place twenty minutes ago.

But that's not what's taking my breath away. Because dominating the whole space is an actual wraparound balcony with the most stunning view right over Grand Canal Square. I can't help myself; I just gravitate right over to the glass sliding door as Will, correctly reading my thoughts, steps up behind me to open it. Stepping outside it's even more impressive, particularly on a warm evening like this, with the sun dancing across the water's edge just beneath.

'Will, this place is astonishing!' I blurt as he looks on bemused, leaning back against the glass doors, hands stuffed into his pockets.

'But how are you able to afford it? It must have cost . . .' I break off here, but all I can think is, a million plus. Easy. Has to be.

'Did a wealthy distant cousin die and leave you a fortune?'

'Now, now,' he says, playfully wagging his finger, 'that's just morbid of you. Although I'm glad to see you're making a joke. Means you're definitely on the mend.'

'Then you're some kind of a hedge fund manager by day.'

'Clearly you never saw my maths exam results back in school.'

'Please don't tell me you're a drug dealer in your spare time?'

'Do I look like a drug dealer?'

'They never do.'

'You and your overactive imagination,' he smiles. 'Tell you something though; I never tire of showing guests the balcony. Rain or shine, it's always a hit. There were thunderstorms the other night and it was a light show out here. I only wished I'd—'

'Wished you'd what?'

'Nothing,' he says, abruptly breaking off. 'Tell you what. Why don't you go into the bathroom and maybe I can get you something to settle your stomach?'

'Cup of tea would be gorgeous, thanks.'

'Could you try to eat something?'

'Oh,' I say doubtfully, 'not sure that my tummy is up to food just yet.'

'Not a problem. I'll rustle up something anyway and if you fancy picking at it, it's all yours. Nothing like a few carbs to sort out a sick stomach.'

He shows me the way to the guest bathroom, which as you'd expect in an apartment like this, is state-of-the-art luxurious with marble floors, mahogany cabinets, the whole works.

'There's a brand new toothbrush in the press behind the mirror,' he shouts at me through the door. 'Help yourself.'

I gratefully accept, but as I'm brushing my teeth and splashing cold water on my face, all I can think is . . . spare toothbrush. Right. For lady-callers, who might just be staying the night, no doubt.

Feeling a whole lot cleaner, I finish up in the bathroom and find Will in the galley kitchen where I swear to God the guy has more gadgets and gismos than Nigella.

'You're certainly looking a whole lot better,' he says, taking me in from head to foot.

'Probably a good sign, now that the sickness has passed, that I'm starting to feel mortified for vomiting on the street. Fair play to you for sticking around, Will. Most blokes would have run a mile.'

'Just sit back, relax and let me get you a cup of tea and something to eat,' he says, efficiently zipping around, whipping onions, garlic, tomatoes and cream from his supersized American-style fridge and sticking them all into a pan. 'Is the smell driving you mad? Making your stomach feel dodgy again? Just tell me if it is and remember, there's a loo just feet away from you.'

'No!' I smile, 'if anything that gorgeous smell is actually making me hungry.'

'Good sign,' he says, chopping onions.

'Here, at least let me do that much for you,' I say, grabbing the knife off him and taking over.

'You don't have to. When you're a guest in my house, your only job is to sit and relax. And if I'm ever a guest in yours, I'll do the same.'

'Ha, some chance of you ever wanting to be a guest in my house,' I smile, chopping away. 'I'm back living with my parents just now and the way things are in that house at the moment, there's a good chance my mother would hand you a bottle of Windolene and a J-cloth, then tell you to get going on the upstairs windows.'

'Why are you back living at home?' he asks, looking up from the pan to where I'm working away on the onions.

'It's a long story. A very long one.'

'That's two long stories that you've got to tell me. That and the reason why you didn't want to go straight home this evening when you weren't feeling well. It struck me as a bit odd.'

'You sure you're ready for it? Be warned, neither is pretty.'

'I'm a good listener, or so my ex used to always say.'

Ah, I think, thoughts flipping. The ex-wife. I look over at Will where he now has his back to me, weaving all sorts of magic with everything he just threw into the frying pan. His tall, lean frame is bent over while he concentrates so I take the chance to really take him in.

An attractive guy, I think, in a rangy, long-limbed sort of way. And obviously not short of a few quid. Generous, thoughtful, attentive, and good company too. So what sort of a nut-job would ever leave a fella like this?

'Jesus, Tess, even from here,' he says, 'I can almost hear the sound of your devious feminine mind whirring.'

'What do you mean?' I ask, blinking back at him innocently.

'When you were in the bathroom, I'll bet you checked out whether or not there were any signs of a woman living here. Bits of make-up, tampons, all the usual. Am I right?'

'Will, I wouldn't dream of being so nosy!' I lie, mainly because that's exactly what I was doing as it happens. The spare toothbrush being a dead giveaway. 'Why would you even suggest that?' I add, for good measure.

'Because I write crime fiction for a living. And if there's one thing I know, it's how a woman's mind works,' he grins over his shoulder at me.

'Just like Mel Gibson in *What Women Want*,' I smile back. 'Must come in handy for you.'

'Certainly does. Not least when I look over at Kate King every day and try to imagine what's going through that woman's mind. Oh and just to save your feminine wiles a considerable amount of bother, the answer is no.'

'No what?'

'No, I currently live alone.'

BERNARD

The present

A character in an Oscar Wilde play once said of another that "they never talk scandal, but they do remark on it to everyone they meet", and at that moment, Bernard couldn't possibly have thought the quote any more apt. You see it was Jasper who'd got him into this fine mess, because with a staggering self-importance, he'd taken himself off to the courts to give testimony on whatever case it was that he'd been asked to serve on.

And although Jasper point-blank refused to divulge any details of the case, however large or small, it was virtually impossible for Bernard and the rest of the faculty not to guess. After all, how many cases that would require an art historian to give testimony were going on at the moment anyway? As Jasper bustled importantly out of college to go to court, Bernard had almost felt like calling after him, 'when you see Tess in the jury box, give her my love, won't you?'

Because that was the other thing. Jasper had developed an intensely annoying habit of letting everyone in the faculty know exactly what he was doing and the full reason for his non-attendance at college lectures for the next few days at least.

Which meant of course that it fell to poor, long-suffering Bernard to cover for him. He'd willingly agreed to do it of course, all for one and all that, but now was vaguely starting to regret it somewhat. Mainly because taking over Jasper's students in addition to his own meant not only having to prepare at short notice an in-depth tutorial on Italian Etruscan art in the second century B.C. – which had never been Bernard's strongest subject – but also having to correct a grand total of thirty-seven undergraduate essays on the subject too. True to his word though, this was exactly what Bernard was now attempting to do, holed up in his tiny, wood-panelled office on the third floor of the college's Art History department.

'No wonder our course tutor is single, he actually looks like a vole' was one comment scribbled across an essay by a fresher student. Despite himself, Bernard couldn't help smiling a little, because this was indeed a highly accurate description of Jasper.

'I'm only here because I couldn't get the points to get into law', was scrawled across another, which Bernard instantly marked with a D and tossed to one side. 'Why am I writing an essay on this boring crap when I could be outside in the sunshine playing football?' another fresher had scribbled across the back page of his offering, and for a split second, Bernard could actually empathise with the poor chap. It was well past seven in the evening and here he was still cooped up in this stuffy little room, effectively doing a colleague's work for him, while it felt that the rest of the world had all gone out to play.

From the window directly behind his desk, Bernard could

clearly hear the thwacking noise of a cricket bat pummel-
ling a ball and envied the spectators, all stretched happily
on the lawns outside, sipping strange-coloured cocktails
and looking utterly at peace with the world. Then his
thoughts turned to the talk at his club tonight that in all
likelihood he'd now have to miss, which was particularly
vexing as it was one he'd been looking forward to as well.

It was to be given by a noted TV historian who Bernard
greatly admired on the subject of the Napoleonic invasion
of Russia. Quite his favourite subject too. However, there
was no option now but to forgo that pleasure, he thought,
feeling distinctly peeved about the whole thing. Just then,
his phone rang and, glad of the distraction, he answered
right away.

'Hello, sweetie, it's Mother,' said Beatrice to the recognis-
able background noise of ice clinking in a glass she was
whirling around with her free hand.

'Hello, Mummy, how are you?' said Bernard. 'I can't talk
for long, I'm afraid, I'm still stuck in work.'

'Oh how very annoying for you. I thought you were
going to hear Dr David Harrison speak at the club tonight?
I know your father is already on his way there, he's greatly
looking forward to it.'

'Duty calls, I'm afraid.'

'Well as a matter of fact,' Beatrice went on, pausing to
take a gulp of her G&T. 'Duty is precisely the reason why
I'm calling you.'

'Oh, really?' Bernard asked, utterly at a loss.

'It's about this accursed evening that's been planned for
Saturday night. At Tess's family's house, you know, darling.'

'Oh,' said Bernard, actually glad of the reminder himself.
He'd been so bogged down in work, he'd temporarily

368

forgotten all about it and for some reason Tess hadn't mentioned it much either. But then Tess had been so caught up with jury service that she appeared to have time for little else these days. And being brutally honest, the way Bernard felt just now, if she'd decided to call off Saturday night, he'd have raised absolutely no arguments whatsoever with her.

A 'sten night' apparently such gatherings were called, which was an Americanism that Bernard personally loathed, but of course he'd said nothing. Tess had reassured him the idea was that all close wedding guests came together for a lovely informal celebratory party, just weeks away from the wedding.

Back when the idea was first mooted some months ago, she'd been the driving force behind the whole idea, as it meant guests would already have met before the wedding, thereby eliminating the need for stilted small talk with complete strangers on the big day. And considering that the idea of an actual stag night was complete anathema to Bernard, he'd been prepared to go along with just about anything that meant he could side-step that ghastly tradition of grooms-to-be being handcuffed to lampposts in Temple Bar. Although somehow the idea of any of his friends from the club or from the college ever setting foot in Temple Bar almost made him smile at the sheer ridiculousness of it.

'So what's the problem with Saturday, Mummy?' Bernard asked.

'Oh, darling. There isn't *really* a problem per se, except that I've only just had a good look at the invitation and it seems the whole affair is to be hosted by the Taylors, at their home and . . . well . . .'

'Yes?' said Bernard, correctly anticipating exactly what she was about to say.

'Well do your father and I really need to be there, dearest? Tess is a very sweet girl, you know, but as for the rest of her family . . . let's just say that Daddy and I feel there isn't really much common ground between us. If you know what I mean.'

As it happened, Bernard knew exactly what she meant, but ever loyal, he said nothing.

'And you know, all your mutual friends will be there too, so it's hardly like you'll miss a pair of old codgers like us, now is it?'

'I completely understand,' said Bernard kindly. 'But you know—'

'Oh, thank God,' said Beatrice, sounding infinitely relieved. 'To be perfectly honest, I was actually starting to dread the whole ghastly idea. I know I mustn't say anything unkind about your in-laws-to-be, but it's such a dreary chore finding anything to discuss with them, isn't it? Do you know that Tess's father actually told me that he'd only ever read one book in his whole life? A thriller of some sort. And he claimed it was so good that he never bothered reading any other, as it couldn't possibly match up. I mean really, what does one even say to that? I can't begin to imagine.'

'Of course I understand how you feel,' said Bernard, aware that he was treading a particularly fine line here. 'But really, you and Dad need only appear at the party for about an hour or so. Now that's not too much to ask, is it?'

'Hmm,' said Beatrice doubtfully. 'I don't know.'

'It's just the Taylors will have gone to considerable trouble and the last thing we'd want would be to appear rude. Duty calls and all that.'

'Duty,' she groaned, like he'd just played his trump card. 'That bloody word gives me heartburn.'

'But for now I'm afraid I really must get back to work, Mummy,' said Bernard. 'One hour of your time, Mummy, that's all, then you can consider yourself fully excused from Saturday evening.'

'Well if we really must,' Beatrice sighed resignedly. 'I suppose we'll just offer it up and do it for you, sweetheart.'

'Good. I know they'll appreciate it.'

'Well, if we must, we must. Alright then, big hugs and see you for dinner before the weekend. I've got some boiled tripe in, your absolute favourite.'

Bernard hung up, dearly wishing that he could miraculously back out of Saturday himself. Not that Tess's friends weren't absolutely delightful. It's just that they were all so very *young* and so full of energy, with their constant stream of chatter about TV shows he'd never heard of and bands with names that sounded borderline obscene to him. They were always talking about clubs and bars that were alien to him and which they'd all doubtless head off to after Saturday's party.

His own tight little group of chums, on the other hand, he knew would be perfectly polite to everyone at this sten night, then as soon as would be deemed acceptable, would want to leave the party nice and early to go back to the club for a lovely gentle nightcap. And Bernard knew exactly which group he'd far prefer to be with.

Suddenly aware that he was feeling quite peckish, he checked his watch and realised he hadn't eaten since a light snack at teatime. There was a brown paper lunch bag on the sideboard opposite him; one Tess had very thoughtfully put a packed meal into a few days previously. Most kind of her and all that, but Bernard had taken one peek inside and decided he'd far prefer to sneak off to McDonald's for a Quarter Pounder with cheese – a snack which he was becoming increasingly partial to these days.

So much so that Tess had begun to notice. Already on more than one occasion she'd remarked that for someone who was trying to lose weight, he was seriously starting to pile on the pounds again.

'Bernard,' she'd said to him just a few weeks back. 'Are you starting to fasten your belt a notch wider these days, by any chance?'

'What? Oh, no, no, good God absolutely not!' he'd automatically lied, the guilt flooding over him almost overwhelming. 'Doubtless just a little . . . erm . . . water retention, that's all.'

'You think you're retaining water?'

'Well, I have been drinking two litres of the confounded stuff a day, as you recommended, my sausage, so there you go!' he'd answered brightly, hoping that he'd got away with it.

Hauling himself up from his desk, Bernard chanced peeking inside the lunch bag again, just in case there was anything remotely edible in there at all which he could salvage. Two packets of what looked like bird seed, an apple which was starting to rot and a wilting salad made with something called quinoa, and which to Bernard tasted exactly like cardboard.

'Oh this is just ludicrous,' he said out loud, packing up the remainder of the essays he'd been correcting and deciding he could always finish them at home later on in the evening. He'd stay up all night if he had too, but right now no grown man could possibly carry on working on an empty stomach.

An hour later, fully back to his usual good humour after the most delightful Chicken McNuggets with fries (large) and a chocolate sundae to follow, Bernard decided to take a gentle stroll as far as his club. The lecture he'd been so looking forward to was long over by now, but still, there was always the temptation of a lovely soothing glass of sherry after such an arduous day.

At the club bar, he bumped into Edgar and Dickie, two old chums of his from his schooldays back at St Gerald's. Both confirmed bachelors and remarkably contented to be so, Bernard often thought.

'Ahh now here's the soon to be condemned man!' Edgar greeted him warmly with a pat on the back.

'All ready for the off?' said Dickie. 'Not long to go now before you're entered into the marriage stakes!'

'Let's have a little toast to you,' said Edgar, motioning to the barman, who without even having to be asked, immediately brought over three large sherries.

'Let's raise a glass to Bernard's last few weeks as a stodgy old bachelor like ourselves!' said Dickie.

'Yes, absolutely, here's to what remains of the bachelor life for you!' said Edgar, clinking glasses.

Well there you have it, Bernard thought, suddenly feeling terribly sorry for himself as he half-heartedly clinked glasses with the boys.

Goodbye to his bachelor life.

Cheers indeed.

TESS

The present

'So come on then, Tess,' says Will. 'You owe me at least one of all these "long stories" that you keep being so secretive about. Can I remind you that I just made you dinner? And OK, so you only picked around the edges of it, but still. Quid pro quo and all that. Now come on, spill.'

We're sitting out on his balcony, having just finished the last of a gorgeous impromptu penne pasta with garlicky tomatoes and basil that he appeared to rustle up out of a near-empty fridge. It's one of those rare, beautiful, almost Mediterranean-like spring evenings too. Right beside us the sun is just setting over the Marker Hotel, and the canal water five floors beneath looks so pristine clean and sparkling that you'd be half tempted to chance your arm and jump in for a swim.

I could be absolutely anywhere, I think. This feels exactly like being in the South of France or somewhere exotic like that. This feels like taking a break from all the stresses of the real world. This really feels like holidays.

Will tops up my glass of fizzy water, reaching over to a bottle he's placed into a cooler beside him. And for my part

I gratefully let him, not having felt this relaxed and chilled in I can't remember how long.

'So out with it,' he says, still waiting on an answer, 'and enough with your secrecy, Greta Garbo. Storytelling is kind of my line of work and I can faithfully promise you, I'm a particularly attentive audience.'

The black eyes are dancing back at me from across the table and I know right well he's not going to let this go.

'Alright then,' I say. 'Any particular long story you'd like to hear first?'

'Well, how about why you felt so sick earlier? Sounds like as good a place as any to start.'

'It's not what you're thinking anyway,' I tell him, rolling my eyes.

'What was I thinking?'

'Oh, I dunno. That I could be pregnant maybe? Because let me tell you, I'm one hundred per cent definitely not.'

'Thought never crossed my mind,' he says with a tiny smile, folding his arms. 'So come on then, what brought it all on? Tummy bug maybe?'

'You have no idea,' I sigh, taking another sip of water. 'It's just all of this wedding stuff is really getting on top of me, the big day is getting closer and closer, there's still so much to do and . . . oh God, every time I even think about it, I really do feel physically ill.'

'Ooo-kay,' he says thoughtfully, and come to think of it, now that I articulate the thought, it really doesn't sound great when said aloud: bride-to-be vomits publicly on the street with three weeks to go till the final countdown.

'Any chance we can change the subject?' I ask a bit weakly.

'Of course,' he says. 'If that's what you'd like. Subject change. Great. Good idea.'

'Ask me about something else. Anything else.'

'Well,' he says, stretching his long legs out in front of him, 'you mentioned that you were back living at home again.'

'And just when I was starting to relax,' I groan back at him playfully.

He doesn't say anything to that though and now a silence falls between us, broken only by a gang of giggly women down on Grand Canal Square beneath us, squealing like dolphins as if they've just met up and haven't seen each other in decades.

'Let me guess, because of . . . maybe a bit of money trouble?' he said softly, misinterpreting my thoughts. 'Don't worry, we've all been there. I know I certainly have.'

'Oh now would you just listen to the poor little rich boy,' I grin back. 'You're here living the bachelor boy dream in penthouse luxury, and you expect me to believe that you know what it's like to be smashed broke?'

'In fairness, this is all quite recent, you know,' he says, gesturing around him. 'I was only able to afford the deposit on a place like this when my books started to sell. Before then, life was very different, I can tell you.'

'Always great to hear a home grown success story.'

'Modesty prevails me from describing myself as a success story. And believe me, I know exactly how lucky I've been.'

'So . . . what was it like for you before your books took off?'

'How long have you got?' he says, rolling his head back and running his hands through the dark head of hair. 'Take it from me, Tess, that until I changed careers, I had more than my fair share of wondering where the next mortgage payment was going to come from.'

'And what did you work at back in your old life?'

'I worked for a software development company.'

'Fancy job.'

'No, not particularly. I wasn't very good at it. I certainly wasn't happy and it came as no surprise to anyone, least of all me, when they eventually let me go.'

'I'm sorry to hear that,' I say. 'That must have been a horrendous time for you.'

'Certainly was. In fact, I often think that's probably what started to put such a major strain on my marriage. My ex used to say that love goes out the door very quickly once financial pressure creeps in. And she wasn't wrong there either. I can tell you that from bitter experience.'

Silence while we both digest this for a bit.

'Although in spite of my romantic history,' he adds, 'I'd like to think that I'm not quite that cynical at heart. Even if I do happen to write about death, murder, blood and revenge for a living.'

It's a strain to keep my mouth buttoned up, but truth be told I'm itching to ask all about the ex-wife and what exactly happened. Call it the *Rebecca* factor. But Will clams up and very annoyingly doesn't drip-feed me anything more on the subject.

'So how did you get in to writing then?' I ask, steering the chat onto slightly safer ground.

'Ah, now there's a question,' he says with a lazy smile. 'Where do I start? Chance, fate and sheer good fortune, really. Though like a lot of the best things in life, it didn't seem quite like that at the time.'

'What happened?'

'Excuse me, but aren't we meant to be talking about you?'

'You first, you're the host.'

'Alright then, you asked for it,' he says, focusing straight ahead across the balcony and onto the water's edge beneath.

'So, about seven years ago just after I lost my job, I found myself stuck at home all day with absolutely nothing to do. And as you can imagine, I was slowly going out of my mind. Audrey – that's my ex – was only working part-time too, and money was tight as hell for us. Anyway, I started writing short stories, mainly to keep myself sane really.'

Ah. So she's called Audrey.

'Jesus, Tess,' he grins broadly, turning back to face me. 'I can read you like a book. In fact you, my dear, are easier to read than the front page of *The Chronicle*.'

'Excuse me?'

'Even from here, I can sense that feminine mind ticking over,' he smiles. 'So just to satisfy your curiosity, yes, her name is Audrey. And yes, my break-up with her was pure hell. I wouldn't wish it on another living soul. The old story of two mismatched souls who somehow ended up together, then subsequently realised we were far, far better apart. And yes, Audrey's with a new partner now who's a great guy and believe it or not who I'm actually very fond of. She and I won't ever be friends, I don't think, not in the real sense of the word, but we do occasionally stay in touch. She and her partner even came to my last book launch.'

His eye catches mine and he twinkles across at me.

'So now, there's nothing more to see here, Tess,' he says, 'no deep murky secrets for you to unearth.'

'Well it's certainly great to hear that you're on such good terms,' I say, slightly morto that I can be read this easily.

'And now can we get back to you?' he says, turning his head away from the view to look at me. 'I've just given you a potted version of my own autobiography, and now it's your go. Fair's fair and all that. Start with why you're living with your folks and we can take it from there. Don't worry, I'll ask questions if I need to. I do a lot of author Q&A sessions; I'm well used to it.'

I take another tiny sip of the water.

'Well, before I met Bernard,' I tell him, 'I was with a long-term boyfriend and we shared a flat together.'

There. Now that wasn't so bad, was it? I managed to get that much out alright and it didn't even make me feel nauseous all over again.

Whaddya know. I must be improving.

'Name, rank and serial number, please?' Will says.

'You really need that level of detail?'

'Writers always need back-stories. Come on, humour me. Fill me in.'

'OK then, he was called Paul,' I say, invoking his name, in a way I never, ever allow myself to. 'He's a physiotherapist and we'd been together for so long I think everyone just assumed he and I were a done deal.'

'So what went wrong?'

'He did. Very, very wrong. So wrong you'd choke on your drink wrong.'

'I'm all ears.'

I sigh, sensing that Will isn't going to let this drop.

'In a nutshell, he went off to Manchester to work and was away for five days a week, but then back home with me for weekends.'

'Ah, the classic five: two relationship. Tell me more and rest assured I promise not to put any of this into a book.'

'You'd better not!' I say, mock horrified. 'Although mine is such a textbook case, I doubt anyone would even be interested.'

379

'Well I am, for one.'

'Your common or garden case of cheating, that's what happened,' I say quietly, feelings that I've long since dealt with and locked away now threatening to bark at the door all over again.

'A cheater?' Will says, and even from here I can see his fists clenching inside his pockets. 'Bastard. No excuse for it. Absolutely none.'

'Turned out that he'd met someone else over there – an actress, to really make me feel good about myself – and that was the end of that.'

'Ouch. An actress? Such a cliché. Might I have heard of her? What has she been in?'

'Panto and five episodes of *Hollyoaks*. I googled her.'

'A truly fitting contribution to world culture. So how did you find out? Did your ex behave like a gentleman and, overwhelmed by guilt, confess all?'

'Are you kidding? That was the worst part of all. I actually found out through her.'

Oh, Christ can I even finish telling this?

'Through the erstwhile Meryl Streep?'

'Via social media, if you can even believe that. She friended me on Facebook, explained that she'd got pally with Paul in Manchester then started posting all sorts of photos of the two of them that . . . well that got me suspicious, let's just say.'

'What sort of photos?'

'Nothing incriminating, it was just that they seemed to be spending so much time together. She'd send photos of them in bars and restaurants and at football matches, then when he'd come home, all he could do was talk about her.'

'And did you confront him? Please say yes. I love a good juicy confrontation scene.'

'Course I did. But it was how he handled it that really was the clincher. He denied, denied, denied that there was anything going on.'

'I'm told they all do.'

'He claimed they were part of a gang of friends who hung out together, and that was it . . .'

'Which may have been true, I suppose.'

'. . . well that's just it, his lies were so convincing that I completely believed him . . . I wanted to believe him.'

'I find there's nothing more dangerous in this world than a good liar.'

'. . . But it was still agony for me every single Sunday night when he'd head back to Manchester for the week ahead and I wouldn't have a clue what he was up to over there.'

'Ah, the erosion of trust. Fatal to any relationship.'

'Then not long afterwards, he came clean and told me he'd actually been seeing this actressy one – sorry, I still can't even bring myself to say her name—'

'She's secondary to the story, don't worry, I don't need a name.'

'Well the upshot of it was that they'd been together, actually properly together for months. And to make matters worse, he'd been living with her Monday to Friday the whole time, then coming home to me at weekends. To my knowledge he's still with her now.'

'Please tell me you did at least get to whack him over the head with the back of a frying pan and rip up his clothes when you found out? Shitheads like him deserve no less. In one of my books, he'd have been murdered in cold blood by now.'

381

'There was a horrible scene of course – more than one – but you know how it is. I think I ended up crying in front of him mainly, then spent weeks afterwards full of Smart Alec indignation thinking of all the stingers I actually could have come out with. Oh God, Will, it was all just such a mess. We'd just put a deposit on a house together, but then when we broke up, I couldn't bear the thought of living there, not to mention the fact that I wouldn't be able to afford the mortgage on my own. You see, I'd really thought that would be a home for us. Our permanent home, *my* permanent home—'

I break off here though, astonished that the memory still has the power to sting with pain. Even from a safe distance of three full years. Even now.

'Anyway, I moved out . . .' I go on, aware that Will is looking worriedly at me across the table now. 'But of course, I lost my deposit on the house, so I ended up losing all my savings. In the space of a few short months, I lost everything. The man I loved, my home, my money, my whole future, everything.'

'Jesus, Tess, that's rough,' he says gently. 'I don't know what to say, except I really can sympathise. What an arse that Paul is.'

'So I'd no choice but to go back to Mum and Dad—'

'With your dignity intact, though.'

'My dignity may have been intact, but I can tell you at the time I felt like a complete failure.'

'Au contraire,' he says, his eyes looking softly across at me. 'Like a very brave girl, who wasn't prepared to compromise.'

'And then not long after, I met Bernard.'

'Who's the complete opposite of Paul, I'd imagine.'

'Gracie, my sister, always calls him the anti-Paul. And yeah, I'd been lied to and cheated on and dumped in the worst way you can imagine, then along comes this sweet, older man who I knew in a million years would never put me through the emotional wringer I'd just been through. You've no idea, my whole faith in men had been totally eroded and I suppose he helped me to heal, in a way. After just a year, he was talking about marriage. Whereas with Paul, we were a full six years together and it was a hard slog getting him to commit to a dinner with my family.'

Bernard, I think, my thoughts drifting. Who I still haven't heard a word from all day. Nor come to think of it, have I been in touch with him either. I suddenly go quiet just at the mention of him.

Then with a sinking heart I think of Saturday night and this sten do that's looming and just about everything that still has to be done in time for it. I texted Mum earlier to say I'd be a bit delayed getting home, but faithfully promised that I'd stay up all night if need be, to get the house ready.

Mum, I think, suddenly sitting up straight. And Gracie. And bloody Saturday night. And the wedding, and all the hundred thousand jobs that still have to be done for it. And just like that, the spell of this beautiful sunlit balcony and the feeling that I'm a thousand miles away from all the stresses in my life instantly shatters. I glance down at my phone, suddenly aware that I've lost all track of time. And sure enough, there's a text I must have missed waiting for me from the Mothership. One of her super-long ones too:

OFF TO BINGO WITH THE GIRLS. SO NOW YOUR JOB, MISSY, IS TO MAKE ENOUGH VEGETARIAN CANNELLONI FOR TWENTY-FIVE PEOPLE FOR SATURDAY. BE WARNED THOUGH THAT IF I COME HOME TO EVEN AS MUCH AS A DIRTY SAUCEPAN IN THE SINK, IF THERE'S AS MUCH AS A STRAY BIT OF PASTA ON THE COUNTER, YOU'LL KNOW ALL ABOUT IT.

Then a second one, as if to reinforce it:

TESS? WHERE ARE YOU ANYWAY? HOME. GET HOME NOW! GET YOUR APRON ON AND GET TO WORK!

'Will, I really need to go,' I say, abruptly getting up to leave. He looks surprised, but stands up with me and politely slides the balcony door open as I head back into the warmth of the apartment inside.

'None of my business of course,' he says, 'but that text message. The fiancé, I'm guessing?'

'Oh, just more wedding crap. So much still to do, you wouldn't believe it.'

'Not such a good sign when a bride-to-be is referring to her upcoming nuptials as "more wedding crap".'

'You'd be very surprised just how much sheer crapology is involved.'

'You never finished telling me about Bernard,' he says. 'Though a lot of things are starting to make more sense to me now.'

'Like what?' I ask, stopping in my tracks, suddenly intrigued.

384

'You really want me to tell you?'

I turn to face him, with my arms folded. 'Go on then, smart-arse.'

'Well, I'd hardly be a million miles off the mark in assuming that this Bernard guy is something of a rebounder for you. So far, so obvious.'

Jesus, I think, freezing on the spot. Deep down I've always known as much, but there's something about another person stating it out loud that's actually frightening.

'It would certainly account for a lot of things,' he goes on. 'How angry and upset you were when I bumped into you last weekend for one thing, after you'd rowed with him. Why you never wear an engagement ring, for another.'

'Will,' I say in a small voice, 'can we drop this? Please?'

But it's like he's not hearing me.

'. . . And so now of course, with the clock ticking down to the actual wedding, it's highly probable that cold, hard reality is finally starting to set in,' he chats on, seemingly unaware that I'm almost glaring at him by now. 'You've been so bogged down in jury service and bridal centrepieces and wedding bands and bridesmaids' dresses, that it's easy to lose sight of the fact there's going to be a man waiting for you at an altar very soon. So now you're at this emotional crossroads, is my guess. You're thinking . . . all this fuss for one day, but come the day after, you could well find your-self looking at someone who was a rebound guy for you at best. One day, Tess, versus the rest of your whole life. I've tried to tell you before and you didn't listen to me then. So I'm only hoping you will now before it's too late.'

A pause and it's like he's suddenly aware that I'm scarlet in the face by now, a red hotness burning through me.

'Oh God,' he says, seeing my expression and instantly

backtracking. 'Forgive me for being so cheeky and for rambling on. You have to understand that we fiction writers have very vivid imaginations.'

I say nothing though. Just grab my jacket and bag and make for the hall door. He follows me, walks with me as far as the lift and presses the button for it. It arrives and we both step into the cool, marble interior. I'm aware of him looking over at me, but still can't bring myself to meet his gaze.

'Tess?' he says softly as the lift zooms down. 'Did I push it a bit too far?'

I don't answer.

'Old habit of mine, I'm afraid,' he says after a pause. 'Making all sorts of rash assumptions and invariably jumping to the wrong conclusions. Authors are ruthless like that, I'm sorry to say. We sense a story and just have to get to the bottom of it.'

Another pause while I just stare into the brass reflection on the lift door. My own face looking blankly back at me while Will looks on, hands like fists shoved into his pockets.

'Tess?' he says gently as the lift comes to a stop. 'Come on, talk to me. Say something. Don't leave like this.'

We step out together and he follows me through the main entrance door and out onto the busyness of Ringsend Road, just adjacent to Charlotte Quay Dock. Automatically, I start looking left and right for a cab, but next thing I'm aware of, Will has swung me around to face him, his hands clamped down on both of my shoulders.

'I'm so sorry,' he says. 'There we were having a perfectly lovely evening and then I went and blew it, didn't I?'

'No, no you didn't,' I say, seeing just how concerned he really is. 'This is something—'

'Yes?'

'Well let's just say that it's a very confusing time for me, that's all. And . . . no . . . you weren't wrong in what you said at all. In fact you were more accurate than you probably even know.'

'Then all I can do is keep saying sorry,' he says, eyes burning into mine. 'Me and my bloody big mouth. Wouldn't be the first time it's got me into trouble. So are you OK?'

A pause that almost throbs as the traffic whooshes past us.

'No,' I say, almost under my breath, shaking my head back at him. 'No, Will, I'm about as far from OK as you can get. So much is happening all at once and . . . oh God, do you ever just feel like events have taken over your life and you're powerless to do a single thing about it?'

'Every single day of my life,' he says wryly.

'And just for the record,' I add. 'What you said back there about Bernard being a rebound relationship for me was—'

His black eyes are scrutinising my face now, just waiting.

'Well, my family certainly do agree with you. Mum, Dad, even my sister Gracie.'

'Then as my little niece always says to me, let's hug it out,' Will says, opening his arms wide. 'Trust me, a good hug makes everything better.'

So I fall into him and we hug, tightly. And it feels warm and secure and he smells just lovely; strong and musky and comforting. Exactly what I needed right now.

A couple more taxis swish by and I let them, and still our hug goes on, both Will's arms locked around my waist now. I snuggle my head against his shoulder and am suddenly aware that he's starting to stroke my hair gently.

'He's a lucky guy, this Bernard fella,' he says quietly. 'I

387

hope he knows that. And I hope he's good to you and treats you well.'

I don't answer though, just stay locked where I am, enjoying this moment of closeness, unable to break away just yet. Bernard and I never hug, not properly, not like this. But then, he's such a big man that I only ever end up bouncing off him.

Then Will pulls back a tiny bit, lightly putting his fingers under my chin and tilting my face up to him.

'Goodnight then, Tess.'

'Goodnight.'

He bends down to kiss me lightly on the lips. Just once.

And then twice. And by the third time neither of us can stop. Then somehow he and I are kissing full-on and it's warm and getting hotter and sexy as hell and somehow even if I wanted to, I just can't seem to break away.

KATE

Friday morning, 8 a.m.

'You all set?' said Mo.

'As I'll ever be,' Kate replied, praying that some of Mo's latent confidence might just rub off on her.

Mo, ever a true pal, had offered to drive Kate in to court today and not only that, but said she'd sit in the public benches too, to lend all the moral support she could from the side lines.

'You know I'll never be able to thank you enough for all this,' Kate said, as they zoomed down the N11 motorway on their way to the Criminal Courts of Justice.

'Don't be so ridiculous,' said Mo briskly, eyes focused on the road ahead. 'Today is a big one for you and there was no way I was letting you face that alone.'

Just then, the eight o'clock news came on the radio and instinctively Mo went to switch it off.

'You don't need to hear this, dearest,' she said. 'And I know I certainly could do without it.'

'Actually,' said Kate, the thought just occurring to her. 'Let's leave it on. See what they're making of all this.'

'Sure?' asked Mo warily glancing at her out of the corner of her eye.

'Certain.'

So Mo raised up the volume as a newsreader's voice filled the Jeep.

The headlines were all about the housing crisis, followed by a report about pressure on banks to cut variable mortgage interest rates. And sure enough, there it was, third item on the news.

'Today at the Criminal Courts of Justice,' the news anchor went on, a man with a voice full of pompous authority. 'All eyes will surely turn to court number seven, where defendant Kate King has called a surprise witness, a noted art historian from City College. The court has been in recess for the past few days, but later this morning, he'll take the stand. And now over to our special correspondent, who has more for us.'

'I'm here at the Criminal Courts of Justice,' began another news reporter, a woman who Kate was starting to recognise by sight, she'd seen her so often outside the court, microphone in hand, 'where there's a considerable amount of speculation about the latest twist in the King case. Mr Jasper Adams from City College is due to take the stand today and the question on everyone's lips appears to be, why? Oliver Daniels for the Prosecution vehemently protested against the inclusion of this witness and was overruled. This clearly points to the Defence possibly having new information to bring to the case, which had previously been withheld. All in all, today should certainly be an interesting one here at court number seven. I'll be back with more, just after the lunchtime news. And now, back to you in the studio.'

Mo leaned forward and snapped off the radio, glancing over at Kate to see how she was taking it.

'Alright?' she asked.

'Better than that,' Kate said. 'Because, just think . . . today it all ends. Everything. For better or for worse.'

'I'll be there beside you all the way,' said Mo encouragingly.

'And I'll never have words enough to thank you,' Kate replied, sitting back against the warmth of the leather passenger seat, silently blessing her good fortune in having a pal like Mo. 'Do you know, I once read a quote that said a friend is someone who'll help you to move house. But you know what the definition of a true friend is?'

'What's that?' Mo asked, slowing the Jeep down at traffic lights.

'Someone who'll help you to move a body in the middle of the night and then never speak of it again.'

For a moment the two women just looked at each other, then smiled.

TESS

Friday, 9.55 a.m.

I'm late into court this morning (nothing to wear, missed bus, heavy traffic, etc.). But I think the actual subliminal reason is because I wanted to avoid facing Will for as long as I possibly could. Puerile, I know, given that we're going to be sitting in court together for the day, but still.

By the time I get into the jury room, Moany Mona looks like she's just about to send out a search party to look for me.

'There you are!' she barks, as everyone else looks over at me, all lined up and ready to move. 'You almost delayed this court session, you know. I'd kindly remind you to be punctual in future.'

'Sorry about that,' I mutter lamely, hobbling over to join the end of the line, eyes constantly attuned to where Will is. Hard to miss him though, given that he's about a foot taller than everyone else here. He's just three in front of me as it happens, sandwiched in between Daphne and Mai. He turns around and gives me a tiny smile, but instead of acknowledging it, I blush, ignore him and pretend I didn't see.

I've got the bad luck to have Edith beside me though, who misses absolutely nothing. She looks first at Will, then at me, then nudges Jess beside her.

'I think I just won a bet,' she says, a bit too knowingly for my liking, before we're ushered through the doors and on into court number seven.

*

It's a charged atmosphere in court today and Hilda Cassidy wastes absolutely no time in calling her late witness to the stand. Jasper Adams turns out to be quite a short man, even Sandra the Court Registrar is towering over him and she herself is petite. He's wearing a bow tie with an immaculately pressed tweed suit that's creased so sharply down the front you could probably cut yourself on it. Gay or else living with his mammy, I immediately decide, giving him the once over.

My eyes then veer across to Kate, sitting serenely composed in a long, elegant cream suit today. First time, I think, that I've ever seen her looking calm and not totally on edge. Damien, on the other hand, is sitting right behind Oliver Daniels, eyes focused like lasers on this new witness, taking absolutely everything in.

Anyway, Jasper takes the oath and coughs discreetly into a hanky as Hilda launches straight into her first question.

'Dr Adams,' she says clearly, hands clamped behind her back. 'Would you care to tell us when you first met Mrs Kate King?'

'Certainly,' he says in a thin, reedy voice. 'Mrs King first contacted me back in April of last year. I was lecturing in UCD at the time and while one doesn't like to blow one's own trumpet, it seems she'd heard I was one of the country's foremost experts on seventeenth-century Dutch Masters.'

'Modest bugger, isn't he?' Beth whispers into my ear and I can't help smiling.

'Can you tell us Mrs King's reason for getting in touch with you?'

'She came to see me at the university and told me that her husband was in the process of purchasing the painting in question, *A Lady of Letters*. And as he was expected to pay a vast amount of money for it, she merely wished to know a little more about it, just out of curiosity and nothing else. Most prudent of her, I thought at the time. After all, it's a work of some note. Who wouldn't wish to know more?'

'And what were you able to tell Mrs King at this point?'

'Regrettably, very little. Although the painting is an important one, it seems that it had disappeared into private hands in the last century and little is known of its whereabouts since the early 1900s onwards. However, I was able to confirm a rather interesting backstory about it, namely that it's rumoured to be cursed. Tracing back to the late-eighteenth century, it appears that during the French Revolution, it was in the hands of the Marquis of Montmarcy, a loyal advisor to Louis VI, who was subsequently executed during the Terror.'

'Your Honour, is this meandering history lesson really necessary?' says Oliver, straight up on his feet, red-faced. 'Rumours of curses and speculation about the painting's history are hardly relevant. This is a court of law, not a college lecture theatre.'

'I'll allow it,' says Judge Simmonds. 'But keep to the point,' she adds as a warning to Hilda.

'Dr Adams,' Hilda goes on smoothly. 'Am I right in thinking that was the end of your dealings with Katherine King?'

'Yes,' he nods. 'She very kindly invited me to her birthday party, where the painting was to be unveiled. Regrettably, however, I was unable to attend as my mother was unwell at the time.'

'Nothing serious, I hope?' Hilda asks politely.

'I'm afraid she's a martyr to her piles.'

Titters around the court at that, but Hilda ploughs on, undeterred.

'However, some months ago, you did begin to conduct more extensive investigations into the painting's history, is that right?'

'Correct,' says Jasper, wiping his nose with the hanky again in an affected little gesture. 'When first approached by the Defence in relation to this court case, I was asked to dig a little deeper into the painting's remarkable history. During the course of these investigations, some new information came to light and then, just a few days ago, I received the concrete proof I'd been hoping for. Which naturally brings me here today.'

'Tell us what it was that you discovered, Dr Adams,' says Hilda, 'in your own time.'

'Certainly,' he nods. 'It seems that Mr King purchased the painting from a perfectly reputable auction house in London in spring of last year. To neither party in this case do I apportion any wrongdoing on that score. After all, although the phrase "caveat emptor" generally holds true, in this case we can exonerate both parties of any blame attached to purchasing the painting in question.'

A few puzzled mumblings throughout the court at that,

which Judge Simmonds silences with a hammer of her gavel.

'Please elaborate further for us, Dr Adams,' Hilda prompts.

'Of course,' Jasper says in the thin little voice. 'You see, Damien King acquired *A Lady of Letters* from art dealers who enjoy the highest reputation internationally. They had naturally authenticated the painting prior to the sale and conclusively proved that it was in fact a particularly rare late-period Rembrandt. One that had been in private hands, for the past number of decades. Legally, that's all they were obliged to do, you know. When selling any painting, any vendor's primary obligation is to prove that it is indeed an original.'

'And what of the painting's provenance?' Hilda probes.

'Ah, now this is where it gets really interesting,' he replies.

'For those among the jury who may be unfamiliar with the term,' says Hilda, 'perhaps you'd explain what art dealers mean when they speak of provenance?'

'By all means,' Jasper says, turning to face the jury box this time, where we're all looking a bit confused, knowing that something potentially game-changing is coming, but not having a clue what it might be. 'When we speak of a painting's provenance, it's generally more of a moral issue, really.'

'Go on,' says Hilda.

'Provenance, you see, is a term we use to describe the chronology of ownership, not just of paintings, but of archives, manuscripts, and even printed books. Its use is primarily to help authenticate historical objects, as so many forgeries can be uncannily accurate.'

'And was such a document available for *A Lady of Letters*?'

'No, it would seem not. However, this wouldn't be unusual

for a painting of this age. Given that *A Lady of Letters* has been around since the late-seventeenth century, it would in fact be highly unusual for a document of provenance to still be in existence.'

'So the painting was authenticated in other ways prior to the Prosecution purchasing it?'

'Yes, naturally. Any art historian would first look at the brushwork and of course the signature, before dating the materials and carrying out a full Morellian analysis. This is a technique we use to examine an artist's repeated stylistic details which again all contribute to establishing the veracity of a painting.'

'However, in addition to that, you have since made one other significant discovery of note?'

'Yes, that's absolutely right,' says Jasper a bit smugly, actually looking like he's enjoying all the attention. 'And it was a difficult task for me, as you can appreciate. *A Lady of Letters* has been held in private collections for many decades now. And that in itself gave me my first hint that there might be more to this than met the eye.'

'Will you elaborate?'

There's not as much as a whisper or a cough to be heard as we all strain forward in our seats to hear. Even the press corps have stopped tapping away on their iPads and all eyes totally focus on the witness box.

'I'd be delighted to,' says Jasper, almost puffing up with the importance of what he's about to tell us. 'It certainly hasn't been easy, but I've found that it's possible to trace the painting all the way from the seventeenth century, right through to the turn of the last century. It seems then that *A Lady of Letters* surfaced in a small auction house in the USA. In New York, to be exact. This was during the First World War and the year, I think you'll find, is quite significant.'

'Can you tell us the year?'

'1915. May 1915, to be precise.'

'Go on, please,' says Hilda.

'Then subsequent to my research, just a few days ago I was successfully able to confirm that the painting was purchased from this auction house for a record price.'

'Purchased by who, exactly?'

'By a Sir Hugh Lane.'

Ripples throughout the court at the name and once again Judge Simmonds has to call for silence.

'For those on the jury who may not be aware,' says Hilda, 'would you tell the court exactly who Sir Hugh Lane was, and the fate that befell him?'

'Certainly,' says Jasper, looking like a man whose moment in the spotlight has finally come. 'Sir Hugh was a noted Irish art collector and as you know, made sizable donations to the world-famous gallery here in Dublin which today bears his name. However, he was unfortunate enough to be a passenger on the RMS *Lusitania* in May 1915, where sadly he perished, along with some twelve hundred other poor souls.'

'And is it fair to assume,' says Hilda, both her hands on the witness box now, 'given that Sir Hugh had just paid such a great deal for the painting in the exact same month he travelled, that it would have journeyed with him as he made the transatlantic crossing?'

'Of course we can never say for certain,' says Jasper, 'but in my opinion, I think we can safely assume that he would most definitely have taken the painting with him. It's thought that Sir Hugh was travelling with many other noted artworks too, a Degas and a Monet included. All would naturally have been sealed in lead-lined cases and safely stowed in the cargo holds of the ship, as was standard practice at the time. Naturally it's not for us to deduce as to how such a painting – and I'm sure many others along with it – subsequently came to reappear in private collections around the world.'

'But what conclusion would you draw, Dr Adams?'

Pin-drop silence as every eye in the room is focused on him.

Jasper coughs once again into his hanky before answering. 'That it certainly can't have been through honest means.'

'Do you mean that it was looted?'

'Most likely, yes. The *Lusitania* sank in shallow water a mere few nautical miles from the Cork coastline and was, and is to this day, readily accessible. It's been rumoured for decades now that illegal looting has gone on. How else can we account for a painting such as this one miraculously resurfacing? It can never be proven beyond all doubt, but it is my firm belief that this is what happened. After all, the painting was being stowed in an air-tight, lead-lined casket. It would have survived the sinking intact. And clearly, it did.'

'I must object most strenuously,' Oliver huffs and puffs, straight up on his feet. 'Rumours have no place in a court of law, Your Honour. Besides, what proof does Dr Adams have that links Sir Hugh Lane to the painting?'

'You're about to see,' says Hilda, before striding over to her desk and taking a sheaf of papers offered to her by one of her junior counsels. 'Your Honour, may I submit this as exhibit A? You'll find it's a record from the archives of the Feinberg and Son art dealership on Park Avenue in

New York. Sadly this dealership went out of business during the Depression, but Dr Adams managed to unearth a record of the sales transaction from the private archives of the family's descendants.'

Judge Simmonds takes her copy and then Hilda steps over to the jury box and hands us each a sheet of photocopied A4 paper, then reads it out to the court. It's difficult to make out, the writing on it is so spidery and scrawly, but I can clearly see the name Feinberg and Son at the top of the page, and the name Hugh Lane at the bottom. And there it is, dated and everything, *A Lady of Letters*, purchased on 1st May, 1915 for fifty thousand dollars.

After Hilda finishes reading it out loud, instead of a hush in court, there's now full-on murmuring. Even from up here in the jury box, you can clearly hear one word being bandied about: looting. The painting was more than likely looted from the wreck of the *Lusitania*. It must have been, there's no other possible explanation.

I look around the jury box and accidentally catch Will's eye. He's nodding, as if he'd always suspected there was more to this case than met the eye and now he's been proved right.

And then my eye wanders back to Damien King, who looks, there's no other word for it, thunderous.

*

No sooner do we have time to digest this latest twist than Hilda calls her last and final witness.

'The Defence now calls Mrs Kate King,' is announced to a crescendo of astonishment from around the court. I swear I can even see one press hack's jaw physically drop, like something out of a cartoon.

'Sweet baby Jesus and the orphans,' hisses Minnie from behind me, 'I think I'm going to need one of my heart pills after all this excitement.'

'Never saw that one coming,' says Beth.

Nor, it's safe to say, did any of the rest of us. But then Kate always seemed so nervy and edgy throughout this, it almost feels like a sacrificial lamb is about to go to the slaughter. As if a woman who's been accused of witchcraft is about to be flung into a pit surrounded by villagers with pitchforks shouting 'burn the witch!'

Not for the first time since this all started, I have the hugest surge of sympathy for the woman, in spite of horrible things I've read and heard about her since all this started. Because no one deserves what Kate King now has to go through. Absolutely no one.

Calmly, moving almost balletically, she glides across the court, steps up to the witness box and takes the oath. Her voice is soft, so quiet in fact that it's almost a strain to hear her. Every eye in the whole court is trained on that beautiful, angular face as Hilda steps up to question her.

'Mrs King,' she begins. 'This case, as you can imagine, has been the subject of much speculation and conjecture since we opened.'

'Yes, I'm well aware of that,' Kate says, immediately putting me in mind of Grace Kelly in *Rear Window*. The posture, the blonde elegance, that whisper of a voice; everything.

'Now, Mrs King, I'm about to ask you a hypothetical question, but one that it appears no one else in this room, not even my learned friend, has even considered asking,' says Hilda.

'By all means,' says Kate quietly.

'Should the jury award in your favour, and should the good people of the jury decide *A Lady of Letters* be established as your rightful property, what are your intentions towards it? What will you do with such a prize? Sell it on at a profit for your own gain, perhaps? If we're to believe what we read in the papers, certainly a great many people appear to think that's the case. Or maybe keep it as a trophy to show off on your drawing room wall?'

'Absolutely not,' Kate says, raising her voice a little so we can all hear her a bit better this time. 'Admittedly, maybe those were my intentions when the case first began, but Mr Jasper Adams's testimony has changed everything for me.'

'So what would your intentions be, should the result of this case go in your favour?'

'My intentions,' says Kate to a dead silence around the court, 'would be to fulfil the wishes of the late Sir Hugh Lane. He intended that *A Lady of Letters* should be kept here in Ireland and exhibited publicly in Dublin, for everyone to see.'

'Can you elaborate further for us?' prompts Hilda.

'Should the painting be awarded to me,' says Kate softly, 'I would donate the painting to the Hugh Lane Gallery in Dublin, as it's now my firm belief that that's where it should have been all this time.'

'No further questions, Your Honour.'

I look around the court and see Damien King and Oliver deep in hurried conversation and then my eye falls on Mo Kennedy, that friend of Kate's who gave testimony yesterday. She gives Kate a wink and a tiny thumbs-up and Kate doesn't just smile back at her, she actually beams. Like a woman who's just had a vast load lifted from those skinny, bony shoulders.

Predictably, Oliver Daniels is up on his feet to cross-question.

'Mrs King,' he begins, 'in consideration that there's not a single shred of concrete evidence to connect the painting with Sir Hugh Lane's passage on the *Lusitania*, we'll glide over that for now.'

'Objection, Your Honour,' says Hilda, straight up onto her feet. 'An expert witness has just told us that it's his considered opinion that was the case.'

'Rephrase your question,' Judge Simmonds says to Oliver.

He sighs, before continuing.

'It is not my business to engage in speculation and conjecture, Mrs King. However, there is one important question that still remains unanswered.'

Kate looks quizzically back at him while just feet away her ex-husband sits back with his arms folded, just like the rest of us, listening intently.

'Where is the painting right now?'

'It's perfectly safe, I can assure you, Mr Daniels,' Kate tells him calmly.

'I repeat the question,' says Oliver, raising his voice so the question actually sounds like a threat now.

'Very well,' says Kate as we all hang on what she's about to say next. 'At this moment in time, *A Lady of Letters* is hanging in the home of Mrs Mo Kennedy, who has been a great friend to me throughout this whole ordeal. Who is, in fact, my best friend. And my prayer is that it'll remain there until such time as I have the pleasure of returning it to its rightful place. Which is, and always should have been, at the Hugh Lane Gallery.'

*

403

It's the strangest and most surreal thing. Whereas a lot of testimony in this case almost seemed to move at a snail's pace, now suddenly there's almost an urgency to it. As though both Defence and Prosecution have laid out their stalls for us and just want to get a verdict in as quickly as possible.

So now it's over to Judge Simmonds for a brief summing up.

'Ladies and gentlemen of the jury,' she says, addressing us directly. 'Over the past week, you've had to digest a great deal of testimony from both parties. On one hand, you have the Prosecution who doubtless have a rightful claim to the painting in dispute. Damien King bought it in good faith and also in the name of the King family trust. His intentions towards the painting are, as you know, to tour it across the United States under the donorship of that family trust. These are noble motivations indeed and for such, the Prosecution can only be commended.

'However, the Defence raise an interesting case too. It's Mrs Kate King's contention that she was gifted the portrait and if you're to believe this, then this matter should never have come to court in the first place. Indeed, had Defence and Prosecution been on more amiable terms, then perhaps the need for this expensive court case might have been side-stepped altogether. However, such was not the case, and now it falls to you to decide on an outcome.

'Nor do I envy you your task,' Judge Simmonds goes on. 'Just this morning alone, the Defence have raised no doubt valid points concerning the painting's rightful provenance. It is not for the jury to speculate as to whether or not the painting – along with others – was indeed looted from the wreck of the *Lusitania*. Of course it has been rumoured

404

for some time now that many such lootings did in fact take place in the years following the sinking. As Mr Jasper Adams told us, the *Lusitania* sank a mere few nautical miles from the coastline. Who knows what might have happened to the wreck in the years that immediately followed? It is certainly not the work of the jury to decide.

'All I charge you to do is to bear in mind that Mrs King now also offers a noble reason for so wanting the painting declared to be in her possession. So that it may be donated to the Hugh Lane Gallery, and displayed there to be enjoyed by everyone. However, and I must stress this, it's natural that your decision may be swayed by what will ultimately happen to such an important piece of art. But please remember that your primary duty is to award the painting to whomever you feel is the rightful owner, regardless of their ultimate intentions towards it.

'And now, ladies and gentlemen,' she says, getting up to rise. 'You will shortly be escorted to the jury room to begin your deliberations. This court is adjourned until you've reached a unanimous verdict.'

'All rise!' says Sandra the Court Registrar as Judge Simmonds sweeps back to her chambers and now – for better or for worse – it's over to us.

KATE

Castletown House, June 2014

'Stockpile.'

Those had been Mo's exact words to Kate that night they lay holed up in the library at Castletown House, and this time, she wasn't taking no for an answer.

'Now just listen to me,' she'd gone on to say, with an urgency in her voice. 'It's past eleven now, my babysitter will have put the kids to bed and Joe is away in New York for a big Globtech conference tomorrow. So it's now or never, babes. We've got to act fast.'

'What are you talking about?' said Kate, looking at her, wondering if Mo had momentarily lost her reason.

'What I'm trying to say is that right now we've got this whole house to ourselves,' Mo said, 'and there's no time like the present.'

'So . . . what do you mean?'

'I'm saying that this ridiculous pre-nup that you were practically strong-armed into signing leaves you with next to nothing. And I know you say you don't care about money—'

'And I don't, as it happens,' Kate said firmly.

'But you may well change your mind, and in the very near future too. So why don't we just put by a little pension plan for you? Just for a rainy day, that's all. A little bit of security, just in case you ever should need to fall back on it.'

'What are you thinking of?'

'Well for a start, how about that ridiculous monstrosity that Damien gave you for your birthday? It's your property after all, so what are you doing wrong?'

What indeed, Kate thought.

*

A Lady of Letters was a dead weight, and it took both women puffing and panting to haul it all the way down the hallway at Castletown and out into the boot of Mo's Jeep. It was just coming up to midnight when half an hour later, they pulled up at Mo's home, swished through the security gates and pulled up at a discreet side door that led directly into the utility rooms.

'Mo, are you sure about this?' Kate asked worriedly, as the pair of them shuffled down the back hallway, out of breath from the effort of lifting the painting. 'Supposing Joe finds it and tells Damien?'

'Trust me, he'll be doing no such thing,' Mo said bluntly.

'But how do you know for certain?'

'Because we're going to leave this baby in the only room in the house he never, ever goes into.'

'Where?'

'The laundry room,' Mo said, with a conspiratorial wink. 'If I gave Joe a map of this house, he still wouldn't be able to find it. In fact, I doubt he even knows that we have a laundry room at all.'

Kate put down the painting for a moment so she could rest, and in spite of herself she smiled. And even through the dimly lit hallway, Mo was grinning right back at her.

TESS

Friday, 11 a.m.

We don't get off to a very good start. After we're led off to, or rather shoved into, the jury room by Mona, we're given clear instructions that we're not allowed to leave the room till the end of the day. Till then, if there's anything we need, all we need do is ask for it.

'In that case,' says Ian cheekily, 'I'll have a pint of Heineken with a packet of salt and vinegar on the side.'

'And a Margarita straight up for me!' says Daphne cheerily, before hissing to the rest of us, 'I haven't a clue what that is, but I've always wanted to try one.'

Cackles around the room at that as we all gravitate towards seats around the huge, round conference table. Will and I lock eyes and there's a moment of will we/won't we confusion as to just how far apart we can sit, but in the end he sorts it out for me by pulling out a chair for me right in between Edith and Minnie.

'Thanks,' I say to him.

'No problem,' he says with a tiny half-smile. First actual words we've spoken to each other all morning. 'So how are you today?' he adds, a bit formally.

'Ehh . . . very well, thank you,' I answer stiffly.

Christ, I think. Last time we were together, we were snogging the faces off each other on a street corner. It was hot and sexy as hell and if I'd not somehow peeled myself away in time, God knows where things might have led. And now we sound like two characters from a regency novel, all over-politeness and reserve as we neatly side-step each other.

'Hmm,' says Edith from beside me, the beady blue eyes taking in this innocent little exchange. And I swear you can almost see her putting two and two together and coming up with about a zillion.

First job is to elect a jury foreman and already there's a row. Will throws his hat into the ring, but Barney is hot on his heels.

'In fairness now, I've a lot more life experience under my belt than you, son,' he says. 'Plus I've a whole mine of case information I've studied that I can draw on to help us. Can you say the same?'

'In that case, please go ahead,' says Will pleasantly.

'Hang on a minute, why does it have to be a man?' says Jane. 'Even the phrase 'jury fore*man*' is pejorative. Won't any of the ladies put themselves forward?'

'Well I would,' says Mai, 'if I thought I might get paid or something.'

'Doesn't work like that, you eejit,' Minnie nudges her.

'If it'll shut you all up,' says Daphne, 'then go on, stick me down for it. Only I have to warn you, I'm inclined to be a bit forgetful these days. I mean, I remember all the testimony we heard this morning, but ask me to go back further and I'm worse than useless.'

'Tess, you volunteer for it for us, there's a good girl,' says Minnie.

'Ehh . . . sorry?' I say, miles away, but then I'd kind of tuned out a bit till they got this sorted between them.

'Yes, that's a great idea,' says Edith, 'I vote for Tess!'

'Seconded,' says Will as we lock eyes again. He gives me a little nod of encouragement.

'Well, OK, then,' I say reluctantly, 'if it'll get us all out of here that bit quicker—'

'Ah, now hang on a minute, what about me?' says Barney to muted groans around the table. He then spends the next half hour – I kid you not – extolling the reasons why he's the best choice by far, so to shut him up more than anything else really, we all vote him in.

'Sweet Mother of Divine,' mutters Daphne, 'will we ever hear the last from that aul' windbag?'

'That man could bore for Ireland.'

Apparently we're not allowed to leave the jury room once deliberations have started, so lunch is brought to us by Moany Mona via a trolley with 'Keane Katering', written across it. Tomato soup, chicken or cheese sambos and a fresh-fruit platter, which everyone immediately ducks and dives into.

At least it's a vast improvement on the Ebola Arms, I think, picking at an apple, which is pretty much all I've got an appetite for. We're allowed a 'brief recess' to eat, as Moany Mona bills it, and everyone is milling around the catering trolley, giving out about Barney being such a time-waster mostly, from what I can discern over in my little perch by the window.

Then Will ambles over, two mugs of coffee in his hands.

'Thought you could use one of these,' he says, handing one over.

'Oh thank you, that's really kind,' I say, again, sounding reserved and over-correct.

'You're welcome,' he says.

Then a pause while in the background all we can hear is Mai and Barney arguing over who should get the last of the cheese and pickle sandwiches.

'I was just . . .' I begin, to fill the awkward silence more than anything else.

'You were just what?' Will asks, looking at me quizzically.

'Oh . . . erm . . . you know. Just . . . ehh . . . looking out the window and wondering if it'll rain,' I say inanely.

'Ah, right. The weather. Sure. Yeah. Rain.'

'And of course it's a lovely view too.'

'Tess, we're overlooking a car park,' he says with a crooked little smile.

'Oh. Yeah. I mean . . . it's nice that we're not locked away in some airless dungeon for this. Well, it's something anyway.'

'Your break is now over and all jurors are requested to resume deliberations,' shrieks Moany Mona from the top of the room as everyone scuttles back to their seats.

'Well, we'd better . . .' Will says.

'Yes. Yes indeed.'

Jesus. There were less stilted conversations in Jane Austen's *Persuasion*. All I'm short of is a bonnet, a corset and a bout of TB.

I slip back into my seat and Edith, who's already in situ, seems to have overheard everything.

'Something happened between you pair, didn't it?' she asks, the beady blue eyes locking onto mine.

'Edith!' I hiss, 'will you keep your voice down?'

'Ooh now, does he have a big willy?' whispers Daphne from the other side of me, innocent as you like. 'I'll bet he does.'

'Will you keep it down?'

'Well, does he or not?'

'Just *shhhhh*! Please!'

'That means she slept with him,' nods Daphne. 'Always does. I know because that's the exact same way my grand-daughters go on.'

'Well?' says Edith.

'Nothing happened,' I whisper back, only thankful that Will is at the other end of the table, so the chances of his hearing are slim. I hope. 'Now can we please drop this?'

'That's a lie, I know by the look of you. And I know by the way the pair of you have been skirting around each other all morning. Something definitely happened, I can smell it a mile off.'

'OK then!' I hiss back, more to shut the pair of them up than anything else really. 'Let's just say for the sake of argument that something very minor happened between us. Now can we just let it go?'

'Minor like what? Kissing?'

'A bit of above-the-bra action?'

I do not know where this pair get their ideas about modern day sexuality from, all I know is that I have to stop this in its tracks right now.

'Maybe,' I say. 'Now for the love of God, let's get back to the case.'

'Sticks out a mile that something happened between you and Will,' Edith says softly, sounding genuinely concerned now. 'But I'll say this much to you, missy. You do realise that you're playing with fire?'

*

Just as it's coming up to 5 p.m., urged on by Barney, we take a vote. Five of us are in favour of Damien King, six for Kate and one undecided. Which is Will, as it happens. I'm Team Kate, as I just feel so sorry for the woman. And since this morning's evidence, all the more so. Despite the fact that all of the Team Damien jurors have spent the last hour yabbering on about the King family trust and its iron-clad hold on the painting, I'm unswayed by any of it. In spite of the fact we're not supposed to care what happens to the painting after the case closes, I do care.

There's just something about knowing that the painting would be restored to the Hugh Lane Gallery that feels so right to me. And besides, I happen to remember a lonely and emotional woman crying her eyes out on a bridge, one dark, rainy night a long, long time ago. A woman who I now think, in spite of the public perception of her, got a pretty raw deal in life. And while it's in my limited power, I'd love nothing more than to right that wrong, in my own small little way.

Moany Mona hammers on the door, and Barney pompously informs her that, 'the jury have so far failed to reach a unanimous verdict.'

'In that case,' sniffs Mona, 'Judge Simmonds has dismissed you for the weekend. Back at 10 a.m. promptly on Monday morning to resume deliberations.'

I can feel Will's eyes on me as I pack up my bag in silence. But I don't give him or anyone else the chance to say a word to me. The minute I hear the word 'dismissed', I'm out of there like a bullet and straight home to face the music.

KATE

As usual, Kate lingered a good half-hour after the day's court hearing until she felt brave enough to chance leaving the building. But if she thought that she could slip into her waiting taxi unnoticed, she was wrong. If anything there were even more reporters and cameras than usual and as she battled her way down the steps, sure enough, they surrounded her.

'Kate! Over here, Kate! Can we just get a few words with you?'

'Kate! Just turn this way, just a quick shot, please!'

'Mrs King,' said one reporter, who Kate recognised, he dogged her footsteps so often. 'After today's sensational developments in court, would you care to comment about—'

'Actually,' Kate said, turning to face him square on, 'there is just one small thing that I would like to say, if I may.'

At that, all the clamour and jostling instantly quietened down and a hush descended, broken only by the noise of the rush hour traffic running along the quays beside them.

415

'What's that, Mrs King?' said the reporter, shoving a microphone into her face.

'I've decided to revert back to my maiden name,' she said, simply and clearly. 'So from now on – for the first time in over fifteen years – I'm Kate Lee once again.'

TESS

Saturday, 6 p.m.

I'm telling Bernard. Now. Tonight. No way out of it. It's Saturday, the day of this accursed sten night which frankly I must have had a blood clot to my brain to ever have suggested in the first place. And I tried calling Bernard after court yesterday, but he was working late in college and his bloody phone was switched off. But then Bernard rarely answers his phone at the best of times, regarding all mobile phone communication as the death of human interaction, civilization, etc.

Being perfectly honest though, half of me is relieved, because it gave me most of today to mentally prepare my speech.

Bernard is a good man who deserves to know the truth. Then he can make an informed decision about what he wants to do and on my own head be it.

Meanwhile the show must go on and like it or not, I've got twenty guests coming for supper this evening who have to be catered for. The very least I owe my pals and Bernard's family is a decent meal, I figure. So I spend the whole day with my head down in the kitchen: baking, whisking, mixing, prepping.

Our kitchen is too tiny to serve people any way other than buffet-style, so I've put together a banquet of goat's cheese and walnut salad, tomato bruschetta with capers and a vegetarian cannelloni with cauliflower and pesto sauce. As a nod to the non-veggies, I even forced myself to make a sweet and sour chicken with pilau rice, so there's something for everyone in the audience.

I'm just in the middle of making chocolate profiteroles for dessert when Gracie comes into the kitchen, sticking her fingers into bowls so she can sample everything and generally making a complete nuisance of herself.

'Gimme a lend of your car tonight, will you?' she says without any kind of a preamble. 'I've a date with Elaine and I don't want her to think I'm a complete tosspot who can't drive.'

'If you stay for one hour at the party, then you can have the car for the whole rest of the night,' I say, raising my voice to be heard over the Magimix.

A pause while she weighs up the lesser of two evils.

'Right. One hour then. But don't put me sitting near anyone whose last name is Pritchard.'

I say nothing, just focus on whisking cream and melting chocolate for the profiteroles.

'What's up with you?' she says suspiciously.

'Nothing.'

'Yes there is. Normally whenever I slag off the Pritchards you're in like Flynn to defend them.'

I say nothing, just keep creaming, beating, blending.

'You've something on your mind,' she nods knowingly.

'Piss off, Gracie.'

'On second thoughts,' she says, sticking her fingers into a bowl of melted chocolate and tasting it, 'maybe I will hang around for a bit longer tonight.'

418

'One hour. That's all I ask. You can do an hour.'

'Right then. Because if there's one rare and precious gift I have, it's that I can smell relationship trouble a mile off.'

'Gracie, will you either help me here, or else shut up?'

'. . . And if there's going to be a bunfight between you and lover boy, then I want to be there. I want a front row seat.'

*

7 p.m. An hour before showtime. I've just finished hoovering our living room and am dotting a few vases of lilies around the place when Mum comes in, still in her dressing gown and with a load of heated rollers wobbling dangerously on her head.

'You're very quiet, Tess,' she says, looking at me worriedly.

'Am I?'

'You know you are. And you've been like this all day. For the last few days, in fact.'

'Oh, just, you know,' I shrug, 'I want tonight to go well. That's all.'

'Is that it, love? Or is there something you want to tell me?' she says, perching on the edge of the sofa.

'Why would you think there was something I wanted to tell you?' I say, putting down the lilies I was arranging.

'Lots of reasons,' she says, looking at me keenly, 'like you've stopped counting down the days and weeks to your wedding, for one thing.'

'Oh . . . I'm just a bit distracted, that's all.'

'If there's anything you want to talk about, you know I'm here for you, don't you?'

'Course I do, Mum,' I smile at her gratefully.

'And remember, pet. There's no problem in this world that you and me can't fix together.'

Instinctively I give her a hug. So full of love for her at this moment that I'm almost close to tears.

'Bernard, can I have a word?'

'In a moment, sausage. Just let me fix Mummy up with another drink; that'll keep her quite contented.'

'Here, let me,' I say, taking the empty glass from him. 'But then can you and I go somewhere private to talk?'

'Yes, yes, good idea,' says Bernard, sounding totally preoccupied, which is most unlike him.

Although mind you, finding somewhere quiet in this house is a challenge. It's just past 9 p.m. and the party's in full swing. God bless my gang of friends, is all I can think, because they all arrived in top form, ready to party and really get into the atmosphere.

My two best friends, Monica and Stella, are here of course and even came by an hour earlier to help me with all the last-minute stuff, bless them. And pals from work are all present and correct too; Sue, Shauna and Rosie, along with a gang of lads that we've all been buddies with since our training days. We've got neighbours here, cousins, aunties and uncles, along with a few of Bernard's pals from college and, of course, Desmond and Beatrice.

I've basically spent the last hour whirring around like a wind-up doll making sure every drink was refreshed and that the buffet kept coming everyone's way. Have to say it's a relief to see my nearest and dearest enjoying themselves, not having a clue about the undercurrents of tension bubbling away. And whenever anyone tells me that I'm acting a bit distracted, I just dismiss it with, 'oh, you know, just hostessy stuff. I'll be fine when you've all had enough to eat!'

Gracie is being impromptu DJ and 'All About that Bass' by Meghan Trainor is blaring out. Meanwhile Edgar, a much older mate of Bernard's, is physically wincing at the sound of it. I'm doing a round of the living room and snippets of one excruciating conversation after another keep wafting my way.

Like Beatrice to my pal Stella: 'I'm reading the most wonderful book at the moment, you know. Have you read the latest on the Mesopotamian Bronze Age? Utterly gripping stuff. Such a page turner.'

'Emm, nope, I'm afraid not,' says Stella, looking a bit baffled. 'Have you read *Fifty Shades of Grey*?'

Then there's Dad and Desmond, stuck over by the telly trying their best to find common ground, while Dad looks wistfully at the blank screen, doubtless thinking of all the Sky Sports he's missing out on.

'I'm told I'm banned from talking about either politics, water charges or how much this wedding is costing,' he says morosely.

'Oh, I know, I have a subject we can talk about,' says Desmond.

'You do?' says Dad, lighting up. 'What's that?'

'Are you an opera fan? Did you see that *La Traviata* is coming to the Wexford Festival later this year?'

You know what? That's it, I think. Enough. This ends right here and right now.

I put down the bottle of Prosecco I'd been circulating with and find Bernard in the kitchen, helping himself to a plateful of quinoa salad and looking very unenthusiastic about it. Without any preamble, I grab him by the elbow and steer him out to the back garden, taking care to close the kitchen door tight behind us.

'What's up, sausage?' he says, plonking down on a garden bench, immediately taking over two thirds of it as he munches half-heartedly at the salad.

I squeeze in beside him and brace myself to tell it quickly and cleanly. Just like ripping out painful stiches after surgery, then it'll all be over.

'Bernard,' I begin, taking a deep breath. 'There's something you need to know.'

'Yes?' he says, the big puppy eyes looking over at me.

You can do it, Tess.

'I kissed someone. Just a few nights ago. And I never meant for it to happen and I swear that it went no further than that, but the guilt has been scorching me inside ever since, and I knew I wouldn't rest easy until I got it off my chest and told you. And, oh God, I really am so sorry, there's no excuse for what I did and I'm not trying to make one . . . I just wanted you to know. That's all.'

I'm rambling now, but feeling so much lighter already, just for having said it.

Then I scan Bernard's face, looking for a reaction. But so far, nothing. Anger? No. Shock? Don't think so. Hurt? Definitely not. Instead he just takes another mouthful of salad and looks thoughtfully out over the garden.

'I see,' he says a bit flatly. 'Well, thank you for telling me, I suppose.'

Is that it? I think. Thank you for telling me? Like I just gave him today's weather report?

'Are you annoyed?' I ask tentatively.

He thinks about it for a bit.

'I suppose I ought to be,' he says after a pause. 'But the funny thing is that I'm not really. Not at all, in fact.'

A long silence while we look at each other.

422

'Bernard,' I eventually say. 'This isn't such a good sign is it? I kissed another guy just a few weeks before we're supposed to get married . . . it's not really how brides are meant to carry on really, is it?'

'And I'm feeling . . . quite nonplussed about it all,' he says thoughtfully. 'Which I imagine isn't quite how grooms-to-be are meant to carry on either, now is it?'

We look at each other for longer this time and in the end, we both say it together, overlapping each other.

'So . . . do you think we should just call the whole thing off?' I say while Bernard beats me to it with, 'so . . . is getting married really such a good idea for us, do you think?'

'No!' I say.

'Yes,' he chimes in agreement.

Then he holds out his big, plump arm for me and I snuggle into it, like friends. Like friends, who'll always remain that way.

'You're the kindest, loveliest man I know,' I say. 'And you deserve so much better than me. And you'll find her. She's out there for you.'

'Whatever,' he shrugs. 'Because, you know, sausage, there's quite a remarkable amount to be said for the bachelor life too.'

And now that he's said it, I can see it so clearly for him, it actually makes me smile. Bernard and his pals Edgar and Jasper, sipping very dry sherries and attending all their lectures together, like a little triumvirate of confirmed bachelors. And more than happy to be so.

'So who's this chap then,' he asks, but I know he's cool about it when he adds, 'this love-rival of mine?'

'Oh, a guy who's on jury service with me. He's called Will and . . . I don't know . . . it's just like we've been in such an intense pressure cooker together with the case and everything that I suppose things just spilled over. But we should have a verdict in another day or two and I doubt we'll ever see each other after that.'

'It was good of you to tell me, sausage. You didn't have to. Commendably brave. I did think you hadn't seemed like yourself these past few days.'

'Oh come on, I had to, Bernard. The very least I owe you is the honest truth.'

'And now can I tell you the honest truth?' he says, looking at me a bit shiftily.

'Of course.'

He looks sadly down at the quinoa salad.

'Tess, you're a dear, sweet girl. But there are no words to describe how much I loathe and detest this utter rabbit food you've been feeding me. And there really is no form of exercise that I don't hate and despise. I like ice cream and chocolate and full-fat dairy, and essentially any meal that doesn't come with the calories written on the side of the carton. I'm so sorry, but in the spirit of openness and honesty, there it is.'

A moment when we look at each other and smile.

'Do you know,' he says, suddenly brightening. 'I saw the most divine plateful of chocolate profiteroles earlier. Now that I'm a single man again, do you think I can go in and help myself? I'm absolutely bloody starving.'

*

Not long after, hand in hand, we go in together to face the room, our families, everyone.

'Bernard and I have some big news to share with you all,' I tell the room, wreathed in happy smiles.

424

'We're both so delighted about this,' Bernard says, standing right beside me with his hand locked tight around mine, 'and we really hope you all will be too.'

'Oh, Christ,' I hear Dad groan under his breath. 'She's pregnant.'

'No!' Bernard and I chime together. 'We're *not* getting married!'

KATE

Saturday, 7.30 p.m.

You and I have had some good times together, Kate thought, as she closed the front door behind her on Castletown House for the very last time. Some fabulous times, in fact. But now it was time for her to move on and that's exactly what she was doing.

With Mo's tireless help, she'd finally packed up the last of her things, bid a fond farewell to the staff who were all staying on, and now her Range Rover was stuffed to the gills with the last of her things as she drove down the gravelled driveway for the very last time.

As it happened though, she didn't have too far to drive. Just a few miles really, to Mo's gorgeously warm country home, so different to the cool elegance of Castletown, where she'd been invited to stay till she found somewhere permanent to live. It couldn't have been more perfect for her really, because Mo's was a proper family home, with kids and cats and dogs all squealing at each other; full of warmth, laughter and fun.

Exactly what she needed right now, in other words. At least till she managed to find a place of her own. Love, comfort and just to be around happy, joyous people.

426

She pulled in through the gates and drove on up the driveway, but was utterly unprepared for the sight that was waiting for her.

It was Josh and Ella, her ten-year-old Godchildren, standing proudly in front of the house with a giant, over-sized banner that said, 'Welcome to our home, Auntie Kate . . . we love you!' scrawled across it in their bright-red, bold paintwork.

The dotes have gone and made a banner for me, Kate thought, almost touched to tears. That's probably the sweetest thing that's happened to me in months.

'Auntie Kate! You're finally here!' said Ella, hurling herself into her Godmother's arms the minute she was out of her car.

''Cept we don't want you to stay for just a little bit,' said Josh, sounding so grown up and so like his dad that Kate almost wanted to laugh. 'We want you here for ever.'

'I want you to sleep in my room, Auntie Kate! So we can tell stories and so I can practise with your make-up and wear all the clothes you don't want!'

Kate hugged them both tightly to her, loving the feel of their small hands clamped tight around her waist. Then she looked up and saw Mo standing at the doorway to welcome her, still in her apron and wiping her hands on a tea towel.

I'll never be able to thank you enough, Kate thought. Never. Not as long as I live.

TESS

Monday, 10.30 a.m.

'Well I'm for Kate.'

'Me too. She's definitely getting my vote.'

'But the painting rightfully belongs to the King family trust! That's the legal position and there's nothing at all that any of you can do about it. We have to respect the law, after all.'

'Have to say though, I really like the idea of the painting being kept here in Ireland.'

'Oh I agree. Definitely. And in the Hugh Lane too, where it looks like it should have been all along.'

'Yeah, but that whole Hugh Lane thing. OK, so we can prove his connection to the painting, but we've no certain way of knowing that it ever travelled with him on the *Lusitania* in the first place. As Oliver whatshisname said, that's nothing more than rumour and conjecture.'

'Yeah, but you heard Jasper Adams's evidence. The odds are overwhelming that it *was*. I mean, come on. One minute Hugh Lane buys it in New York, which we know for certain. Just days later, he's on the *Lusitania* – of course the painting must have been with him. If he'd left it behind in America, surely it would be hanging in the Guggenheim or some-where like that now, wouldn't you think?'

'You know I once saw a documentary about the *Lusitania*,' Beth chips in, 'and it definitely claimed that not long after the sinking and before the First World War ended, all sorts of illegal looting went on. It's so close to the shoreline, you see, apparently it wasn't that difficult to get at.'

'Such a horrible thought,' sniffs Daphne disapprovingly. 'Mind you, I felt the exact same when they started bringing up all manner of trinkets from the *Titanic*. Just like grave robbing, if you ask me.'

'Oh, I couldn't agree with you more,' says Mai from across the table. 'Like digging up your grandfather's coffin just so you can get the gold watch off his wrist. So morbid.'

'Yes, but ladies, the point is we're here to decide ownership,' Jane interrupts in her no-nonsense manner. 'And as the judge told us, what Kate or Damien King decide to do with the painting afterwards is none of our business really, is it?'

It's Monday morning in the jury room and here we are, all assembled and with everyone anxious to give their opinion and fighting to get their two cents worth in. Well, everyone except Edith that is, who's sitting right beside me and won't give up nudging and hissing right into my ear.

'Do you know there's something very different about you today, Tess,' she says, eyeing me up suspiciously. 'I've six granddaughters, you know. I can tell a mile off.'

'*Shh*, will you? We're supposed to be reaching a verdict here.'

'Spotted it from the very minute you came through the door this morning,' she insists.

'What? What are you talking about?' I whisper back, flushing a bit pink at that.

'Well now, it's hard to put my finger on, but you look different.'

'Different how?'

'You came in here this morning looking . . . lighter. Yes, that's it. No other word for it. Like a big weight has been lifted from your shoulders.'

In the background, everyone else is busy debating, arguing and point-scoring. Well everyone expect Will, that is. He's at the far end of the table from me again this morning and so far we've barely exchanged two words to each other. Just came in, gave each other a quick, curt nod hello and took our seats, where Edith hasn't stopped grilling me ever since.

Meanwhile Barney, our jury foreman, has clearly been busy reading up on similar case studies all weekend and won't stop droning on about it until he's bored the whole room into a coma.

'There's an important legal precedent I read of, you know,' he's lecturing us all, to eye rolls and groans we're barely even bothering to hide at this stage. 'In *Kinsella versus Shaw*, in the year 2007. In that case, the painting was a Jack Yeats and it was awarded to the person who'd bought it in the first place, because he was the one who'd actually shelled out for it. Now correct me if I'm wrong, but Kate King didn't actually buy that painting in the first place, did she? Her ex did. Fair is fair, you know.'

'I don't like agreeing with that aul' eejit,' whispers Jane from the other side of me. 'But he does have a point. As long as it was bought by Damien and the King trust, how can it be taken away from them?'

After debating a bit longer, we take another vote and this time it's nine in favour of Kate King, with two against and one abstention. From Will, as it happens. All our eyes swivel towards him, where he's sitting back in his seat, arms folded, shaking his head slowly. He looks up, aware that we're all focused on him and for a flicker of a second our eyes lock.

'I just don't get it,' he says to the room.

'Don't get what?' Ruth says, or rather half-shouts, as she's prone to doing.

'Oh God, where do I start?' he says, dropping his head and running his fingers through his hair. 'But for what it's worth, here's the big sticking post for me. Like most of you, I'm fascinated by the whole notion that the painting did in fact go down with the *Lusitania* and that it was illegally salvaged in the years to come. And if that's the case, then chances are it probably did wind its way from one private collection to another, until it eventually ended up on a wall in that palace the Kings live in. But I still can't help wondering—'

'What, son?' says Barney imperiously from the head of the table.

'OK, so here's what's on my mind,' Will says, sitting forward now, arms folded and looking thoughtful. 'It just seems odd to me that Kate King breached one court order after another, because she was so determined to hang on to that painting. Mark my words, she wanted it, and badly too. Probably figured it was her pension plan. And I'd like to state for the record that up until this morning, I was pretty much on Team Kate anyway.'

'Why so?' Barney asks him.

'Mainly because I thought Damien King is one of the wealthiest men, not just in the country, but in the world,' Will says, looking directly back at him. 'He could easily afford ten Old Masters if he wanted them. And yet he was prepared to take his ex-wife all the way to court just to get this one back. Why?'

I'm silent here though. Mainly because Will's just articulated a niggle that I've had myself all along.

'Well, I think it's not a coincidence that Damien King's new girlfriend is some kind of a world expert on seventeenth-century art,' says Beth quietly as everyone else nods along.

'Agreed, but let's just get back to Kate,' Will says. 'Because prior to this new information coming to court, it looked to me like she wanted to hold on to the painting so she could possibly sell it in years to come, then use the cash as her own personal nest egg.'

'Well that's not illegal, you know,' says Jess. 'Is it?'

'I'm not suggesting for a minute that it is,' he goes on calmly, 'but the fact is that since Jasper Adams's testimony about the whole Hugh Lane link, everything has shifted, hasn't it? Now we've got Kate King saying that if we award it to her, she'll donate it to the Hugh Lane Gallery. The clear implication being that she doesn't care about the money.'

'Well maybe she did want to sell it at some stage,' says Mai, 'but now this new evidence has made her change her mind. What's wrong with that?'

'Nothing at all. Except that for better or for worse, it's swung a lot of us in her favour. And I think that's what's really bothering me. Up until that evidence was admitted, my concern is that Kate's legal representatives were worried that this case might go against her. Because till then, it didn't look too good for her, now did it?'

'No, definitely not,' a voice says from my left.

'Well up until that evidence, I was definitely voting for

Damien. But now I'm pretty much forty-five fifty-five, leaning towards Kate,' Ian chimes in.

'You see?" says Will. 'So was that information a tactic that Kate's barristers used to manipulate things her way? Were they afraid they'd lose, unless Kate took the stand and stated her clear intention that the painting would end up in the Hugh Lane Gallery?'

'But does it matter?' I blurt out. 'The fact is, we're here to decide who we think has the greater claim on the painting. And for one, I'm on Kate's side. All the way. And if she did originally intend to keep it and sell it, then isn't it all the more noble of her now to say she'll donate it to the Hugh Lane Gallery?'

'Hear, hear,' says Daphne.

'Now, son, if you've a problem with this,' says Barney from the top of the table, 'then we can always go back to court and request more information to clarify. It happened in *Hamilton versus Smith* only four years ago, you know. Legal precedent is on our side.'

'There really is no need, thanks,' says Will. 'My vote is for Kate King . . .' Then he glances around the room, aware the eleven other pairs of eyes are zoned in on him and him alone.

'It's just bugging me, that's all,' he says with a shrug, sitting back in his seat and looking away.

KATE

'Why are they taking so long?' Kate said to Hilda, as the two women sat side-by-side on the court benches, while barristers and junior counsels bustled around them.

'Juries have a habit of taking as long as they take,' said Hilda calmly. 'The critical thing is not to try and read anything into it. It's neither a good thing nor a bad thing; it's just a matter of playing the waiting game now. So don't worry.'

Kate said nothing. Just fidgeted nervously on the uncomfortable bench and still worried anyway.

She honestly felt like this whole court case had cost her life's blood. The question now was this: how would it all play out?

TESS

Monday, 4.55 p.m.

Still no verdict by the end of the day. We take another vote and we're now divided ten to two, with the majority in favour of Kate, and just Barney and Jane against. But because we've been instructed to come to a unanimous verdict, that means we're still classed as a hung jury. So we're all dismissed and sent home, to come back tomorrow morning and try again.

We're all just gathering up bags and jackets and making our way to the private jury staircase when Will falls into step beside me.

'So,' he says, looking right at me, 'looks like we're almost there.'

'This time tomorrow, it should all be over,' I stop to say.

An awkward pause as he holds the door open for a troop of the old biddies, led by Edith, all deep in chat about what they're planning to watch on telly later on. I let them all pass and leave last.

'Good weekend then?' Will asks, as we troop down the stairwell.

'Better than good,' I smile brightly back at him. 'Fantastic, in fact.'

435

'Ahh, I see,' he nods.

We arrive at the downstairs doors and I'm first out into the warm sunshine.

'Well. Till tomorrow then,' he says, not looking me in the eye this time.

'Yeah. That's right. Tomorrow. Bright and early.'

There's an awkward pause, and things have been weird enough between us all day, so I wave a quick goodbye and head off in the direction of my bus stop. Next thing from the bottom of the court steps, I turn over my shoulder to see Edith tottering over to Will and getting into what looks like a fairly involved conversation with him.

And more than once, both of them very definitely glance in my direction.

*

It seems Will was right. There's an indescribable shift in public opinion now that's hard not to notice. And the astonishing thing is that the barometer seems to have swung in Kate King's favour. The whole way home on the bus, fragments of overheard conversation keep filtering over to me.

'I never used to like her, you know . . . such a cold fish with that snooty glare . . . but somehow I just *believe* her now.'

'Kate King? Oh yeah, me too. After all, at least she wants the painting to be kept here in the country . . .'

'. . . where it should have been all along . . .'

'And she's got so thin too, hasn't she?'

'Must be all that worry. You know what they say, stress is a great diet.'

'If you ask me, Damien King is a complete bastard for putting his ex-wife through all that in the first place.'

'Oh, I couldn't agree with you more. Poor old Kate. She's well rid of him, if you ask me.'

Even Mum and Gracie are at it right the way through dinner when I get home.

'Now I never had any time for that one, as you know,' says Mum.

'But at least she's prepared to do the right thing and give the painting back to the Hugh Lane,' Gracie chips in, 'unlike her ex.'

'Oh yeah. I'd say he only wanted to keep it so he could impress his new girlfriend. Isn't she all into art too?'

'So how are you voting, Tess?'

'You know I'm not supposed to talk about it,' I say, with my mouth stuffed full with a veggie burger.

'Not supposed to talk about what?' says Dad, only getting home now from helping a pal decorate his house. He still has his white overalls on and has splodges of fuchsia pink paint all over his hair, a bit like psychedelic dandruff.

'The King case,' says Gracie. 'What do you think?'

'Ah Jaysus,' Dad groans, taking a can of cider from the fridge and ripping the lid off the tin, 'can I not have one minute's peace in my own home from talking about that bleeding case? It's been on the radio non-stop and all day long in work, the lads kept harping on about it. I've a pain in my arse just hearing about that shagging painting. They can donate it to a local pub and use it as a dartboard for all I care.'

KATE

Monday night, 8.30 p.m.

'Eat,' said Mo.

'Can't,' Kate replied, shaking her head.

'The choice is yours,' Mo said calmly. 'Either you can eat or you can be force-fed. So choose. You're skin and bone these days, you need fattening up.'

Kate couldn't though. Even the smell from the plate of beef casserole that Mo had put together for all the family was enough to make her stomach churn.

Will I ever have a normal appetite again, she wondered. Whatever the verdict, would life ever go back to normal?

'If you don't like yours, you can always have some of mine, Aunt Kate,' said little Josh loyally, shoving his own plateful of casserole in front of her.

'And don't worry,' Ella whispered, 'I have a bag of mini Mars Bars up in my room. Call up when Mum and Dad are asleep and we'll have a midnight feast. For only you and me, just us girls. And then maybe you can teach me how to do proper make-up? The kind Mum won't let me near? With smoky eyes and everything?'

'Oh, you guys are so good to me,' Kate smiled, leaning

down to kiss the top of each of their heads. 'Do you realise you're keeping me sane?'

'What does sane mean, Auntie Kate?'

Kate thought for a moment before answering.

'It means being at peace with yourself, pet. For the first time in as long as I can remember, totally at peace.'

TESS

Tuesday, 9.30 a.m.

The following morning in the jury room, and by some miracle, I actually got here early. So now I'm being subjected to yet another grilling by Edith over by the window. Meanwhile everyone else is arriving and helping themselves to mugs of tea and coffee, to kick start the morning.

'There's something up with you, Tess,' she says to me, the cornflower blue eyes looking beadily at me. 'You can try and hide it all you like, but I'm onto you, missy.'

'What are you talking about?'

'I just know by you. By the way you look, by your whole manner, everything. Oh you may laugh us aul' ones off as a pack of interfering gossips, but I've only got your best interests at heart, you know, love.'

Realising that she just isn't prepared to drop this any time soon, and also the chance that we'll reach a verdict today and we'll probably never see each other again anyway, I decide what the hell. Why not just tell her the truth and have done with it. After all, Edith and the rest of the Granny Gestapo aren't going to have it any other way.

'Right then,' I sigh, steering her even further away from everyone else in the room, so there's no chance of being overheard. 'If you must know, it's my wedding. And fiancé. And engagement. The whole thing.'

'I knew it was something like that,' says Edith, eyes busily scrutinising my face. 'I knew it without being told. Women's intuition. Very powerful thing, you know. Never under-estimate it.'

'Well the thing is . . . it's all off.'

She looks at me, instantly softening.

'Ahh, come here to me, love, and give me a big hug,' she says, arms outstretched and pulling me towards her. She smells of lavender and fresh soap and it's actually lovely. 'You poor old thing. Did he get cold feet on you?'

'No! Not at all . . .'

'What a bastard! I'll give him a right wallop with my umbrella if I ever get to meet him.'

'No . . . it's not like that at all'

'I know it must be heartbreaking for you right now, Tess, and you probably feel like you can't ever hold your head up in public again, but it'll get easier, you know. And isn't it miles better to find out now that your fiancé is a messer, rather than after the wedding, when it's too late to do anything about it?'

'No!' I say, sounding a bit panicky now. 'Edith, you don't understand! This is totally by mutual agreement. Bernard and I both decided at the weekend that really, neither of us were in it for the long haul and that we're miles better off as friends.'

'Oh,' she says after a pause, her face falling a bit disap-pointedly. 'Never heard of anything like that happening before.'

'Honestly, that's the truth,' I insist. 'And I'm really happy about it. Please believe me.'

'Although,' she goes on, almost like she's thinking aloud. 'I did used to worry about you, you know.'

'Why's that?'

'Well, ever since the case started,' she says thoughtfully, 'you'd chat away about getting married, but you never had that glow about you. Daphne was only just saying it to me the other day. Something didn't seem quite right, you know.'

I sigh, realising that this is probably going to spread around the jury room like wildfire.

'Edith, one last favour to ask you, if you don't mind,' I say.

'What's that, love?'

'Can we just keep this to ourselves?'

She swivels her head around to where the others are all congregated around the catering trolley, helping themselves to mugs of tea and coffee, and surprisingly fresh croissants. Most of us are already here, from Mai, Ruth, Daphne, Minnie and Barney, to the younger brigade, Jess, Ian, Beth and Will, who's just come in and is taking off his jacket and flinging it on the back of a chair.

Edith spots him instantly and turns back to me.

'Ahh right,' she says knowingly. 'Well, if you want me to keep quiet, then of course I will, love.'

'Much appreciated,' I smile back at her.

'Pity though. We all thought you and Will would have made such a lovely couple.'

*

Heated debate around the conference table once Moany Mona barks at us all to get started. The shock news is that

442

Jane, who up till now has been voting in favour of Damien King, is now wavering.

'Just think of it,' Will is saying to her, leaning forward on the table, fully focused on her and her alone. 'We've got concrete evidence in front of us that the painting was personally gifted to Kate King. Whereas if we give this back to the King family trust, then there's a chance *A Lady of Letters* will probably tour some remote gallery in Minneapolis and then end up hanging on a Globtech boardroom wall somewhere.'

'But it's not our job to speculate as to what either Damien or Kate choose to do with it when this case is over,' Jane retorts, but Will comes straight back to her.

'Agreed, but we do have to think long-term too. Kate has said under oath that she intends to gift it to the Hugh Lane Gallery. Now whether you buy into the whole *Lusitania* connection or not, wouldn't it be wonderful to see a Dutch Master on permanent display here in Ireland? And now we've got the power right here in our hands to achieve just that. Don't do it to yourself, Jane,' he adds for good measure. 'Don't wake up in a few weeks' time and live to regret this. You've got the chance now to do the right thing. So come on then, what's it to be?'

God, I think, looking at him. Will can be very persuasive when he wants to be. There's a pin-drop silence around the table now as we all digest what he's saying.

Then a discreet cough from Barney.

'Right then, everyone,' he says. 'How about we take another vote?'

KATE

Tuesday, 11.20 a.m.

'They're coming back,' whispered Hilda to Kate, where she sat bolt upright in court, tight with tension.

'Already?'

'Looks like it.'

'So this is it, then.'

'This is it.'

Kate reached out her thin, white hand and gripped Hilda warmly. She turned around to the public benches to see Mo waving brightly at her and giving her the 'fingers crossed' sign. Kate gave her a quick wink back and a tiny wave, then turned back to Hilda.

'Whatever happens,' she said to her, eyes sparkling with sincerity. 'Whatever the outcome, I just want you to know how very grateful I am to you. You've been amazing in every way. And no one could possibly have done more.'

'All in a day's work,' Hilda smiled.

Next thing, Kate's eyes inadvertently wandered across the courtroom to where Damien had obviously just been given the same news as her. In total contrast to her, though, he sat back calmly and confidently, legs outstretched as

444

Oliver Daniels whispered discreetly in his ear. For a split second their eyes met.

Good luck, she tried to telegraph. *And may the best man win.*

But he just pretended not to see her and looked away.

TESS

Tuesday, midday

Bloody hell. If I'd thought the atmosphere in court was tense before, that was absolutely nothing compared with how it is right now. We're all guided into the jury box, like we've been a dozen times before, except this time it's like we're the sole focus of attention, as every eye in the packed room looks to us for any kind of clue. It almost feels like our body language is being studied, the way we're moving, taking our seats, even the way we're whispering among ourselves. Will is sitting just two down from me, and I'm wedged in between Barney and Minnie.

You OK? He leans forward to mouth silently at me and I give a curt nod back, keenly aware that everyone is looking our way.

Then there's dead silence as Judge Simmonds swishes in and for the last time, takes her seat at the top of the courtroom.

'Ladies and gentlemen of the jury,' she says crisply and clearly. 'In the case of *King versus King*, have you reached a unanimous verdict?'

'We have, Your Honour,' says Barney, standing up as

446

jury foreman and looking delighted with his moment in the sun.

'Will both the Plaintiff and Defendant please rise?' says Judge Simmonds, as both Kate and Damien do as they're told. Kate looking shaky and a bit weak, Damien almost seeming to radiate that cool self-assurance that's been his hallmark throughout the whole court case.

More silence, and out of the corner of my eye I can see the press box with their iPads poised, ready to start reporting the result the second it's announced.

'And who do you find for?' asks Judge Simmonds.

Barney gives a little cough, almost like he's determined to savour every last second in the spotlight.

'In the case of *King versus King,* Your Honour,' he announces importantly, 'we find for the Defendant, Mrs Katherine King.'

Instant cheers from around the room as I look across to Kate. She's white-faced, genuinely shocked and looks as if she can't believe what she's hearing. Next thing she's surrounded by a cohort of barristers, all clamouring to shake her hand, but she almost seems to be looking through them, as if there's one person in particular that she's seeking out.

And then she finds her. Her friend Mo Kennedy steps down from the public gallery and not even caring that the whole court is watching, the two women hug warmly as Kate bursts into huge, relieved, gulpy sobs.

*

The minute the jury is discharged, we're guided back through the jury room and on down the quiet, private staircase. Mona even astonishes us by thanking us all perfectly civilly for serving and wishing us a good day. I catch a raised eyebrow from Will at that and have to resist the urge to giggle.

As you can imagine, it's only bloody mayhem on the steps of the courts outside. There's press everywhere, all clustered around Damien King, who's just made his grand exit through the main doors. They've swept down on him like vultures, just waiting to hear what kind of a spin he's going to put on this and even from where I'm standing, over by the side entrance, I can hear the impromptu speech he makes, loud and clear.

'Ladies and gentlemen,' he smiles confidently into the cameras. 'Firstly thank you so much for your patience throughout what's been an unnecessarily long hearing,' he begins. 'Naturally, my team and I are disappointed at today's result, but some you win and some you lose. I didn't get to where I am today without taking a few knocks and doubtless there are plenty more still to come. But for now, let me just thank you all for your time.'

Oliver Daniels whispers something discreetly to him and Damien nods along to whatever is being said.

'We have no further comments at this time.'

'But Mr King!' goes up in a chorus from the press hacks gathered around him. 'Just one more question, please!'

'Mr King has already made his statement and I'm afraid that's all you'll be hearing from us today,' says Oliver Daniels in that booming voice.

And just out of the corner of my eye, while all of this distraction was going on, I see Kate and Mo slip discreetly out another side exit and into a waiting Jeep with blacked-out windows. Two seconds later, they've gone, leaving Will and I along with the rest of the jurors at the top of the steps just staring after them.

'God love poor Kate King,' says Minnie. 'I'd say she's shattered after this whole case. No wonder she just wanted to make a quick getaway.'

'Nice cup of tea and a chat with her pal will set her to rights,' says Daphne kindly. But then Daphne, I've noticed, seems to think that there's no problem at all in this world that can't be fixed with a good heart-to-heart chat with your nearest and dearest over a pot of Lyons tea.

We're all hugging and waving each other goodbye, swapping phone numbers and saying, 'oh yes, we must definitely keep in touch!'

'Good luck with the wedding, Tess,' says Jess coming over to give me a hug. 'Post loads of pictures on Facebook, so I can see you in your dress, won't you?'

'Oh yes! She'll have to show us all the photos afterwards, won't she, Edith?' Ruth says.

I say nothing, just smile, give her a hug and silently thank God that Edith has kept her mouth shut too. At least, so far. Will is just behind me, but I can feel him tuning into all this, as ever, missing nothing.

And pretty soon, it's just him and me alone as the others disperse and we stroll down the steps to go our separate ways.

'So,' he says.

'So.'

'You must be relieved, now it's all over.'

'How do you mean?'

'Well now you can get back to all your wedding planning. You can get back to full-time bride-ing. If that's even a verb.'

I say nothing.

'Tess?' he says, stopping and turning to me.

'Yes?'

'Is there anything you want to tell me?' he says, that bit softer now.

I take a minute just to look around me. We're halfway down the court steps by now and from here, I can see all the way across to the green treetops of the Phoenix Park. It's peaceful and soothing, and just taking in a few deep gulps of fresh air is helping me think more clearly.

'No,' I eventually say. 'No, I don't think that there is. I mean, maybe sometime in the future, but just not now. If that's OK.'

'Sure,' he says with just a flicker of something in his eyes. Disappointment? Hard to tell.

We walk on a bit in silence and this time, I catch him frowning.

'Will?' I ask, stopping him. 'Your turn now. Is there something on your mind? You seem preoccupied. Miles away.'

He takes a deep breath and shakes his head.

'It's Kate King,' he says.

'But aren't you pleased at the verdict?'

'Course I am, but . . .'

'But what?'

'That late witness. Jasper Adams, the art historian. It's still baffling me. I just can't shake off the notion that the whole connection with Hugh Lane and the *Lusitania* was nothing more than a last resort tactic that the Defence used to swing things their way at the eleventh hour. It was driving me nuts all last night.'

We walk on in the vague direction of my bus stop and then from out of nowhere, something else strikes me.

'Look, Will,' I say. 'I might not be able to answer any of your questions, but maybe there is something we can do.'

'What's that?'

'Well you won't believe this . . .'

'Won't believe what?'

'And you're not to ask any questions . . .'

'Can't guarantee that, I'm afraid . . .'

'But it just so happens that I know exactly where Kate likes to go jogging first thing on a Sunday morning.'

The Chronicle
Tuesday 24th May, 5 p.m.

WE'RE FOR KATE!

Jubilation in court number seven earlier today as the jury found for Kate King, nee Lee, in the King criminal theft case. It's reported that Kate became emotional in court as the verdict was read out and was seen hugging not only Hilda Cassidy, her Senior Counsel, but also her best friend Mrs Mo Kennedy. Throughout the court case, Mrs Kennedy was frequently to be seen in the public benches, lending loyal support to her friend.

The verdict is seen as a huge vindication for Kate and the judge even added as she dismissed the case that it was one 'which should never really have come to court in the first place.'

This, however, leaves a lot of unanswered questions for the Plaintiff, Mr Damien King. Chief amongst them why he ever put Kate, from whom he's legally separated, through such an ordeal in the first place. A further court hearing is due to take place in a month's time, in which the issue of costs will be awarded. After today's ruling though, it's a virtual certainty that costs will be awarded against Damien King and could, as one highly placed source tells us, 'run into seven figures'.

'Well, it's not like he can't afford it,' one observer on the public benches was heard to quip.

'And it serves him right if you ask me,' came her companion's reply.

Here at The Chronicle, *we find this a hard sentiment to disagree with.*

TESS

Sunday, 6.45 a.m.

So it's stupid o'clock on Sunday morning and I'm at home, lacing myself into my trainers and gearing up for an early-morning rendezvous with Will. Not that we've got the slightest guarantee that we'll be successful or anything. After all, only once did I ever bump into Kate King having a Sunday morning dawn run on the pier, so like it or not, this really is in the lap of the gods.

And then with a groan, I realise something else. I loaned Gracie my car last night and she's still not home. Which means I've no other way of getting to the pier in time, other than to run. No harm though, I think laterally, to arrive sweaty and stinking and without even a scrap of make-up on. Mainly because Will doesn't know that the wedding is off. So for the sake of pride if nothing else, the last thing I'd ever want is for him to think I'm getting all dolled up to impress.

I check myself in the hall mirror before tiptoeing out of the house, so as not to wake the folks. Manky Lycra leggings? Check. Scraped back hair? Check. And will I be in a lather of sweat by the time I get there? Stupid question.

Nah. There's no way in hell this girl looks like she's out to impress anyone.

*

'Well, good morning,' says Will, when we do eventually find each other at the base of the pier, as pre-arranged since the other day.

'You made it,' I say, out of breath and panting.

'So how did you find your first few days without having to turn up for jury service, then?' He smiles at me with the dark eyes dancing. And he looks great in his workout gear too, I can't help noticing, in between big gulps of the fresh sea air. Nice tight arse, muscly arms in black Lycra, the whole package.

'Oh, you know, just back to business as usual for me really,' I say, as soon as I get my breath back. 'Work. Seeing family and friends. Catching up with everything I've been missing out on. How about you?'

'Back to the coalface for me too, I'm afraid,' he says, as we both fall into step and start walking down the pier. 'I'm editing a new book right now, so it's a case of no rest for the wicked, really.'

He doesn't ask about the wedding, which is frankly a big relief. Saves me all the bother of having to come up with a good, stout lie. And seeing as how it's peaceful here this morning, clear, bright and sunny, with not another sinner in sight, the two of us automatically start to jog at a nice gentle pace.

'Bet if felt strange though,' he says, as we head off.

'What?'

'Not listening to the Granny Brigade complaining about their IBS every day and how long the wait is to get knee replacements.' He grins as we start to stride that little bit faster, him slightly ahead, me panting to keep up.

'It's the Ebola Arms I really miss,' I say teasingly.

'Ahh, did you have to? Just the thought of their cabbage soup with bits of congealed fat off a cow's bum floating on top of it is enough to start my stomach rumbling. I'll cry off this run in a minute and head straight back there. And it'll all be your fault.'

I grin and we run on for a bit, but there's absolutely no sign of her. Nothing. Not a soul about in fact, bar one early-morning dog walker who nodded briefly at us as he passed by, with a pooper scooper in one hand and a very scary-looking Alsatian in the other.

'This could turn out to be a bit of a wild goose chase, you know,' I say a bit worriedly through mouthfuls of air, as we eventually both slow down a bit.

'Do you think?'

'Well,' I say doubtfully, 'she did tell me she came here every Sunday at dawn, but you couldn't rely on that. After all, how do we know that she hasn't gone away since the court case?'

'Tess Taylor,' Will says, shaking his head in mock anger. 'The things you'll do to get me out of bed at the crack of dawn on a Sunday morning.'

And that's when we see her. It's her, unmistakably. Coming towards us. Tall and lean, dressed in pale-blue workout gear, with a baseball cap pulled down low over her eyes and an iPod strapped to her arm. It's definitely Kate King – sorry, Lee – obviously just finishing up her run and slowing down her pace as she strides towards us.

She looks miles away, utterly focused on her own thoughts and I hate interrupting her early-morning peace and quiet, but in the end I don't have to. She spots us too and before we know it, has slowed down to a walking pace and is tentatively making her way over.

'It's you,' she says to me. 'Again.'

'I'm so sorry if we startled you,' I begin to say, but then she spots Will.

'I recognise your face too,' she says, as Will stretches out his arm to shake hands.

'I'm Will Kearns,' he says, 'and I know that this must look unorthodox to say the least—'

'Put it this way,' says Kate wryly, 'I can't help feeling that your both being here, right now, at this very time, is hardly a coincidence.'

'It's not,' I tell her as gently as I can, so as not to alarm the poor woman. 'And we give you our word, no one will ever know about this. That's a faithful promise.'

She looks at me and it's unspoken between us, but the thought is there all the same. I kept it to myself last time I met her too. So maybe, just maybe, she'll trust me one last time.

'Besides, just think of it this way,' I add. 'If it were ever to come out that we'd come to speak to you after the case, we'd be in as much trouble as you. So you can trust us. Genuinely.'

She looks at me for a moment, thinks about it, then gives a tiny nod.

'It's just there were one or two loose ends that we'd love to ask you about, if possible,' says Will. 'Strictly off the record, of course. And as Tess says, it goes without saying that absolutely none of this will ever go any further. Just put it down to me being a nosy bastard and nothing more.'

Kate smiles a bit at that, then spots a low stone bench running alongside the pier and goes to sit down, with Will and I automatically following behind her.

'Do you know, I think I knew,' she says, taking a seat and looking thoughtfully out over the calm, blue sea. 'I knew when the jury took so long to come to a verdict that you must have had some concerns. And frankly, I was stunned when you decided in my favour, I really was.'

'I was voting for you all along,' I say loyally, sitting down beside her.

'Me and all,' says Will, sitting on her other side. 'But there's just something that we'd love you to clear up for us. And of course, you're under absolutely no obligation to answer.'

'Go ahead,' Kate says calmly, still looking out to sea.

'That last-minute witness, Jasper Adams,' says Will.

'Yes, the art historian,' says Kate. 'The guy that you indirectly knew,' she adds, turning to me as I nod. 'Yes. I thought it might be something to do with him alright.'

'It's just that he introduced the whole notion of the painting having survived – and probably been looted from – the *Lusitania*.'

'So he did,' says Kate.

There's a moment while Will and I both look at her beautiful sculpted profile, while she still gazes calmly out over the water's edge.

'And I'll bet that now you're both wondering why we even bothered introducing that information at all,' she says.

'Well, umm . . . yeah,' I say weakly, 'we did, actually.'

'Because once the information came to us,' she goes on, 'we – that is I – decided that it was only the truth. And that for better or for worse, it had to come out. Regardless of what anyone said or thought.'

'But,' says Will, 'weren't you at all afraid that once you took the stand and said you intended to donate the painting to the Hugh Lane Gallery instead of keeping it, that it might look like you were deliberately trying to swing the jury in your favour?'

'That's not hard to answer really,' says Kate thoughtfully, pulling up one leg onto the stone bench and massaging her calf muscles. Which is why my barrister Hilda and I used to refer to the Hugh Lane link as our 'in case of emergency, please break glass' strategy. Only to be used as a last resort, if things really didn't seem to be going our way.

'It was never conclusively proven, you know,' she goes on, 'that whole *Lusitania* link. Really all it amounted to was rumour and conjecture and that's not good enough for a court of law. So we held it back, hoping that it wouldn't be needed and the jury would be swayed in my favour by the pre-nup argument; that all birthday gifts would be left to me.'

A silence falls and I catch Will's eye.

Say nothing, he seems to be silently telegraphing across to me. *Just let her do all the talking.*

'Besides, I was worried sick,' Kate says after a pause. 'After all, if *A Lady of Letters* had been looted, it wouldn't look too good for Damien, even though it wasn't his fault and he did buy the painting in good faith. And that's the last thing that I'd want, for either of us.'

'Even for your ex?' I can't help asking. Sorry, the words just came out of my mouth before I could help it.

'No, I wouldn't even wish that on Damien,' Kate says

459

with a tiny smile. 'In spite of everything that's been written and no matter what people may think. He and I had a pretty good marriage back in the early days, you know. Everything was wonderful, till it all went pear-shaped. But I'm afraid I hadn't taken into consideration just how dirty a fight Damien was prepared to put up. All I ever wanted to do was end it quietly and with a little bit of dignity, no matter what people might think of me.'

'You haven't read any of the weekend papers then?' asks Will, raising his eyebrow.

'I've been deliberately avoiding them for weeks,' she winces. 'It's something I can live without. Particularly as Kate Lee-bashing seems to be something of a national sport these days.'

'Because you might just be in for a pleasant surprise.'

It's the truth too. All week long, in fact, there's been a massive public swing in Kate's favour. Now every time I open a paper or turn on the radio, there's someone on complaining about what an absolute bastard Damien King was to ever put his wife through a court case like that in the first place.

I sense we've only got a minute or two left before Kate gets up to go again and I don't want to push our luck. This feels a bit like we've trapped a gazelle that might just bolt at any second. Still though, there's one last thing I've been dying to know.

'So what will you do now?' I ask her as, sure enough, she stands up and makes to leave.

'I'm staying with my friend Mo for the moment, at least till I figure that one out,' she says. 'So who knows? I may possibly even move abroad, to rest up after this whole thing and think about where I want to go from here. After all,

Damien has moved on, so maybe it's time I did too. The Kings, you see,' she adds, looking down at both of us with a shy smile, 'were a couple made and minted in the media. So I suppose a fitting way to bring an end to the whole myth was via the media too. Which this court case has neatly seen to. I went in as Kate King and came out as Kate Lee again. And now life goes on.'

'Plus now you're free to do whatever you want,' says Will.

'For the first time in a long, long time,' she nods. 'Yes. I'm free. There's just one other thing that I need to take care of first. Something important. But all in good time.'

'What's that?' I ask.

'You'll see.'

We both stand up with her then, as she clearly is anxious to get off.

'Well, we've taken up enough of your time,' I say.

'But, thank you again,' says Will. 'You've certainly cleared up a few things that were really bugging me.'

'And it goes without saying that this conversation never happened?' she says. 'That we never met?'

'You have my word,' I tell her stoutly. Then thinking, what the hell, I throw in something else that had been playing on my mind.

'In fact, you'll hardly remember this,' I added, 'but you and I did sort of meet on another occasion, long before the court case. You'll have forgotten I'm sure, but it's something that's always stayed with me.'

'Really?' says Kate, with fresh interest. 'When was that?'

Even Will is looking at me now, with an expression that clearly says, 'and you're only telling me this now?'

'It was about two years ago,' I tell her, 'on the Ha'penny

Bridge. In the lashing rain. I recognised you and was just worried because – well, you seemed so upset.'

Kate looks at me and goes very quiet for a moment.

'The funny thing is that I do remember,' she eventually says, 'not that it was you, just that a young woman stopped and well, was very kind to me. And I'm sorry if I wasn't exactly polite. I'm afraid I was going through a very tough time back then.'

'Husband trouble?' Will asks her gently.

'I'd just discovered he was having an affair, yes,' Kate says, sounding astonishingly calm about it. 'Or another one, I should say.'

'It's none of my business of course,' I tell her, 'but you deserve so much better.'

'Well,' she says thoughtfully, 'now that I'm finally free, who knows what the future holds?'

We bid her a warm goodbye and she strides off, then stops just a few paces later and turns back to us.

'Oh, just one more thing,' she says, with an impish little smile.

'Yes?'

'Forgive my nosiness, but here you both are, out running together at the crack of dawn. Does this mean that you two are an item now?'

'No!' I say, probably a bit too loudly.

'We're . . . more like friends really,' says Will, scanning my face as if to say, is it OK to say that?

'Ah,' says Kate, her beautiful face falling just a little. 'Such a pity. I often used to look at you both across the courtroom and think, what a sweet couple that pair would make.'

*

As I'm car-less this morning, Will very kindly offers to drive me home and as soon as we leave the pier, he steers me towards a very swish-looking sports car in sexy black, with leather seats, bum-heaters, the whole boy-toy works.

'Are you kidding me with this?' I laugh when I see it. 'What are you, like Bruce Wayne in your spare time or something? Do you secretly keep this in your Batcave at night? So Alfred the butler can polish it?'

'Very funny,' he says dryly. 'Now, do you want a lift home or not?'

I jump in and we're just zooming off when he glances over at me.

'You know, I was just thinking . . .'

'Yeah?'

'Absolutely nothing worse than an early-morning run on an empty stomach.'

'Gotta hate that.'

'So how would you fancy maybe . . .'

'If the end of your sentence involves any kind of food, then my answer is and always will be yes.'

We pull up in Monkstown village, right beside a gorgeous-looking restaurant that's open for breakfast, called Salt Café. And it's lovely inside too, all brightly polished wooden tables and floors, with a menu that couldn't be more mouth-wateringly perfect for this time of day. So we order, scrambled eggs for me and the full fry-up for Will, with two cappuccinos to get us started.

Then the place slowly starts to fill up with other diners; some with friends and family, some on their own clutching the Sunday papers. And no prizes for guessing what the main story is most feature editors have run with this week.

A silence falls between us as our coffees arrive and I take

a first delicious mouthful, instantly feeling a whole lot perkier.

'So,' says Will, sitting back now and really focusing on me.

'It's been quite a few weeks, hasn't it?' I say.

'Certainly has, in every possible way.'

'How do you mean?' I ask, raising an eyebrow across at him.

A pause while he plays a bit with the spoon on the side of his cup.

'Mentally. Emotionally. Come on, Tess, you know what I'm getting at here.'

'No,' I say, genuinely baffled. 'I don't.'

He leans forward and takes my hand, looking, there's no other word for it, a bit anxious now.

'They told me. And I just wanted to make sure that you were OK. That's all.'

'They told you what?' I say automatically, as of course, the answer already hits me before I've barely finished my sentence.

'The Granny Brigade as you so endearingly refer to them,' he says softly. 'About your wedding. About everything.'

'Oh, right. That,' I say flatly. Serves me right for asking Edith to keep a secret. She's a lovely, sweet old lady and everything, but about as discreet as a hang gliding flasher.

'Look, Tess,' he says, in no rush to let go of my hand. 'You can tell me to mind my own business here, but I just wanted to make sure you were OK about everything. Can't have been an easy time for you. And I'm so sorry, I really am.'

'That's good of you,' I say, 'but it's all been fine. Really. Honestly. And of course no one ever believes a bride when she says that she's got no problem whatsoever with the fact that her wedding has just been called off, but I can promise you, in my case, it's the absolute truth. And Bernard feels exactly the same way as I do.'

'You're not just putting on a brave face?' he asks, watching me closely. 'Because you don't need to. Not with me anyway.'

I smile back at him.

'I'm positive. I even told Bernard about what happened between you and I, by the way.'

'You did?'

'All in the spirit of honesty and transparency,' I shrug. 'He and I were having a heart-to-heart the other night and so I came clean. You know, it's never a good sign when a woman who's meant to be getting married in a few weeks suddenly starts kissing the face off someone else.'

'Ahh,' he says. 'That.'

Silence now, just as our food arrives, but in spite of the delicious smell of fresh toast, neither of us makes the slightest attempt to eat. Instead we just look across the table at each other.

'Because you know,' he says, 'I've thought about that night too. And now that you're officially single again, I just wanted to say that . . . well . . .'

'Yes?' I ask, thinking how cute he is when he's flustered and out of his comfort zone.

'Well, if you ever wanted to go out . . . I mean . . . like . . . on a proper date, you know? Then . . . that might be . . . nice . . .'

'Nice?' I grin. 'That's your adjective? And you call your-self a novelist?'

'You know what I mean,' he says, reddening a bit now.

'It would be lovely. More than lovely. If you were up for it, of course.'

I take another sip of coffee and this time, it's my turn to take his hand.

'Will,' I tell him after a beat, 'here's the thing about me. I went straight from one ill-judged relationship into another one. You said so yourself that night, I was Rebound Girl. And although it's so sweet of you to ask me out . . . I just think that right now—'

He nods and looks like he can guess what's coming next.

'I need to be on my own again,' I finish. 'I'd like to remember what it is to be single. To be independent and, as Kate King – sorry Kate Lee – said earlier . . . free.'

'I totally understand,' he says. 'And for what it's worth, it sounds like you're doing the right thing for you. But you know, if you ever . . .'

'If I ever . . . ?'

And then he grins as the black eyes start to dance again.

'Tell you what,' he says, sounding a bit more playful now, 'in the spirit of romantic adventure, why don't we arrange to meet in exactly . . . say . . . six months' time. You name the date and place and let's just see what happens. If we both turn up, then maybe it'll turn into a *date* date. And If only one of us does . . .'

'Or neither of us . . .'

'Then it's a case of no harm, no foul. Gives you a bit of time-out to clear your head and let's just see where we both are then. So come on. What do you say?'

'Here,' I tell him firmly. 'In six months' time, here at this very table in the Salt Café.'

'Why not?' he smiles. 'Say 8 p.m., for dinner?'

'Oh no,' I say doubtfully, 'not dinner.'

'Why?'

'Because if the other doesn't turn up, then you're . . .'

'OK, yeah, I get it,' he says, finishing the sentence for me. 'Then you're the poor sap that's sitting all alone for dinner at a table for two. How about breakfast then? So if one of us doesn't show, it's still cool to have breakfast on your own with the papers. What do you say?'

'In six months then,' I say.

'In six months.'

*

About an hour later, Will's flashy car pulls up at our house, just as Gracie is parking in the driveway, still wearing the same clothes she had on last night and looking like a big, dirty stop-out. She comes over to us and I make the introductions.

'Although you've both actually met before,' I say. 'That night, when you and I were at that awful dinner in the club and you were at a fortieth birthday party, Will, remember?'

'Don't remind me,' groans Gracie. 'I'm still having therapy to recover from that bloody night.'

She waves to Will through the open car window and is just about to say hi, when suddenly her jaw physically drops, cartoon-style.

'Oh. My. Actual. God,' she says, staring at him, like she can't believe her eyes. Meanwhile, Will just looks faintly embarrassed, like he's quite used to generating this sort of a reaction.

'What's wrong?' I ask, looking at her.

'Tess, you moron! Don't you realise who this is? You're W.T. Kearns! *The* W.T. Kearns! I've read every single line you've ever written! I'm your number one fan!'

'Guilty as charged,' says Will with a shy little smile.

'Tell me this. Will you ever write a sequel to *Murder at Merrion*? Please, say yes! Your hero is my favourite fictional character ever!'

KATE

Dublin
Two months later

The Hugh Lane Gallery was packed out and not only that, but the press was out in force too. The whole place seemed crammed with social diarists, the whole works. It had got to the stage where Kate could almost pick out their faces, even in an exhibition room as crowded as this one. She looked around nervously as Jasper Adams made his way to the podium to introduce her. And sure enough, her eye very quickly picked out Mo in a bright lemon-yellow dress, good old loyal Mo, standing right there at the back to cheer Kate on.

'Ladies and gentlemen,' said Jasper, addressing the room importantly and, not for the first time, Kate almost wanted to smile at just how much he reminded her of the quintessential Mammy's Boy, right down to the neat crease down the front of his immaculately pressed suit. He'd insisted on coming here today from the Art History department at City College and had even brought a friend along with him; an overweight, rotund man, a bit like Billy Bunter from the comics. He looked strangely familiar to Kate too, but she couldn't quite put her finger on where she'd seen him before.

'Much has been written,' Jasper went on, 'particularly of late, about the painting which is about to be unveiled here today. She's been the subject of a lengthy court battle and it's so wonderfully satisfying to have her returned here and now to the beautiful Hugh Lane Gallery. So without further ado, allow me to introduce you to our incredibly generous benefactress, Miss Kate Lee!'

A hearty round of applause went up as Kate made her way to the podium, aware of a whole bank of flash photography going off in her face.

She paused, took a moment to look around the packed gallery, then steeled herself to make the little speech she'd prepared.

'Thank you all so much for coming today,' she began. 'It truly is an honour to see such a great turnout for *A Lady of Letters*. We're particularly fortunate to have some representatives from the Art History world here this evening as, unlike me, they'll certainly be able to answer anything you wish to know about the painting.'

There were a few titters around the room at that, which gave Kate the courage to go on.

'However,' she continued, 'there's one thing I'm afraid you won't find in any history book. Did you know that apparently *A Lady of Letters* comes with a curse? Some people believe in it and others don't. But up until recent events, I'd certainly have gone along with the whole notion alright.'

Laughter at that, and even a brief smattering of applause.

'Yes, indeed,' said Kate, growing in confidence as she warmed to her theme. 'Whether or not you believe in

470

the whole *Lusitania* story or not – and for the record, I certainly do – it seems that no private owner of this portrait has ever had a day's luck from it.

'But today that all changes. Because today, the painting's previous owner now gets to see his dying wish fulfilled. And so, can I ask you to charge your glasses and raise a toast to Sir Hugh Lane, who one day dreamt that *A Lady of Letters* would hang here in the gallery that bears his name. And today, I have the very fortunate privilege of being in a position to make that dream come true. Ladies and gentlemen,' she went on, tugging at a discreet little rope so she could officially unveil the portrait, 'I give you . . . *A Lady of Letters*. And after the longest journey imaginable, now she's here for good.'

With that, loud applause broke out as Kate smiled at the room. It had indeed been a long journey – and not just for the painting either. And yet take a look at me now, she thought. She was in a better place than she had been for years, she was far more fulfilled, more independent, much more like the Kate Lee of old. Work offers had begun to pile in for her – she'd been invited to be a spokeswoman for several charities and even better, the gallery had even offered her an honorary position on its board, something she was particularly excited about.

Meanwhile she was still living with Mo while actively house-hunting and loving every minute of it. And as if that wasn't enough, to her total astonishment she'd even been asked out on a date. By an old friend of Mo's, as it happened, a sweet, genuine man, who was almost the complete and total opposite to Damien.

Yes, life was most certainly looking up, Kate thought, as loud cheers now began to break out all around the room.

She took a moment to look proudly around her, before her eyes lingered back on the painting.

You're home, was all she could think. *You've finally come home.*

Hugh Lane can be at peace now and you know something? Maybe I can too.

*

'Wonderful speech, wasn't it?' said Jasper to Bernard, where they both stood at the side of the room, champagne flutes in hand.

'Absolutely top-notch,' said Bernard. 'And did you hear that the gallery have invited Kate Lee to take a position on its board? A most welcome addition too, I should think.'

'Absolutely,' Jasper nodded in agreement. 'So when this bunfight is over,' he went on, 'how about a little nightcap back at the club?'

'Oh, I'd love nothing more,' Bernard beamed delightedly, thinking what a perfect evening this had been too. A Rembrandt restored to its rightful place and now a lovely sherry at the club to round things off. Bliss.

'Wonderful,' said Jasper. 'In that case, I'll just call Mother and tell her I'll be a little late home.'

EPILOGUE

TESS
Six months later

Tess checked her watch for the hundredth time that morning. 9 a.m. on the button. Neither too early nor too late, just bang on time. She was driving through Monkstown village scanning the streets for parking, and her mind was already made up. She'd walk in, grab a paper, order a coffee, wait exactly the same length of time as it took her to drink it, then if he hadn't turned up by then, she'd hand the paper back and leave. No raised eyebrows from anyone else, nothing. She'd just look like someone who was just on their way to work and who'd dropped off for a quick caffeine hit, nothing more. Potential for mortification? Zero.

The weird thing was that she'd had absolutely no contact from Will in the past six months, nor he from her. She purposely hadn't given him her mobile number and, probably sensing that she needed time out, he hadn't pushed her for it either. So absolutely anything at all could have been going on in his life in the interim, she thought, her mind racing.

He could have met someone else by now. He could even

be in a serious relationship. He might have forgotten all about her and this daft arrangement, which was frankly starting to feel a whole lot dafter by the minute.

As for Tess, though, the last few months had flown by. She'd busied herself in work and taken on a shedload of new clients. And she'd had a great time while she was at it, catching up with Monica, Stella and all of her other friends and really getting to spend quality time with her family, as opposed to just rowing over wedding arrangements the whole time. Thanks to her promotion to Assistant Manager at work, she'd even saved up enough to put a deposit on an apartment in town, close to where she worked. It was tiny, of course, but that didn't bother her. As soon as the sale went through, it would be her own, lovely, independent home – hers and no one else's.

Not only that, but her mum and dad were both doing fantastically well too. Her dad had proven to be such a dab hand at painting and decorating, that he'd gone into business with another pal of his and already, they had more work than they could handle.

'Just think, we'll soon have enough money saved to be able to go out and visit Gracie in Canada,' her mum had told her delightedly. Because that was the other big development in Tess's world; Gracie had finally saved up enough to make the big leap to Toronto, to take up her dream job as a graphic designer. Tess missed her of course, but the whole family Skyped her regularly, in fact so much so that Gracie had started to complain, 'ah here, I don't talk to you lot this much when I'm back home.'

So all in all, Tess had been having an absolute ball for herself, loving every minute of being single and free and having fun.

And yet somehow Will had lodged himself into the back of her mind and just wouldn't go away.

Bingo. She discovered a free parking space and was just about to reverse in . . . and that's when she saw it. It was the same one, unquestionably. A black convertible sports car that she'd once joked about, saying it reminded her of the Batmobile.

Opening her car door, she stepped out into the nippy autumn morning and strode across the street to Salt Café.

I have absolutely no idea what the future will hold, she thought. But I do know one thing. I'm ready to take a risk again. I'm ready for something. And maybe this whole thing with Will would just fizzle away to nothing, or maybe they'd go the distance. Who knew?

But one thing was for certain. Nothing would come of it unless she took this one leap of faith.

So smiling to herself and taking a deep breath, she walked up to the café door. Opened it and stepped inside.

THE END

Acknowledgements

Thank you, Marianne Gunn O'Connor. I'm very lucky to be your client, but even luckier to be your friend.

Thank you, Pat Lynch, for everything. Next lunch in The Farm on me.

Thank you, Vicki Satlow, for all your tireless hard work. Really hope to see you very soon.

Thank you to Charlie Redmayne for your incredible generosity and for making all your authors feel so special.

To all at Avon, what can I say? There really are no words to thank you all for everything you've done for my books. You're a fabulous team and it really is a joy to work alongside you. Special thanks to Oli Malcolm, Helen Huthwaite, Caroline Kirkpatrick, Helena Sheffield, Kate Ellis, Hannah Welsh and Jennie Rothwell.

Special thanks to Natasha Harding, whose incredible hard work shows on every page of this book.

Thank you to Rachel Eley for being such a fabulous copy-editor.

Thank you to all at HarperCollins Ireland, especially Tony Perdue, Ann-Marie Dolan and Mare Byrne. What a terrific team you make.

Thank you to all at Kate Bowe PR, especially Kate and

Sarah Dee. And thank you to Light Brigade PR in London, with a special shout-out to Sabah Khan.

Thank you to my family and friends, for putting up with me when I need to shut the world away 'so I can just make this deadline'. Mum, Dad, you're the best. Paddy, Sam, Richard, Maria and especially my Aunt Lilla, thank you all.

Thank you to my lifelong friends, Karen, Susan, Clelia, Marion, Fiona, Alison, Pat, Fionnuala, Frank and Tony. What would I do without any of you?

Thank you to my writer buddies, for all your friendship and support. Special thanks to Sinead Moriarty, Liz Nugent, Monica McInerney, Patricia Scanlan, Aidan Storey, Morag Prunty, Martina Devlin and Sarah Webb.

And in case you were wondering, there's one very special person who I've left till last, my editor Eleanor Dryden. Dearest Eli, there are no words to thank you for everything you've done. It's been a privilege to work alongside you all this time, and I wish you nothing but joy and success in the future.

Which is why this book is fondly dedicated to you.

If you loved *All She Ever Wished For*, we think you'll enjoy the following reads too . . .

Love Me or Leave Me

Claudia Carroll

Breaking up is hard to do …

'An original & poignant story'
SHEILA O'FLANAGAN

CLAUDIA CARROLL
THE NUMBER ONE BESTSELLER

Me
&
You

'Full of warmth,
humour and emotion'
MELISSA HILL

'A very modern
fairytale, full of
wit and humour.'
SHEILA O'FLANAGAN

A Very
Accidental
Love Story

Is there such a thing as the *perfect* man?

Claudia Carroll

'It bubbles and sparkles
like pink champagne'
Patricia Scanlan

Absence makes the heart
grow fonder... doesn't it?

*Will You
Still Love Me
Tomorrow?*

Claudia Carroll